THE BLACK
AND THE GREEN

The Sequel to PRELUDE IN BLACK AND GREEN

A Novel

Ada Nicolescu

   www.trafford.com

North America & international
toll-free: 1 888 232 4444 (USA & Canada)
phone: 250 383 6864 ♦ fax: 812 355 4082

*To the memory of
my Aunt and Uncle, Mela and
Doctor Cornel Iancu.*

ACKNOWLEDGMENTS

I OWE MANY THANKS TO my guide and mentor, CAROL EMSHWILLER and the caring support of my writer friends, GABRIELA CONTESTABILE, BARBARA FLECK-PALADINO, IRENE GLASSGOLD, FLORENCE HOMOLKA, MARGARET SWEENEY, GAY PARTINGTON TERRY, and MARIA TAMMICK who have contributed to the creation of this book with important critical suggestions.

MIHAELA COSMA, a fellow Romanian, has been an inspiring presence for the recollection of the past, and SYBIL H. LANDAU, an accomplished historian, has helped me gain a historical perspective of those years.

CAROLE PAUL has shared her gifts of creativity, practical knowledge and experience, while LINDA F. SULLIVAN's exceptional technical skills, sharp attention to detail and great patience have been essential to the emergence of the book.

And, as always, my husband, LAWRENCE L. LE SHAN, has been my Rock of Gibraltar.

TABLE OF CONTENTS

THE LIST OF CHARACTERS

The Stein Family

Adrian Stein ....Electrical Engineer, 44.
Nina...His Wife, 40.
Suzy...Daughter, 17.
Nadia ....Daughter, 12.

Nina's Relatives (all maternal)

Aunt Josephine Gold ....Nina's mother's youngest
                                             sister, 68.
Uncle Leon Gold.......................Her husband, 74.
Joel Gold ....Their son, Pediatrician, 32.
Mathilda Gold...........................Joel's wife, 26.
Stella Frühling...........................Nina's sister, 36.
Sorel Frühling ....Stella's husband,
                                             Pediatrician, 39.

Others

Zalman Bier ....President of the Jewish
                                             Community, Istanbul, 56.
Domnişoara Braunstein.............Adrian's Secretary, 31.
Sigmund Dorfman ....President of the Jewish
                                             Community, Moghilev, 47.

Dr. Eugen Milo..........................Psychiatrist, Assistant to
Dr. Georgescu, Legionnaire
leader, 31.

Nissim...First Mate, the DORINA, 28.

Rabbi Alexander Naftali ....Chief Rabbi of Romania, 46.

Paul Radin..................................Romanian Diplomat, 61.

Silvia...Dr. Milo's fiancee,
member of Legionnaire
Organization, the IRON
GUARD, 27. Has been Suzy
and Nadia's governess.

Professor Gheorghe Ursu...........Physician, Dean, Bucharest
School of Medicine, 45.

Hans Waldo.................................Journalist, Courier for the Swiss
Embassy in Bucharest, 26.

Max Wiener ....Famous Jewish Historian, 75.

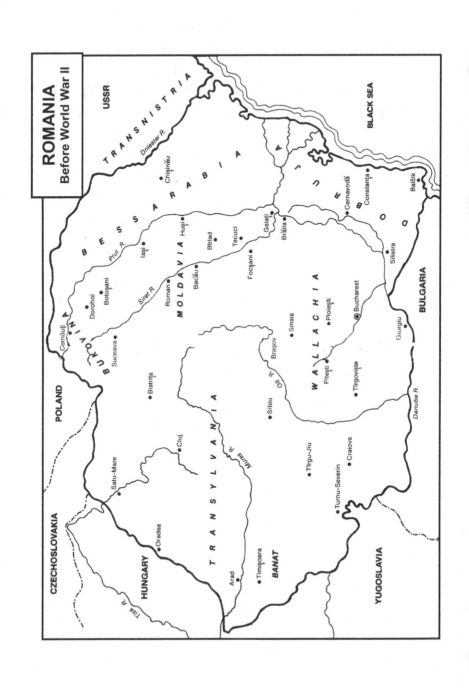

ROMANIA
Before World War II

POLAND

CZECHOSLOVAKIA

HUNGARY

Tisa R.

Satu-Mare

Oradea

Arad

Timişoara

BANAT

Cluj

Mureş R.

Bistriţa

T R A N S Y L V A N I A

Sibiu

Braşov

Olt R.

Sinaia

Tîrgu-Jiu

Turnu-Severin

Craiova

Piteşti

Tîrgovişte

W A L L A C H I A

Ploieşti

Bucharest

Danube R.

Giurgiu

YUGOSLAVIA

BULGARIA

Silistra

Balčik

Constanţa

Cernavodă

BLACK SEA

D O B R U J A

Galaţi

Brăila

Tecuci

Bîrlad

Focşani

Bacău

Roman

Huşi

Iaşi

Prut R.

Sirat R.

Botoşani

Dorohoi

Suceava

Cernăuţi

B U K O V I N A

M O L D A V I A

B E S S A R A B I A

Chişinău

Dniester R.

T R A N S N I S T R I A

USSR

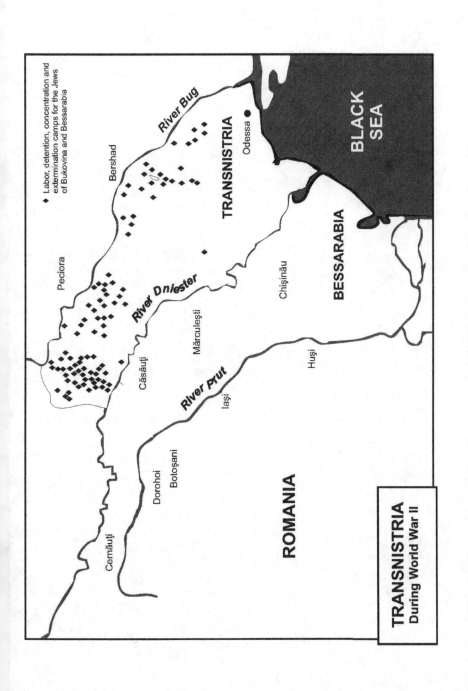

Labor, detention, concentration and extermination camps for the Jews of Bukovina and Bessarabia

River Bug

Bershad

Peciora

River Dniester

TRANSNISTRIA

Odessa

BLACK SEA

BESSARABIA

Chişinău

Mărculeşti

Căsăuţi

River Prut

Huşi

Iaşi

Cernăuţi

Dorohoi

Botoşani

ROMANIA

TRANSNISTRIA
During World War II

PROLOGUE

Juda verrecke!
(Nazi slogan)
Die Juden sind unser Unglück!
(*Der Stürmer*)

JUDA VERRECKE! JUDA PERISH! WAS the battle cry howled by thousands of Nazi demonstrators in Hitler's Germany.

Die Juden sind unser Unglück! The Jews are our curse! was the written slogan which adorned the front page of *Der Stürmer*, the Nazi Party newspaper.

But Fascism was not limited to Germany. In other countries in Europe, similar slogans and demonstrations dominated the scene.

The increasing violence and a string of political assassinations made the Jews realize that there was no one and nothing to protect them.

Like many Jewish families, the Steins and their relatives from Romania are caught in this turbulence. They have to live with Fascism and the forthcoming war.

What will their future be? Will they survive?

How will they cope with the challenges they have to face?
These questions are on everybody's mind.

This book is a work of fiction, inspired by historical events. All characters are imaginary, and any resemblance with real people is coincidental.

Part I

ANOTHER SPRING, ANOTHER SUMMER

THE SPRING OF 1939 WAS an unusually beautiful season in the city. The days were mild and sunny, the snow melted slowly, without giving birth to the floods of other years.

In spite of the international convulsions of that year, the song birds also came back to Bucharest. One could hear the cooing of the turtle doves, the chirping of the swallows and the trills of the nightingales in the gardens. For a while, one could hear, during the night, the calls of the wild geese flying over the city. Sometimes they were so loud, they woke Nadia up. Once, on a full-moon night, she got out of bed and stepped out on the terrace. The air resounded with the distant calls. When she looked up, she saw the black silhouettes of the birds flying across the moon.

Adrian, her father, had also heard the calls of the geese and joined Nadia on the terrace. He brought with him his field binoculars, and together they watched the winged travelers pass over the moon. He told her that other birds, like eagles, owls and storks would also be flying this way. On these full-moon nights, they scanned the sky with the binoculars, trying to see these other flocks.

Sometimes it seemed to Nadia that she could hear the barking of eagles, the hooting of owls, or the clappering of storks. But even with the binoculars she couldn't really see where they were.

For Nadia, this spring was unusual not only because of the mild weather and the migrant birds. It was important because she was graduating from elementary school and was going to be admitted to high school.

It was a great event in her life, since the admission exam to the high school of Nina's choice—the best, most prestigious, and sought after—was difficult, competitive and selective, and outright discriminatory against Jewish students. Only a small quota of the best Jewish students was accepted to this school. Suzy was in the last year in the same school, and now Nadia was expected to follow in her footsteps.

It was Nina's conviction that a superior education at a first rate school was essential for a successful career. This had been the case for Nina's two older brothers, who had been encouraged to go to first rate schools and universities and had become accomplished professionals. Her older brother, Emil, was a well-known construction engineer, and her second brother, Liviu, a much respected internist.

Nina envied both of them. She would have loved to have gone to the university and become a teacher of literature or history. But in her youth, girls of her generation were not allowed to have a profession. She and her sister Stella attended only four years of elementary school. After that, giving in to Nina's tears and supplications, her mother had hired a private tutor who came to the house and taught the two sisters bits of French and German literature. It

4

was at that young age that Nina promised herself that her daughters would go to the best schools and universities and have successful careers.

Now, this year since the admission exam consisted of a written and oral math test and a written spelling test, Nadia was seriously drilled for several months in the spelling of complicated words and sentences with many hyphens and apostrophes. She also had to solve difficult math problems which involved multiplication and division.

Even though her cousin Mathilda, who was a teacher, came regularly to the house to tutor Nadia and gave her difficult assignments, Nina was afraid that Nadia wasn't going to make it. She was unhappy that Nadia didn't have the exceptional mathematical skills Suzy had shown. Also, given the progressively severe anti-Semitic rules, she felt that Nadia was too immature to understand the seriousness of the situation and make the effort needed. All these worries gave Nina nightmares.

To motivate Nadia in this struggle, Adrian promised to help her buy "the bicycle of her dreams," if she passed the exam.

Nadia had been saving for this bicycle for at least one year. She envied Suzy her own bicycle, even though it was old and rickety. She wanted her own bicycle so badly, she agreed to do all kinds of odd jobs around the house, for which her parents gave her a weekly allowance. For many months now Nadia helped Gheorghe, the gardener, trim the bushes and water the lawn, clean the swimming pool during the spring and summer, and sweep the dead leaves from the garden paths.

Since she no longer had a governess, she had to keep her room, her armoire, and her schoolbooks neat and clean.

Nina was a tough supervisor. However, since Nadia behaved herself, she received her allowance. Since she was obsessed with having her own bike, she lived up to her tasks. On holidays and on her birthday, Nina and Adrian gave her money instead of gifts, and Nadia gathered her savings in a bank shaped like a fat, rosy pig with pointed ears and a grinning face.

The day she passed the exam, the piggybank was smashed in front of the whole family, and Nadia retrieved its content. Adrian promised to round up the sum if necessary.

The next day they went to the best and most elegant bicycle store in the city. Even though she had never been there, Nadia immediately knew where to find what she wanted. She marched quickly through the store, pulling her father by the hand. Then she stopped right in front of a graceful, silvery bicycle. It was all nickel and chrome, and had a light, elegant shape. A small winged horse was engraved on its body.

"Look at the winged bicycle!" Nadia said with shining eyes, which reflected the gloss of the two-wheeler. She stroked it lovingly and imagined that, under her touch, it would grow real wings.

"I'll call it Pegasus, my winged horse!" she said, as she climbed on its seat. "All my friends will envy me!" she added, as she stretched her legs to reach the pedals. She couldn't reach the ground when she perched on the seat.

Of course, the new bicycle was twice as expensive as Adrian had expected. But he took out his wallet and paid the difference. No way would he let Nadia down.

Getting the bicycle was a major event in Nadia's life. Passing the admission exam and going to the new school was another.

Nadia loved this school. The imposing white building, with its tall windows, the large, high-ceiling classrooms, the wide, airy corridor made her think of a fairy tale palace. But what she liked most was the gym with its rich and varied equipment—the ladder, the trapeze, the parallel bars, the climbing ropes and the rings. Then, there was the biology lab, well endowed with microscopes, colored slides, and "real" stuffed animals such as small and large birds of prey, two monkeys, a small lion cub and a baby alligator—the last two believed to be trophies of royal hunts in India and Africa, since the Queen had endowed this lab herself. It was said that the lion cub was actually shot in the Punjab by Albert, Prince Consort of Queen Victoria, Queen Marie's paternal grandmother.

Next to the biology lab was the geography and astronomy room which housed many maps of the five continents, a large terrestrial globe in the middle of the room, and an astronomical globe of the universe with all the planets and galaxies.

Nadia was happy here. She was proud of her new uniform of "*strajer*," a boy-scout type uniform with a white shirt, navy-blue skirt, green cravat, and wide leather belt with a large brass buckle engraved with the royal crown. The white shirt was outfitted with gold trimmings and a golden silk royal badge on the right sleeve.

But what Nadia liked most was the shiny whistle attached to the left breast pocket with a golden ribbon. She was particularly proud of this uniform, since it was the official costume worn by the Crown Prince Michael, the King's son. He was the leader of all the students in the country and looked very handsome and dapper in this uniform.

Large photos of the Prince and the King, standing at attention were hanging in all the classrooms. Nadia had a few small pictures of Prince Michael tucked away in a secret corner of her desk. Skender had been forgotten, since in the last two years she hadn't been to the seashore. Now, all her attention went to the Prince and his handsome appearance.

That year, the students had been ordered to wear the uniform all the time. When Nadia raced down the streets on her new bicycle dressed in her proud attire, she imagined herself to be the mythical hero Bellerophon riding his winged horse Pegasus, challenging the gods on Olympus.

Did she indeed challenge the gods? When she first got the bicycle her legs were short; she barely reached the pedals. She certainly couldn't reach the ground. But as time went on, her legs grew longer, her skirt got shorter. During the summer Nina realized that her daughters needed new uniforms. She immediately bought fabric for the navy skirts and white linen for the shirts. Doamna Avramescu, the old seamstress with the thick eyeglasses, was back in the house, cutting, sewing and patiently doing the fittings for the two girls.

Toward the end of August, Nina went to school to enroll her daughters for the new school year. As it was still summer, she put on her pink linen dress and a delicate gold chain. She packed a small bottle of Arpège, her favorite French perfume and the book, *La Vie de Victor Hugo*, the most recent biography by André Maurois, which her brother had sent her from Paris. These were gifts for the school principal, Doamna Tacorian. Nina had known the principal for many years, since she had first registered Suzy at the school. They had met regularly since then.

Doamna Tacorian, a respected teacher of French literature, was a tall, majestic woman with large blue eyes and blond hair gathered in a bun. There was a calm, but authoritarian air about her. Every year, at registration time, Nina and the principal had sat down with a cup of Turkish coffee in the wood-paneled office and discussed either a prize-winning French book, or an author whose work Doamna Tacorian was going to teach during the year. Nina had always brought gifts. They had lively discussions, and Nina had always looked forward to these meetings.

This year when she arrived at school, the secretary gave her a cold look and asked her to wait. "Doamna Tacorian is very busy," she said as she pushed a chair toward Nina.

She sat down and waited. But after a while it became obvious that other mothers, who had arrived later than she had, were going in to see the principal. She was getting impatient, but she told herself that she must be waiting because she had two children to register, while the others probably had only one. Finally, after more than an hour, the secretary came out and asked Nina to follow her into her cubicle. She was holding two large envelopes and offered Nina a chair. Then she sat down at her desk, facing Nina.

"Doamna Tacorian cannot see you today," she said, avoiding Nina's gaze. "As a matter of fact, she cannot see you at all. I must inform you that your daughters are not permitted to enroll in this school anymore."

The secretary spoke quickly, examining her fingernails and then looking away from Nina. "Jewish students are not permitted in this school any longer nor in any Romanian schools. Here are your daughters' folders, with their transcripts and all their documents." The secretary handed Nina the bulky envelopes and then led her out the door.

Alone in the corridor, Nina felt dizzy and had trouble walking. She held onto the wall and advanced slowly toward the stairs. The secretary's words kept spinning in her head: "Jewish students not permitted in Romanian schools . . . Jewish students not permitted in Romanian schools . . ."

How was she going to break this news to her children? How was she going to explain this to Nadia, particularly after she had forced her to make such a big effort to get into this school? And what would the girls do about studying in general? The Moriah school had only elementary classes. Outside of this, Nina knew only about one old Jewish school, far away, at the end of the Jewish quarter. It was very old and very small. Nina didn't even know whether it was still functioning. Besides, it had never been officially recognized by the Department of Education!

But was schooling of Jewish children actually allowed? She had heard rumors about places in Germany where all Jewish schools had been closed or destroyed. When teachers and parents gathered a small group of children in somebody's house, they were all arrested and deported to camps.

Nina told herself that this happened in other places, not here, in Bucharest. On the other hand, maybe she should have been more prepared for what happened today! The times were so unpredictable! Nevertheless, whichever way she looked at these events, she couldn't accept this painful reality—the annihilation of a cherished dream for her children!

When she walked into the house carrying the envelopes, the bottle of Arpège and the book, she was relieved to see that neither Suzy nor Nadia were home. Before even taking off her dress and her pumps, she decided to call her sister Stella and ask her for advice.

"Sorry that you had such a bad experience!" said Stella. "But the new law about the schools has been published in all the newspapers today. It will probably be broadcasted on the radio at lunch. You ask how to tell the children?" Stella went on. "We should gather them all together, and Sorel should tell them, quite matter of fact, that this year they must go to other schools. It will be a new experience for them, maybe even a good way to learn about Judaism!"

"Yes, maybe!" Nina mumbled." She was not convinced. But she felt relieved that she didn't have to deal with the children by herself.

The next day the two families gathered at Stella's house, and Sorel told the children the news about the school. Corinna and Theo shrugged it off, since they figured that they'd be in the same school with their best friends, Mona and Dan, who were also Jewish.

Nadia however was troubled by the news. She didn't know what to think about her friend Liudmila. They had been best friends and schoolmates for several years, but Liudmila was not Jewish. What was going to happen to their friendship? Nadia was so worried that she took her bicycle and rode to Liudmila's house. She needed to make sure that they'd always be friends, even though they weren't going to be together in school. She needed to know that Liudmila was going to be there for her.

As she got on her bicycle it started to rain. The streets were wet and slippery, but Nadia didn't slow down. When she arrived at Liudmila's house, she rang the doorbell. There was no answer. She rang again—once, twice, several times. Still, there was no answer. Maybe Liudmila had gone out, with Mishka the dog, but would come back soon.

Nadia propped her bicycle against the lamppost, and sat on a low brick fence. She didn't wait long. After about ten minutes the concierge came back from the market. Her hair and her glasses were wet from the rain, and so was her net bag, in which she carried a cucumber and a live chicken. With the other hand she held a dog on a leash.

Nadia recognized her friend's dog, Mishka. He wagged his tail, jumped up and licked Nadia's hand.

"Where is Liudmila?" asked Nadia, as she stroked the dog's head. "Will she be back soon?"

"Oh, no!" said the concierge. "She won't be back. Not very soon, anyway. Haven't you heard? Liudmila and her aunt left in a hurry last night. They took only two small valises and left everything behind. They're from Kishinev, which is in Bessarabia, and it was given back to the Russians two days ago. Liudmila and her aunt are Russians, so they had to leave. Only Mishka was born here, so he is

Romanian and could stay behind. If you want him, I can give him to you. I really have no use for a dog!"

Nadia thanked the concierge. "No, no!" she said and shook her head. "I can't take Mishka!" She knew that her mother wouldn't let her have the dog. She never even liked Puck.

Nadia was sad, and she felt like crying. First losing the school and now losing Liudmila! She might never come back and Nadia might never see her again! It was like death, like when her dog Puck was killed, two years ago! She remembered how heartbroken she was then, how much she had loved him, and how much she missed him. She felt like crying, just thinking of him.

But Liudmila is not dead, she told herself, after a while. She could still come back, one day, God only knows when! Nevertheless, Nadia felt sad and lonely. What was the sense of making good friends, if they then disappear or have to leave? She sighed, as she rode home slower than usual. She turned one last corner and was now close to the house.

But what if Liudmila had not left at all? she asked herself. Maybe it was just a story concocted by the concierge? Maybe her friend was going to call her. Or maybe she had just gone away with her aunt, on a short vacation, before the beginning of school!

It made no sense to become all upset right now, she thought, as she locked up her bicycle in its regular place under the stairs.

FROM THE DIARY OF DOCTOR MILO

9/10/1940.

THE KING IS GONE! HOORAY! King Carol has finally abdicated, two days ago, and has left by train with his disgusting Jewish mistress.

My good friend Horațiu and the Mareshal are now the leaders of the country, and we have been proclaimed a "National Legionnaire State" which means a National Fascist State. We also have a puppet king, since the Crown Prince Michael is the new king.

It is a great pity that our cherished commander, our Căpitan is not here to lead us through these glorious days. But I am sure that he is watching us proudly from his golden throne in Paradise!

King Carol had to pay for murdering the Căpitan and his thirteen comrades in secret in a most despicable way. It is true the Căpitan and his men were in jail for the assassination of the corrupt prime minister and other politicians. But then, murderous King Carol engineered a most perfidious plan of liquidating them.

He ordered the prisoners to be transferred from one prison to another. During the night of the transfer, they were strangled with ropes and leather thongs in their van. Their bodies were covered with quick lime and destroyed. The official version was that the captives tried to run away from their guards and were shot in the back.

The old King deserves punishment with death for these murders and his duplicity. I have sworn not to let this go by without retaliation. The mere sight of this criminal makes me sick! We had to avenge our great Căpitan! But it wasn't easy to get rid of King Carol.

Following the loss of our great provinces, Bessarabia, Bukovina, Northern Transylvania and a good part of the seacoast, the Romanian people came to hate the King. We, the Iron Guard, decided that this was the best moment to get rid of him.

We mobilized tens of thousands of our Legionnaire members from all over the country, brought them to Bucharest, and demanded that the old King abdicate.

Every day a green sea of our militants gathered in front of the royal palace carrying banners, shouting for the King to step down and leave. But he ignored our appeals. He gave a proclamation saying that he will never abdicate. He called, to his defense, the Mareshal whom he had previously sent to prison. To his surprise, it was the Mareshal who told him that he must abdicate—the people hated him and the army was not going to stand up for him. He was in great danger.

The Mareshal promised to put at his disposal a train with twelve cars which the King could fill with all his precious belongings—famous paintings including those of the great El Greco, ancient carpets, gold, priceless jewelry, hand-carved furniture, crystals and silver—all the riches of his five palaces. His Jewish mistress and his corrupt "royal entourage" could go with him.

The Mareshal assured the King that nothing was going to happen to him. He was going to travel safely to the western border of the country and then continue his trip to Western Europe.

But when we heard about this plan, we decided otherwise. We were angry that the Mareshal would allow the King to run away carrying with him the riches of the country's palaces. Horațiu ordered that the train be stopped at the border and searched by our militants. All the riches were to be unloaded and the King assassinated. It was the proper punishment for this murderer.

In reality, things didn't work out this way. The royal train with its precious cargo indeed left Bucharest at midnight. The border station of Jimbolia was entirely occupied by hundreds of our militiamen. But to everybody's surprise, the train never stopped. It raced through the station at full speed.

Our men posted in the station shot at the moving train. I was told that the frightened King and his mistress threw themselves on the floor. One of his beloved hunting dogs was cut by broken glass.

What went wrong? Why did the locomotive never slow down and never stopped? Were we betrayed? By whom? This is the mystery which must be solved.

I had a discussion on this subject with Doctor Georgescu. He hasn't changed his position or his convictions. He is shocked and depressed by the new developments. He keeps accusing our movement of violence and organized political assassinations. He is convinced that the Legionnaire State will be nothing more than the continuous reign of a criminal regime. He doesn't understand the beauty of the "New Man," a young being full of energy and dynamism, driven to action by the "Will to Power."

Dr. Georgescu thinks the concept of the Nietzschean New Man which embraces violence as essential to creativity and for which assassination is an act of religious freedom is criminal. But we want our youth to be unencumbered by old bourgeois lies. Compromises only lead to weakness and corruption. And, of course, our youth will be proud of the national greatness of our country—a shining star—brighter than many other countries.

I wonder about Doctor Georgescu: is he too old to learn to accept the laws of our new world? Or, worse, are there traces of Jewish blood in his veins, which make him cling to these rotten beliefs? I worry about him and about his friendship with those stinking Jews!

By contrast, Silvia has made astounding strides in our movement. From "Aspiring Junior Member," she quickly advanced to "Junior Member of the Iron Guard" and then to full membership. In her enthusiasm she has volunteered to perfect herself in sharpshooting and is now the chief of a group of six distinguished sharpshooters.

During our demonstrations in front of the palace, she has accompanied me every day carrying banners with the large portrait of the Căpitan, or with the word "abdicate!" I can say without hesitation that she is one of the most passionate demonstrators in the Palace Square.

Nevertheless I am wondering about something: it is a long time since she had a booster hypnosis. I thought it wasn't necessary. But as we stood in front of the palace, something happened. Silvia's face turned suddenly pale and her blue eyes grew large. She started to shake. I followed her gaze. I saw Joel Gold standing in the crowd, staring at us.

Silvia seemed paralyzed by this encounter. I took her hand and led her away. She followed me without resistance, as if in a trance, but it took more than a few minutes before she was herself again. I think it is time for a booster hypnosis. I must remind her that she is the Joan of Arc of our Iron Guard Movement and is always protected by the Archangel Michael, and that Joel Gold, the Jew, was the evil cause of her troubles.

It was because of her unrequited love for him that she tried to strangle herself, while she was still a governess in the Stein family. Doctor Georgescu admitted her to the Psychiatric Hospital and referred her to me for treatment. Since then we are sharing everything in our existence.

THREE MEN

I N THE FALL OF 1940, three men came from the Center of Romanization to take Nadia's bicycle away. They were very young and did not know how to operate the intercom. At first they kept ringing the doorbell. Then, as they didn't understand the meaning of the buzzer, they started to shout and pound on the entrance door. Finally, Adrian came down to see what they wanted.

It was a rainy evening and was already dark. The three men wore wet and rumpled green shirts. Their long and dishevelled hair was also wet.

"Is this the house of the Jewess Nadia Stein?" asked the tallest of the three, who wore glasses with thick lenses. "Under the new law of Romanization, we have to take her bicycle away. She has to sign a paper that she is complying with the law. Otherwise she will be punished and will have to go to jail."

How mean, how petty they are! thought Adrian. To take away a child's bicycle! He had heard that in some places they confiscated "Jewish" skis. What will they take next? The children's scooters? Their roller skates? It's just a monument of pettiness!

Then he turned to the men. "My daughter Nadia is a child of 11. She is still a minor and has no right to sign. I'm her father and I'll sign for her."

"I don't care whether she is called minor or minora, I must have her signature. Call her down!"

Adrian was about to say no, when the oldest of the three, a short youth with a protruding belly said, "Let's get the bicycle first and worry about the signature later."

They stormed into the lobby and pushed Adrian out of the way. The bicycle stood right in front of them, chained to the radiator, gleaming in the faint light.

The third young man was carrying a tool kit. He crouched by the bicycle, opened his tool kit, took out a hammer and started to break the lock.

Adrian wanted to say this was not necessary. He could go upstairs and fetch the key but he really didn't want to make it easy for them. He also remembered that the key was in Nadia's desk and he didn't want to make her suspicious.

The operation was more difficult than expected. The lock resisted the blows. The man pounded harder and harder until the hammer broke.

"You shithead!" screamed the man with the fat belly. He seemed to be the leader of the group. "I told you your tools stink and you must buy a new set! What are we going to do now?"

The youth with the tools turned red and clenched his fists, ready to start a fight.

"Stop!" said the tall man with glasses. "Let's try the pliers!"

While still cursing under his breath, the man with the tools took out a large pair of pliers and applied them to the lock. He squeezed hard and, after several squeezes, the lock broke open with a loud crack. After that, they quickly removed the chain and got ready to walk out.

But the short man with the big belly was still not pleased. "Idiot! That's what you should have done from the beginning with your shitty tools!" He was so angry at his colleague that he forgot about Nadia and allowed Adrian to sign the papers.

"Shithead yourself!" screamed the tool man who had not given up. He jumped with the pliers toward the aggressor, ready to hit him. But the short youth was quicker. He punched him, making him drop the pliers and they ended up in a fistfight.

They were battling outside on the landing. Suddenly there was a loud bang. The bicycle had fallen off the landing, and one of the men was lying on top of it. Adrian went out to look: the handlebars and the front wheel were bent out of shape. Nobody could use this bike again.

Now the three men were quarreling about who should carry the bicycle.

Near the garden gate they were again ready for blows. But a sudden burst of rain made them run, all three holding onto the bike.

After they left, Adrian wondered how he was going to break this news to Nadia? He felt relieved that she hadn't been downstairs with the men. She might have burst into tears or tried to stop them from taking the bike, which would have created much trouble. She even might have been hurt in the scuffle.

The next day was Sunday. As Nadia didn't have to go to school, Adrian waited for her at breakfast. He started by reminding her that times were difficult for Jews, and nobody could hide or protect himself from the unfair laws. Then he told her what happened the evening before, without mentioning that the bike had been damaged.

She burst into tears, crying "It's unfair! It's unfair! Why do they need my Pegasus? You shouldn't have let them carry it away!"

Adrian took her in his arms, stroking her and saying "I know, I wish I could have done otherwise!"

When she grew calmer, while still holding her in his arms, he gently told her that she wasn't a baby anymore and that she was expected to act like a big girl. Nadia immediately stopped crying, looked at him with wet eyes, and said that yes, in that case he and Nina should also treat her like a "big girl" and give her more freedom! Adrian smiled and promised to do so, as long as she kept her end of the bargain.

Later that day, when Fritz, the chauffeur, came to work, Adrian told him what had happened with the bicycle. Fritz remembered that, in the furthest corner of the garage, was Suzy's old bicycle, which had been partly dismantled when some important screws had been lost. Suzy hadn't used this bicycle in some time.

"This old bike hasn't been registered in many years. Nobody knows that it exists," said Fritz. "I can put it together, make it work again, and Nadia can use it!"

Adrian's face lit up. "I forgot about the old bicycle. A great idea! It will make Nadia very happy. Suzy doesn't seem to care about the bike."

Fritz set to work, replacing the missing screws and putting the bicycle back together. Then he covered its rusty body with black paint, making it look slick and unobtrusive.

Nadia sighed when she saw it. It wasn't her gleaming "winged horse," her beloved "Pegasus." She tried it in front of the house. It was light and went almost as fast as the lost bicycle.

Nevertheless, in the beginning she didn't like the "new" bike. It was ugly. It was old. The handlebars were old-fashioned. But she had to admit that it ran fast and smooth. Finally she got used to it and decided to take good care of it.

Every day she dusted it with a soft piece of suede Fritz had given her. Slowly, it became her own cherished "winged horse" which only she would ride.

That's why she became angry when Aunt Stella suggested that she should teach Rachel Guttman, the little Polish girl who lived with the Frühlings, to ride her bike.

Rachel and her brother Boris were the two Polish children from Krakow who had been staying at Aunt Stella and Uncle Sorel's apartment for about ten months. Rachel was 11 years old and Boris was 17. They had arrived in Bucharest with their uncle, Doctor Henry Guttman, in September 1939.

In the fall of that year, at the beginning of the war, many Jews from Poland had sought refuge in Bucharest. Boris, Rachel and their uncle were among the refugees, but the parents were not with them. They didn't know where they were; they had lost them in the chaos of the German invasion. Of their large family, only their uncle, Doctor Henry Guttman, had arrived with them in Bucharest.

While the two children were staying with Aunt Stella and Uncle Sorel, the doctor was now sleeping in Adrian and Nina's living room. They all wished to leave by boat for Palestine, as soon as this was possible.

Nadia didn't like the Polish "guests." She resented the doctor who had now taken over the living room. She didn't like the children who spoke only Polish. Boris knew some French, so he could speak to Suzy and the grownups, but Rachel spoke only Polish. She was a pale and thin girl with stringy hair. She missed her mother and ate poorly.

Nadia felt ill at ease with the two children. If this had happened to them, could it also happen to her? Bad things were now happening to children! She had already lost her good friend Liudmila!

She tried not to think about it. She tried to avoid the two newcomers. So she got angry when Aunt Stella suggested that she should teach Rachel to ride *her* bicycle. She told herself that Rachel would fall and damage the bike. Then Nadia couldn't ride it anymore. This would be a terrible loss. What could she do? Aunt Stella kept insisting, and Nadia could no longer say no.

But then she had an idea: she took some tools from the garage and raised the seat of the bicycle. Now she herself could barely reach the pedals when she climbed on the bike. It would be definitely too high for little Rachel, who needed a more comfortable, lower seat to learn how to ride.

Nadia felt proud of her victory. Life was worth living again!

THE MEETING

T HE FIRST MEETING OF THE Underground Jewish
Council took place at the end of September in Adrian's
living room. The new committee was formed as soon as
the old Federation of the Jewish Community had been
dissolved by the Legionnaire government. The new council
consisted of the Chief Rabbi, Doctor Alexander Naftali,
Sorel and Stella Frühling and two other Zionist leaders, the
principals of the two Jewish schools, a lawyer, a journalist,
and Adrian.

This was an emergency meeting in which urgent
problems had to be solved: all the synagogues, the Jewish
cemeteries, the newly formed Jewish schools had been
ordered closed by the Legionnaire Minister of Education,
Professor Bunescu.

Immediately after the expulsion of the Jewish students
and teachers from the Romanian schools, new Jewish
schools had been organized: three for boys and three for
girls. The two old schools were too small to accommodate
all the children.

In no time buildings had been rented; desks, benches,
blackboards and maps had been obtained. But now,
suddenly, Professor Bunescu had announced that he was

going to close all the schools and take away their furniture and equipment. He told the principals that the schools had no authorization to function and no recognition would ever be given to their students. If they didn't obey the minister's orders, the whole committee, including the teachers, would be arrested.

In addition, the synagogues and all Jewish cemeteries were also to be closed.

"What shall we do with our dead?" the Rabbi had asked.

"Whatever you please. Throw them in the Danube!" came the answer.

But in spite of the threats, these orders were unacceptable to the Council.

"We have to invalidate Bunescu's decisions or make him change his mind!" said the Rabbi. "And this has to be done quickly, before he locks up all the buildings and the cemeteries and puts his green shirts in charge! Does anybody know how we could prevail upon Bunescu? Make him change his mind. Do you know anybody who is friends with him?"

"I heard that this man is very stubborn and authoritarian. He is ferociously anti-Semitic!" said Sorel.

"What can we do? Get an order from the Mareshal to invalidate his decision!"

"Good idea!" said several voices.

"But who can talk to the Mareshal? Is anybody friends with him?" asked the Rabbi. There was a moment of silence.

Then Adrian said, "I was in school with the Mareshal. He was doing poorly in math. I helped him along. I both tutored him and wrote his homework. Later he even wrote me a note thanking me for helping him pass the baccalaureate. But that was long ago, before he went to the military academy and became the important person he is today. I don't know whether he would do anything for us!"

Then Adrian told the council about his more recent encounter with the Mareshal only two years ago.

It so happened that during that summer, while he was vacationing with Nina and the children at the mountain resort of Predeal, a cat got stuck in a tree in the backyard and couldn't come down. It meowed so desperately that Nadia climbed the tree and brought it down. It was a small, striped cat like a miniature tiger, which, the landlady said, belonged to the family next door. Nadia took the cat in her arms and, together with Adrian, they went to return it to their neighbor.

The man who opened the door had thick, very red hair, and a face covered with freckles. Adrian had seen only one person with such a mane of red hair and so many freckles. It was the Mareshal of his youth.

The man also recognized Adrian. His face lit up, he smiled and thanked his visitors for returning the cat. Then he called his wife and introduced her to "the person who was largely responsible for his successful military career."

"Without Adrian Stein I would have never made it into the military academy," he explained. Afterwards his wife served Turkish coffee and homemade cake.

These recollections and the fact that Adrian knew the Mareshal "personally" produced great excitement among the members of the committee.

"You must call the Mareshal immediately!" cried several voices. "We cannot waste any time!"

"And I propose that we elect Adrian Stein as President of our Council, since he can talk to the people in power!" said the Rabbi. Everybody agreed. The vote was unanimous.

Adrian was flabbergasted. He didn't expect this turn of events. But he promised to contact the Mareshal as soon as possible.

To his surprise, his request for an audience with the Mareshal was immediately granted. In the ministerial office, the Prime Minister came to the door himself to welcome his visitor.

Once again, Adrian was stunned by the color of his hair. It looked even more flaming red than ever. There also seemed to be more freckles now.

The Mareshal's military tunic was unbuttoned and he was wearing a Legionnaire shirt under it. He was standing under a large photo of himself and the Iron Guard leader, Horațiu, both raising their right arms in the fascist salute, wearing the green shirt with the satchel of earth suspended from their necks. Next to this picture was an equally large photograph of the Mareshal shaking hands with Hitler. They were relaxed and smiling, like two old friends having a good time.

Besides the pictures, the room was dominated by a large mahogany desk which supported a heavy lamp. A shiny revolver lay at the foot of the lamp.

The Mareshal was all smiles and repeated how pleased he was to see Adrian again. "I am very indebted to you," he said, as they sat down on two brown leather armchairs. He again said, "Without you I wouldn't have had my successful military career. Nevertheless I had a rough time when King Carol arrested me and threw me in jail. It was a difficult time! But now, thank God, it is different." His face turning very serious, he asked, "What can I do for you? Do you have a problem?"

"Yes," said Adrian. "An urgent problem which needs an immediate solution."

He told the Mareshal about the Legionnaire minister of education's new order to close all the Jewish schools, synagogues and cemeteries. He even told him how Bunescu had commented about the dead, saying "throw them in the Danube!"

As he heard this, the Mareshal got very angry. His face turned as red as his hair. He pounded the desk with his fist and shouted: "The imbecile! Who does he think he is? I give the orders here and he has no business changing them! The synagogues and the cemeteries will stay open, and so will the schools. You can even have a Jewish university if you wish! I'll speak with him immediately. Bunescu should know his place and not challenge my orders! Go back and tell your community that I am the boss and I make the laws in this land!"

Adrian thanked him and got up to leave. His host saw him to the door and shook hands with him. His face was still red and his eyes full of anger.

Adrian felt disturbed by his looks. Could he have faith in his promises?

A question he couldn't answer.

THE CAR

THE CEMETERIES, SYNAGOGUES AND SCHOOLS indeed remained open, but new anti-Semitic laws appeared every day. The Mareshal had granted the Council's request, but didn't do more than that.

The decree which ordered all Jews who possessed cars to deliver them within twenty-four hours to the local Romanization Centers appeared in all newspapers and was broadcast on the radio. Insubordination was punishable by arrest and imprisonment.

On this beautiful September morning, Adrian asked Fritz to drive him with the Dodge to the Romanization Center in Cotroceni. The center was located in the former palace of a princess who had fled the country with King Carol.

To Adrian, the loss of the Dodge felt like a personal attack. It was not simply the loss of a car. It felt like a wound inflicted on his own person. Over the years, the Dodge had become a close companion, a cherished friend with whom he had spent many hours. Not only did he use it every day to go to work, but he had always driven it to Grozăveşti in the mountains, where the electrical plant he had designed, was being built. Overtime he had watched the construction develop and grow, like a child grows into an adolescent.

In addition, many trees in his garden in Bucharest—oaks, pine trees, junipers and silver fir had been picked in the mountain forests he had reached with the Dodge. Adrian remembered the Sundays and holidays when he, Nina and the children had picnicked on green or rocky peaks. Then, he and Fritz had carefully uprooted small shoots of trees which he had later replanted in the garden. They had been very small at that time, maybe five or six inches. Now they were taller than Nadia!

Adrian was also worried about Fritz, wondering what he could do now? The order to deliver the cars had been given with such short notice, there had been no time for him to apply for another job. Fritz had four children, and his wife was expecting a fifth!

He had been the Steins' chauffeur for about fifteen years, ever since Adrian had married and bought his first car. Adrian had been best man at Fritz's wedding. Over the years, he had become part of the family. Fritz had known Suzy and Nadia since they were born. Just as Adrian couldn't imagine life without the Dodge, he couldn't imagine life without Fritz. It was going to be a sad separation. Since he was so worried about Fritz's future, he had decided to pay him his salary for the next two months.

As he stepped out onto the street, Adrian saw Fritz speaking to a man in a gray uniform. They were standing next to a black Mercedes adorned with a small Nazi flag. The Mercedes was parked behind the Dodge.

"This is my brother-in-law, Hans. He will drive us back from the Romanization Center," said Fritz. "Hans works for the German Embassy. Today is his day off. The Cotroceni Palace is some distance from any public transportation, so I asked him to come along. Besides, the buses and trams will be crowded all day."

Adrian shook hands with the young man and thanked him for his help.

The morning traffic was heavy with trucks, trolleys, buses and peasants' carts. They arrived at the Palace early.

The Romanization Center, which was run entirely by the Iron Guard, was awash with green banners, adorned with the portrait of their dead leader, Captain Zelea Codreanu.

In front of the center inside the large courtyard, young men wearing green shirts were parading in military formations and singing anti-Semitic anthems. Others scurried between cars, distributing official papers and declarations.

"Jidani! Hurry up with your forms!" they kept shouting and pushing people around. The noise was deafening.

All the Jews had to stop in front of a booth by the entrance to the Palace to deposit their keys and car registration.

Fritz had driven the Dodge under a tree to a spot indicated by a green-shirted youth. Then he joined Adrian in the line which had formed in front of the registration booth. They had to wait for a while. When Adrian arrived in front of the window, he was told that he must go inside.

A young man in Legionnaire uniform, holding a revolver pointed at Adrian, made him climb a majestic staircase covered by an expensive rug. The carpet reminded him of the antique oriental rugs brought by Uncle Leon from the Punjab for the King's palace. But the once resplendent floor covering was now stained with mud and grease.

As he walked, Adrian could barely catch his breath. That gun pointed at him . . . He wished that Fritz could have joined him inside the palace, but he knew that was not possible. He had heard about beatings inside these centers. He tried to walk faster and not look at the gun.

The room to which he was taken was small and elegant. It must have been the private salon of the princess. The furniture consisted of a small desk made of inlaid wood, a few Louis XVI armchairs, and a gilded mirror. The walls were covered with French style wallpaper decorated with bucolic scenes. The curtains had the same motifs. Stains, where paintings once hung were visible on the walls. A pile of leather-bound books were lying in a corner, next to a heap of broken vases.

Adrian imagined that the princess must have left in a hurry, carrying with her only a few precious possessions. Everything else was left behind.

After a few minutes, two men wearing green shirts entered the room. To Adrian's surprise, one of them was Doctor Ionescu, his neighbor from across the street. He looked older and thinner in his green uniform. His face was more yellow. He looked like a man afflicted with jaundice. As usual, he held his pipe in his stained and leathery fingers. The other man was a tall, broad shouldered stranger with a gray moustache. He was holding a folder.

Adrian felt troubled meeting Doctor Ionescu in this place. Why was he here? What was this all about? He had known the doctor for many years. It was Doctor Ionescu who had sold him the land on which his house was built. It had been part of a large orchard—several blocks wide—which the doctor had inherited from his family and which he had needed to sell after losing much of his fortune to gambling at the Monte Carlo casino.

Even though Adrian had paid the whole cost of the land with gold coins, and had provided the doctor with a modern American stove and refrigerator for his household, he always felt that his neighbor regarded him as an unlawful intruder. He also felt that the doctor was envious of him.

Adrian remembered how, just a few years ago, when the Ionescus came over for a short visit, the doctor kept repeating: "Our trees are doing so much better and are much more beautiful since they are under your care! What is your secret?" He had also shown great admiration for Adrian's car. "I wish it were mine!" he had once joked.

"Well," said Doctor Ionescu after he sat down at the table. "The day of justice has finally come. I wanted to inform you personally that your smart, fashionable Dodge will now belong to me. It wasn't easy to get it. I wasn't the only one who wanted it. But justice has finally prevailed!"

He lit his pipe and went on. "You, Jidani, have benefited too long and too much from privileges you don't deserve. It is high time that you return all your gains to the lawful inhabitants of this country! So, I must tell you, I can hardly wait to receive the car keys and registration papers directly from you." With these words he stood up and reached over the desk.

Adrian hesitated. He wanted to shout, "You are a thief! You don't deserve anything! I will never give you my car!" He bit his lip. He felt the blood throbbing in his head. Then, in the mirror behind them, he saw the gun pointed at him.

Slowly, he put his hand in his pocket, pulled out the keys and registration papers and placed them on the table.

"Perfect! Well done!" said Doctor Ionescu with a grin. He put the keys in his pocket and slid the papers into the folder. "Now let's go and find your chauffeur, since he will drive me home in the car!"

Adrian was surprised by these words, but said nothing.

They found Fritz waiting outside by the registration booth. Doctor Ionescu looked radiant. "Hello!" he said. "Everything's done. Now the Dodge is mine, and I expect you to drive it to my house. You'll be working for me from now on, as nobody knows that car better than you! We'll have a swell time from now on!"

Fritz, who was much taller than the doctor, looked down at him. He shook his head.

"No!" he said. "I won't drive you home and I won't work for you. I'm not tied to the Dodge and you can't order me around. Besides, I already have a job. I'll be working for the German Embassy. I speak German and my family comes from Austria. I've already signed the contract with the Embassy."

Adrian and Doctor Ionescu were both stunned. Adrian never expected this. Fritz had never mentioned a word about the German Embassy.

But the doctor was furious. His yellow face turned red. "I can't believe you!" he shouted. Turning to Adrian, "This is another Jewish trick! One of your eternal schemes and Jewish plots! But you will pay for it! The day will come when you'll pay!" He kept shouting at Adrian.

A few minutes later, Fritz and Adrian walked quickly toward the black Mercedes with the Nazi flag. It was parked just outside the gate.

"It isn't true. I haven't signed any contract with the German Embassy," Fritz said when they were seated in the car. "I haven't concealed anything from you. I didn't know that this was coming. But I may just do it!" he went on, after a moment of silence.

"My brother-in-law Hans is exploring it for me. It would be better to work for the Embassy than for a man as lousy as Ionescu. Anyway, I will never work for that crook!"

They drove in silence, and when they were close to Adrian's home, Fritz turned toward him again. "It's too bad that the doctor got your beautiful car! But who knows, things may change if we live long enough." Adrian nodded. He couldn't say anything.

Finally, they stopped in front of the garden gate. As they climbed out of the car, Fritz promised to come back the next day to collect the money Adrian had offered him.

THE OFFICE

A DRIAN HAD BARELY TIME TO get used to life without his car, when another new law was proclaimed. Now, all Jewish engineers were excluded from their professional organizations and prohibited from working in their specialty.

Adrian quickly realized that, like his car, his office was also going to be taken away. It had already happened to Jewish lawyers and their offices. They were first banned from their professional organizations, then prohibited from practicing law, and finally their offices were taken away.

He had learned, from the moment the new law appeared, everything would have to remain in the office; nothing could be removed. He had decided to be prepared and, ahead of time, to take out everything which was important to him. He couldn't bring himself to abandon his papers and documents to the hands of strangers. He knew that what he was doing was risky, but he felt that he had no other choice.

At the office, he opened the safe and checked its content. He had planned to take out only the most important papers. But he spent a whole morning combing through his documents. He pulled out, one after the other, the folders containing the plans of the power station in Grozăveşti which he had designed, then a series of important articles and publications in the field of electrical turbines and transformers. His own collection of original articles by Nicola Tesla, the scientist who had inspired him in his youth and who had given him an inscribed photograph of himself sitting next to his electrical transmitter surrounded by cascades of sparks.

Then there was his entire correspondence of many years with Charles Kass of Brown Boveri in Switzerland and his insistent offers to work with him in Baden.

There were the receipts of the sums of money which he had sent to Switzerland. He certainly didn't want the authorities to know about his money abroad. They would take everything away. They could even arrest and torture him. Jews were not allowed to hold money abroad. They had to declare it to the authorities, and then it was confiscated. Blackmail and torture were serious matters.

Finally, there were the keys to his villa in Lugano. He took them in his hand and stared at them. How well he remembered Lugano! He and Nina had been there on their honeymoon and had found their dream house on the shores of the lake. It was a stone villa with an orange tile roof, surrounded by lemon and cypress trees. Nina was ready to refurbish and decorate it. They were going to buy furniture, rugs, crockery and move in, spending their holidays by the lake.

But time passed, the children were born, and, fifteen years later, when Adrian returned to Lugano and bought their "dream villa," Nina had changed her mind. She said she could not live abroad without her siblings, particularly her sister Stella. Adrian could not even convince her to join him and visit the house. It made him very sad.

Now he kept staring at the keys in his hand, contemplating, with his mind's eye the big loggias hung with blooming wisteria and the small red boat sailing in the sunlight.

The bronze keys were heavy in his hand. Adrian couldn't decide whether they were a symbol of the past or a sign of the future. He slipped them into their brown velvet pouch and placed them inside the safe.

In addition to the keys, journals and documents, there were important professional books. They were irreplaceable. He couldn't abandon them.

He had brought with him two suitcases in which he thought he could crowd everything. But now he saw that this was not possible. He had to take out the whole safe. He called Fritz, his old chauffeur, who now worked for the German Embassy. He came with a van and his brother-in-law Hans.

They worked hard to move the safe. It was heavy and so large that it was difficult to carry through the doors. They all wondered how it had been brought into the office in the first place! But they succeeded at last.

Before leaving, Adrian looked at the window which was engraved with the large figure of a naked devil that covered a factory chimney with his hand. The smoke billowed out through the windows and doors of the factory, while the frightened crowd of tiny workers spilled out into the street.

He had this window engraved with the figure of a naked devil as the symbol of an industry based on coal burning. It seemed to Adrian now that the grinning devil was watching him. And, even though this image had always represented the evils of the coal industry, Adrian had grown attached to the naked devil and knew that he was going to miss him.

On Monday morning at 7:30 when Adrian came to work, the men who were going to take over the office were already there. They were three youths in green shirts with guns, and a middle-aged man, the chief of the group. He was tall and gaunt, grim-looking, with thin lips and a pointed nose. A deep frown on his forehead. He was pacing nervously in front of the building, while one youth armed with a rifle stood guard by the door. Adrian had to show his ID before he could enter the suite.

"We're from the Romanization Center. Here to take over your office," said the grim-faced man as he entered the room. He sat at the desk and took a bunch of forms out of his briefcase.

"Sit!" he barked at Adrian, motioning to a chair opposite him. The three youths had posted themselves in front of the windows and in front of the door, guns pointed at Adrian. He felt like a prisoner ready for execution.

The grim-faced man started filling out forms. He kept tapping the desk with his fingers while completing an inventory of the room. When he finished, he needed to take measurements of the office. Adrian offered him a sheet with measurements, but he refused.

"Measurements from a Jidan are always unreliable!"

He had his assistants do the work, and when it was finished, he made Adrian sign a statement saying that he had voluntarily put his office and its contents at the disposal of the Romanization Center.

The commander slipped the forms into his briefcase and pulled out another bunch. Now he stared fixedly at Adrian, and started to ask questions:

"Money. What money do you have abroad and where is it?"

"None."

"Don't lie, Jidane! We know that all of you have money abroad. If you lie, you'll pay with your life."

There was a long silence, while the man kept staring at him.

"I repeat: what money or other property, assets, do you have abroad?"

"None," said Adrian again, without blinking.

"What money or gold do you have here in your office? You must declare it immediately." He handed Adrian a blank sheet of paper and a pen.

"None. I have none."

"None? I don't believe you."

Adrian repeated: "I have none."

"Then declare it on this sheet of paper."

While Adrian wrote, the man kept drumming with his fingers on the desk. As soon as he had finished, the man spoke again.

"What weapons are you hiding in this office?"

"Weapons?" Adrian asked in surprise. "I have no weapons!"

"No weapons? And no gold? I don't believe you! All Jews hide gold and arms at their business quarters. We must make a search. Get up and face the wall! You Gheorghe watch him. If he moves, shoot!"

They pushed him, face to the wall and he closed his eyes. He heard loud noises. The men were pulling books from the shelves, they were ripping pages, and dumping the books on the floor. Drawers were opened and emptied on the parquet one on top of the other.

The man in command was pacing back and forth. He lost patience and started yelling at the three youths. There was a cracking sound as a cabinet was shattered and wrecked, then a loud sound of broken glass told Adrian that the crystal which covered the desk had been smashed. In the end, there was a very loud crash which made Adrian turn around in spite of himself. He had just enough time to see the big window with the engraved devil plunge to the floor, breaking into a hundred shards.

"Was this your grandfather? Your Jewish God?" asked the grim-faced man with a snarl.

Adrian glanced at him and turned to the wall.

Finally, they were ready to leave. Outside, the captain of the group made Adrian lock the door and hand him the keys. Adrian watched the men get into their car and take off. Then he turned back and opened the door with a key he had kept. He searched through the bits of glass on the floor and when he found the face of the grinning devil he wrapped it in a piece of newspaper and took it home.

SCHOOL DAYS

T HE HIGH SCHOOL WHERE NADIA was now enrolled was in the heart of the Jewish section. It was a somewhat large, old building of red bricks with arched windows, located at the end of a street of small, ancient, one-family houses. It was only twenty minutes by bicycle from Nadia's home.

The street was very quiet. There were old trees and bushes in the schoolyard and even older trees in the gardens which bordered the street. The only noise was the chirping of sparrows and the laughter of the girls in the schoolyard. Occasionally a sleepy dog would wake up and bark.

There were about sixty students in Nadia's class and the desks were so crowded together that it was difficult to move around. Nadia found herself seated next to Dorothea Waldman, a 12-year-old girl with thick, brown braids. But most striking about Dorothea were her eyes. Particularly her right eye, which was larger than the left. It was also more luminous since it was filled with tiny specks of gold which sparkled in the light.

Sitting so close together in the crowded room led to a tight friendship between the two girls. Also, Dorothea lived right around the corner from Nadia. Every morning they packed their schoolbooks and sandwiches in one bag. Then, perched on Nadia's rickety bicycle, they both rode to school. Dorothea climbed on the seat, while Nadia pedaled, standing, without sitting down. She had dubbed this unusual arrangement, "the two-headed bicycle monster."

In the beginning of the semester, Nadia hated this new school. It couldn't compare with her old, distinguished lyceum. There were no labs, no gym, or geography room, not even a library or reading room. The corridors were dark and narrow; paint was peeling from the walls. Some of the classrooms were dark, humid and smelled of mold. Nadia had seen a rat scurrying away among the weeds in the courtyard. She had told her parents that she wasn't going to go back to that school.

Nina got very angry and cried. She told Nadia that she was "killing her." But Adrian talked patiently to her, telling her to keep trying to stay in school and not give up so easily.

"You can do what other children are doing!" he told her. "How will you feel when everybody else will know science, history, and literature and you alone will remain a dummy?"

These words made her doubt her decision. But more convincing than her father's advice was the news that Domnişoara Braunstein, Adrian's old secretary who had a doctorate in French and English literature and whom Nadia liked very much, was going to teach French and history.

Aunt Mathilda, who had drilled her for the admission exam to the old school, was going to teach math. Nadia hoped that these two ladies whom she was fond of, weren't going to be too tough with her!

For some time she kept thinking of her old friend, Liudmila, wondering where she was and what she was doing. She tried to imagine her life in the far away river town. But as she couldn't receive any letters from Liudmila and didn't know anything about her life, she thought less often about her and grew closer to her new friend, Dorothea.

She often visited Dorothea at her home, particularly in the afternoon, after they had finished their homework. Each afternoon Dorothea had to practice piano, and Nadia would settle herself in a cool place beneath the grand piano. Dorothea had to practice for at least two hours. It always started with Czerny's exercises and was followed by a short piece, such as *Moment Musical*, which she repeated again and again, until it was perfect, or nearly perfect. Eventually she progressed enough to play Mozart's *A la Turca* and Beethoven's *Mondschein Sonata*.

Every afternoon at 4, Mrs. Waldman, Dorothea's mother, would interrupt the piano practice, call Nadia and Dorothea into the dining room to serve them tea or hot chocolate and almond croissants which she had baked herself. She would sit with them at the table and ask questions about school, about the teachers and even about the other students. After the short break was over, Dorothea returned to her practice, and Nadia again took her place under the grand piano.

On a Monday in the middle of October, when Nadia and Dorothea came to school, they found the street closed to traffic. A huge German tank was barricading one end of the street. It had a long gun barrel pointed at oncoming traffic and was flanked by Wehrmacht soldiers wearing metal helmets and battle gear. A deafening metallic rumble came from the tank, even though it wasn't moving. The two girls were frightened and didn't know what to do. The tank was very large, and the soldiers looked threatening in their dark uniforms holding machine guns and revolvers. The noise from the tank was frightening.

Nadia and Dorothea got off the bicycle and wondered whether they should turn around and go home. But the soldiers pointed to a narrow passageway near the tank and signaled them to advance. The girls hesitated but then decided to keep walking. They squeezed past the rumbling tank and, as they marched toward the school, they saw that the entire street was filled with armored cars, cannons on rolling platforms and more tanks. The rumble made by this machinery was deafening.

The schoolyard too was filled with the same military arsenal. The whole street and schoolyard had been turned into a huge parking lot for the Wehrmacht. The soldiers hurried back and forth between their vehicles, stomping their boots on the pavement.

Nadia and Dorothea advanced cautiously, walking the bike, stopping from time to time. Should they turn around and go home? they wondered. But when they entered the schoolyard they met other students and a few teachers. They kept walking slowly between the canons and tanks, and finally reached the entrance to the school building. Here they were met by another German soldier in battle gear, who stopped them from going to the classrooms on the ground floor. He directed them to the upper floors. All the classrooms and offices on the main floor had been taken over by the German troops.

The encounter with the German soldiers at the school came as a big shock to Nadia and Dorothea. In fact, the presence of the German troops in Bucharest surprised everyone. They appeared one morning in the city with their tanks and cannons, as if out of nowhere. Now, suddenly, they were everywhere: the officers in their elegant uniforms lodging in the best hotels and the motorized troops taking over the entire Jewish section of the city. It was said that they had come as "friends" and "protectors." But, with the signing of the Hitler-Stalin Pact, this wasn't clear: What protectors? Against whom?

A week earlier, a number of German "civil engineers" had come to the country to "inspect bridges and railroads." They were staying at the most expensive hotels in the city. Then, one morning, without warning, they shed their civilian clothing and appeared dressed as German officers. At the same time Wehrmacht troops in battle gear appeared everywhere. Rumors had it that they were hiding for some time in the forests surrounding the town.

On Embassy Row, the British Consulate closed shop after the press secretary was found shot dead in front of the building. A red swastika had been painted with his blood on his forehead.

At school, the situation remained unchanged for a few weeks. Nadia and Dorothea had to squeeze past canons and tanks, even though they were frightened by them. The engines kept rumbling all day under their windows and, when they stopped, the soldiers marched in the schoolyard singing Lili Marlene and other war songs. With so much noise, it was hard to hear what the teachers said.

By the end of October the bad weather started, with icy rain, wind and mud. The streets were wet and had become slippery. Nina told Nadia to stop using the bike and to walk to school like the other children. Dorothea had decided to stop riding the bicycle and walked to school instead. But Nadia was stubborn and kept using the bike. She put on her red slicker, gathered her books and her sandwich in her schoolbag, and pedaled as fast as she could through the windswept streets. It was hard to advance: the freezing rain was whipping her face and her hands, while the wheels of the bicycle were slipping on the wet cobblestones. After half an hour she arrived near the school, breathless, with frozen hands and teary eyes. As she tried to avoid a slow moving tank, the wheels of the bike slipped and she fell.

There was a sharp pain in her left knee. Blood was running down her leg and into her shoe. The next minute she was lifted and carried inside the building by a German soldier. His face was hidden by his big helmet.

At first, Nadia didn't recognize the room where she was taken. It was a light and clean medical office, with an examining table in the middle, two white cabinets with glass doors against the wall, and a wooden desk in a corner. A large photograph of the Führer in military uniform and a banner with a black swastika were hanging from the wall. It was only the embroidered curtain by the window and the brown garbage can which made Nadia recognize the old office of the principal.

The doctor who examined her was young and handsome, with blond hair, clear blue eyes and rosy cheeks. He wore a stethoscope and a white coat over his military uniform. He disinfected Nadia's cut and wound a big bandage around her knee. Then he gave her a tetanus shot which hurt so much, it brought tears to her eyes.

From the beginning of the consultation Nadia spoke German to the doctor, which made him very friendly. He told her that she was lucky that she didn't need stitches, and ordered her to come back after three days to clean the wound and change the dressing. Before she left, he gave her a piece of Stollwerk chocolate.

At home, Nina scolded her for her stubbornness and was angry that she had to be treated by a "Nazi" doctor. She said that it was a bitter irony that, under the present laws, a Romanian doctor was not allowed to treat a Jewish patient, and a Jewish doctor was not permitted to treat a Romanian patient. But of course, a German military doctor could take care of a Jewish child!

Nina decided that it was definitely the end of the bicycle rides. And this time Nadia went along with her mother—mainly because she couldn't bend her leg with the huge bandage around her knee.

She went a few more times for treatment to the doctor, and every time he gave her a bar of Stollwerk chocolate. On the second visit he showed her a picture of his 12-year-old daughter. Her name was Irma and she lived in Berlin. He told Nadia that he missed his daughter very much and that Nadia reminded him of her.

On the morning of November 10, Nadia went to her last treatment. The doctor removed her bandage and gave her a large piece of chocolate with marzipan. Nadia thanked him. She felt sorry that she had finished treatment and wasn't going to see him anymore. She said goodbye and went upstairs to her classroom.

It had rained all morning that Saturday so the soldiers were not rumbling around in their tanks and armored trucks. In the now quiet classroom, the students could listen to their history lesson, given by their new teacher, Domnişoara Braunstein. (Nadia knew her well, since she had worked in her father's office.) She was a passionate lecturer, enjoying the opportunity to teach, rather than being forced to work as a secretary in an office.

Today's lecture was about the French Revolution and the execution of the aristocrats by guillotine. She spoke about "Les Tricoteuses," the lower class women who kept knitting, while watching the spectacle of the nobles being beheaded by the guillotine.

Domnişoara Braunstein taught her students "La Marseillaise." She had written the words on the blackboard. Everybody was singing:

> *Allons enfants de la patrie*
> *Le jour de gloire est arrivé!*
> *Contre nous de la tyrannie*
> *L'étendard sanglant élevé . . .*

when a deep clamor like a hundred tanks was suddenly heard. The girls sang louder to cover the noise, but the clamor grew more intense. Then the whole room, the entire building started to shake. It was rocking and rolling like a ship on a stormy sea. The windows were rattling, the doors were opening and shutting by themselves, the blackboard fell off the wall with a big thud, books tumbled down from the shelves. A rain of plaster fell from the ceiling. And on the front wall, by the window, a black crack suddenly appeared. It grew longer and wider, exposing the bricks, until the sky could be seen through the opening.

When the earthquake stopped, the frightened students ran to the door. But only half of the double door opened. The other half was stuck on broken hinges. They pushed and shoved through the narrow space trying to get to the stairs. But the steps were covered with plaster and pieces of bricks. The stairway was shaking dangerously under their feet. A part of it had come loose from the wall and was now hanging in midair.

There was no way they could get down by the stairs. They panicked and started to scream. They ran back into the classroom and some girls were so frightened they burst into tears. Domnișoara Braunstein had great difficulties keeping them calm. To get some help, some attention from the Germans, she called the soldiers downstairs, but her voice was covered up by the rumble of their machinery.

She then wrote S.O.S. on a blank piece of paper and wrapped it around a big piece of chalk. She also tied together a few large handkerchiefs from her students, took them to the window and let them wave like a flag of surrender. At the same time she threw the chalk wrapped in the S.O.S. paper down into the courtyard. It landed on the engine of an armored car.

Immediately the soldiers who were clearing away the rubble which had fallen on the car picked it up and became aware of the students' plight. They raised a firemen's ladder to the second floor window. One by one, all the girls climbed down. Domnişoara Braunstein was the last to be rescued.

As soon as she stepped off the ladder, Nadia looked at the window of the medical office: it was badly cracked. She could see the doctor in his white coat standing on top of the desk, trying to fix it with surgical tape.

Even though it was only 10 o'clock in the morning, school was finished for the day. The students went home. On their way, Nadia and Dorothea were met with unusual sights: people in pajamas and nightgowns, bundled up in blankets or winter coats, were huddled on the sidewalk in front of their houses. They said they were waiting for the second earthquake, which was expected to occur within the next two or three hours.

The streets were littered with bricks, broken chimneys, and tiles fallen from the roofs. A freezing November rain was falling. But the frightened and shivering people kept waiting outside in the cold, risking pneumonia and frostbite, rather than end up buried alive inside a collapsing building.

When the two girls reached the end of the block, near the corner, Nadia turned around and looked at the school. "Will we ever come back to this building with its broken staircase and cracked walls, and all the German soldiers?" she asked. "What will happen to us, to our school, to our classrooms?"

Dorothea looked at her and shrugged. "I don't know. I bet *nobody* knows the answer!"

A VIENNESE DINNER PARTY

THE SECOND EARTHQUAKE DIDN'T OCCUR in the next two hours. It didn't happen on that Saturday at all. As a matter of fact, later in the day, an official communiqué was given on the radio, stating that the imminent danger of another earthquake had passed.

That evening, Nina and Adrian were invited for dinner at Domnişoara Braunstein's apartment. She was celebrating "the launching of her new teaching career."

The closure of Adrian's office and the need for qualified Jewish teachers in the new schools was a blessing for Domnişoara Braunstein. Her brother Erwin who had arrived in Bucharest on the day of the Anschluss, two years ago, was also looking for a teaching position. He had been a lawyer in Vienna. As such, he knew Latin perfectly and hoped to become a Latin teacher in one of the Jewish schools. He also played the violin and could teach music or give private lessons. But so far he had only succeeded in making some translations from German into Romanian and vice versa.

Dinner was set for seven o'clock in the evening. Nina and Adrian didn't want to be out too late. The streets were dangerous now. Only a few days before two cousins of

Nina's and their friends were severely beaten by Iron Guard bands who roamed the streets after dark. One cousin almost lost his eye; the other ended up with broken ribs.

For this visit Adrian had bought a box of marrons glacés, and Nina took out of her armoire a bottle of French cognac which her brother Emil had given her for her birthday two years ago. As they were getting ready to leave, Nina stood in front of the mirror arranging her pillbox hat with the small voilette. When she finished, she draped her silver fox over her dark winter coat. Adrian had taken the packages and was waiting for her by the door. He was not in a bad mood. After the shock of losing his office had worn off, he had received a phone call from an old colleague at Grozăveşti, engineer George T., who stated that there was some trouble with one of the turbines. Would Adrian be willing to look into it? Actually, would he be willing to become an "unofficial consultant?" His identity would be fully protected, his colleague assured him.

Adrian accepted the offer with great relief. Now he suddenly realized that his colleague, George T., had the same address as Domnişoara Braunstein: they both lived in the Carlton, the newest high-rise in the city.

The rain had stopped, so they walked to the dinner party. On the big boulevard, the litter from the earthquake had been removed. Only the small side streets were still covered with pieces of broken chimneys and tiles.

Domnişoara Braunstein's home, the Carlton, was the most modern high-rise in the city. It had been built above a large movie theater, which could seat a great number of spectators. The entrance to the residential wing, which was next to the movie theater, was impressive. Two big columns standing near the glass door which opened onto a lobby as spacious as a small theater. There were comfortable armchairs, green plants, a dark marble floor with small specks of gold and soft, indirect lighting.

No additional decoration. Everything was in simple geometrical lines. A very modern, very "Bauhaus" inspired construction, thought Adrian. And very solid since there was no trace of damage from the earthquake.

Upstairs, on the 11th floor, Domnişoara Braunstein, her mother and her brother were waiting for them. Erwin's wife, Sophie, didn't join them; she stayed home with the baby.

The apartment was small, but furnished with taste. A comfortable sofa and armchairs, a coffee table, a large bookcase with books in four languages. Framed reproductions of French impressionists—Monet, Renoir and Degas—and a few abstract pictures by Mondrian, Kandinsky and Braque hung on the walls. Everything was simple and modern, with the exception of a small collection of Lalique vases and lamps, scattered in various corners. They matched surprisingly well the modern character of the apartment.

"I love this ornate French glasswork," said Domnişoara Braunstein as if apologizing. "It may be old-fashioned, but I love it. Thank God, only one vase fell and broke during the earthquake. But I have gathered the shards and I think I can have them glued back together."

"Will it hold water? Will you be able to put flowers in it?" asked Adrian.

"Yes, of course!" said Domnişoara Braunstein, staring at him with her big grey eyes. "The owner of the antique shop around the corner has magical hands. He can glue anything back together, so it's as good as new!"

She straightened out her big, practical skirt with deep pockets, and went on. "I feel so privileged to be able to live in this great building! I sank all my own and my mother's savings in this apartment, but it is worthwhile. Just look at the view!" She pointed to the large window from where one could have a bird's eye view of the city. "I also have a wonderful terrace where, on a clear day, you can see the Bucegi mountains in the distance!"

While she was speaking, her mother, a woman in her 70's with a wrinkled but friendly face, her silver hair gathered in a bun served everybody with hot cheese patés and glasses of Fernet Branca. She still had beautiful hands with perfectly manicured fingernails. She was wearing a light grey angora sweater and a thin strand of pearls.

They drank to the success of their new careers and to the uneventful ending of the earthquake. Over a dinner of roast chicken Viennese style washed down with an Austrian wine, the conversation skipped from Grinzig sausages and Sacher torte to Beethoven's *Symphonie Pastorale*, which he had composed on the outskirts of Vienna. Then it turned to the German and Austrian writers in exile, and the numerous books burnt by the order of Hitler. Finally it concentrated on the anti-fascist speeches and articles written by Einstein and Thomas Mann. Everybody admired the courage and fighting spirit of these two great men.

However, Adrian and Erwin didn't agree on everything. The young man was a confirmed Marxist, who had studied *Das Kapital* and believed in Communism and the Soviets. He admired Berthold Brecht, Bernard Shaw and Stalin. "Our hope is with the Soviets, and Communism is the future," he proclaimed. "It is the only hope we have against Fascism!"

Adrian didn't agree with him. He kept shaking his head and challenging the young man with controversial issues, such as the Hitler-Stalin Pact, the lack of freedom in Russia, Stalin's purges and the recent assassination of Trotsky.

They had finished dinner and were sipping the French cognac Adrian had brought for the evening. Erwin put down his glass and lit a cigarette before answering. He tried to stay calm, but his face was flushed and his eyes were shining.

"We cannot know, we don't have enough information to understand the situation in Russia," he said. "So many rumors, we really don't know the truth." He added that he was sure that Stalin acted in the best interest of the people and that Trotsky's death had nothing to do with Stalin. "It was just a madman, a crazy Mexican murderer!"

"Then how about Mayakovsky's suicide?" Adrian too was red in the face and his voice was louder than usual. Nina put her hand on his arm, trying to keep him calm.

But Domnişoara Braunstein interrupted the discussion by clapping her hands. "You will never be able to answer these questions. There are no answers," she said. "I have a better idea: why don't we ask Erwin to play the violin for us? He is an accomplished musician. And if you play a Fritz Kreisler piece," she said turning to Erwin, "mother will accompany you at the piano."

Everybody agreed with this suggestion. The young man finished his drink and rose to get his violin. He was tall and thin, with a slightly stooped back. Meanwhile, his mother arranged her seat in front of the piano. A few minutes later, the sounds of the violin and the piano filled the apartment.

Nina and Adrian went home at about 10 o'clock. Since it was windy and rainy again, they took a taxi from the row standing in front of the Carlton. They felt safer in the car than walking the dark streets where they risked being attacked by gangs of Legionnaires. At one point they heard singing, shouting and screaming, but their cab drove away from the noise.

When they arrived home, Suzy and Nadia were already in bed. Nina and Adrian took off their coats, kissed the girls good night, and went to their bedroom. Nina sat in front of the mirror and smiled while combing her hair. "It was a beautiful evening!" she said. "It's been a while since I had such a good time!"

"Yes," Adrian answered. "I too had a good time, in spite of my discussion with Erwin. He is a bright, idealistic youth, perhaps too naïve! But he is very talented with the violin. I think he could be a successful musician. We had a good evening, indeed."

Adrian stroked Nina's hair and kissed the back of her neck. He took her in his arms and brought her to bed. They fell asleep in a tender embrace.

In his dream, Adrian was listening to the sound of the violin. He and Nina were still at Domnișoara Braunstein's, but the violin player had changed from Erwin Braunstein to George T, the engineer who had offered Adrian the consulting job and who also resided at the Carlton. (He had given Adrian a business card with his own name and the word "Carlton" inscribed in bold print.)

While he was playing, the man got up suddenly and started to dance. He turned, jumped and swayed so fast that the room started to shake. Other people who were there joined him in his wild hopping and spinning, making the walls rattle and creak.

When Adrian woke up, the lights were on and he saw Nina bent over him. She was pulling his arm and screaming: an earthquake! an earthquake! The bed was shaking. The clock showed four in the morning. He jumped out of bed and ran to the children, but at that moment the lights went out and the violent rocking threw him to the floor. There was a deafening rumble, the walls made loud, cracking noises, and, in the dark, heavy objects were falling. He heard the sound of breaking glass followed by the crash of the crystal chandelier hitting the floor. Pieces of plaster were raining from the ceiling, striking him as if it were hail. Nadia and Suzy came running from their bedroom, and they all ended up huddled on the floor, holding a blanket over their head. It felt as if the shaking and rumbling were getting stronger and stronger and would never stop.

After a while the tremors became less violent and eventually they stopped altogether. Nina got up in the dark and walked to the kitchen to get a candle and matches. She was barefoot, and as soon as she took a few steps, she cut her foot on the broken glass.

With the burning candles, Nina and Adrian walked through the rooms to look at the damage. They had to advance carefully because of the rubble which covered the floor. They were stunned by what they saw. In every room, paintings, mirrors and lamps had fallen off the walls. Books were lying in heaps on the floor. In the dining room, the display case with fine china and crystal was lying on one side, and everything inside was broken. In the kitchen, cups, saucers and glasses had been flung from the shelves and were smashed. In the living room, the big glass door to the terrace was cracked.

When the lights came back on, they could see the trail of blood left by Nina's cut. As soon as the telephones were working, Nina called Stella, her sister. "We're okay and Emil's family is okay. Just a lot of plaster and broken glass," she said. "But—the Carlton is gone! Look out the window: it is no more. It has collapsed! And it's weird: the telephones are working. You can reach the people inside, even though they're buried under fallen walls! Sorel has taken the bicycle and gone there. He has patients, two families with children who live in the Carlton!"

Adrian immediately called Domnişoara Braunstein. She picked up right away. She was crying. "We're in the dark. We're buried under collapsed walls and ceiling. We called the police and the firemen, but we couldn't get through. I don't know what they're doing out there."

Adrian called the police and the firemen himself. The calls didn't go through.

He called his old colleague, the engineer George T. who also lived in the Carlton. The phone kept ringing, but there was no answer.

Then he called Domnişoara Braunstein again. She was sobbing and sounded desperate. More plaster and bricks had come raining down. It was dark, the three of them were locked in a tiny space and couldn't reach the doors or the window. The floor was shifting, and they could hear the loud thuds of falling walls.

Adrian decided that he had to do something: he had to go to the Carlton himself. He got dressed in a hurry, put on his heavy winter jacket, his fur hat and his woolen scarf. Then he unlocked Nadia's bicycle and started toward the Carlton.

Nina was angry at him for leaving like that. She was worried for him, for his health, for his safety. She was also afraid of another possible earthquake. But Adrian didn't listen.

It was almost 6 o'clock on a rainy Sunday morning. The traffic was worse than on a weekday rush hour. Everybody was running some place and many streets were closed because of falling debris. All the roads were littered with rubble, making it hard to advance. People were angry and frightened, and kept swearing and cursing.

When he finally arrived at the Carlton, it was in ruins. He couldn't get close, since the site had been cordoned off and was surrounded by police and firemen. What had once been a twelve story high-rise was now a mound of debris, barely as high as the second or third floor. From time to time Adrian kept hearing telephones ringing and people speaking from under the ruins.

The whole scene was lit by enormous floodlights, giving it an eerie feeling. And the picture became even more surrealistic, when, in all the confusion, he clearly heard men singing. He saw a large crowd of Iron Guard youths, dressed in their green shirts advancing from around the corner. They were carrying big banners with their symbol, the image of the Archangel Michael killing the dragon. They were accompanied by priests wearing their ceremonial garb and carrying incense burners.

The youths stopped in front of the ruins and kept singing their anthems. Then they fell to their knees, and the priests started praying and reciting a special Mass.

The workers and the firemen on the site were hindered by the religious ceremony and by the crowd of demonstrators. They tried to chase them away. Some firemen turned their hoses on them, but others didn't dare hurt the priests. A big scuffle ensued between the police, the firemen and the Iron Guard Legionnaires. Adrian heard the screams and the loud noise of fighting. He had stepped aside, so as not to be caught in the tumult.

Suddenly, there was a loud explosion. Flames shot up from the mound of rubble, and a cloud of black smoke engulfed everything. The ringing of telephones stopped. Then, Adrian heard the rumble of heavy machinery in the distance. And, when the smoke lifted somewhat, a convoy of German troops armed with heavy digging equipment and specially trained dogs arrived.

The German soldiers surrounded the demonstrators and pointed their rifles at them. Their captain climbed on top of an armored truck and ordered them to leave. At his command, the Legionnaire youths and the priests disappeared in a hurry.

Finally, after so many hours, serious work was to be started. The German troops and the firemen closed the whole boulevard and everybody had to leave.

Adrian was cold and exhausted. It had been raining and his jacket was soaked. His hands and feet were frozen. He felt crushed, overwhelmed by the catastrophe. He was devastated by his own helplessness and pessimistic about the fate of the Braunsteins. The incompetence and disorganization of the local authorities infuriated him.

When he arrived home, Nina told him that she had spoken twice with Domnişoara Braunstein. The young woman was crying and asking for help. She said that her mother and brother were not talking at all and she didn't know why. Maybe they were unconscious.

The second time they spoke, her voice was faint, and the words came out slowly. Then, Nina said, there was a loud thud, and the telephone went dead.

While listening to Nina, Adrian turned on the radio. The announcer said that the earthquake which had occurred at 4:15 on Sunday morning had measured 7.6 on the Richter scale and had lasted four minutes. Saturday's earthquake had measured only 6.7.

The announcer then added that no survivors had yet been found at the Carlton, with the exception of a tiny baby which had been propelled from the twelfth floor in its crib.

This news was later confirmed by the papers.

THE RABBI, THE MEETING AND
THE MARESHAL

Another meeting of the Underground Jewish Council took place in Adrian's living room, a few days after the earthquake. Everybody was there: the Chief Rabbi Alexander Naftali, two Zionist leaders, the two school principals, the lawyer, the journalist, and of course, Stella, Sorel and Adrian.

They were happy to see each other, relieved to have survived the earthquake with only minor destruction. They complained about broken windows, leaky roofs and damaged walls which had to be mended and plastered.

And then they all remembered the Carlton and its many victims. Everybody in the room had a dear friend or a relative killed in the building, and was now mourning his disappearance. Adrian recalled the death of the Braunstein family whom he and Nina had visited the evening before the earthquake. Sorel who, as a physician, had gone to the Carlton to help those trapped in the ruins, talked about a group of Jewish physicians who had come to help, but were arrested by the Iron Guard. They were taken to police headquarters and savagely beaten. They were accused of being "spies for a foreign country," even though some of them were wearing national military decorations which they had received as soldiers in World War I.

Professor Jakubov and the other principal worried about the future of the Jewish students and of the school buildings which had been either severely damaged by the earthquake or were now completely occupied by German troops.

It was Rabbi Naftali who made the Council aware that the Jewish cemeteries at the outskirts of the city— which were still in use by the community—had begun to be ploughed over by so-called "farmers," members of the Iron Guard. The Rabbi had brought with him a briefcase from which he extracted a thick pile of letters and claims describing abuses and acts of violence suffered by the Jews all over the country.

"Shall I read all the letters to you?" asked the Rabbi. "They are worthwhile, but I'm afraid it will take at least a thousand and one nights, just like in the story of the Sheherazade. So, since we don't have a thousand and one nights, I'll select only a few representative claims."

Rabbi Naftali smoothed his pointed black beard with his left hand and read a few letters describing how, day or night, Jews were picked up randomly from the street or from the synagogues. They were then taken to Legionnaire centers or police stations where special torture chambers had been set up in the basement. There they were beaten unconscious or forced to sign over to the Iron Guard their houses, their savings or their stores.

Other letters described posters with the words: "Jewish store! Do not enter! Do not patronize!" "Who shops at the Jidani is a traitor. He will be photographed, and his picture will be made public!" "Entry forbidden at the Jidani!" All the posters were signed by the Legionnaire Iron Guard.

These notices were pasted on the doors and on the windows of the stores. Green-shirted armed guards were stationed in front of the shops, ready to arrest or beat up anybody who dared enter the store.

The Rabbi then produced other letters which described how the Iron Guards forced their way into Jewish homes, banks, businesses and even factories and beat up or threatened the owners into signing over "everything on the premises" to the intruders or to the Legionnaire movement. Wealthy, prosperous homes and enterprises were plundered at the same rate as hovels and shacks.

And how about the synagogues, the houses of worship? The Rabbi gave an account of many temples, all over the country, which had their stained glass windows shattered and their silver candelabras stolen. In addition, many religious Jewish men who attended services had had their beards shaven by force.

Sometimes, the Rabbi continued, the entry into Jewish homes or businesses was presented as a "Search for Suspects." In those instances, the Legionnaire intruders scattered fake Communist leaflets inside the rooms, and then the entire family or the head of the household was accused of being Communist spies and arrested.

There was a particularly poignant case of a 15-year-old schoolboy accused of "Communist propaganda" whose dead body was returned to the family after such an investigation.

And there was another letter, describing the story of an old lawyer who was found dead, after "jumping out the window" during an Iron Guard interrogation.

The members of the Underground Jewish Council listened in silence to the Rabbi's presentation. Yes, it was true. They all knew that these attacks and abuses were going on. Everybody in the room knew people or had relatives who had suffered at the hands of the Legionnaires. But they didn't like to think about it. With the exception of Adrian who had already lost his car and his office, the others felt lucky that nothing had happened to them. However, now they had to face up to the severity of the problem.

"Well, what are we going to do about this? Just sit here and let it happen?" asked the Rabbi.

"What can we do?" answered the lawyer. "We have no legal rights! We have no power at all!"

"Then we should use illegal rights!" said Stella. "Are we going to sit passively and lick our wounds?"

A big discussion followed during which all the members of the Council expressed their opinions. They had different convictions. The lawyer, one of the school principals and the journalist favored a passive approach, being afraid of provoking a worsening of the situation. But the others leaned strongly toward action.

It was finally decided, like the previous time, that Adrian should ask for an audience with the Mareshal. He should show him the letters and memoranda, inform him of the abuses of the Iron Guard, and have them stopped.

Everybody felt better at the end of the meeting. Most of the Council members had a smile on their face, hoping that Adrian's visit with the Mareshal would succeed in turning things around.

When Adrian went to see the Mareshal, he had to wait for half an hour in a small ante-room with a few leather armchairs and a desk in a corner. A guard in military uniform armed with a revolver was sitting at the desk. The door to the Mareshal's office was slightly open, and Adrian could hear an animated discussion inside.

The Mareshal sounded angry. He was shouting "No, no, no" and he pounded the desk. "Of course I'm part of the National Legionnaire Government! And I'm wearing the Green Shirt! But I will not pledge loyalty and submission to the leader of the Iron Guard, Horațiu! I'm the head of the government, and he's the second in command. I'm the State, and the State is me! He should pledge loyalty and allegiance to me!"

After a while the voices became softer and Adrian couldn't make out the words. A few minutes later, two officers wearing green shirts under their military tunics walked out of the office, and Adrian was invited inside.

The Mareshal was seated at his desk, bent over some papers. His freckled face was deep red. He was frowning. He looked very angry and he didn't get up when Adrian walked in. He motioned his guest to sit down and lit a cigarette.

A new photo of himself with the Führer, a framed picture with Hitler's dedication and signature, stood on his desk.

"Why are you here again?" he asked with a gruff voice.

Adrian was surprised by this unfriendly reception. But he didn't lose his courage. He took the Rabbi's memoranda out of his briefcase and explained point by point the abuses and injuries the Jewish communities had suffered in the last months. Many times he mentioned the names of the people, the date and the place where the offense had occurred.

The Mareshal didn't interrupt him. He listened carefully. When Adrian finished, he placed the memoranda and the letters on the desk. The Mareshal stared at them, then browsed through the stack of papers.

"I'm sorry about all this," he finally said. "I promise it will not happen again. I will speak to the people in charge and order them to stop these abuses. It will not happen again!"

He was friendly now, and his voice sounded reassuring. "Thank you for bringing all this to my attention. Things will be straightened out, and the culprits will be punished. Please let me know if other harassments occur." He stood up, shook hands with his visitor and saw him to the door.

Adrian went home feeling hopeful. The Mareshal had listened to him and had offered to help. He seemed sincerely moved by the Rabbi's memorandum and the many claims. In addition, Adrian thought the Mareshal seemed disenchanted with his friends, the Legionnaires. After all, the goods and the monies taken from the Jews went into the deep pockets of the Iron Guards and their organization. Nothing had benefitted the coffers of the State! One more reason, Adrian thought, to have faith in the promise of the Mareshal. He had helped them in the past, keeping the

Jewish schools and cemeteries open. He would certainly help them again.

Back in his living room, the members of the Council who had gathered there for his return, greeted Adrian like a hero. Everybody was hopeful. Things were going to be normal again! Even though the Mareshal was wearing the Green Shirt, he wasn't going to let them down.

FROM THE DIARY OF DOCTOR MILO

11/13/1940.

YESTERDAY, AFTER A LONG MEETING at the Casa Verde, my old friend Horațiu, who is now Vice President of the country and the leader of our Legionnaire Party, asked me to accompany him home. There were problems he wanted to discuss with me, and only with me. We are old friends; we used to live on the same block when we were children.

Horațiu now lives in the elegant villa of Prince S., a first cousin of King Carol and a former member of his parliament. The prince is now in jail, like many of King Carol's former ministers.

We drove to the villa in Horațiu's new Mercedes and we were followed by another car filled with his bodyguards in green shirts. At the villa, when we sat down in front of the fireplace, I noticed that Horațiu was wearing a silk green shirt with large gold buttons. The gold buttons seemed even larger than those of the Mareshal.

The small pouch of earth, which hung from Horațiu's neck, was also made of silk and its string had a thread of gold. Come to think of it, all the Legionnaire members of our government now wear green shirts made of silk. But their buttons are made of silver, and the threads which hold their satchels are also made of silver. Only Horațiu and the Mareshal have gold buttons and golden threads.

We sat down in the deep, comfortable armchairs, and Horațiu offered me an expensive Cuban cigar and a glass of țuică, made from the plums of his uncle's orchard. He looked tired and discouraged.

We watched the fire for a short while and puffed at our cigars. Then Horațiu started to tell me how disappointed he was with the Mareshal.

"My confidence in him is gone! I trusted him completely when he first put on his green shirt! I really believed him when he swore absolute loyalty to our cause!" he lamented. "Now I see that it isn't true. He is out for himself and doesn't care about us. He could even turn against us!"

I reminded Horațiu that the government of our country was formed almost entirely of Legionnaires and the power was in our hands. But he shook his head. He looked sad. He agreed with what I said, but he was convinced that the Mareshal had fallen under the influence of the Jews. They had made him wish power only for himself, forgetting about our movement and our common goals.

He finished his glass of țuică. As he put it down, he added with a sigh, "And then there is Hitler. The Führer likes the Mareshal. They are great friends. He is closer to Hitler than to us. So, here we stand with the Mareshal: the Jews on one side and the Führer on the other. Where does this leave us?"

I tried to remind him that the reality was not so bleak. Our organization had received money and weapons from the Germans and Himmler and the entire Nazi party were standing by us. I mentioned the special reception planned at the German Embassy. Himmler himself was going to be there, and the reception was to be given in honor of the Iron Guard only. Neither the Mareshal nor any of his associates were invited. It was a special banquet given for us.

I also reminded him of the approaching visit to Berlin. Both he and the Mareshal were invited by Hitler for November 20th. I was sure he was going to go, and make the most of it. Everybody knows how vain Hitler is, and this visit could be very important for us!

11/15/1940.

The reception at the German Embassy was a great success. The occasion was Himmler's visit to Bucharest. The celebration was entirely devoted to our Iron Guard organization. Horațiu and all the other leaders of our movement were the guests of honor, as well as all the Legionnaires who are in the government. Neither the Mareshal nor any of his representatives were invited.

It was a most elegant affair. All the German officials were dressed in the black SS formal attire, with white insignia and piping. They looked very smart with their white ties, white gloves and tails. And, of course, with large swastikas around their arm. Many of them wore shiny medals pinned to their chest. We too had put on our green silk shirts and had pinned gold medals on our chest.

Silvia looked very beautiful in the uniform which perfectly matched her eyes. And her blond braids, which she had wound around her head, had great success with our German hosts. She waltzed continuously with the two consuls and their associates, and even Himmler danced only with her. Silvia was at the reception not only as my companion, but mainly as the official representative of the Legionnaire women in our movement. She has taken the example of Joan of Arc to heart and has developed organizational skills beyond my expectation.

Silvia has changed so much. She is nothing like the governess of the Stein children, she was four years ago! Nor has she kept any semblance to the hysterical patient who was admitted to our mental hospital, after trying to strangle herself because Joel Gold didn't love her! My treatment with hypnosis has worked wonders for her!

But coming back to the reception: the ballroom was full of banners with black swastikas, interspersed with our green banners sporting the Archangel Michael, our patron saint. Large portraits of Hitler and of our dead Captain Zelea Codreanu dominated the hall. Crystal chandeliers hung from the ceiling, and special flower arrangements were placed around the walls and on the tables.

The reception started with the orchestra playing the *Horst Wessel* song, the anthem of the SS, and was followed by our own anthem, *Sfîntă Tinerețe Legionară* (Holy Legionnaire Youth).

Then Himmler and Horațiu gave a short talk each, in which they praised their collaboration and pledged to continue their "righteous" fight against our Jewish enemies. The audience responded with enthusiastic shouts of "Sieg Heil" and with our Fascist salute.

After the dancing and refreshments, toward the end of the evening, Horațiu and two of his associates—Viorel and Miron—went into a small salon with Himmler and the German consuls. Horațiu asked us to wait for him. When he came out, he was all smiles. I have rarely seen him so radiant.

Later, in the car, he told us that Himmler and the Germans had promised to give our organization a large sum of money. A big transport of weapons—machine guns, flame throwers and tanks—was headed our way.

"Did Himmler and the consuls mention the invitation to Berlin?" I asked him.

There was a short silence and I could imagine him frowning in the dark.

"Yes," he finally said. "They absolutely think that I must go with the Mareshal and visit Hitler. They say they are on our side, but that we must continue to collaborate with the Mareshal."

Horațiu sounded annoyed with this conclusion. I would have liked to talk more about this issue, but we had arrived home. I had to get out of the car.

11/18/1940.

Horațiu seems troubled these days. He calls me every day to confide in me, since he has nobody else to talk to.

The day of the State Visit to Berlin is approaching, but he is still undecided. He makes many excuses not to join the Mareshal. He told me that it is dangerous to have both leaders—him and the Mareshal—out of the country at the same time. "These days are too troubled," he says. "One of us has to be here to mind the ship."

He also says that he has to be here for the "unearthing" of the remains of Captain Zelea Codreanu (the Legionnaire leader murdered by King Carol) and for the subsequent "Grand Funeral" at the Cathedral. A grandiose festivity is being planned with armies of Legionnaires from the entire country gathered in Bucharest and with the participation of many foreign dignitaries, particularly German and Italian.

The "unearthing" of the remains of the Căpitan and the new entombment are set for November 28th and 30th and the visit with the Führer in Berlin is planned for November 20th. I see no reason why Horațiu couldn't attend both. Except, of course, if he doesn't want to go. Is he afraid of being upstaged by the Mareshal?

11/24/1940.

The visit of the Mareshal with the Führer has been a triumphal event. They have been photographed riding together in Hitler's

Mercedes, playing with the dogs, toasting at the Berghof. They were smiling all the time and seemed to enjoy each other's company. It is a great pity that Horațiu missed the opportunity to join in the fun and the politics!

Meanwhile, things have been turbulent here. Our Legionnaire police have intensified the cleanup—I mean the arrest of King Carol's politicians who have been our enemies. About 70 or 80 ex-legislators are now in jail at Jilava, getting ready for trial. Other former parliamentarians have been so frightened by our police that they committed suicide by swallowing cyanide capsules as soon as they heard the knock at the door. Doctor Georgescu, Victor Georgescu, tells me that not only Jews, but also Romanian private citizens, known to be unsympathetic to our movement, have been arrested and tortured. This has created panic among the population and rumors run rampant that we have a long list of at least 5,000 enemies marked to receive punishment!

I laughed when I heard these exaggerations. I told him that these are only tall tales invented by the Jews! Our path is straight and narrow. Yes, we are punishing those who are against us and those who betray us. But we always protect those who are innocent!

It's only the Jews, always the Jews who invent these rumors and make all the trouble.

11/29/1940.

The seventy former politicians who were awaiting trial in Jilava prison were shot last night. The newspapers are saying that, while digging up the remains of the Captain Zelea Codreanu from the solidly frozen earth, our men got so enraged with the Captain's cruel assassination by King Carol and his minions, they stormed the prison, shot the guards, and killed the prisoners in their cells. Some other famous intellectuals who were not in the prison but who were known to be archenemies of our movement were also murdered last night. Their bodies were thrown in a ditch.

I know that this is not a democratic, liberal way of action and Horațiu never told me about this plan. But we are not a liberal, democratic organization and we don't follow a traditional code with trials, courts, judges and juries. Our code is: "Assassination is a gesture of religious liberation and an act of justice."

I can only commend my friend Horațiu and his buddies for their courage and deed.

But I suspect that the Mareshal, who is under the influence of the Judeo-Masons, will have a different take on these events.

12/12/1940.

The war between the Mareshal and Horațiu is now hard to conceal. Even though the Mareshal still wears the green shirt—he had it on at the great ceremony of Captain Codreanu's entombment at the Cathedral—he is furious with Horațiu. He has forced him to write an official pledge of loyalty for the good of the country!

There are rumors that persons close to the Mareshal were related to the politicians murdered at Jilava. Also, there is gossip that our movement is getting too rich and too powerful as we have pocketed the money and the assets of our wealthy Jewish victims. (This, of course, is a rumor spread by them.)

But the situation is not simple. The rank and file of our organization is angry and feels deceived by Horațiu for pledging loyalty to the Mareshal. They were hoping for an uncompromising show of force—in the style of Captain Codreanu.

At the same time, Horațiu is still hurting from the betrayal of the Mareshal. He had sincerely believed that the Prime Minister was going to espouse our sacred cause and pledge loyalty to Horațiu as the leader of the Iron Guard movement. On the contrary, the Mareshal is now disrespectful and rude, using foul language and curses when he speaks to our representatives. Horațiu takes it as a personal insult.

He has told me that he once had a dream about the "disappearance" of the Mareshal.

12/15/1940.

The conflict with the Mareshal is getting "hotter" all the time. He treats our organization as the "enemy," and this is no secret anymore. He has dismissed our Legionnaire police units without consulting us. He has accused them of excessive abuses, cruelty and incompetence. He has not discussed this in any government meeting with our representatives.

He has also dismissed, without any debate, Prince L. from his position of Secretary of Foreign Affairs. The pretext for this dismissal was "incompetence." The Mareshal has replaced him with a military man from his inner circle.

It is impossible not to recognize the hand of the Judeo-Communists pulling the strings behind the scene.

But we are determined to fight back. My friends Horațiu, Valeriu and Radu tell me that in many places our men are absorbed into the regular police force, where they remain active leaders and continue their work. In other cities, the order of dismissal given by the Mareshal was simply ignored.

I have participated in a secret meeting at the Casa Verde where it was decided that, if we're going to be attacked by the Mareshal's military force, we will defend ourselves.

1/8-10/1941.

I met Horațiu at the Casa Verde. He was furious with the Mareshal and obsessed with the idea of getting rid of him. After everybody left, he asked me to join him in his office. He told me that, a few days earlier, he had gone to see the Mareshal for government business, something pertaining to the new budget. As soon as he saw him, the Mareshal started screaming. It seems that in Moldova his wife's relatives had been attacked and threatened by members of the Legionnaire police. And this was not the only case in which Romanian, not Jewish, citizens were harassed by our men.

Horațiu made a good imitation of the Mareshal, when he shouted, "Didn't I order the liquidation of the Legionnaire police? Why don't they obey my commands?" and "Why don't you keep them under control?"

When Horațiu tried to answer him, the Mareshal ordered him to get out, before he could say another word. He opened the door and asked one of his guards to escort Horațiu out of the room.

"You can talk to me only after you bring me proof that the Legionnaire police have been completely liquidated! Until then get out and stay out!" he shouted. Then he slammed the door. Since then, Horațiu is obsessed with taking the power away from the Mareshal, or even doing away with him.

1/18/1941.

The events now speed up. After his most recent "triumphal" visit to the Führer, the Mareshal has engineered a well-organized attack against us. In addition to the liquidation of our police force and the dismissal of Prince L, he has gotten rid of all the governors of the country who were active Legionnaires. He invited them to a "conference" in Bucharest. While they were dining and wining at an elegant banquet, he secretly replaced them with military men who were loyal to him. Of course, all communication between Horațiu and the Mareshal stopped. Horațiu stayed away from the party of officials who welcomed the Mareshal at the airport on his return from the Führer.

It is sad to see that this split is happening only four months after the inauguration of the Legionnaire State. In the beginning of September, the Mareshal was so fond of our organization, that he called the Legionnaires "his beloved children." He also declared that his own fate, his life and death were forever tied to the fate of the Iron Guard.

At the same time, Horațiu assured our followers that the Mareshal—who was wearing the green shirt over his military uniform—had been "wearing the green shirt in his heart for many years."

What made the Mareshal change so radically? I am convinced that only his Jewish friends can be responsible for this transformation!

1/20/1941—Early morning.

There is no respite.

The latest: a mysterious political assassination. I was at the Casa Verde yesterday when we heard that a high German official, the head of the German espionage agency was shot in front of the Hotel Ambassador. Another Judeo-Communist provocation, helped by the Americans, we thought. It turned out that the murderer was a Greek boxer, probably hired by the Americans.

But this assassination had unexpected consequences: the German Ambassador immediately complained to the Mareshal that the Reich's offices and residences were insufficiently protected. When he heard that, the Mareshal exploded and immediately dismissed the Secretary of Internal Affairs, an experienced and well known Legionnaire. He was, of course, replaced with a military officer well trusted by the Mareshal.

This was too much for us. We felt that it was more than we could tolerate. In a secret meeting we decided to organize a large demonstration. A hundred thousand of our people would march, thus showing the entire country that we were more numerous and more powerful than the Mareshal.

The call for the next day's demonstration went out the same afternoon. It was broadcast on the radio, as soon as the decision was made.

But then Horaţiu disappeared. He couldn't be found. We needed him. We had questions, we needed to work out details about tomorrow's demonstration. We started to worry. He had never vanished like this, without saying a word to anybody.

What happened to him? Did he have an accident? Had he been kidnapped by the troops of the Mareshal? We didn't know what to think and we didn't know what to do: should we prepare for tomorrow's demonstration, or should we search for Horaţiu?

Finally, much later in the day, he reappeared at the Casa Verde. He was radiant. His face, his hands and feet were frozen, but there was a glow about him, like a halo.

"We will be victorious!" he shouted. "We will win this war with the Mareshal! The Germans are on our side. I went to the German Embassy, I spoke to the consul, and he promised us plenty of weapons. If we need them, we'll be well provided." He clapped his hands. "The order is out: all night long, machine guns and even tanks will travel to our depots."

1/20/1941—Midnight.

I can't sleep. I'm too excited, so I have decided to write down the events of the day.

This evening at 6 o'clock, we all gathered in Piaţa Universităţii, at the foot of the statue of Michael the Brave. The general mobilization had worked. Thousands of young people were crowding the large plaza and the side streets. Even though it was bitter cold—a freezing night without stars—they had all responded to our appeal.

Silvia insisted on being counted and so were her friends, Nicoleta, Eugenia and Ana. They are all women under Silvia's command.

Recently, her sharp shooting skills had come to light. One weekend we went quail hunting in the field, and she hadn't missed one shot. Since then and because of her talent, she has moved up in the organization, even higher than Nicoleta. This makes all the women look up to Silvia.

As I mentioned before, she still thinks she is Joan of Arc, the French heroine I suggested to her as a role model, when I hypnotized her in the hospital a few years ago. The picture of Joan of Arc still hangs in our bedroom next to the icon of the Archangel Michael, our patron saint and protector of Joan of Arc. This model has been magical for Silvia. But I never expected her to have so much talent and so much drive!

Back to our demonstration: there were a few short speeches, after which our columns marched toward the Royal Palace. When we arrived, we sang the Royal Anthem and shouted the King's name, hoping that he would appear on the balcony and welcome us. (The King's name is Michael, just like our patron saint, the Archangel Michael.)

But nobody came. The Palace remained shrouded in darkness, and I noticed that the national flag had vanished. This was a sure sign that the King was not in the city. Surely the Mareshal had whisked him away to prevent him from any contact with us.

We were disappointed, but we marched on. In front of the German Embassy, Horațiu gave a speech expressing our deep regrets for the murder of the German official. He also pledged loyalty to the Führer and the Nazi party. We all shouted "Sieg Heil" and raised our right arm in the Nazi salute. Then we sang the Horst Wessel song and our own Legionnaire anthem, Sfîntă Tinerețe Legionară.

Next we marched to the Italian Embassy, where we pledged loyalty to Il Duce. We sang the Fascist anthem, "Giovinezza," and shouted "Viva il Duce" and "Viva Fascismo."

Then we started toward the Presidential Palace. As we approached the grand, majestic building, some demonstrators became more vocal. "We want a Legionnaire government!" "Down with the kikish leaders!" And the name "Horațiu! Horațiu!" as head of the new government was heard repeatedly.

We stopped in the large plaza, right in front of the Mareshal's palatial building. The darkness here was even more complete. I could barely distinguish "nests" of machine guns, hidden behind piles of sandbags. There must have been soldiers guarding them, but they didn't move, and they made no sounds. An eerie silence was hovering over the entire space. It lasted what seemed a very long time. Then, suddenly, the silence was broken. "We want Legionnaire government!" a voice called out. The cry was then picked up by many others. "Horațiu! Horațiu!" they shouted. "Down with the Judeo-Masonic government!" came other cries, followed by "Death to the Kikes!"

The whole plaza chimed in at these calls and applauded loudly. Then our anthem filled the air. We were jubilant! We were victorious! Not a single shot had been fired, but victory was in our hands.

As we were leaving the plaza, special editions of newspapers made their appearance, and proclaimed our victory: faced with such a large number of demonstrators, the Mareshal had been overwhelmed. He would now have to resign.

On the streets, our young people were singing and dancing.

Horațiu joined us at home. We opened a bottle of old palincă and turned on the radio. The speaker announced our certain victory and his words were followed by the blessings of the Head of the Church and his thanks to the Lord.

We called in Horațiu's driver and his bodyguards, poured some palincă in their glasses, and toasted to our total victory over the Mareshal and revenge against his Judeo-Masonic clique.

WEDNESDAY MORNING

E ARLY WEDNESDAY MORNING JOEL GOLD and his father Leon were getting ready to leave the house. Joel, Nina's cousin, was a young pediatrician and worked at the Jewish hospital. On this day he decided to take his father with him since the old man suffered from diabetes and needed a blood test and an insulin shot. He had had fainting spells and his insulin dosage needed to be adjusted. They had also run out of insulin at home and needed a new supply.

Joel was looking forward to this trip to the hospital. In a weird way he had benefited from the racial laws: he had always dreamt of becoming a pediatric surgeon. This was not possible before, since, as a Jew, he was not allowed to work in a hospital. But now, with the existence of the Jewish hospital, he was finally able to use his skills.

On their way, the two men were going to stop at their cousin Nina's to pick up a letter which had just arrived from England. Joel had heard that their uncle Ariel, the Chief Rabbi of London, was not doing well.

As he was combing his unruly hair Joel remembered the big family party Nina had given about four years ago when the Uncle had come to Bucharest on a visit.

He remembered that the Uncle had been received with enthusiasm by everybody. Both the family and the entire Jewish Community of Bucharest were proud to have one of their own as the Chief Rabbi of London! Of course, Uncle Ariel and his daughter Clara seemed to have enjoyed the attention lavished on them.

But Joel also remembered that visit for another reason: it was at the end of Nina's party that Silvia, the governess, had tried to strangle herself with a blue scarf Nina and Adrian had brought her from Venice. And it was because of him, Joel, because she felt betrayed and rejected by him, she had tried to commit suicide! In the end he had succeeded in getting hold of the photo which she was holding in her hand. It had been a picture of him as a boy on a bicycle and it was covered with red lipstick kisses.

All this had happened a long time ago but Joel still felt guilty about it. Even though his wife Mathilda assured him that the suicide attempt was not his fault, he still felt that he had led Silvia on and then had abandoned her, by promising to take her to the opera and then going with Mathilda, instead.

The grandfather clock in the dining room tolled 7:30 and Joel rushed to put on his coat. He kissed Mathilda goodbye and ran downstairs to pick up his father. His parents lived in the first floor apartment, having given the smaller apartment on the second floor to Joel and Mathilda.

It was a very cold January morning. The trees were covered with frost. Both Joel and his father were dressed warmly, with heavy coats, fur hats, woolen mittens, scarves and boots. The street was very quiet. In a house next to theirs they could hear a radio talking, and further down the road somebody was chopping wood.

They had barely taken a few steps when they ran into Doamna Popescu, their next door neighbor who was coming back from the market. "Why are you going out?" she asked. "Don't you know that there was a radio announcement telling people to keep off the streets? There seems to be trouble in the city!"

Joel and his father were surprised. "No," said Leon, "we don't know anything. Our radios have been taken away by the Romanization Commission."

Doamna Popescu shook her head. "If I were you, I would stay home, not promenade on the streets!"

"Oh!" said Joel. "We're only walking a few blocks. Just to our cousins Nina and Adrian, and then to the hospital for my father."

"Do as you please . . ." said Doamna Popescu. "But if I were you . . . ," she didn't finish her sentence. She turned and stepped into her house.

Joel and his father continued their walk. The air was warmer now and it started to sleet. The sparrows were hiding under the eaves, and only the fat black crows and hungry dogs were roaming the streets. After ten minutes of walking, they turned onto Nina and Adrian's block. There were many gardens on that street, and all the trees looked as if they were made of silver because of the frost.

They were close to the Steins' house. Across the street Joel saw Adrian's Dodge parked in front of Doctor Ionescu's residence. It felt strange, Joel thought, to see the familiar Dodge in front of another man's house. But he was even more surprised when he saw two black Mercedes with swastikas in front of Adrian's gate.

As Joel and Leon arrived in the living room, Adrian told them the Mercedes were those of Fritz, his former chauffeur, and his brother-in-law. "He and Fritz sometimes come to visit us. They told us today not to venture outside. Probably nothing will happen, but they said there were warnings this morning on the radio. The Mareshal wants to get rid of the Iron Guard. He wants to get them out of police headquarters, the radio and telephone stations and all government offices which they occupy. He may use the army to get them out. Maybe you and Leon should stay here rather than walk out on the street."

"But the police headquarters and all the government offices are far from here, while the hospital is practically next door!" said Joel.

"First take a look at Clara's letter and decide afterward!" said Adrian, while Nina brought them two cups of tea.

The news wasn't good. Uncle Ariel had had a stroke which had left him half paralyzed. The doctors were not optimistic about his recovery.

When they finished reading the letter, Joel slipped it back in its envelope and gave it to Adrian. "I hope he does get better soon," he said as he got up.

"Won't you stay here with us?" Nina asked.

Joel was ready to accept this invitation, but when he looked at his father he changed his mind. Leon's face was pale; he was shivering, while cold sweat kept dripping down his cheeks. He was complaining of severe thirst, even though Nina had brought him two glasses of water and two cups of tea. Joel now had no doubt that he had to take his father to the emergency room.

"Maybe Fritz can drive you?" said Adrian. They went downstairs looking, but Fritz was cleaning the engine and was not ready to leave. Joel didn't want to wait so they said goodbye and started to walk.

The cold air refreshed Leon and gave him more energy. The hospital was less than ten minutes away so they should be there in no time. They kept walking, Joel supporting his father's elbow. They soon reached the end of the block. They began to cross the street when the shooting started.

Joel stopped and listened, trying to figure out where the shots were coming from. The first volley was loud and had come from the west. Joel thought that it must be the local police station. But it was immediately followed by a second volley which came from the opposite direction. Was it the Jewish Community Center, the building where the Rabbi lived?

"I think we should go back to Adrian's house," said Leon. "This isn't good. You're taking risks for my sake! Let's go back." But Joel couldn't make up his mind. He stood still, trying to think. The shots were loud, it was true, but the hospital was near. Then, also, if his father didn't get his insulin injection, he might slip into a coma. It had happened about two years ago, but then they had found a lost insulin vial at the eleventh hour and brought him around.

As they stood at the street corner, they heard trucks rumbling and voices singing the Legionnaire anthem. The songs were interrupted by occasional shots.

The trucks turned the corner and stopped next to them. Four young men in green shirts jumped down, surrounded

Joel and Leon and pointed their guns at them. They ordered them to show their ID papers. "We knew right away that you were stinking kikes!" they said, as they pushed them into the truck.

It was dark and cold there. When Joel's eyes got used to the darkness, he saw that there were eight other men crouching on the wet floor. They were guarded by a giant of a man wearing a green shirt and armed with a braided leather whip. He ordered the newcomers to sit on the floor which was covered with sawdust.

The truck started moving again. Joel looked around and saw that it was old and rusty. There were holes in the walls, which let him watch what happened outside. In a short time the truck stopped in front of Adrian's house. The four Legionnaires jumped off the truck and tried to open the garden gate. But they were immediately stopped by Fritz and his brother-in-law who were wearing German Wehrmacht uniforms.

Joel could hear fragments of their conversation. "The Stein family isn't here anymore and we don't know where they are." Fritz told them. "The whole house belongs to the Gestapo. It is German property and you can't go in."

The Legionnaires finally left and the truck rumbled on. The next stop was the Jewish Community Center, where the Rabbi's home was also located. Joel thought that he had heard shots coming from that direction.

There was a loud commotion at this stop: shooting, screaming, cursing and crying. Joel wondered whether this had been one of the "torture and beating places" into which Jews had been herded and then tortured. Now about ten men were pushed into the van; among them were the

Rabbi and his two young sons. They all looked disheveled, with torn clothes and pale, swollen faces. The left part of the Rabbi's beard had been pulled out, and his face was a bleeding, open wound. While the newcomers were pushed into the van, Joel watched a group of green-shirted youths carrying big bundles of clothing, bedding and baskets filled with china, cutlery, vases and tableware out of the house. Others were loaded down with carpets, pillows and even chairs.

Joel was frightened by the sight of the Rabbi and the injured men. He was shaking and wondering what was going to happen to them? Where were they going to take them and for what purpose? He held his father's arm and tried not to move, for any movement or change in position could be punished with a blow from the whip.

The Rabbi and his sons were sitting, facing Joel and his father. The boys looked to be at most 10 and 12. The Rabbi had draped his arms around their shoulders and was reciting the *shema* in a low whisper.

As the truck advanced into the Jewish Quarter, more men were picked up from the street and pushed into it, so that the space was very tight. Eventually they came to a halt inside the court of the Spanish Synagogue. This place looked like a crowded bus station: the large courtyard was filled with trucks. Pale, frightened men who had come to the temple to worship were now loaded into the trucks. An army of Legionnaires were streaming in and out through the doors of the sanctuary. Joel could clearly see the broken stained glass windows, the smashed candelabras, and pieces of Torah scrolls ripped from the ark, which littered the floor and the courtyard.

Then he saw a bunch of Legionnaires rolling barrels of gasoline into the sanctuary and setting up others outside at the base of the building. The liquid was then spilled on the ground and set on fire. In no time flames leaped inside and outside of the temple. A large crowd of jubilant green-shirted youths danced around the burning building.

Meanwhile, Joel's truck, loaded with desperate people, was slowly leaving the grounds. Inside, the space was so tight, nobody could move or change their position. Joel was hungry, thirsty and tired. His legs, his arms, his shoulders, his neck were hurting and cramped. His father Leon was not talking and not responding to Joel. His eyes were closed and he was only moaning from time to time.

There wasn't much air in the car. Fortunately the two men were getting a breeze from the cracks in the walls.

Joel was tormented by endless questions and fear. Where were they going? What was going to happen to them? He was terrified of being tortured or beaten, afraid of pain and of death. He felt helpless and vulnerable. Like many physicians who had seen death up close, he had learned to fear it.

A thin man with sparse grey hair who was sitting near Joel was sobbing quietly and repeating the words "dead . . . dead . . . dead . . . they shot everybody, even my dog and my cat."

The man's wailing made Joel worry about his wife Mathilda and about his mother. Were they all right? Were they safe? Had their house also been attacked? Even though he knew that he couldn't save them, he still wished to be there with them.

The truck kept rolling and, when it finally stopped and the doors were opened, an intolerable stench of rotten meat hit him: they had arrived at the main slaughterhouse of the city.

Now, everybody had to climb down. They were arranged in a row and marched toward the killing pavilions. The men formed a long column and were flanked by loud swearing and whip wielding Legionnaires. They were led down a road. At the end he could see a brick wall. From here volleys of shots could be heard.

Joel was walking next to the Rabbi and his two sons. He was struggling to support his father, who could barely stand up. When the first fifteen men reached the wall, they were pushed forward, facing it. A big, green-shirted man armed with a gun took Joel's father out of the line and propped him against the wall, with the first fifteen people. The man was surrounded by a group of youths holding revolvers. The big individual took a cigar out of his pocket, lit it with a match presented to him by one of his followers and took a long puff. Then he raised his free hand, waved it slightly and ordered: "One, Two, Three—Fire!"

The bullets flew with great speed. The fifteen men, including Leon were lying motionless on the ground.

Joel couldn't feel anything. He couldn't think either. All he knew was that he and the Rabbi were next in line.

But this didn't happen. Without any explanation, after a short conference between the big man and another officer, Joel, the Rabbi with his sons and about another twenty men were ordered to turn around and go back to the trucks.

On the way to the parking lot they had to walk past a hall where the slaughtered cattle were usually processed. The doors were wide open and there was a lot of activity in this space. Were they processing slaughtered cattle today? Joel wondered. Dead carcasses were dragged in, and fastened on heavy metal hooks while green-shirted Legionnaires were fussing around them. When he came closer, Joel saw that these weren't animal carcasses at all; they were naked human bodies which the Legionnaires dragged in from the piles of corpses, after stripping them of their clothes. They hung them from individual hooks and slit open their stomachs with butcher knives. Then they pulled out the intestines and wound them around the neck of the dead like a special tie. In the end, the men branded the corpses with a large stamp, reading "Kosher Meat."

The men engaged in this ritual were having a great time. They had built a fire near the entrance to the hall and were singing, laughing and emptying bottles of beer.

Joel felt sick at this sight. His stomach was turning. He could barely breathe.

Back inside the packed truck, Joel could barely move. The doors were locked. It was suffocating inside, but he could watch the route they were following through the holes in the walls.

They were at the outskirts of the city, driving past factories, miserable looking shops and tavernas, past small hovels surrounded by barren trees. They were far away from the heart of the town. A few times Joel saw armored military cars and once he saw a procession of three or four tanks. At times, he could hear gunshots far in the distance.

The Rabbi and his sons were sitting next to Joel and he could hear the Rabbi praying without interruption. "Maybe he prays for the soul of my father also!" Joel thought, trying to give himself courage. He was choking with tears, but he couldn't cry.

He couldn't get rid of the stench of the slaughterhouse. He still felt sick to his stomach. But stronger than that was his obsession with the human bodies displayed in the slaughterhouse. Was this going to happen to his father too? Was this his fate? Joel clenched his fists. His father shouldn't have died here like a dog!

His father had been a proud, decorated soldier of The Great War, a devoted Romanian patriot, squarely set against Zionism! He was proud to be the King's purveyor of precious oriental rugs and to be invited, as a guest, to official, elegant balls at the palace.

Leon had always resented being a Jew. Joel remembered his father's determined opposition to Joel's bar mitzvah, and his anger when he learned that Joel had joined a Zionist organization and dreamt of going to Palestine! Now, he thought, this miserable ending was his, Joel's own fault: he should have listened to Nina and Adrian and stayed in their house.

The truck made a sharp left turn and he saw that they were now following a highway flanked on both sides by barren fields. The factories, the shops and the miserable looking hovels had disappeared. All he saw was a low, fort-like construction in the distance. It was surrounded by woods.

After a while, they stopped at the edge of the forest. The doors were unlocked, and the men were told to get off. They were marched into the woods, toward a clearing in the middle of which stood a small building with a large porch. There were tables and chairs in the garden surrounding the villa and on the porch. It all looked familiar to Joel. He recognized the small garden restaurant where, as a child, he used to come with his parents in the summer or spring. He remembered his parents bringing him here and inviting some of his friends at the end of the school year to celebrate and reward him for having been a good student. They liked to sit at a round table in a far corner of the garden, next to a fence covered with roses in bloom.

Now, Legionnaires, armed with revolvers, were moving around or sitting on chairs. Empty and broken beer bottles were scattered all over the place. The wooden fence was still standing at the end of the garden, even though a part of it had collapsed. Piles of bloodstained clothing were lying at the foot of the fence.

Joel and the other men were lined up in a row, Joel could count, from the left, three or four men, then the Rabbi's sons, then Joel, followed by the Rabbi and the other men.

Standing by the fence and looking down, Joel saw that the mounds of clothing were not garments as such, but the dead bodies of men shot in the head. A cold shiver ran down his spine. He felt that his heart was going to stop beating.

When he turned around and looked up, he didn't see a firing squad, but a young woman facing him, holding a pistol. She was surrounded by other Legionnaires, but she alone aimed the pistol at them. She wore boots and the green shirt of the Iron Guard, and she was bareheaded. Her thick blond braids were wound around her head like a crown. She stood tall and looked like the queen of the Amazons.

Silvia!

Joel recognized her at once. He kept staring at her without blinking.

She pulled the trigger and the first shot was heard. The volleys followed one after the other as the dead men slumped to the ground. Joel kept staring at Silvia fixedly, without blinking. The shots were coming nearer: it was the Rabbi's first son, then the second, and now Silvia was staring at him. Her blue eyes grew larger in recognition. Her face twitched. Her hand trembled. The bullet went astray.

She gave a sudden moan and fell down unconscious.

A big commotion followed. The Legionnaires couldn't decide whether to help her or to go on killing their prisoners. In the meantime, Joel slid to the ground, hiding behind a pile of corpses. He stayed there, without moving while the other men ran away into the forest.

This prompted the Legionnaires to chase after them. Unfortunately, the fugitives couldn't run fast enough and the Legionnaires, acting like blood thirsty hounds, caught up with them and shot them at once. The snow was splashed with blood stains as dead bodies were scattered at the foot of old oak trees.

From his hiding place, Joel saw Silvia being carried to a small car and driven away.

Soon darkness fell and there was no more movement in the woods. The Legionnaires marched to their trucks and drove back to the city.

When everything was very quiet, Joel climbed out from under the bodies and looked around. But he quickly went back under cover when he saw a shadow moving not far from him. The shadow kept coming nearer and, from the sound of his mumbling Joel recognized the Rabbi who had come back to be near his sons.

"Iskadal ve Iskadassmei rabo . . ." he was saying the Kadish, the prayer of the Dead.

Joel joined him, reciting the prayer for his father. He kept thinking of the powerful Angel of Death. A few years ago, his father had dared to challenge the Angel by cheating Him. In a special ceremony in the Geller Temple, he had "bought" Nadia—at that time a sick, dying child—from her father, Adrian Stein. By changing her name he had made believe that she was his own child, not Adrian's. In this way the Angel of Death would be misled and couldn't find her. Was Leon's death in the slaughterhouse the cruel revenge of Melech Amuvis?

A great pain filled Joel's chest at this thought. He remembered that the Rabbi too had offended the Angel of Death. It was he who had conducted the ceremony at the temple. Was the death of his two sons his punishment for this crime? Joel looked at the Rabbi and wondered whether he was aware of his sin.

After a while the Rabbi stopped praying. It was dark now and they heard men's voices coming from a distance. The sounds were coming nearer. Joel realized that they had to get out of the forest. They crawled away and after a while they found a ditch which ran along a narrow footpath. They advanced slowly and cautiously, ducking down into the ditch whenever they sensed danger.

Men came to the forest, villagers from the nearby communities who had heard the shots or knew about the massacre. They bent over the corpses and stripped them naked. Joel saw them taking everything they found: coats, suits, pants, underwear, socks, shoes, watches, spectacles, money, belts. Then, at the light of matches or an improvised torch they forced open the mouth of the dead and searched for gold teeth and crowns. They then extracted them by force using big pliers, mutilating the faces.

More villagers kept arriving, leaving behind naked and maimed corpses scattered in the snow. At one point two peasants got into a fight over a gold tooth. One of the peasants hit his opponent in the face with the dead Jew's boot. The second man grabbed a butcher knife and jumped to slit his throat. The other villagers had great trouble keeping them apart.

Because of these peasants, Joel and the Rabbi could barely move. They watched the men carrying their heavy loot home on their backs or on sleighs. Finally, when it was quiet again, when all the corpses had been stripped naked, all the gold teeth had been pulled out and all the clothes had been carried away, Joel and the Rabbi came out of the ditch and followed a path which led them to the road. In the distance they could see the lights of what looked like a few houses or a small village.

The road which they followed turned right, and they suddenly found themselves in the glare of an oncoming car. The car stopped abruptly. Two men in forest ranger uniforms opened the door and climbed down. They were followed by a large German shepherd who started growling and barking.

Joel ran toward the forest, but he slipped on the ice, fell, and hurt his knee. He couldn't get up. Now the dog was next to him, barking furiously. Meanwhile the Rabbi had disappeared into the woods.

The two men pulled the dog away. They then lifted Joel and carried him to the car. As soon as he landed on the back seat he closed his eyes and passed out.

When he came to, he didn't know where he was. It was cold, and the air was full of smoke. He opened his eyes and saw that he was lying on the street. There were burning buildings around him. He heard shots and people singing the Legionnaire anthems. He sat up and realized that he had been dumped in the middle of the Jewish Quarter. His knee was hurting, but he dragged himself to the end of the block and saw that he was close to the Geller Temple. He thought he was dreaming: Sinagoga Mare (The Great Synagogue) across the road and the Malbim Temple further down the street were on fire, but the small Geller Temple—his family's temple—was unharmed.

A light was burning in the caretaker's lodging—a one story cabin which stood in the courtyard. A big cross had been painted on the door of the cabin, above the words "Christian Residence."

Joel knocked at the window and Ştefana, the caretaker, opened the door and pulled him inside. When she looked at him, she started to cry. She had known Joel for many years, since his bar mitzvah, as she had been the caretaker of the Geller Temple since she was very young. She brought him a big bowl of soup and a thick slice of bread.

"How come the Geller Temple is alright, when everything around us was looted and burned?" he asked, when he finished his meal.

"Oh! we were lucky! God and Jesus Christ have protected us!" she said as she made the sign of the cross. "Early this morning, they came to the temple, a large group with axes, guns and barrels of gasoline. They wanted to loot the building and set it on fire. But I came out and started to cry, I recognized their leader; he comes from my village. I wept and I said if you destroy this temple you take away my livelihood! Where shall I go with my sick husband and my small child? Leave this temple alone, it's a small synagogue, you won't find many riches inside. Go next door and across the street to the Sinagoga Mare and the Malbim Temple, those are much bigger and richer temples with much better loot.

"Gheorghe, the young man who was their leader, listened to me and thought it over. "Yes," he said. "Ştefana is right. Let's leave this place and go across the street. I thanked him and prayed God to bless him. I always thought the man had a good heart!"

Joel stayed at Ştefana's for three days and three nights until the shooting, burning and looting were over. He wasn't able to talk to Mathilda or his mother since their telephones had been taken away by the Commission of Romanization. He did reach Doctor Georgescu, who, in turn, spoke to Mathilda and told her that Joel was okay. But he couldn't tell anybody, not even Doctor Georgescu, about his father's terrible death.

PART II

THE FOLLOWING DAYS

W HEN JOEL AND ADRIAN WENT to the morgue to look for Leon's body, they had to stand in a very long line. It seemed as if half of the Jewish population of Bucharest was looking for the other half. It was cold and it had snowed again during the last few days. The long line of mourners formed a black ribbon on the street leading to the morgue.

They had gathered early in front of the building—as soon as the shooting had stopped and victory for the Mareshal had been proclaimed. They saw the convoy of military trucks loaded with corpses line up at the back of the building, but a cordon of armed soldiers stopped them from getting too close.

Finally, after a long wait, people were allowed inside the morgue, about twenty at a time.

It so happened that Joel and Adrian found themselves close to the Rabbi. He was very pale, with a large, dark, oozing crust covering his face, where his beard had been pulled out. His eyes were red and unfocused. His hands and his lips were trembling. His hair had turned all silver.

He greeted Joel and Adrian. He told them that after Joel had been taken away by the forest rangers he had continued to wander alone in the forest, until he was met by two policemen who had taken him to the next Legionnaire site. From there he was again driven to the forest with another group of Jewish prisoners and shot at by the young fascists. The bullet zipped by his head. He fell to the ground but was unharmed. He started again toward the village, but again he was caught by Legionnaires, taken back to the forest and shot at. The bullet missed him again.

During the three days and three nights of chaos and murder he had been shot at three times, but miraculously escaped unharmed. "I wish the bullet had hit me at least one time, but good," he said. "It is an excruciating pain to be condemned to survive the death of one's children. But this is God's will. I feel that I'm sharing Job's fate and, like him, I must say the Lord gave and the Lord hath taken away. Blessed be the name of the Lord."

They were standing inside the morgue. The whole building, every room—the tables, the floors—were covered by naked, dead bodies tightly packed together. The specialty labs and the basement were also crowded with corpses. Meanwhile more trucks were arriving, loaded with more bodies. A loud argument broke out between the soldiers who wanted to get rid of the corpses and the director of the morgue. The soldiers threatened to unload the bodies in the middle of the street in front of the building. The director of the morgue told them to take the bodies directly to the Jewish cemetery.

As they entered the first room, Joel, Adrian and the Rabbi could barely tolerate the sight which confronted them: the faces of most of the dead were mutilated beyond recognition following the peasants' search for gold teeth and crowns. Other bodies had had their noses broken and tongues cut out, so that they no longer looked human.

Luckily for the Rabbi, he found his sons in the second room. They were among the few whose appearance had been spared.

But Joel and Adrian went on looking for Leon. Walking through the many silent rooms, Joel could hear, in his mind, the shooting, the singing and the screaming of the past few days. He was sighing heavily. He even turned around a few times to see where it was coming from. Adrian kept watching him with worried eyes.

They searched through the entire building. They even descended into the basement and they waited for all the trucks to unload more corpses. But it was in vain.

The next day they drove with Doctor Georgescu to the Jewish cemetery, where a transport of severely mutilated corpses had been left. But Leon's body remained among those that were never found or identified.

FROM THE DIARY OF DOCTOR MILO

2/20/1941.

WE HAVE LOST THE BATTLE and the Mareshal and his army have won. It is a major catastrophe for us. Le coup de grâce, a deadly blow for our organization.

The Mareshal is taking his revenge: 2,000 executions in the entire country, 30,000 young Legionnaires thrown in jail or condemned to the salt mines for the rest of their lives. Our former friend and ally has shown himself to be crueler and more bloodthirsty than our archenemy, King Carol.

Nevertheless, in this big disaster, a few of us ended up lucky: Horațiu, Viorel, Radu and a few of their friends were able to escape to Germany with the protection of the German consul. I myself owe my freedom and the privilege of keeping my job to Doctor Georgescu and his friendship with the Queen. He claimed that he needed me like his right hand and couldn't attend to his patients, his students and his lectures without me. I am immensely grateful to him, for I know, without his intervention, I too would have been locked up in prison, or sent to a salt mine or labor camp.

The only major problem today is Silvia. To say that she is not well is a serious understatement. She is ill. She has been very sick since the day of our rebellion when she was suddenly confronted with Joel Gold as her target. That stinking Jew is haunting us and poisoning our lives with his presence. As far as I'm concerned, he certainly deserved to die there and then from Silvia's shot or any other bullet.

As I said before, Silvia is far from well. She doesn't know who she is any longer. She has forgotten about our organization. She thinks she is still the governess of the Stein children. Even worse, she is constantly looking for Joel and calling for him. She is treating me and Doctor Georgescu like strangers and is afraid of us.

A few days ago she picked up her guitar and started to sing her old German children's songs. Two songs which she likes to repeat are: *Frère Jacques* which she sings in variations of French, German, English and Romanian and an English song, *My Bonnie Lies Over the Ocean*, which she repeats endlessly, like a broken record. If I ask her to sing or play any of our Legionnaire songs, she looks at me with big eyes and an air of incomprehension, as if I were speaking Chinese.

I must add that Silvia too was in danger of being locked up for her role of executioner during the rebellion. But Doctor Georgescu was able to waive her indictment for reason of insanity. That is why he admitted her to the mental hospital and put her back in the same guest room where she had been five years ago. (I only hope that she doesn't try to commit suicide again.)

I have started to treat her with hypnosis, like in the past. But she has not yet responded to these attempts. Even if she responds, we still have to keep her in the hospital to prevent her from being locked up in jail.

STELLA'S AFTERNOON

A T FOUR O'CLOCK IN THE afternoon, Stella woke up in Victor Georgescu's embrace. Even in his sleep he was holding her tight. She yawned silently and stretched her legs, trying not to wake him. He mumbled something in his sleep and held her even tighter.

She looked out the window and watched the white smoke billowing out of the chimney from across the street. Then she looked at her watch; it was 4 o'clock. Soon she would have to get dressed and leave. But for a few minutes she stayed quiet and remembered her dream.

They were at the seaside, in Victor's villa, standing on the terrace and watching the sunset over the sea. Soft music was playing and they started to dance. Victor was kissing her and reciting a poem by Baudelaire . . . Was it a dream? Yes, she had dreamt it now. She could still hear the music and Victor's voice reciting the poem. It seemed so real. Then Stella remembered that it had happened in reality: yes, four or five years ago, the summer they had all gone to Eforie. Sorel, her husband, had brought with him the golden orchid. Afterwards Victor had told him that it was a gift for the Queen! It had been a wonderful summer, they had had a few charmed days in spite of all the political troubles.

It was getting time for Stella to get up. At 6 o'clock she had to meet with Professor Jakubow at the Moriah school, near the Geller Temple and discuss the repairs which needed to be made to the school. The building had been first damaged by the earthquake—all the chimneys had fallen down. Then a part of the school had been set on fire during the days of the pogrom. Fortunately, the library which was the pride of the school with its collection of rare books inherited from Rabbi Ariel Geller (Uncle Ariel Geller) had survived undamaged and could be used.

Victor too would have to get up and prepare for his private patients here in the office.

As Stella slipped out of her lover's embrace, he opened his eyes and smiled. His cheeks were rosy from sleep and his smile made him look younger than his 58 years. "I don't want to get up and face the rest of the day!" he mumbled, as he stretched out his hand and stroked Stella's breast. "Why don't we both run away and take a long vacation on the Riviera?" he said.

"Dreams, dreams, old dreams," Stella answered. "They won't take us anywhere."

"You never know, maybe one day . . ."

". . . if we're still alive," said Stella, while buttoning her blouse.

"Yes! of course, we will be alive!" Victor had put on his shirt and pants and walked into the small kitchen to prepare two cups of Turkish coffee. (He felt lucky that he still had a provision of coffee, since it had started to be in short supply on the market.) When he finished, they sat down in his office with the coffee and a pack of Gauloises cigarettes.

"Yes," he nodded, continuing the conversation. "We will be alive after these bad days and we must prepare for the years after the war, when life will be peaceful again. We must keep our courage and our morale . . . I listened to Churchill's speech yesterday. I heard about the bombing of Genoa and the British advances in Africa . . ."

"Since you speak about courage and high morale, I want to mention that my friends, the Jewish actors who have been thrown out of the National Theater, now want to reopen the Jewish theater, the Barasheum, which had been closed by the Legionnaires. They need a stage. They need to act because they're out of money and have nothing to eat. As a matter of fact, when I spoke with my friend Bella F. she told me that they have already started to rehearse two productions, even though they have no permission for any theater. They're already fighting with each other over what to produce: a drama, a comedy, or a musical!"

"Would anybody go to a musical or a comedy now?" asked Victor Georgescu.

Stella started to laugh. "You don't know the Jews! The more serious the danger, the better the jokes! The more they enjoy a good laugh. It is said that the best jokes are made during a pogrom. Seriously now: could you talk to your patient, the Queen? I know that both she and her son, the King, are passionate theater lovers. If the application goes through and permission is granted, we can send them free invitations to the gala performance on opening night!"

Stella and Victor finished their coffee and put out their cigarettes. As they walked toward the doctor's car, they were struck by the darkness of the streets. A total blackout had been ordered. There were rumors about a possible British air raid, now that the British legation had been forced out of the country. "We're not at war but an attack may be possible, now that they have left on unfriendly terms," people were saying.

The doctor drove the car toward the Moriah school, passing through the center of town. He and Stella were surprised by the great number of German cars and German military men they encountered. In the last six months they got used to the German troops in the city. But now it seemed that they had not only doubled, but increased many times.

There were Germans crowding the luxury stores, food shops and restaurants, taking over tavernas and hotels and gathering in large groups on the sidewalks. The roads were clogged with their shiny Mercedes and their heavy army trucks. They were speaking and singing at the top of their lungs in the tavernas and on the streets.

The combination of the city blackout and the large number of German troops gave Stella a sense of danger and dread. What was going to happen? What was in store? she was asking herself even as she tried to keep calm and not lose all hope.

To reach the Moriah school, they had to drive through the Jewish Quarter, which they hadn't seen since the pogrom. As soon as they entered Calea Dudești, the main thoroughfare, they were confronted with an unusual sight: charred houses, shops with smashed windows, a grocery store with blackened walls, deserted buildings with doors hanging from broken hinges. A burnt mattress lying in the middle of the road. Here and there, ghostlike figures hiding in the shadows. The Big Synagogue and the Spanish Temple had turned into heaps of black stones and ashes.

Stella and Victor kept looking out the window without saying a word.

The Moriah school building looked undamaged from the street. Only the back of the school, adjacent to the Malbim Temple had been touched by fire.

Professor Jakubow, the principal, was waiting for them. As usual and in spite of the cold, he was wearing a sport shirt with an open collar under his sweater. Stella remembered that he always looked ready to go hiking in the mountains. He never wore a tie. As she looked around, she saw one change in the room: the map of Palestine which was hanging on the wall had been replaced with a large map of the world, on which the most recent British conquests were marked with small, colorful flags.

The Professor took his visitors to the back of the building to show them the damage. A window was broken. In a corner, the ceiling was blackened by smoke. A small hole was visible, large enough to allow the rain to come in. They all agreed that it had to be fixed quickly.

"But this will cost money, which we don't have, particularly now!" said Professor Jakubow.

"What do you mean, particularly now?" asked Stella. "I don't understand."

"I am going to show you." The Professor opened the door to the kitchen. Here, at a long table, a row of hungry men and women were sitting in silence and eating soup. Professor Jakubow closed the door gently. "These are our neighbors. They have lost their houses and everything in the pogrom. Now they come here for a meal. And every day there are more people coming. For them too we will need funds. We cannot wait!"

Stella nodded but didn't have an answer. "Let me think about it and speak to my husband, Sorel. We should certainly bring it up in our next committee meeting!"

After that the two visitors said goodbye to the Professor and walked out the door. They took a few steps and as they drew close to the car, they heard a strange noise, a faint cry. It stopped for a little while, then it started again. Every time it started anew it was a little fainter than before.

They followed the sound which led them to a garbage bin. When they opened the lid, they found inside a tiny baby swaddled in towels. At first, Stella was so shocked, she put the lid back in place. But then, quickly, she made a decision: she took the crying baby in her arms, wrapped the towels tightly around him, and announced that she was going to take him home.

"We have no choice," she said. "If we leave him here, he will surely die. So what else can we do?"

"How will you manage?" asked Doctor Georgescu, as he turned on the engine. "You already have your own children, the two Polish youngsters, and now this!" Stella shrugged as she lit two Gauloises cigarettes. "I'll find a way!" she said, giving Victor a cigarette and keeping one for herself.

She was silent for a moment, watching the smoke. "I got it!" she suddenly said. "We can organize a raffle and the winner gets the baby! How about that? I think it's brilliant!" She laughed, as she gently rocked the infant who had fallen asleep in her arms.

NINA'S BIRTHDAY

THE NEXT MEETING OF THE Underground Jewish Council took place in the afternoon two weeks later in Adrian's living room, as usual. It was the first meeting since the pogrom. Everybody was looking forward to this gathering. They were glad to meet again and happy that the Iron Guard had been smashed.

"We should celebrate!" said Professor Jakubow who was chairing the meeting. "Most of the Legionnaires are now in jail, under lock and key, and very few have escaped to Germany," he added, rubbing his hands.

"Yes, but they are the most important and dangerous ones," said Joel. "Should Hitler get angry at the Mareshal or become disappointed with him, he could always bring them back and get rid of his old friend."

"This is possible, but not probable. It's not happening now, so today we should just celebrate. Today is also Nina's birthday and Adrian has invited all of us to a surprise party for this occasion."

Cheers of Bravo! Bravo! and loud clapping of hands greeted his words.

"But before discussing anything else, I want to announce two important accomplishments of our committee: the first news is that in two days, on Monday, the doors of the new Jewish university will open. Our children will be able to start or continue their graduate studies. They'll be able to pursue any specialty: medicine, architecture, electrical engineering, art, chemistry and so on. We have the location, the teachers, and, above all, we have obtained the Mareshal's permission to function!

"It was Adrian's doing: he made a list of all the scientists and intellectuals friendly to us, and then had them convince the Mareshal that this was a splendid idea. Now our children will be able to go to the Jewish university, and the professors who were dismissed from their universities will be able to teach their specialty and earn an income."

These words were also received with enthusiastic applause. When the room became quiet again, Professor Jakubow made another announcement.

"The second news is that, in two weeks, the Jewish Theater, the Barasheum, will reopen. This too is due to Adrian's intervention. He convinced Doctor Victor Georgescu who, as you all know, is the Queen's doctor and friend, to take the actress Bella F. to visit the Queen at the Palace. Everybody knows that the Queen is a great theater fan and she particularly adored Sarah Bernhardt. So when Bella F. made a memorable impersonation of Sarah Bernhardt with her amputated leg, the Queen was so impressed, she immediately ran to the telephone and rang the Mareshal on a private line asking him to reopen the Jewish Theater and allow the actors to perform.

"Adrian, who had urged Doctor Georgescu to speak to the Queen, knew that the Mareshal was also a great theater fan. He had a great passion for Madeleine Renaud. As a matter of fact, when she was on tour in Bucharest, some years ago, he had spent so much time with her and gave her such lavish gifts, his wife became jealous and threatened him with divorce. Naturally, when he received the Queen's message, he had no choice but to say yes to her request.

"This is great news—not only will we be able to enjoy our theater, but there will also be work and income for actors, directors, playwrights and everybody else connected with show business. Two plays, a drama and a musical, are already being rehearsed at the theater."

More cheers and applause met these words. As the meeting ended, the big sliding doors to the dining room were pushed open, revealing a table lavishly set and covered with many delicacies. There were platters of smoked salmon and whitefish, paté de foie gras, luscious greek olives, deviled eggs, delicate endive salad in vinaigrette, next to deep crystal cups filled with black sevruga caviar and ruby red salmon caviar.

A vase with perfumed violets—the first flowers of the season—which Adrian had picked in the garden that very morning, stood in the middle of the table. Bottles of Vin de Cotnari, the best Romanian wine and champagne had been placed on the sideboard.

"How did you get all this, now that there is nothing on the market?" asked the Rabbi in awe.

"A parting gift from the Iron Guard!" joked Adrian.

"A remarkable accomplishment in these times!" said the Rabbi, shaking his head.

In reality, the day before, Adrian had driven to Leonida's, the fanciest gourmet store in the city in Doctor

Georgescu's car. There they looked for Sofica, the manager, an old friend of Adrian's.

The big store was full of German officers buying a lot of treats, but very few local customers. It looked as if the many military uniforms had frightened away the usual civilian clientele.

As soon as they found Sofica, the plump lady with hairy legs and a squint in her left eye, Adrian handed her a large banknote and the list of foods he wanted.

Sofica thanked him profusely and was happy to see him. She complained that these hard times had driven away her best customers. It seemed to Adrian that her squint had gotten worse since he last saw her.

While they were talking, she put the money in her pocket, and handed the list to one of her assistants. Then she told Adrian and Doctor Georgescu to step out of the store and wait for the packages near the back door.

Before leaving, Adrian gave her another banknote, for which he received a supplement of fresh white rolls, a case of juicy oranges, and a bunch of fresh bananas.

Then, everything was loaded into the car, taken to Doctor Georgescu's house and kept there overnight. The next day, the day of the meeting, the doctor brought the packages to Adrian's apartment. But since Nina was supposed to be surprised by the party, he had to wait in the car until he saw her and the children leaving the house. It was only afterwards that he brought the packages upstairs and gave them to Mathilda, Joel's wife. She was to put them on platters and trays, and arrange them on the dinner table.

Nina came home as the meeting adjourned and was stunned as she entered the dining room. She first stepped back, ready to run away. Luckily, Joel was standing near the door and stopped her.

"What's this? What is going on? What are you up to in my own house?" she kept asking. She looked bewildered, embarrassed, her eyes, wide open. Her face was flushed. The children, Suzy and Nadia, standing next to her, also looked very surprised.

"We are celebrating your birthday, my dear!" said Adrian, taking her hand, and kissing her fingers. "We could barely wait for your return!"

"But . . . But . . . ," Nina stammered.

"No but, now!" Adrian filled a glass of champagne and handed it to her. Then Doctor Georgescu stepped forward, bowed deeply, and presented her with a gorgeous orchid with golden blossoms.

"This is the finest, the purest Catleya, the prize-winning flower in my collection," he said, placing it in front of her.

In the next minute they were all singing "Happy Birthday dear Nina" and clinking their glasses of champagne. Nina was so moved by this demonstration, her eyes filled with tears and her lips started to tremble.

As soon as they finished singing, her close relatives, Stella and Sorel, Joel, Mathilda, Josephine, as well as Suzy and Nadia surrounded her, wishing her a long and happy life. Aunt Josephine, Joel's mother and Leon's widow (Nina's mother's youngest sister), was the first to embrace her and Nina made her sit on an armchair next to her. Aunt Josephine was hard of hearing and was spoken to through an ivory horn made from an elephant tusk which she wore suspended from her neck on a silver chain.

"I am very touched that you came to my birthday party," Nina said, shouting into the ivory horn. "I am really glad that you came. It makes all the difference to me. I am so sorry that Uncle Leon is not with us anymore! But I do hope that things will now change for the better."

"From your lips to God's ear, as they say. Life must go on, no matter what," said Aunt Josephine. "But to tell you the truth, I'm worried about my son, Joel. Ever since the pogrom and his father's death, he is not the same. He has lost his enthusiasm for medicine. Remember how passionate he was about pediatric surgery? But now he obsesses, he only speaks about leaving the country, about emigration. He is angry that we didn't leave earlier, when it was easy to leave. He even blames Leon, his father, for his own death!"

By coincidence, Joel was standing not far from his mother, and he picked up her last words.

"You are wrong. I not only blame my father, but I hold everybody present in this room responsible for what is happening to us now," he said. "We should have seen it coming. We should have left years ago when it wasn't a problem. We could have done what Liviu and his family did, pretend that we were going on vacation abroad and never come back. Besides, we could still do it now, if we really wanted to!"

"Leaving, how? Going where?" asked Adrian, who had heard Joel's words.

"Everybody knows that we can't get visas to Switzerland. The borders are closed to Jews. Also now the British White Paper has cut down all emigration to Palestine. We can't even sail there."

"Yes, we can!" Joel answered him. "We could use the clandestine ships of the Aliah Bet. Some of my Zionist friends have traveled on them to Palestine."

"But they're dangerous. They're very unsafe. Quite a few have been sunk or torpedoed. I, for one, think that they are so dangerous as to be criminal."

"Well, that's fine—if you choose to stay here and if you can trust your friend, the Mareshal," Joel said with a smirk.

Their conversation was interrupted by Emil, Nina's oldest brother and his wife, Dora, who had just arrived. Adrian poured out champagne and Emil raised his glass in a toast to his sister. "Happy birthday to you and many returns! Let's drink to your happiness and good health, to the victory over the Iron Guard, to the Great Churchill who will smash the Germans to pieces, and to the health of the Mareshal who is protecting us!"

Everybody cheered and clinked glasses. Nina's face was flushed and her eyes were shining. Even Aunt Josephine, sitting between Nina and Joel smiled from time to time while stroking her son's hand.

After he finished his drink, Adrian put his glass on a tray and went to the window. He opened it a crack for a breath of fresh air. There were no clouds in the sky and the moon shone peacefully from above. The clear sky and the full moon reminded him of another family party they had organized four and a half years ago, when Nina's uncle, Ariel Geller, the Chief Rabbi of London, had come to visit them in Bucharest.

The party had started as a pleasant and joyous evening, with plenty of food, wine and dancing. But then Silvia, the girls' governess, tried to strangle herself because of her unrequited love for Joel. The evening had turned into tragedy. Silvia had to be taken to a mental hospital and never came back to the Stein family.

On that evening the subject of emigration had also been hotly debated. It was before the existence of the British White Paper, so trips to Palestine were still feasible. At that time, the Zionist family members—Uncle Ariel, Sorel and Joel—had wanted to go to Palestine, while the "Patriots"—Emil and Uncle Leon, both of whom had been decorated in the Great War for their courage and heroism—were set against emigration. They believed that total assimilation was the solution to anti-Semitism.

He, Adrian, had wanted to go to Switzerland.

Had these people changed their opinions during this last year, since the advent of Fascism? Adrian wondered. Not very much: the patriots still favored assimilation in spite of the many deaths at the hands of the Legionnaires. The Zionists—Sorel, Joel and Professor Jakubow—were still ready to go to Palestine, even without entry visas.

Yes, they would be willing to board rickety, old, unsafe vessels and sail on the dangerous seas. Even though a number of these ships had been attacked by the British and

Germans alike, many young people continued to prepare themselves for these trips. As a matter of fact, Stella had told him that one day last week, after Nadia and Theo had visited the Zionist training camp at Buftea (where Joel and Professor Jakubow had taken them), they had both announced they were going to leave for Palestine to build the new country. They had stars in their eyes and were very excited.

Stella had watched them for a moment and then told them that if they stayed here and studied medicine and went to Palestine later, as doctors, they would be of much greater help to the country. Stella promised them that she and Sorel, as well as Nadia's parents would pay for their studies.

To her relief, this new suggestion seemed to satisfy the two children. They decided to postpone their travel plans.

But how about Stella herself? Would she now go to Palestine? Adrian wondered. He remembered that there had been a point in 1938 when they were all ready to emigrate to Switzerland. But at the last minute the Swiss border was closed to the Jews, and they ended up being trapped here. So how about Stella now? Would she opt to leave with her Zionist husband, Sorel, or would she stay?

The answer was no, she wouldn't leave, Adrian knew Stella was too involved with Doctor Georgescu to abandon him. In addition, she was deeply committed to other projects, such as raising funds for the Moriah school and the impoverished Jewish community, in addition to caring for the new baby. If Stella didn't plan to emigrate, neither would Nina. Adrian knew that Nina would never separate from her sister. So, in conclusion, they would be forced to stay here and depend on the humanity of his old friend, the Mareshal.

Adrian closed the window. As he turned toward his guests, he heard music and laughter coming from the children's room. He followed the corridor to the bedrooms to see what was going on. He peeked into the room through the glass door. He saw Suzy dancing cheek to cheek with Boris Guttman, the young Polish refugee who was staying at Stella's house. The victrola was playing, while Nadia and Rachel, the boy's younger sister, were sitting at the table playing dominoes.

As he watched the four children, Adrian remembered that in two days Suzy and Boris were going to attend classes at the new Jewish University. He smiled and told himself that there was something else worth celebrating besides Nina's birthday!

THE THEATER

T HE SHOW AT THE BARASHEUM Theater was planned for Sunday, March 20th, at eight o'clock. Since it was opening night, Nina decided to wear her black silk two-piece suit and the Marlene Dietrich brooch with rubies and diamonds which Adrian had bought her in Zürich on their last trip. With the famous brooch pinned to her jacket and her silver fox draped over her shoulders, she knew she would look very elegant.

In the past, on opening nights she had worn a long evening gown and Adrian a tuxedo. This was the rule when they still had a car and Fritz drove them to the theater or opera. But now, since the car had been taken away, walking in a long gown with high heels on a dark street seemed too difficult, even dangerous.

Nevertheless, before dressing, Nina couldn't stop herself from trying on her "latest" ball gown which she had bought some time ago but which she had worn only once at an opening night of the opera. It was a burgundy moiré dress with a low neckline and a wide sash, and it still fit her just as elegantly as the day she bought it.

Even though she was a confirmed homebody who stayed in the house as much as she could, Nina was excited about this evening. She hadn't been to a show in a very long time.

Adrian, too, was looking forward to the evening. It wasn't only the music, the entertainment, which excited him, it was also a sweet sense of victory—a sign that the Jewish community was coming back to life.

On the street, the blackout was so complete and the theater building so wrapped in darkness, they almost missed it. Once inside, beyond the heavy doors and thick curtains, they found themselves in a space flooded with light. The chandeliers glowed, their light reflected in the mirrors which covered the walls. As the theater had been damaged by fire in the pogrom and repaired afterwards, the air smelled heavily of burnt wood, fresh paint and French perfume.

The place was crowded and everybody was wearing their best attire. The women were showing off their minks and silver foxes while the men were sporting custom-made dark suits, French silk ties from Beau Brummel and expensive aftershave lotions from the house of Guerlain.

The mood was as festive as in a synagogue on a high holiday. Special invitations had been sent to the King, the Queen, and the Mareshal. The Royals had thanked by telegram but excused themselves. There had been no answer from the Mareshal.

When they looked at their program, Nina and Adrian realized that this wasn't going to be a musical as they had expected, but rather a vaudeville with a medley of different performances. Adrian recognized that this presentation was going to give more artists an opportunity to be on stage and earn some money.

The curtain was raised on the two beautiful Gambrinus Sisters, singing the then fashionable song, *Bei mir bist du schön*. This was followed by a handsome young musician with a violin, singing and playing *Yoschke mit der Fiddle, Berl mit dem Bass* and then by two tap dancers who looked so much like Fred Astaire and Ginger Rogers, that, for a moment, Adrian thought the two world-class stars were performing in front of him.

It was a lively show, in which fashionable hits of the time—*J'attendrai, Le Bateau des Isles, C'est à Capri*—alternated with Yiddish songs like *Of'n Pripichik, A Yiddische Mame* with witty, sometimes saucy, sometimes thinly disguised political skits. The actress Bella F. performed her famous impersonation of Sarah Bernhardt in her role of "La Tosca," which had gained her the name of "Divine Sarah." To emphasize the actress's amputated leg, Bella F. wore a stocking which looked like a wooden prosthesis and moved more stiffly than usual. The actor Virgil P. recited a parody of Hamlet's "To Be or not to Be" in Yiddish.

There was, of course, a magic show in which a Houdini impersonator pulled five white rabbits out of his top hat, released a dozen pigeons from his breast pocket, and sawed his beautiful female assistant in two.

A mime, dressed like Pierrot, declared mute adoration to a paper rose with which he had fallen in love, and a family of jugglers and acrobats made everybody gasp in terror as they threw sharp knives at each other, and then summersaulted so high in the air they almost touched the light fixtures.

The show was a great success. Adrian also admired the avant garde and abstract stage designs in brilliant colors, which conveyed great movement and energy. Some were made of collages.

Several actors wore bizarre costumes and masks. They all were the works of one of Nina's cousins, a co-founder of the international Dada movement. Both creators of this revolutionary movement were related to Nina and had been born in Romania. Adrian had met the poet, Samuel Rosenstock aka Tristan Tzara, only once at his avant-garde Cabaret Voltaire in Zürich.

That evening he had also met Lenin, who had been living in exile and lived across the street from the café. During that time, Lenin often attended the shows. Insiders used to say that the artists and poets at the cabaret Voltaire were more revolutionary than the Bolshevik leader.

Adrian remembered that the whole Dada movement had started as an artistic protest against the cruelty and violence of The Great War and against those who had fomented it. "How could the artists fight against war?" was the question of the time. The answer they gave stated that the poet could write poems, plays and manifestoes in which he said "No," to the mass bloodshed and violence. The artist could rebel against and condemn the tastes and artistic values of the traditional bourgeois society which had produced the war.

After meeting the artists in Zürich, Adrian lost track of the poet. But after a few years he had reestablished contact with the master architect and painter Marcus J.

As the Dada movement spread over Europe and artists traveled from country to country to propagate their new ideas, Adrian had met him briefly in Germany and later in

Bucharest. He had come back to his country in the 30's in an attempt to bring modernism home.

Nina had known him in his youth, before the first time he had left the country. She remembered him as a young man full of dreams and ambition, a visionary full of imagination and enthusiasm. When he came back, she saw that he hadn't changed. He had been successful abroad. The proof was that he was on Hitler's list of "Creators of Degenerate Art."

In Bucharest, he was the architect and interior decorator of several large, official buildings and a few elegant private villas. He had designed the decoration of the modern lobby of the Carlton. He told Nina that he had warned the builders that the construction was not safe, but they had paid no attention to him.

Nina and Adrian had asked him to draw the basic plan of their house. Many of the decorative features of their home, particularly the abstract, surrealist stained glass panels, were entirely created by him.

The Jewish Theater had also been rebuilt by him: he had added a new wing with an elliptical shape, a curvature which contrasted sharply with the surrounding old-fashioned houses. People said that this revolutionary design had greatly offended and irritated the conservative Iron Guards, making them feel justified in setting fire to the theater. But even before the pogrom, the architect was so hated by the Legionnaires, he received numerous death threats. He took them seriously and embarked on the first available ship that sailed to Palestine.

When the curtain finally came down for good, Adrian, Nina and other members of the Underground Jewish Council were invited to join the entire cast at a dinner sponsored by an anonymous benefactor.

Adrian found himself seated next to Bella F. It was the first time he could see her close up and admire her unusually deep, dark blue eyes. They gave her an air of mystery, a magical power to control and seduce, and even hypnotize. He thought that it was due to these deep, dark eyes set in a luminous face, that she had become very successful in impersonating Sarah Bernhardt, who was also famous for her exceptionally beautiful eyes.

He also noticed that her jewelry matched her eyes. She wore a gold ring with a large sapphire and a long necklace of lapis lazuli. When Adrian told her how much he admired her jewelry, she explained to him that these jewels—which she adored—had a history of their own.

"My dear friend of many years, one of the great industrialists of this country who is now far away, gave me the ring and the necklace as a goodbye gift. The irony in this situation is that everybody thinks that he left the country because of the threats of the Iron Guard. But this isn't true! He had to leave because of the jealousy of a military man who is now in power. This man stalked and harassed me for many years. He wouldn't take 'no' for an answer. Wherever I went, I ran into him. He sent me a thousand letters, chocolates and armloads of flowers every day, and sometimes he even showed up, unannounced, when I toured in the provinces. It was unbearable and ridiculous.

"When he found out about my lover, he became mad with jealousy and swore to destroy him. There was nothing else for him to do, but leave. I will probably never see him again!"

A tear trembled on the edge of her eyelashes. She fumbled in her bag, pretending to search for a cigarette, but brought up a small handkerchief with which she daubed her eyes.

Adrian waited, then offered her one of his own cigarettes and lit it for her. He was impressed by her revelations and wanted to know more about her. But a live band suddenly started to play. People got up and went to the dance floor. The music was so loud it was hard to carry on a conversation.

Besides, the actress had disappeared. Only her cigarette was still burning in the ashtray. Adrian turned around and saw her twirling on the dance floor in the arms of the stage director.

When Nina and Adrian came home, they found Nadia and Suzy peacefully asleep. Their bags of books for the next school day were neatly packed and waiting on two chairs—a big bag for Suzy, a smaller one for Nadia. Adrian watched them for a minute, then went to the master bedroom. "Maybe some good days are closer than we think!" he told Nina, as he kissed her good night.

THE NEW LAW

THE DAYS BECAME SUNNIER AS spring approached. Adrian saw an ad for a ping-pong table for sale, in good condition. He was concerned about the approaching long, hot summer so he decided to buy it for his daughters.

As Jews, they were not allowed to travel out of the city, nor were they allowed to go to the public swimming pools. What were they going to do during their vacation?

He had seen that, in the past, the girls and their friends had enjoyed the small pool and the swing in the garden. The ping-pong table would be a wonderful addition.

Maybe things would be better by summer. All kinds of rumors were going around, mostly optimistic, stating that, after the liquidation of the Iron Guard, the fate of the Jews was going to improve. In the meantime, the purchase of a ping-pong table seemed to be a good decision.

But to everybody's surprise, one morning, not too long after the reopening of the Jewish Theater, an article appeared on the front page of the major newspapers, declaring that the "Romanization Program" (begun in the summer of 1940 under the Iron Guard regime) had reached its goal and had been a great success: Jewish doctors, lawyers, clerks, professors, librarians, and other skilled workers had been fired from their jobs and replaced with Romanian nationals. The process would continue until no trace of a Jew remained in any place of employment.

The next day, the old Romanization Centers organized by the Legionnaires reopened all over the city. Adrian hoped that this measure would not affect him, since he still worked as an unofficial consultant for an associate of the engineer who had been killed in the big earthquake.

But the article was a serious disappointment for those who had expected the Mareshal to be more humane now—without the influence of the Iron Guard. There were speculations that Hitler was putting pressure on him or some hidden groups of Legionnaires were blackmailing him.

The news about the Romanization program was followed shortly by the "Law of Urban Expropriation." This was a direct blow to Adrian and his family. The order stated that, not only did the Jews lose ownership of their houses, but now they were obligated to open their doors to anybody who wished to view or take their apartments at any time of the day or night. The visitors' only condition was to show an authorization from the Romanization Center. There were no other regulations, no specified visiting hours. It was another blow, another disappointment regarding a leader from whom something better had been expected.

What were they going to do now? How were they going to cope with this calamity? How long was it going to last? Adrian was concerned, knowing that Nina already had difficulty sleeping under the best of circumstances. He also worried about interruptions to the children's sleep. He himself would have no difficulties, since he could always fall asleep even in times of trouble.

But he couldn't see himself moving with his family to another place in Bucharest. This was his home, the house he had planned together with Nina, and then built from scratch, stone by stone.

The only alternative he could imagine was his villa in Lugano. Yes, he would move there. Any time. Tomorrow. Even today. It was spring there too. The orange trees and wisteria must be in bloom. He would take a ride in his boat on the lake, or he would sit on the terrace with Nina and admire the view.

But Lugano was far away. It was another world. He knew it was only a dream.

Visitors appeared one day after the publication of the new law. To Adrian and Nina's surprise, a line quickly formed at the entrance, so many people wanted to view their home. The Bauhaus style and avant-garde decoration of the building attracted many visitors. Neither Nina nor Adrian believed that all these individuals wanted to acquire their house. A few of them, yes, but most of the others came out of curiosity, for their own entertainment, or maybe just to annoy the Jewish owners.

Most people came during the day or in the late afternoon. But some came at the crack of dawn, before breakfast, or very late in the evening, or sometimes even in the middle of the night. The Steins always had to be prepared. People rang the doorbell, showed Adrian their authorization, and wandered leisurely through the rooms, as if it were a public place. Sometimes a man would come alone and later return with his wife, and then he would come a few more times with other members of his family or even friends.

People who came in with children were a special problem, for the youngsters liked to run back and forth in the long corridor, or they took Nadia's roller skates or used her scooter. If there were several children, they started to play hide and seek, crouching behind the big armchairs or under tables and desks. The parents made no effort to control them. Once a small boy crawled into an armoire and couldn't be found for some time. The father got angry and threw furious looks at Nina and Adrian as if accusing them of kidnapping.

If it rained, the people did not wipe their shoes, bringing the mud with them into the living room. And if they had a dog, they wouldn't care if the animal relieved itself on the expensive rugs.

It was not unusual for the men to make themselves comfortable on the overstuffed armchairs or on the sofa and light a cigarette or a pipe, letting the ashes drop on the floor. Meanwhile, the wives wandered through the house opening the doors to the armoires, peeking into chests of drawers and inside closets.

A few people who came were polite and respectful, but most acted as if nobody were around, as if Nina and Adrian were invisible.

After a few days of this "open door" policy, Nina noticed that small objects had started to disappear. So she collected all the knickknacks and locked them inside a closet which was out of reach. By now, Adrian could see that she was not doing well. At night she could not fall asleep for fear of being disturbed. If she woke up in the small hours of the morning, she was too nervous to doze off again. She was always tired, but could never get enough sleep. Her face had turned pale and drawn. She had dark shadows under her eyes.

She had also lost her appetite. She could barely eat and had lost weight. Soon her clothes became too large for her. Adrian was worried, but didn't know how to help.

One evening there was a loud ring at the door. The person who came in was a tall military man with broad shoulders and heavy boots. There was an angry look on his face, as if he had been forced to make this call against his will. As soon as he arrived, he ordered Adrian to take him through the whole house. In every place he asked specific questions: he wanted to know the exact measurement of every room, the doors, the windows, the height of the ceiling, and so on. He was never satisfied with the answers.

Finally he got ready to leave. He buttoned his tunic and walked to the door. But on the stairs he stepped on the tail of the neighbor's cat who was sitting there, licking its paws.

The cat leaped in the air, gave a big yowl and spat at the man. The shocked, dumbfounded officer landed on his behind with a loud thud. His dignity was shattered. He looked so miserable and perplexed, that Nadia, who was standing next to her father, burst into laughter.

Adrian shushed her and tried to make her stop, but the more he tried, the more she laughed. Tears were running down her cheeks and she started to hiccup, but she couldn't stop.

The officer got up, brushed the dust off his pants, and regained his composure. Then he straightened his tunic and turned toward Adrian, who kept apologizing for Nadia's behavior.

"Don't waste your time with useless excuses. Prepare yourself for a trip to a forced labor camp. That is the place for Jidani who show no respect for the officers of the Romanian Army," he said as he walked out the door.

Even though he could always sleep no matter what, that night Adrian couldn't. He was convinced that he was going to be arrested and deported to a forced labor camp. It had happened to people who had had conflicts with the military. Nina suggested that he contact his old school friend, the Mareshal. But Adrian hesitated. He was not sure it was the right thing to do. He decided to wait.

The next morning Nina packed up Nadia's school books, her uniform and her pajamas, and sent her off to stay with her aunt Stella, uncle Sorel and their children. Adrian insisted that Nina go there with Nadia, but she refused.

A short time after Nadia's departure, Doctor Ionescu, their neighbor from across the street walked in. Nina and Adrian led him into the living room. He held a briefcase in one hand and a cane in the other.

"Good morning!" he said cheerfully. "I told you a few months ago that the day of reckoning would come," he said to his host.

Adrian remembered well that meeting at the Legionnaire Center when Doctor Ionescu had succeeded in appropriating his car. He remembered the banners, the green-shirted youths with their bloodthirsty songs and their revolvers. He remembered the insults, the threats, and the gun barrel stuck in his back, which forced him to sign his car away.

Obviously even now, without his green shirt, Doctor Ionescu was still a powerful man.

"Do you mind if I sit down?" he asked as he made himself comfortable in one of the overstuffed armchairs. "We have a few things to discuss and you must sign some papers." He pulled a folder out of his briefcase.

"I am sure you have guessed by now why I am here. And if you don't, let me tell you that I am the one who has won your home." He stared at Adrian with his small, yellow eyes set in an equally yellow and leathery face. His lips and teeth were stained brown from smoking. As a matter of fact, as soon as he sat down, he took out his pipe and asked for a light. "It wasn't easy getting your house. It is quite popular! I had to compete with four other serious contestants. One of them, a heavy set cavalry officer, was so angry at you and your family that he swore to have you all arrested and sent to a forced labor camp!

"But I am here for another reason: as I told you in the past, I have decided to get back the big chunk of land which was my family's orchard. The land was cut into smaller lots, all bought up by Jidani like you. Even though everybody has paid for their lots, some even with gold coins as you did, the land should belong to me, a Romanian, not to a foreign Jidan!"

The doctor pulled out a map from his briefcase, and showed Adrian a big piece of land divided into several smaller lots. Adrian recognized the plot on which his own house and garden had been built.

He remembered Doctor Ionescu and his wife's visit to their house a few years earlier. The couple was always saying "our trees" when speaking about the mulberry tree, the pear tree or the apricot tree in Adrian's garden. He had told Nina at that time that the Ionescus still considered the Steins' home and garden as their own property.

"This is the beginning of my campaign," said the doctor. "It will be successful. So you must sign here on the dotted line." He handed Adrian a sheet of paper which the latter signed after reading it carefully.

"Very good, very well done." The doctor slid his document back into the briefcase. "In three days I'll be back to get the keys. The rooms must be empty by then, so we can move in." With these words he walked out the door.

Nina and Adrian looked at each other. They couldn't speak. They couldn't move. In their heart, they had both known it was coming. Still, they couldn't believe it.

Three days later the big space was empty. Adrian had called Fritz and his brother-in-law, Hans, to take the furniture and put some pieces in storage.

Since the time had been too short to find another home and sign a new lease, with the intervention of Doctor Georgescu and his friends, they were allowed to move into the attic to the old rooms once used by the maids.

THE NEW LIVING QUARTERS

A s ADRIAN AND HIS FAMILY had moved upstairs in a great hurry, there was no time for moping or angry feelings. Settling into the attic was not easy, but Nina and Adrian had decided to make it work.

The maids' rooms were now used as bedrooms, while the space in the attic proper was divided so as to form a small living and dining room and a den or study room for the girls. A few area rugs and low cabinets separated the various living sections. The maids' bathroom was not elegant but functional and part of the laundry room, which now had a stove, was used as a kitchen.

The feature of the new living quarters which the family liked best was the large roof terrace which spanned the length of the living and dining rooms of the apartment below. This compensated for the fact that they now had no access to the garden.

Adrian decided to make use of the terrace in the best way possible. The outdoor chairs, tables and chaise longues from the garden were brought upstairs, the ping-pong table which he had recently bought was set up in a corner, under an awning. In addition, Adrian made the place really beautiful. With a little coaxing, he convinced Suzy and

Nadia to help him plant geraniums, petunias and marigolds in the flower beds.

A long hose attached to a faucet would serve both as a watering source and as a cooling shower in the heat of the summer.

When he finished work on the terrace, Adrian unpacked the boxes of books which they had brought from downstairs. There were many boxes containing the most popular novels of the last ten years which Nina and Adrian had collected and had carefully bound in leather or cloth.

As he rummaged through the boxes, Adrian found, in a corner, an old, moldy valise which he remembered from his high school years. He hadn't seen it in a very long time. Nina must have hidden it at the bottom of their large bookcase, so that it was out of reach. He had forgotten about it.

He opened the valise now and found the books he had cherished most as a teenager: *Twenty Thousand Leagues Under The Sea*, *Robinson Crusoe, Winnetou*, the story of a mythical American Indian hero, by Karl May (which he had learned was also the favorite book of Adolf Hitler and Albert Einstein).

Next to *Winnetou* and *Old Shatterhand*, also by Karl May, was Darwin's *Origin of the Species* and his account of the *Voyage on the Beagle*. Last but not least was *The Scarlet Pimpernel* by Baroness Orczy. This, it was said, was Churchill's preferred and inspiring book.

Each of these volumes was a story of adventure and courage. Adrian greatly admired the heroes of these novels and had wanted to emulate them. As a teenager, he had often imagined himself in the role of one or another of these unusual men. Later, when he discovered the miracles of electricity, his worship of these idols was replaced by a great passion and enthusiasm for Nicola Tesla and his magical turbines.

But now, as he browsed through the old volume of the *Scarlet Pimpernel*, the heroic English nobleman who risked his life to rescue the French aristocrats from the guillotine, he came to realize how important such a rescuer would be in today's world. Yes, he told himself, these legendary heroes live forever inside the hearts of each of us. We only have to remember to turn inside and look for them.

Adrian gathered the books scattered around him and placed them in the highest drawer of the bookcase, where they would be protected from dust, mold and unwelcome strangers.

About two weeks after their move to the attic, a new meeting of the Underground Jewish Council was called. The committee had not met for the whole month of April and part of May, since most of its members had been victims of the new Law of Urban Expropriation and Rent Hike. Many of them had to abandon their apartments either because they were taken away or because their rents had become too high. Some people had found smaller apartments on the outskirts of the city, while others had moved in with relatives, while still others were searching for affordable living quarters.

Finally a meeting was set for May 18th. This time they were going to gather at Sorel and Stella's apartment instead of Adrian's. There was no room in his attic and to reach his living quarters, they had to pass by Doctor Ionescu's kitchen. Nobody wanted to run into the doctor or his wife.

By contrast, Stella and Sorel had no problems. Not only was their apartment very spacious, but it belonged to Emil Regen, Stella and Nina's oldest brother (who had bought it from Adrian a few years ago). Emil was an important railroad engineer who had built and repaired a strategic bridge over the Danube. This enabled him to be classified as a Category 1 Jew, allowing him to keep all his rights and privileges, including ownership of his apartment house. In this exceptional situation, as tenants of a Jewish landlord, Sorel and Stella were not forced out of their apartment, nor did they have to pay higher rent.

When they all gathered at Sorel's apartment, Professor Jakubow started the meeting with what he thought was the most important subject, namely the money needed to rescue the families who were still homeless and hungry after the pogrom. His talk was followed by Solomon Klein, the director of the Barasheum Theater who also asked for contributions in order to finish repairing the building.

Adrian noticed that, as the speeches went on, people in the room looked progressively gloomier. There was a heavy, uncomfortable feeling in the air. Finally, at the end of the talk, an angry voice came from the back of the room.

"Where should we get the money for these donations, when we can barely subsist ourselves? We cannot work, yet our rents have tripled!" said Serge Levine, a young lawyer in charge of the legal matters of the committee.

"There is nothing in the market. The stores are practically empty," added a very thin journalist who sat next to him. "The lines in front of the stores are unbelievable. My wife got out of bed at the crack of dawn for a loaf of bread. Two hours after the store opened, it was already empty!"

"And this happens in spite of the fact that everything has been rationed," said the lawyer. "Sugar, oil, meat, bread. And you can't find milk, soap, cheese or eggs. All you see are countless German military trucks loaded with food which they carry away."

There were murmurs of agreement in the room. But then Joel got up and started to speak. "We are wasting our time talking about food and money," he said. (He and Doctor Georgescu had recently joined the committee.) "You are ignoring the most important question, which is: will there be war? Will Hitler and the Mareshal attack Russia? In that case, what will happen to us, to the Jews? Nothing good, I assure you! I think we should gather all the money we have and get hold of those ships. We should immediately contact the organizers, give them the money and get out of here before the start of the war!"

Joel's words were drowned out by loud noises and shouts of: "What war?" "There will be no war!" "You're crazy!" "You should be locked up!" "And those ships? Some lousy wrecks! They shouldn't be allowed on the sea!" "They're nothing but floating coffins, and besides, the British stop them from landing in Palestine!" Everybody was screaming.

"Churchill will save us. He is our hope!" said the Rabbi.

"Churchill doesn't give a damn about us," answered Joel. "If he did, he would cancel that White Paper and allow us to go to Palestine. Besides, he has sent British spies here to hunt down and even kill the Mossad agents who organize the emigration by ships. I myself have seen them in operation and I know how they manipulate the Romanian authorities to sabotage the emigration."

"Well, perhaps . . ." the Rabbi tried to say.

"And how do we know that Churchill isn't negotiating a separate peace with Germany?" Joel went on. "Rudolf Hess is in Britain, surely sent there by Hitler to convince them to make a separate peace. After those terrible bombings in London, the British may have had just enough of the war."

"No," said Adrian, who now stood close to Joel. "Churchill will never make a separate peace with Hitler. Didn't you hear the famous speech he made last summer, just before the fall of France? It went like this: . . . whatever the cost may be, we shall fight on the beaches, we shall fight on the landing grounds, we shall fight on the fields and in the streets, we shall fight in the hills; we shall never surrender . . . Words like these come only from a man's heart. And, besides, there won't be any war with the Soviets. Hitler has a lot to gain from his peace treaty with Russia. He gets oil, iron, coal, meat, grain, which are badly needed. After all, he is not Napoleon!"

Even though Adrian spoke with conviction and passion, he couldn't sway Joel, who stuck to his opinions.

After a while everybody was quiet. They looked cranky and tired. Thoughts and fears which they didn't want to acknowledge had come to the surface.

Nobody could return to the earlier subjects. They slowly sipped their ersatz tea which had a suspicious color, was nauseatingly sweet and tasted like medicine.

Then it was time to leave. "There will be no war!" they whispered to each other, as they stepped into the pitch dark, blacked-out street.

Every evening at 7, Nina and Adrian, as well as Stella and Sorel gathered at Doctor Georgescu's home to listen to the BBC. It was actually the BBC's Romanian program. All radios had been taken away from the Jews, so that, if they wanted to know the "real" news, they had to find a non-Jewish person with a radio. Sometimes Joel and Mathilda, sometimes Professor Jakubow and the Rabbi also joined them in the evening. It was a dangerous activity for everybody: Listening to the BBC was punishable with imprisonment and listening in the company of Jews was ten times worse.

The war in the Balkans was not going well. Greece and Albania had fallen to the Germans, Yugoslavia was ruined, and only Crete was still fighting. London was being bombed night after night. Hitler appeared invincible.

Then, the sinking of the German battleship, the Bismarck, by the British, was a great victory hailed by the BBC and all its listeners.

But soon after that Crete too fell to the Germans. Oddly enough, this was followed by a sudden lull in the fighting.

Adrian and the others were asking themselves what was going to happen next? The city was chock full of German troops. Where were they planning to go? The faithful listeners to the BBC hoped for an answer from this oracle.

But nothing came. The local newspapers said that friendly negotiations were going on between Russia and Germany.

But the city was full of rumors: Ştefan, the milkman, told Nina that the German and Romanian troops were going to attack Turkey and Macedonia or possibly start an offensive in Gibraltar, Tunis or Algeria.

Joel and Professor Jakubow had not abandoned their theory about a war with Russia. Meanwhile the newspapers firmly denied this possibility. Adrian was convinced that these war theories were only chimeras. Churchill hadn't said anything on the subject. Adrian told himself and others that the fall of Greece and Yugoslavia was not important. As long as England resisted, there was hope. He trusted Churchill completely.

But at the end of May, not too long after the sinking of the Bismarck and the fall of Crete, the mood in the city changed abruptly. Suzy and Nadia told their parents that the schools were going to close on June 14 instead of June 27 as planned. A few days later they came home saying that their schools and universities were going to close even earlier, on June 7, not on June 14. All baccalaureate examinations had been cancelled for this year.

At the same time, Ştefan, the milkman, told Nina and Adrian that in the country side the military were requisitioning the peasants' horses, oxen and carts. In some communities, people were also ordered to dig trenches for protection against air raids. In addition, there were rumors about draft orders; the milkman's cousin had told him so.

Meanwhile all newspapers and local radio stations denied any rumors of war, insisting upon friendly relations with the Soviets.

As time advanced into June, however, there were more whispers about strange preparations: more draft orders, more talk about government offices and even schools being evacuated in Bucharest. The confusion was such that everybody now had a theory of his own—whether or when the war would be starting. People kept arguing with each other.

Sorel had heard that a Romanian government for Bessarabia (which belonged to Russia now) had been secretly formed and that a Romanian mayor for Cernăuți (which was also Russian) had been named. Stella had seen a long convoy of German military trucks loaded with soldiers driving East. Adrian had run into a column of Jewish men flanked by police and soldiers, being led down the boulevard. He couldn't find out who they were or where they were going.

On the same day, the American ambassador made an official declaration that there wasn't going to be any war between Russia and Germany. Meanwhile, the BBC made no comments on this subject.

Adrian decided that there wasn't going to be a war. He figured since the American ambassador had denied such a possibility and the BBC never mentioned it, it was highly improbable that a war would be declared. It was in nobody's interest!

Joel had a different opinion: the British would benefit from a war since German troops would have to be deployed in the East, thus decreasing the number of German troops fighting in the West and elsewhere.

On June 10th he claimed to have heard that the Romanian-German army and the Russian troops were facing each other on the opposite banks of the river Prut. The war could start any minute now.

The next day he had new information: the date of the offensive was set for June 20th, if it didn't rain. Adrian still didn't believe him. He couldn't take these rumors seriously. He kept waiting for a sign from Churchill or the BBC. But nothing came.

Nevertheless, war was declared on June 22, 1941 at 4:15 in the morning, as soon as the rain had stopped.

PART III

THE FIRST DAYS

That Sunday was an exceptionally beautiful summer day—mild, clear, drenched with sun. The linden trees were blooming and the whole city was saturated with their perfume. Through the open windows, Nina and Adrian could hear the neighbors' radios blasting the Mareshal's order to the Army:

"Today the hour of the most holy war has arrived, the battle for our and the Church's ancestral rights, the battle for our eternal Romanian hearths, our eternal Romanian borders.

"Soldiers! I order you to cross the river Prut. Destroy our enemy from East and North. Liberate our beleaguered brothers from under the red yoke of bolshevism. Bring back into the body of our country the ancestral glory of the Bassarab dynasty, the majestic old forests of the Bukovina, our beautiful fields and meadows!"

The words of the Mareshal were followed by the national anthem and a short report about the success of the advancing Romanian army and the enthusiasm with which the soldiers were welcomed in each community.

The proclamation was repeated every hour, so that Adrian, Nina and the children soon knew it by heart.

At about three in the afternoon, Nina and Adrian decided to take a walk in the neighborhood. The streets were unusually quiet. It felt as if it were a big religious holiday or as if they were walking in a dream. The streets which were usually teeming with Sunday strollers were deserted now except for a few children playing soccer in the middle of the road and a sleepy cat watching them.

There were more people and more activity when they reached the boulevard.

As they stopped in front of a red and yellow tram, they saw that large cartoons had been pasted on its sides. One, a poster with the title "The Butcher of Red Square" showed a Jew with a yarmulka and a crooked nose pulling the strings of a Stalin-like figure with bloody hands and a blood-stained apron. Another cartoon showed another Jew with a crooked nose and sidelocks hiding a bunch of armed Russian soldiers under his caftan. The caption read: "The Real Master of the Red Army." A third one displayed a grinning Jew squeezing a bleeding globe in his claw-like hands. This caption read: "The Jews Are The Curse of the Earth."

As they looked around, Nina and Adrian saw that other, similar posters had been pasted on buildings and fences. Next to the cartoons were large posters warning that spreading rumors was punishable with harsh prison sentences, even death.

They walked another block. When they reached the newsstand they saw that it was filled with "Special Editions" of the Mareshal's declaration of war and "Extra" issues of *Der Stürmer*," the official Nazi publication. Under its large subtitle, "*Die Juden Sind Unser Unglück*" (the Jews are our catastrophe), the newspaper published its own series of anti-Semitic cartoons.

The man at the newsstand who knew Nina and Adrian told them that a group of policemen had arrived very early in the morning and had pasted the cartoons and posters on the buses and trams and on the walls of buildings and gardens.

"Hitler and the Mareshal have started this war, but the Jews are being blamed for it!" said Adrian.

"That's right," said the vendor. "I wouldn't like to be in the shoes of the Jews."

Nina and Adrian walked home in silence. When they reached the gate to the garden, they saw that two large posters had been pasted on their fence.

"No, not on my wall, they won't!" cried Adrian. He dashed toward the fence, ready to rip the posters from the wall.

"It's not your fence. It's not your house anymore!" said Nina, as she stepped in his way. She grabbed his arm, trying to stop him. But he pushed her aside. With a gesture of sudden violence, he ripped the posters off the wall and tore them to pieces.

Nina turned pale and her hands were trembling. "You shouldn't have done that! If anybody saw you, they could arrest you! Let's go upstairs quickly!" she begged him, as she tried to pull him inside.

"Whatever you say, it's still my house, it's still my fence and I won't put up with this nonsense," he answered as he kept tearing the paper.

Nina looked at him, but didn't say anything. Adrian's face was red and a big blue vein was throbbing at his temple.

"To hell with it! We can't just sit here and pretend that nothing is happening!" he said as he threw the last bits of paper in the garbage.

At that very moment the door opened and Doctor Ionescu's wife stepped into the garden. She nodded coldly and gave Nina and Adrian a hostile, suspicious look.

"Madam Ionescu will report us to her husband and we'll be in trouble," said Nina when they were back in the attic.

"I hope she won't!" Adrian shrugged and lit a cigarette. His voice was calm, but the big vein was still throbbing at his temple.

Two days later, on Tuesday, they heard the first air raid alarm. A government order forced everybody to get into a shelter or basement during an air raid. Under penalty of law, anybody who disobeyed this law was considered a foreign spy in the process of sending signals to the enemy. Such individuals would be punished with death. Special militiamen were patrolling the streets and the buildings to make sure that everybody was obeying the law.

But in spite of this, when the sirens started to wail, Nina refused to descend into the basement, which the family had to share with the Ionescus.

"I don't want to share anything with Doctor Ionescu and his family!" Nina declared. "Not my days, not my life, and not my death."

The wailing sirens and the rumbling planes reminded her of World War I, of the German bombings, the destruction of the house, the urgent evacuation in the armored train which had been attacked by the Zeppelin . . . then the flu epidemic, her mother's death in 1918 from the Spanish flu, followed by her own suicide attempt with the kitchen knife following the loss of her mother! It all came back. The pain was still there, as if it were yesterday.

"No, I won't go to the basement. Don't try to convince me. You're wasting your time. I won't share anything with those people."

"But what about the children?" asked Adrian.

"Oh, they can go downstairs with you. It's only me. I just can't sit in the same room with those Jew haters."

"But it's dangerous to be upstairs! The Ionescus can report you for staying in the attic. They can say that you send signals to the enemy planes. Then you'll be arrested and God knows what next!"

"Tell them that I'm not here. That I'm spending several days with Stella."

As the rumbling of the plane engines grew louder, Adrian grabbed Suzy and Nadia by the hand and ran down to the basement. They reached the bottom of the stairs just as the first bombs exploded in the distance.

Adrian felt unhappy and anxious about the bombings, leaving Nina alone, upstairs, and sharing the basement with the Ionescus. But he had no choice. This was the law.

To his surprise, the cellar was empty. Nobody was there and nobody came later. The next day, Nina found out from the milkman that the Ionescus had left the city for an indefinite length of time.

The air raid alarms continued for the rest of the week. Nothing could be accomplished since everybody had to spend time in the shelter. Sometimes they had to stay downstairs for many hours, while nothing happened. Other times the ending of the air raid alarm was sounded immediately after they went downstairs. Then, as soon as they were back in the attic, the sirens sounded again. One day there had been six air raid alarms without a single bombardment.

One evening, Sorel stopped by for a visit on his way home from the Jewish hospital. It had been a warm day. He was tired and hot. Nina served him cold ersatz tea and a few dry biscuits. The ersatz tea was made from a sweet yellow chemical powder which dissolved in hot water and tasted like medicine. She apologized for the meagre treat and explained that because of the food rationing and the continuous air raids, she hadn't been able to get any food. But Sorel interrupted her saying that he and Stella had the same problems.

Soon after Sorel's arrival the air raid sirens started to wail. They descended into the basement. They were sitting on a wooden bench at a narrow table in the dim light of a storm lamp. They were not allowed to turn on electric lights during an air raid. Adrian had brought a few sandwiches with margarine, since they didn't know how long the air raid would last. Dry biscuits and a few bottles of water were always kept downstairs.

It was quiet for a while. Sorel told Nina and Adrian that he had been summoned to report to Iaşi, his city of birth, within two days. "This is another bureaucratic harassment like the one four years ago when they decided to check my birth certificate. Victor Georgescu, our friend, suggested that I disregard this summons and go there at a later date, since the situation is now unstable so close to the frontline. But I am afraid of the severe punishments which threaten those who disobey the order."

While they were talking, they could suddenly hear the airplanes rumbling in the distance. This was immediately followed by antiaircraft fire.

In the next few minutes they heard the loud noise of exploding bombs. Even down in the cellar they felt the walls shake from the force of the impact.

"Nadia! Where is Nadia?" Nina suddenly cried.

Nadia and Suzy had been sitting quietly on the banquette near the table, playing rummy and half listening to the conversation of the adults.

Nobody had noticed when Nadia had gotten up and left. They called her and started searching the basement to find her. Nina looked into the old armoire where her own and her mother's wedding gowns, as well as their old-fashioned lace petticoats had been kept.

But Nadia wasn't there.

At the same time, Adrian walked into the dark furnace room, although he knew that Nadia was afraid of the hellish contraption. They kept calling her and exploring every corner of the basement, but they couldn't find her.

Meanwhile the explosions grew louder and louder. They heard windows rattling. They saw the storm lamp which hung on the wall sway dangerously. They looked again everywhere, but she wasn't there.

So they opened the door of the basement and ran up the stairs shouting "Nadia! Nadia!" There was no answer.

Up in the attic they looked in all the closets and under the beds, thinking that she may be playing a childish game of hide and seek. But this too was for nought. Finally, as they were getting sick with worry, Adrian saw that the door to the roof was ajar. He immediately climbed the few steps which led outside.

It was dark now. The sky was crisscrossed with bright, shiny searchlights. The sound of the antiaircraft volleys was deafening. Far above everything, high in the sky, the small, silvery silhouette of a plane was caught in the blinding beams of the searchlights.

Then, suddenly, Adrian heard the unmistakable whistle of a bomb close to him. It was followed by the unreal, magical light of the explosion. A strong gust of wind, like the blast of a hurricane, caught him, almost lifting him and pushing him off the edge of the roof. Fortunately he held onto the door of the staircase.

In the next minute, the air turned solid with dust and debris which fell on the roof like hale. Adrian covered his face to protect his eyes.

When the dust settled and the air became clear again, he saw that the house two blocks away—at the far corner of the street—had disappeared. All that remained was a heap of smoldering rubble.

But where was Nadia? The airplanes kept rumbling overhead, the antiaircraft gunners were shooting at them and Adrian needed to find Nadia. He stumbled, his mind clouded with terror and pain. He could not think; he could only search.

The roof was not even. In front of him, a raised platform supporting the large stained glass panel which formed the ceiling of the bathroom, obscured his view. To the right, his way was blocked by the tall chimney of the furnace.

Adrian walked carefully around these obstacles. When he reached the other side, he finally saw Nadia's white frock shimmering in the dark. He took her in his arms. She was trembling and crying and held onto him tightly. He led her down the stairs gently, just as another explosion shook the building.

When they reached the basement, he signaled Nina not to scold her and not to ask any questions. Nina was so angry she didn't speak to Nadia and wouldn't look at her for the rest of the evening.

Later, Nadia confided to her father that cousin Theo had confronted her about having enough courage to stay alone on the roof during a bombardment. "No girl has the guts to do that!" he had scoffed. She had felt strongly that it was a matter of honor to live up to his challenge.

Adrian listened to her and made her promise never to do that again. But it took a long time for Nina to forgive Nadia for her dumb foolishness.

THE TRIP TO IAŞI

A S HE HAD TOLD NINA and Adrian, Sorel decided to comply with his summons and set out for Iaşi to register with the authorities on June 27th. He arrived in the city the afternoon of June 28th.

He was excited about this trip. Even though he had been somewhat anxious about traveling since Jews were not allowed to journey by train except under very special circumstances, he was looking forward to this visit. He didn't plan to stay long—just long enough to see his younger sister and her family and mainly to go to police headquarters on Monday morning to take care of his papers. He had done the same thing four years earlier when he went to Iaşi for his birth certificate and passport application. Now he wanted to return to Bucharest quickly. He was still planning to explore—with Joel and Adrian—the possibility of leaving the country by ship.

He didn't have much luggage—just a small valise in which he carried a clean shirt and a change of underwear and socks. Of course, as on all his trips, he had also packed his medical kit, i.e. his stethoscope and a sterile syringe with a few needles.

Stella had prepared for him a hearty package of grilled chicken, four hard boiled eggs, two tomatoes, feta cheese and plenty of bread. She had obtained these delicacies with the help of Doctor Victor Georgescu who was not only the Queen's doctor, but also treated the Palace Majordomo for diabetes. At the insistence of Stella and Victor Georgescu he took plenty of money with him. "You can never have too much money," Stella told him.

Even though the voyage was long and the train was filled with Romanian and German military brass, he didn't mind it. He had a comfortable window seat in a quiet compartment and nobody bothered him. He was able to take a few naps and, while he was awake, he reflected on this visit to Iași. He hadn't seen his younger sister and her family in four years. He was looking forward to seeing them now.

He was also planning to take a walk through the picturesque Copou Garden. The last time he was there it was winter and very cold. A severe blizzard had made it impossible to promenade in the park. Now it was just the right time to wander through the park and sit near the bust of Eminescu (the great national poet) under the blooming linden trees. As in Bucharest, the many linden trees in Iași would be in bloom and permeate the "city on the seven hills" with their intoxicating perfume.

Sorel found himself nostalgic for old Iași, the Moldavian Rome, which, like its Latin counterpart, had also been built on seven hills. He was looking forward to seeing the house in which he grew up, which would be full of tender memories. It was a large, comfortable home with many high-ceilinged rooms. It was surrounded by a lush garden filled with rosebushes and oak trees, in which nightingales came to nest. It was in this garden, under the full moon, that he had first kissed his pigtailed sweetheart and recited his own passionate love poems, which had sounded like childish imitations of Eminescu.

It was only six months before that romantic event that he had celebrated his bar mitzvah in the majestic old synagogue of Iași which had been built in the 1600's and looked very much like a medieval Arab fortress. The Rabbi who prepared him for the bar mitzvah also took him to the Yiddish theater (which had its beginning in Iași) and to his first Zionist meeting. It was here that he learned to sing *Hatikvah*, the inspiring Zionist anthem, and learned that its creator, the musician Naphtali Herz Imber had composed the anthem in Iași.

These early sentimental episodes were later followed by his lifelong passion for medicine. It started on his fifteenth birthday, when his father bought him a real black, shiny microscope and a book about the life of Louis Pasteur.

When he got off the train and went to hail a taxi, Sorel was surprised by the number of troops and military vehicles in the streets. There seemed to be a nervous mood in the air, a sort of agitation, which he attributed to the great military concentration, and to the fact that he was so close to the frontline—only six kilometers beyond the outskirts of the town.

The ride to his sister's house, the old home of his parents on Păcurari Street in an affluent Jewish section of the city near the Copou Gardens, took much longer than usual. Many streets were closed. He saw many destroyed and damaged buildings. The taxi driver told him they had all been ruined in a heavy Soviet bombardment only two nights ago on the 26th. Official buildings had been razed by the bombs and many people had died in the attack. The air was still filled with dust and smoke. He felt that the fragrance of the linden blooms was replaced with an acrid, nauseating odor.

When he arrived at the old home, Sorel was warmly hugged and greeted by his sister, Diana, and her husband, Marcu. He was led to his old room where he left his valise and jacket. A few minutes later, over a glass of hot tea from the samovar and dry cookies served with cherry preserve, he noticed that both his sister and her husband seemed nervous and looked very pale. They had lost weight since he had last seen them. They had dark shadows under their eyes. There was also more gray now in Marcu's hair.

They tried to smile as they inquired about Sorel's family in Bucharest, but they fell silent after a few words. They seemed preoccupied.

Finally, after Sorel asked them about themselves, Diana told him that weird and serious things were happening in Iaşi proper and in the surrounding areas.

It had all started suddenly, ten days earlier, even before the beginning of the war, she said. On that day, at the crack of dawn, soldiers and policemen came to the house of her husband's family in S and ordered them to pack their bags and report to the railway station before 7 o'clock in the morning. All the Jews from that community and from other communities near the river Prut were evacuated by train to unknown destinations.

Her husband Marcu had gone to the Rabbi to find out more information. He only told Marcu that the Jews had been officially evacuated to assure the security of the frontline. But he didn't know where they were.

"The mood in Iaşi proper is very tense," she added. Marcu then told him the same thing the taxi driver had already told him. Namely, two days earlier, on June 26, the city had suffered a severe Russian bombardment which had caused heavy damage and killed many people. A number of official buildings had been destroyed during the bombardment. Unfortunately, soon after the attack, rumors had started that the Jews had been sending signals to the Russian pilots (who themselves were nothing more than other Jews from Iaşi) directing them where to drop their bombs.

An article in the newspaper claimed that a Jewish baker from Iaşi and a female Jewish medical student, also from Iaşi, had been identified among the downed Russian paratroopers. Other paratroopers and pilots from Russian planes which had been shot down were never found: They were obviously hidden and protected by their fellow Jews in the city—all in the service of the Soviets and sending signals to the planes. These signals consisted of messages from radio-emission sets hidden inside Jewish apartments, attics and cellars. Other "special" signals had been transmitted with the help of red light bulbs and flashlights, or with colored clothing, blankets and underwear which hung on clotheslines on Jewish rooftops.

"I know that all this sounds ridiculous, but the newspapers and the radio spread these rumors, and the people believe them!" said Marcu. He then took Sorel across the street and showed him a large poster with the handwritten words: "Romanians! With each kike you murder, you kill a communist. The moment of vengeance has arrived."

After a light dinner, Diana put her two children—Sarah, 4 and Robert, 9 months—to bed. And at about 9:15, Sorel, who was very tired after the long trip, retired to his old room and started preparing for bed.

The room now served as Marcu's den. Besides a large desk, a new chair, an art deco desk lamp, and a few photos of the children, the room was the same as it had been in Sorel's student years. He recognized his old low couch, the Persian rug, the sagging bookshelves, and the tall armoire. It smelled the same—a mixture of lavender, mothballs and a slight trace of dust, probably from the heavy curtains.

It was 9:30 and Sorel had just taken off his shoes when he heard the air raid sirens. He slipped his shoes back on and ran out the door. In the living room he met Diana holding Sarah by the hand and Marcu with the baby in his arms. They all ran to the shelter, which was a trench dug in the courtyard behind the house.

The trench was long and narrow, about six feet deep. There were rain puddles on the bottom. Diana took Sarah in her arms to protect her from getting wet. They saw the family next door hiding in the shelter which had been dug in their own backyard.

At first they heard the noise of a few airplanes. Then Sorel, who had stopped at the entrance to the trench, saw a luminous blue flair in the sky, probably launched by a plane. It was immediately followed by a loud burst of shots. The volleys came from many places. Marcu said that they sounded as if they were released from military centers. But they were met by "counter shots" and other volleys which came from street corners and even private houses.

There was chaos in the entire neighborhood and even farther away in the city. German troops and Romanian military patrols seemed to be moving about noisily and shooting. Sorel and Marcu heard shouts which sounded like "The kikes' revolution has begun!" and "The kikes are shooting at the army!"

No bombs were dropped the rest of the night. No other planes appeared after the blue flare. But the noise and the shooting went on for a long time. Nobody could close an eye that night.

At 8 o'clock in the morning the doorbell rang repeatedly. There were loud knocks at the door.

"Open immediately or we'll break the door!" angry voices shouted.

When Marcu and Sorel unlocked the door they were faced with two policemen in uniform and a fat civilian who looked familiar to Sorel. The man reminded him of a young Legionnaire he had known during his student years in Iaşi—Vasile Ion, who always wore his green shirt and beat up Jewish students. Yes, indeed, it was the same man. Sorel recognized his hairy birthmark on his left cheek.

"There were shots fired from your house last night," said the older policeman who had a big moustache. "You have to come with us to police headquarters."

"Nobody fired shots from here," said Marcu. "We don't even have weapons in the house."

"We have witnesses that saw shots being fired from here," said the second policeman. From behind him, the next door neighbor suddenly stepped up. He was unshaven, still puffy from sleep and wearing a dark jacket over his pajamas. Sorel now remembered that his sister had often complained about this man and his wife who were envious of their house and had made trouble in the past.

"Yes," the neighbor said. "I heard it very clearly. They kept shooting at our troops all through the night."

"But this can't be true! You can check. We have no weapons!" Marcu protested again.

"You have to come with us to headquarters. If you are found innocent, you'll be given a document stamped REGISTERED, which will prove that you are now free and can go home again. But before leaving, you must empty your pockets and put everything on the table," he ordered Marcu, pointing his pistol toward him.

When he did so, the policeman slipped all of Marcu's money and his ID cards into his own pocket, promising to give them back at headquarters. As he was in a hurry, he didn't take Sorel's money or papers.

When they stepped out onto the street, they saw many other Jewish families flanked by policemen and soldiers, headed in the same direction. The guards pointed their guns toward the people and forced them to walk with their arms raised over their heads. They pushed and hit them if they did not comply.

A police car with a loudspeaker was moving slowly toward headquarters, broadcasting the message that once the Jews had registered, they could return safely home.

Diana was walking next to Sorel, holding the baby in her arms. When they turned the corner, they came face to face with an acquaintance from across the street. She was a non-Jewish woman who loved the little boy. When she saw the convoy, a worried look appeared on her face. She stretched her arms toward the child. Without any hesitation, Diana threw the baby into her arms.

Taken by surprise, the guards didn't stop her, but pushed her hard. They ordered her to stop playing games and turned their pistols toward her. This infuriated Marcu. He lost his temper and screamed at the guards which caused him to receive a blow on his head and a warning that he could be shot. Gunfire was indeed heard in the distance which made him keep quiet.

Nevertheless, as they advanced toward Headquarters, they encountered people walking in the opposite direction. They were holding sheets of paper stamped REGISTERED in their hands, which allowed them to go home.

Sorel was confused about what was going on. Was this a simple formality, or was it something else? He tried to make sense of it, but all he succeeded in doing was to notice that the number of the people going home was much smaller than the number walking in their direction.

Then, when they turned another corner, they stumbled over the first Jewish dead. It was the body of a 12-year-old boy, shot in the head, sprawled in the middle of the road, lying in a puddle of blood. Shot by whom? Why? Who could feel threatened by a 12-year-old child? Sorel asked himself. He found no explanation.

The column slowed down and almost stopped as they passed by the dead boy. But the guards screamed at them to keep going and pushed them along. Shots were still fired in the distance and sometimes close by.

At Police Headquarters

The police headquarters of the city of Iaşi was an imposing building, surrounded by a very large courtyard. When they entered the gate, Sorel saw the yard was filled with a great number of Jews. On one side, two policemen were sitting at a heavy wooden desk, checking documents. The Jews were standing in two long lines, waiting their turn. Sorel noticed that those who presented the right documents, received the paper stamped REGISTERED and were allowed to go home. The others, particularly those who had no ID papers, were ordered to remain in the courtyard.

After a long wait, it was finally their turn. Marcu was immediately in trouble. He was not allowed to go home, since the policeman who had come to the house, never returned the ID papers he had taken away. Sorel was told to wait for further clearance, since his current city of residence was Bucharest and not Iaşi. Of course, Marcu's wife and daughter had to stay with the two men in the courtyard.

The noise was deafening. People were screaming, calling out to each other. Children were crying. Wounded and bleeding men who had been beaten or shot were lying on the ground, moaning. Volleys of shots could be heard from time to time. Sorel saw that they were coming from the Romanian soldiers and the German SS troops who had climbed on top of the wall which surrounded the courtyard, on the roofs and balconies of neighboring houses, and atop the bell tower of St. Sebastian Church across the street. They were even perched in the branches of several linden trees. All the military men had their guns pointed at the crowd gathered in the courtyard.

It was a very hot day. Sorel's small group kept looking for a cooler place. Luckily, they found a spot in the thin shade of an acacia tree. Next to it stood a small tool shed, whose walls offered some protection. A partly crumbling wall with a sign saying, "Do not cross!" blocked the space behind the tool shed.

As they were sitting down, little Sarah was crying from thirst. A young man who was sitting not far from them, let her have a few sips from his bottle of water. When she finished drinking, he climbed over the wall with his bottle. But as he came back, they heard two shots. They saw the man fall, his head bleeding, his bottle smashed. A German SS officer standing not far from them was slipping his pistol back in his holster. It seemed to them that he had a grin on his face.

Little Sarah was now crying even louder from fear. Her parents tried to calm her down, but with no success.

As Sorel kept watching the Jews who were brought into the courtyard, he saw that people who had received papers allowing them to go home, were now being brought back. It seemed as if fewer of them were now being released.

When the bells from St. Sebastian Church tolled twelve, a tall general with broad shoulders and many decorations on his chest walked to the middle of the courtyard. Armed with a loudspeaker, he made an announcement.

"I have to inform all of you that red banners and red lanterns, the tools of the enemy have been smuggled into this courtyard and into the basement of the police station. This is a murderous conspiracy, aimed at sabotaging our holy war. If the author of this criminal act doesn't step forward within the next half hour, we will shoot all of you, ten people at a time. Your fate will be sealed in the next thirty minutes. Do you understand? We will put all of you against the wall and start shooting, ten people at a time."

Silence followed these words. Nobody spoke. Nobody budged. Everybody was stunned. Even the children felt the fear of the adults and were quiet.

But nothing happened. The two officers sitting at their desk went on checking papers, while the Jews waited in lines which grew longer and longer. At two o'clock the officers got up and announced that they were taking their lunch break. They were going to be back in less than one hour. An hour passed, but they did not return.

Sorel saw that more people were being crowded into the enclosed space. He started feeling like a trapped animal. The people around him were silent; they spoke only in whispers. Meanwhile, more soldiers and German SS troops armed with machine guns and automatic rifles surrounded the courtyard.

Suddenly, at the shrill sound of a whistle from a German army official, the shooting began. Hundreds, thousands of bullets flew through the air. The sound of countless explosions covered the screams of the victims. In no time, a great number of people lay dead or wounded, surrounded by puddles of blood.

Hidden behind the acacia tree and the low tool shack, the small group saw that the shots came from all the buildings close to police headquarters, including the bell tower across the street.

The bloodbath went on for a long time as more Jews came in. When the soldiers got tired, there was a short break during which they were replaced with more vigorous troops. During these intervals, the Jews who were still unharmed were ordered to drag the bodies of the dead to the wall of the courtyard and stack them in piles.

Then the shooting would start again and the operation was repeated during the next break. In one of these lulls Marcu, who knew the old janitor of the police station, was able to sneak out of his hiding spot to obtain a bottle of water for Sarah.

At about 7 o'clock in the evening when the shooting had stopped for a while, a four star general appeared on the steps of the building and declared, "The gathering of the people here has been a grave mistake. They would soon be allowed to go home."

When he heard these words, Sorel felt enraged. A mistake.! All these deaths a mistake! What stupidity! What gall to say so! Why on earth should they be locked up here and slaughtered like cattle?

Everybody who could, stood up and got ready to go. They waited, but nothing happened. The gates didn't open and nobody could leave.

All of a sudden there was an air raid alarm. The wailing sirens made the Jews crazy with terror. They started screaming, running and hurling themselves against the gates. Immediately the machine guns and the automatic rifles went into action. Hundreds of people were killed at once.

The March

Late in the evening when it got dark, the Jews in the courtyard were ordered to form a long convoy. They were then led out into the pitch black street. It was a very hot, moonless night. There was no light anywhere. It was war; everything was blacked out. Only some of the officers were carrying flashlights.

The convoy was headed by German and Romanian soldiers and flanked by tanks. Two tanks manned by armed troops brought up the rear.

As they were marching, they were not allowed to speak or make any noise. Anybody who broke the silence was shot on the spot.

Sorel didn't know where they were going. The streets were so dark that he could not recognize anything. They were ordered to walk faster and faster, sometimes even to run. He could hear shooting all around him. To his left, in his row, an old man gasped, stopped in place and fell. A soldier who was flanking the convoy came over and shot him.

Sarah was crying softly from exhaustion and hunger. She was too weak and too tired to walk. Marcu and Sorel carried her in their arms.

Finally, after crossing the city, they reached a wide open area at the foot of a very large building. When he heard trains whistling nearby, Sorel realized that they had stopped at the main railway station.

The guards now instructed them to lie on the ground, face down, each person's head wedged between the legs of his neighbor, so there would be enough room for everybody.

They were still forced to keep silent: a moan or a whisper could bring forth a shot in the head. Even Sarah kept silent now.

Later, when they were all settled, the order for roll call was given. The last number Sorel remembered hearing, was 4,012.

The Train

It was about midnight when they were told to board the train. The cattle cars had no stairs. It was not easy to climb inside, particularly since this had to be done very quickly. Those who didn't succeed in climbing up at once were pushed into the cars with the help of a bayonet. The pointed tip penetrated through the layer of clothing and pierced their skin.

Sorel helped Diana and Sarah into the train, but Marcu was stopped by a soldier and pushed away.

When she saw that he was not with them, Diana tried to jump out of the train to join him. But she was pushed back by the crowd of people still coming in and by the soldiers who stood behind them. She started to cry hysterically which frightened Sarah and she too started to cry.

It was pitch dark inside the car. As more people were forced in, it became so crowded, they were pressed against each other so tightly, they couldn't move. When the car was full, the doors were closed and locked.

The only small window at the end of the cattle car was nailed tight with boards, which were then covered with a thin sheet of tin.

It was unbearably hot and no ventilation. Nevertheless, Sorel managed to place himself with Diana and Sarah near the small window, hoping that, when the train started to move, a breeze would penetrate through invisible cracks.

But the train did not move. It stayed put in the same place for many hours. After a very long time—Sorel could swear it was daylight—the train started to move. But even then, it advanced very, very slowly.

Where were they going? What was their destination? Nobody had said anything. It was a total mystery.

Next to him, Diana was still crying and calling for her husband, Marcu, even though she knew that he was not with them. Sarah was also crying. She needed to urinate and had to do it in her pants. She then climbed in her mother's arms. She was afraid of being squashed or trampled to death. Even though the space was filled beyond capacity, the restless crowd was pushing and pressing in all directions. In the total darkness, people were searching for each other and calling each other's name.

The air was suffocating. The heat and the stench were insufferable. They were so crowded together; they could only stand up, without moving.

The train advanced slowly, stopping for hours. People clamored for air. A few men started working at the sealed window. They succeeded in piercing the boards which covered it and making a hole in the sheet of tin. But the soldiers who accompanied the train became aware of it. They loosened up and lifted a part of the sheet of tin, wedged their gun between the boards, and started shooting at random, thus causing the first deaths on the train.

One bullet hit a man standing next to Sorel. He gave a cry and slumped onto Sorel's shoulder. He could feel the man's blood flowing down his arm. Even though the lifeless body couldn't support itself, it remained standing, propped up by Sorel and his neighbor. There was not enough space for the body to fall to the floor.

Later the train stopped again for a long time. When it started again, it crawled along very slowly. Sorel, Diana, Sarah and all the others were tortured by the heat, by hunger, and by unbearable thirst. Water was not available. It felt as if they were inside a furnace. When some of the travelers, crazed by thirst, started knocking at the doors and kicking them, the guards again opened a corner of the window and shot at random inside the car. This time, not far from Sorel, a few more people were fatally wounded, adding to the number of those who had already succumbed to heat and thirst.

The train continued its mysterious crawl. Days and nights passed. Nobody could keep track.

As no water was available, people started drinking their urine. Mothers particularly would squeeze their urine-soaked dresses or skirts into the mouths of their children.

Sorel was aware how, for as long as she could, Diana kept Sarah alive with the gift of her urine. After some time, she herself had nothing left. She asked Sorel for help and he did for as long as he could. But after a while, without any water to drink, he had no urine either. Soon he realized that the child was getting weaker and weaker.

In the beginning, her cries had been loud and angry. Then they had grown faint. As time went by, she became almost silent. Only from time to time did she utter a weak moan. Finally, Diana gave a loud cry of pain as she became aware that Sarah had died in her arms.

Not long after that, the doors were opened by a group of soldiers assigned to remove the dead. Diana was sitting next to Sorel, holding the child.

When a young soldier tried to take Sarah away, Diana resisted and started to fight. She kept screaming, "No, no!" holding the girl tight to her breast and kicking the man in the shin. The soldier let go and stepped back. But a German SS officer appeared from behind the soldier, pointed his pistol at Diana, pulled the trigger and shot her. Sorel watched in silence as his sister and the child were both pulled out of the car and thrown on top of a mound of corpses piled up near the train. He felt great pain. He had always loved his little sister and had tried to protect her. He wanted to cry, but the tears wouldn't come.

While the train was standing idle in this small railway station and the soldiers were busy removing the corpses, a few peasants approached the cattle cars, trying to sell water to the Jews. Some carried bottles of water, while others brought the water in their felt hats. Some of the men asked for money, while a few gave it away for free.

One man brought water in his felt hat. As Sorel reached down to take it, his hands were trembling. The peasant refused the money Sorel tried to give him. He smiled and Sorel saw that he had kind, blue eyes. The man gave him the water for free. Sorel touched his hand in thanks.

At that moment he heard the shots. The peasant and two others were lying on the ground in a puddle of blood.

Sorel's heart skipped a beat. He felt a pain in his chest. In his mind, he kept seeing the man's kind eyes and his friendly smile. It made him very sad. He then tried to drink from the hat. But his throat was so dry and constricted, he could barely get down a sip.

After some time, the doors of the cars were closed and sealed again. The train resumed its slow crawl to nowhere. It moved, huffing and puffing for many hours, until it again stopped. Sorel saw it was at a station not too far from a pond.

The doors were opened again to throw out the new corpses. Looking at the station, Sorel saw several young people jump out of the cattle car and run to the pond. They threw themselves to the ground, and started drinking the dirty water. They were followed and watched by several SS officers, who seemed to enjoy the spectacle.

Sorel saw the soldiers point their pistols at the young Jews and order them to climb in a tree which leaned over the pond. As the men did so, the SS aimed their guns at the youths and pulled the trigger. As the wounded Jews dropped into the puddle, the officers took pictures of the event.

It was an occasion of great entertainment and merriment for the SS men who laughed heartily every time a youth fell from the tree. Then they finished off every one of them.

Sorel was content that he didn't feel the need to rush to the pond. He could sit quietly in his corner and suck at the hat. Also, he felt too weak to run or to climb a tree.

The train stood longer in this station, since a great number of corpses had to be removed and stacked up in heaps.

Sorel could only sit in his corner and suck water out of the peasant's hat. He could only do it very slowly, a small sip at a time, since his throat was still dry and constricted. Swallowing was painful and difficult. He took a break after some time. As he looked up, he saw a noisy crowd advancing toward the train. They were shaking their fists and screaming "Death to the communist kikes! The kikes have attacked our troops!"

Volleys of rocks aimed at the cattle cars accompanied their screams.

The officers who were guarding the train ordered the crowd to stop and disperse. But the angry people did not obey. When they went on screaming and throwing rocks, the soldiers grabbed their machine guns and fired shots in the air. This show of force frightened the demonstrators who panicked and ran away.

Sometime later, the doors of the cattle cars were shut and locked. The train left the station chugging slowly along the tracks. Where were they going? It seemed to Sorel that they were rolling backwards, heading in the direction from which they had come. Were they going back to Iaşi? He couldn't be sure. It was already dark when the train got in motion and the doors were sealed shut.

There was more space in the car now. More than half of the people had died. Sorel was able to stretch out on the grimy floor. It was indeed dirty beyond belief since it had never been cleaned during this trip. He would have never stepped on such a floor, but now he was so weak and exhausted he could not care about cleanliness.

While he was still busy trying to sip water out of the hat, the image of his sister and her child haunted him. It then turned into the picture of the peasant's kind eyes and finally the image of the boys being killed at the pond. It made him feel hopeless while at the same time he was numbed by exhaustion. He had been on this death train for several days and several nights.

When was it going to end? What would happen next? How was it going to end? He fell asleep and dreamt that Stella, not Diana had been shot on the train. She was holding Corinna and Theo on her lap.

He woke up with a jerk. He opened his eyes but did not know where he was, or what was happening.

The doors of the car were wide open. Somebody was pulling at his legs, trying to get him up. The hat with the water had been turned over and his left shoulder was wet. Several very young soldiers, almost boys, wearing white coats over their military uniforms, were ordering the travelers to get off the train. At the same time, other soldiers were collecting the bodies of the new dead.

Sorel got slowly to his feet and out of the car. He was so weak and lightheaded, his legs were folding under him.

As soon as he was standing on solid ground, he saw that the name of the station was Roman. He realized that the train had indeed gone back to the city where it had stopped one or two days earlier. Only this time the aimless travelers were received in a different way.

To his surprise, they were all taken to a sanitary train, where they were bathed, disinfected and deloused. In his state of exhaustion, he hadn't even been aware of the thousands of tiny red itchy spots which covered his body. Afterwards, specially assigned barbers cut their hair and shaved their beards.

His only regret was that they didn't let him keep the good farmer's hat, as they felt that the sweaty thing must be infested with lice. He tried to hide it in order to hang on to it. In the end, he lost it.

Sorel couldn't believe what was happening. He thought he was dreaming. But he found out from his barber that these measures were taken on the orders of the president of the local Red Cross, a woman as formidable as a witch who intimidated both the mayor and the police commissioner. She had mobilized the local Jewish community to bring water, bread, sugar and milk to the travelers, as well as clothes. Everything had to be done in three hours. At the same time the cattle cars were cleaned, washed, and sprayed with a disinfectant chloride solution. In addition, two buckets of drinking water were requisitioned for, and one medic was assigned to, each car for the next stretch of the trip.

If Sorel could not understand what was happening, he was aware, nevertheless, that he had been given a new lease on life, if only a temporary one.

Back in his car after the bath and the disinfection, he tried to eat some of the bread. He chewed and chewed, but it wouldn't go down. His throat was still too dry and tight to accept solid food. Even the milk with the sugar went down slowly and painfully. It was only after repeated attempts to eat bread soaked in milk that he finally achieved some success.

After the stop in the city of Roman, they received water and bread at every station. A few more days went by and they arrived in the town of C, a port city on the Danube.

Here Sorel found out from a porter that eight days had passed since they had left Iași.

The Camp

They were now ordered to leave the cattle cars and were led to a huge hangar which belonged to an Army base. The hangar was open and empty. It had only a roof and a cement floor on which they were going to sleep.

Sorel was glad to be wearing a new shirt and a new pair of pants, which he had received after bribing one of the medics in Roman. He was lucky to still possess all his money. He had worried about it at the police station in Iași and on the train, but he still had his wallet and his papers.

Many of his companions weren't so lucky. They hadn't received any clothes since there weren't enough to go around. They were forced now to sleep on the floor half naked or in their old rags.

In the first days their diet was very meagre. They were given only a thin corn mush, which was more water than corn. It left them hungry, day after day. But Sorel struck up a friendship with a young medic in the camp. His face was covered with acne, he stuttered and had very little experience. Sorel showed him how to put a man's broken leg in a splint and helped him with other procedures such as cleaning deep wounds, setting up special bandages and splints for complex fractures and a few other procedures.

The young man thanked him by bringing bread, cheese and even sausages from home.

But one day the food in the camp changed for everyone. The corn mush disappeared completely. It was replaced with a more nutritious diet of potatoes, beans, rice, pasta and sometimes small pieces of meat. What had happened? This sudden change remained for some time a total mystery.

Eventually, Sorel's friend told him the story, after making him swear to complete secrecy.

In the beginning, when the nearly 800 starving passengers were unloaded in the city of C, the mayor was surprised and overwhelmed. He didn't know what to do with them. Nobody had notified him of their arrival. He immediately telephoned the Ministry of Internal Affairs in Bucharest. But they couldn't help him, saying that they had no knowledge of this train and its passengers. They told him to call the Council of the Jewish community in Bucharest and order them to deal with the problem.

As soon as they were contacted, representatives of the Jewish community raised the necessary funds for the refugees and immediately sent them to C.

But when the money arrived, the merchants in the city at first refused to sell any of their goods. A rumor had spread throughout C that the Third Communist International had sent loads of money to buy all the food available in the city for the Jews in the camp, thus enabling the Jews to gorge themselves with delicacies, while the rest of the town would starve to death.

It took strict orders from the mayor and from the police commissioner to convince the merchants to sell their produce to the camp administrator.

But this was not all. One morning Sorel was awakened by a loud noise and a barrage of rocks. A crowd of soldiers had assembled in front of the hangar and were shouting: "Death to the Kikes! The Kikes have attacked our troops."

The screams and the volleys of rocks became more and more furious, making the prisoners fear that they were going to be massacred at any moment. Luckily they were saved by the commander of the army base, who ordered his troops to disperse the attackers.

"What had caused this attack?" Sorel asked his young medic friend. Instead of an answer, the man showed him a newspaper which described the Mareshal's recent visit to Iaşi and the published declaration he had made on that occasion:

"The Soviet Union tries to promote sabotage and to cause disorganization behind the frontline. To this purpose they parachute spies and terrorists who then contact agents who live in the country, as well as the Judeo-Communist population in order to perform acts of aggression.

"Some of these agents have been captured and they have already been punished. In Iaşi, 500 Judeo-Communists who have shot from their houses at German and Romanian soldiers have been executed. Anyone who in the future will attempt to disrupt the order and the peace will be punished without pity.

"The residents of any city have the duty to inform the authorities of all suspicious individuals and foreigners who have recently appeared in the town. Those who do not inform the authorities of these suspects will be executed with their entire family."

The following day, the newspapers had published a second communiqué, stating:

"In recent days, foreign individuals who hate our interests and who sabotage our wellbeing have shot at Romanian and German troops. Any future acts of aggression will be punished without pity. For each German or Romanian soldier, fifty Judeo-Communists will be executed."

When he finished reading, Sorel was convinced that indeed these declarations made by the Mareshal must have triggered the hateful reaction of the demonstrators.

As time went by Sorel became more and more active as a physician in the camp. He diagnosed the first case of diphtheria and obtained the isolation of the patient in the city hospital, thus preventing the outbreak of an epidemic. (The fact that the patient was Jewish was less important than the danger of a diphtheria epidemic.)

There were practically no doctors left in the city of C, since all the physicians had been mobilized and sent to the front. So it was Sorel who had to perform a breech delivery on the wife of the camp commander. In return, he was allowed to move into a private room of a small barrack which stood behind the hangar.

Other privileges, however, were forbidden to him. He was still a prisoner. He was not allowed to step out of the camp and walk into the city. He also could not communicate with his family, Stella and the children, in Bucharest. Not having any news about their situation made him worry about them constantly. He sometimes dreamt that they were sitting next to him on the train and they had met the same fate as Diana and Sarah. It would wake him up with a start, bathed in cold sweat.

One day all the inmates were given postcards inscribed with the words: "I am well. Please send money and packages." They were only permitted to sign their names on these cards which had a coded return address, so that nobody could find out where they were. No words or messages could be added.

Sorel sent out his card. After some time, he received a package with food and clothing from home. But he found no letter or money in the box which had been opened and inspected by the camp administration before reaching him.

After nine weeks in the camp, during which time some men were taken by trucks to work on roads while others worked making bricks for construction, Sorel and the others were told that, according to a government order, they were going to be sent back to Iași.

Was that true? Were they indeed to be taken back to Iași? Or were they going to be sent on another deadly journey? Sorel couldn't trust any promise any more after so many lies and deceits. He had learned that out of the 3,000 individuals who had boarded the train in Iași, only 700 men and 80 children were still alive. All the women and small children had perished, most of them on the train.

In the morning before going to the railway station, the camp commander assembled all the residents and made a short speech:

"You are leaving this place as good, loyal citizens," he said. "You should walk proudly, since you are people without a stain. Try to forget the agony and the sufferings you have wrongly endured."

In normal times, Sorel would have been enraged by this speech. It was all a mistake! All these deaths, a mistake! But now, strangely, he felt moved by these words. It was the only time in two months that he had been spoken to as a human being.

Return to Iaşi

During his trip to Iaşi, Sorel kept thinking of Stella and the children, wondering how they were and worrying about them. Were they in good health? How did Stella manage during his long absence? How were things in Bucharest? In the back of his mind he was agonizing about the possibility of a pogrom like the one which took place in Iaşi! But he tried to dismiss these fears. His thoughts kept coming back to those terrible days, to Sarah's lifeless little body and to the splash of blood on Diana's face.

He was still haunted by their deaths. He wondered about his brother-in-law, Marcu, and the little boy, Robert, whom Diana had abandoned into the arms of their kind neighbor. What had happened to them? Was Marcu still alive?

Sorel had heard about a second train in which another 3,000 Jews had been crowded and taken to an unknown destination. How many people had survived that nightmare? He had no information about this second train, but he hoped that Marcu, who was young and strong, had made it through the hardship.

Sorel's plan was to go straight to their house on Păcurari Street, his parents' old home, hoping to find Marcu and the little boy. He also wanted to check on the house, fearing that it may have been looted during his absence.

But things didn't work out that way. As soon as the train arrived in Iaşi, at 2 o'clock in the morning, all the passengers were assembled in the station and told by the chief of police that there was a curfew for Jews in the city. They were not permitted to be out on the streets between 8 o'clock in the evening and 8 o'clock in the morning. Anybody found walking about during that time of night would be shot dead on the spot.

The police chief went on to inform them of the new regulations, which affected mainly the Jews who lived in the Păcurari quarter, an area inhabited by many affluent Jews. This section had now been declared a "military zone" and was off limits to Jews. All their houses on these streets had already been evacuated three days ago. The residents were allowed to take with them only money, jewelry, and clothing. Everything else—furniture, carpets, curtains, lamps, paintings, bedding, towels, kitchenware and crockery—had to be left in place, so that the houses could be immediately inhabited.

The keys to the homes were to be handed to Romanian and German officers.

The next announcement regarded the obligation of all Jewish residents to wear the Jewish star—made of yellow cloth—on the left side of their chest.

The police chief then added a warning that all those who didn't respect these orders were to be considered foreign spies and were to be executed.

Before ending his speech, the police chief fell silent for a moment. Then he coughed, cleared his throat and went on speaking in a softer tone:

"We are welcoming you back to Iaşi," he said. "You have been tried and found to be innocent. You are good, loyal citizens. Remain the same, continue to be who you are, and go home in peace."

Sorel was troubled by these words. He and the other survivors had been "tried and found innocent." But how about those who had perished? Were their deaths proof of guilt? of wrongdoing? of criminal behavior? He was angry at the police chief for making these implications!

He was also angry at not being able to go to the family home on Păcurari Street and find out about Marcu and his little nephew. He was disappointed and sad.

But while he was still trying to find a solution to these problems, his thoughts were interrupted by a loudspeaker who summoned all the Jewish travelers to report to triage. Here he was given a return ticket to Bucharest on a train which was leaving in the next thirty minutes.

He suddenly realized that he had no choice but to run for the incoming train.

THE YELLOW STAR

WHEN SOREL CAME HOME, EVERYBODY was excited. Stella embraced him and started to cry. The children too were excited, particularly Corinna who was happy to see him. She threw her arms around his neck and kissed him many times.

Theo was more reserved: he couldn't understand why his father had left him for such a long time. He was angry with his father. He stood at a distance and kept repeating: "Promise me you won't go away again! Promise me you won't go away again!"

Sorel told Theo that he wasn't going to leave again of his own will. At that, Theo came closer to his father and took his hand. Suddenly, he turned all red in the face, jumped into his father's arms and kissed him, whispering in his ear, "I was so afraid you were never coming home!"

Sorel felt good to be home with Stella and the children. He had been worried for a long time about their fate. Many times he had imagined the worst. Was there a pogrom in Bucharest like the one in Iași? Would he find them alive when he came home?

The haunting images of the dead little girl and her mother, of the good peasant killed when he gave him his hat filled with water which saved his life, of the young men shot down from the tree by the SS made him wonder whether his family in Bucharest had met the same fate. It was a great relief to be back with Stella and the children.

Nevertheless, Sorel couldn't speak about what had happened to him. He very much wanted to tell Stella and Adrian what he had seen and experienced, but every time he opened his mouth to speak about his trip he choked. He couldn't get out a word. It felt as if his throat and his vocal chords went suddenly tight and dry like when he had no water to drink on the train.

At night, he would often cry out in his sleep. "No, no, no!" He would raise his hands as if protecting his face from a blow. One night his screams were so loud and went on for such a long time, Stella decided to wake him up. She turned on the light. When he opened his eyes, he looked as if he didn't know who she was. When he did recognize her, he burst into tears and hid his face in her lap.

He cried for a long time. He felt guilty and depressed because he hadn't been able to save Diana and Sarah and because a good man had lost his life trying to rescue him. After that night, he was able to tell his story to Stella and later to Adrian.

Adrian listened to Sorel in silence, sometimes shaking his head in disbelief. How, in God's name, could all this happen? Why? Where is Marcu? Is he still alive? What about Robert, the little boy? Would they be able to find him?

Adrian was silent when Sorel stopped talking. He and Adrian didn't speak for a while. They smoked in silence. Finally Sorel asked about news in Bucharest.

Adrian didn't answer immediately. He lit another cigarette and contemplated the burning match for a moment.

"The news is not good," he finally said. "Actually the things happening now are quite serious."

He told Sorel an order had been issued by the government forcing all the Jews in the city to wear the yellow badge of the Star of David. The new law was to go into effect within the next seven to ten days.

"This yellow star represents the mark of shame, humiliation and dehumanization," said Adrian. "None of us, no Jew in the world should wear it. Remember, it was born in the dark years of the Middle Ages, when the Jews who were forced to wear it, were despised, hated, ridiculed and spat on in addition to being banished from their homes and murdered. I don't want my children to wear it.

"Just today I heard that two Jewish children from a small town in Moldova, who were wearing the yellow star, were killed as punishment for the ritual murder. Their dead bodies were left on the street, covered with a piece of paper saying, "Punishment for Ritual Murder."

"Those children had paid with their lives for the idiotic superstition that we, the Jews, murder Christian children to use their blood in our Passover matzoh.

"I don't want my children's lives endangered because of the Yellow Star. I don't want them to grow up being despised and feeling less than a human being for the same reasons.

"Besides, this sign would forbid us to ride on buses or trams and go to the market. I don't want it. I'll fight as hard as I can against it."

Adrian looked very angry. A blue vein was throbbing on his right temple and his body was very tight.

He then told Sorel that he had already sent several memos to the Mareshal, asking him to cancel the order, but no answer had come yet. Later he learned, the Mareshal was in Germany visiting Hitler. Nobody knew when he was due back.

In the meantime, since the deadline for the order was very short, Adrian went to see Inspector General P., the Mareshal's right hand in these matters. The inspector, Adrian told Sorel, was a distinguished looking man with graying hair and delicate, manicured hands who spoke with a slight French accent.

"He claims his maternal grandmother was born in Paris. He received me in the most courteous manner," said Adrian. "We spoke about Maurice Chevalier and Charles Boyer, Les Folies Bergères and Le Moulin Rouge. Only after our conversation did I give him the memo regarding the Yellow Star. He read it carefully. When he finished reading it, he told me how disgusted he was with such an uncivilized and barbaric measure. He promised to cancel the order immediately."

"'I stand with you,' he said at the end, as we shook hands. His words gave me hope. But nothing happened. Time passed, but no regulation has come through.

"When I tried to contact the Inspector again, his secretary told me that he couldn't be found.

"As the deadline for the implementation of the law was coming closer, we decided to use a different strategy. Our Chief Rabbi was to meet with the Head of the Romanian

Orthodox Church. With the help of Doctor Georgescu and the Queen, the meeting took place in the priest's study, near the sanctuary of the old Metropolitan Church."

As Adrian started to tell Sorel the story of the meeting, he interrupted himself, to say that the Rabbi was expected to come by that very afternoon and would tell the story himself.

The Rabbi did visit and, while sipping a cup of tea Nina had brought him, he told them what had happened at the meeting.

"The Patriarch received me in his office which is lined with books from floor to ceiling—heavy tomes in Greek, Latin, Aramaic and Hebrew. As you know, he is a very learned man. He greeted me politely, even though a little coldly.

"I told him that I had come in the matter of the Yellow Badge, the distinctive sign that the Jews of Bucharest were now ordered to wear. The Patriarch knew what I was talking about and invited me to speak.

"I told him that the introduction of this sign would have severe repercussions on the public order, on the national economy and national finances.

"But more importantly, given the fact that this distinctive badge of shame, humiliation and dehumanization is the Star of David and given the fact that this symbol is equally sacred in the Christian and Jewish religions, it becomes obvious that this government order changes the Star of David into a shameful symbol and desecrates both the Christian and Jewish religions. In reality, the Star of David is a sacred symbol. It is the symbol of the unique ancestor of Christ. Doesn't the divine quality of Christ derive from the fact that He is a shoot from the tree of David?

"So that a profanation of the symbol of the ancestor of Christ exposes the most sacred symbols of both religions to blasphemy and sacrilege by the Christian worshipper.

"It will also undermine the faith of the Christian believer. Imagine a worshipper who, in church, has taken part in the singing and the glorification of the psalms of David and in the preaching of love for his fellow man. What will this believer think and feel when, upon stepping out of the church, he sees how the Star of David, the symbol of the true ancestor of Christ, has been used to provoke hatred and violence against his fellow man?"

The Patriarch listened to me with much attention. When I finished, he praised me for my words of wisdom and promised to think about the issues I raised.

I reminded him that there wasn't much time left and that we had to act promptly. He did not respond.

In leaving, I asked him again to safeguard the respect of religion and the respect of man. He nodded and repeated that he was going to think about what I said.

A short time after this conversation, the Mareshal came back from Germany and a meeting was promptly arranged between the Mareshal, Adrian, and Professor Gheorghe Ursu. This doctor was the dean of the Bucharest School of

Medicine. He was also the president of the now abolished Liberal Party.

The three men had been classmates and close friends in high school. In later years, life had taken them in different directions so that they had little contact with each other.

Professor Ursu was a plump man with a round, bald head. He had a very short neck. His head rested almost directly on his shoulders and he was always wearing bow ties with polka dots.

Adrian went to the professor's home. Together they walked to the Mareshal's presidential office.

They found him in a very good mood, happy to see his old friends. The trip to Germany had been a great success. Hitler had been very friendly, a generous and cordial host who entertained his guests with good food and amusing anecdotes.

The war in the East was going well: the German and Romanian troops had occupied a good part of the Ukraine and kept advancing toward Moscow. This allowed the Führer to take some time off and arrange a hunting trip in the mountains, accompanied by Eva Braun, Doctor Goebbels, the Mareshal and three of the Führer's beloved wolfhounds.

After a most successful hunting expedition in which Hitler shot and killed a deer and two rabbits, a very elated Führer decided to donate to his friend, the Mareshal, two purebred wolfhound puppies.

At this point in the conversation the Mareshal got up and opened the door of his office. The puppies ran into the room taking over the whole space, jumping on chairs, barking happily, and wagging their tails. The Mareshal smiled and watched them with fatherly pride, saying he was going to train the puppies to become both his bodyguards and his hunting dogs like their parents, who were Hitler's pets. The Führer had also loaned him, for a few months, the special trainer of his own dogs.

In this jovial mood, the Mareshal opened a bottle of fine French cognac and offered his guests luxury cigars both of which had been gifts from Hitler.

He then pulled out of his desk drawer an old photo of the three friends during their high school years. They were standing together, arms draped around each other's shoulders, squinting and smiling in the sunshine.

Professor Ursu reminded Adrian and the Mareshal of the tricks they played on the pedantic and sadistic geography teacher, smearing mustard on the seat of his chair, tying a dead mouse on a string and making it jump when the music teacher, Domnişoara Florescu, walked into the classroom. The Mareshal and Professor Ursu imitated her high pitched scream. They laughed with gusto at these recollections.

Adrian remembered clearly the scene with the dead mouse. It was he who had caught the small animal and had pulled the string, since he couldn't stand the music teacher. But he was too tense to laugh.

They had another round of drinks. When they had emptied their glasses, the Mareshal became thoughtful. He poured himself another glass of cognac and confided to his guests that his only headache was Horaţiu and the other Legionnaire leaders who had escaped to Germany and who were protected there by some German officials.

"Not only are they active in Germany," he said, "but Horaţiu has been caught several times trying to cross the border illegally and sneak back into Romania, where he still has many friends and followers."

"You are right," said the Professor. "They do try to infiltrate your power structure and want ultimately to take over. With the help of some SS leaders in this country and in Germany, they've tried to concentrate the power in their hands. I have a few examples of this behavior. For instance the order which will force the Jews of Bucharest to wear the Yellow Star. I know for a fact that this law has been warmly embraced by Horațiu and his Legionnaires. I have heard from Baron von Mansky, an SS officer attached to the German Embassy, who is also Göring's cousin, that the Legionnaires pride themselves with this law saying it is their creation and demanding credit for it. As soon as it will go into effect, they will exploit it as a show of their power and your weakness."

"What do you mean?" asked the Mareshal, "You mean to say they will pretend to have power in this country?"

"Yes," said the Professor. "That is exactly what I mean."

"So what should I do?" asked the Mareshal who now looked confused.

"If you ask me, you have only one choice. Cancel the order with the Yellow Star. You must do it immediately before it goes into effect."

The Mareshal kept silent and finished his glass of cognac. He was also puffing at his cigar, trying to weigh the facts in his mind.

Finally he picked up the phone and called his adjutant. In the presence of his guests, he ordered the adjutant to annul immediately the new law of the Yellow Star in Bucharest.

"Well done!" said the Professor as he and Adrian took leave from the Mareshal.

"I am stuck between Hitler, on one side, and Horațiu with his green shirts, on the other. It is not a comfortable position!" mumbled the Mareshal as he walked his guests to the door. "But I will show them who is the boss!"

The next day the German newspapers protested against the decision to repeal the new law, claiming that the Yellow Star was an essential part of the "New Order."

But it was not reinstated in Bucharest.

UNTITLED

THE SUCCESS OF ADRIAN'S YELLOW Star intervention was a festive occasion, celebrated by the "heroes" and their families. They all gathered in Stella and Sorel's living room and savored the delicacies brought by Doctor Georgescu with the help of the Queen's majordomo. They particularly enjoyed the black caviar and sable which had disappeared from the stores.

But their celebratory mood was of short duration. As early as July, deportations beyond the river Dniester had started in the cities of Bessarabia and the Bukovina. In August, just about the time of Sorel's return from Iaşi, some people living in Bucharest but who were born in Bessarabia or Bukovina were summoned to return to their cities of birth. They were forced to live in a ghetto before being deported or liquidated.

Mathilda, Joel's wife, had been born in the city of Czernowitz, in the Bukovina, and her parents were still living there. Mathilda worried every day for her parents and for herself, fearing she might be summoned to return to Czernowitz.

This new development was discussed in an urgent meeting of the Underground Jewish Council. Adrian went immediately into action. As soon as he heard about these ghetto-izations followed by deportations or liquidations, he started sending memos of protest to his old school friend, the Mareshal.

But this time the Mareshal was not in a friendly mood, even though Professor Ursu and even the Queen intervened in favor of the Jews.

Adrian sent memo after memo to the Mareshal, asking him to stop the deportations and the massacres. At first he received no reply. After more time and more memos, the Mareshal answered with an angry letter. He accused the Jews of having attacked, shot and killed Romanian troops a year earlier, following the Hitler-Stalin pact, when the Romanian army had withdrawn from Bessarabia and Bukovina and had been replaced by Soviet troops.

The Mareshal said, "Did you ask yourself why the Jews of Bessarabia burned their homes before fleeing? Can you explain why we found 15-year-old Jewish children with their pockets full of hand grenades when we reoccupied this land? Did you ask yourself how many of my people were treacherously killed by Jews? How many were interred alive? If you want proof, you shall have proof!"

Adrian responded that indeed, some Russian Jews had resisted the Romanian occupation. But there had been no massacres or organized violence carried out by the Jews against the Romanian troops that would justify the present deportations and killings. Adrian also pledged the loyalty of the Romanian Jews to the Mareshal and the Romanian Army.

But the Mareshal's reply was even angrier. He stated, "Only the Jews from the Old Kingdom, who had arrived here before 1914, would be allowed to stay as long as they respected the laws of the land and did not engage in Communist activity, propaganda or attempt sabotage. We now have to defend our Romanian rights in our own country, because our tolerance and hospitality have allowed others, mostly Jews, to take advantage of us."

Joel and Mathilda were very troubled by what was going on. They were afraid that at any moment Mathilda could be forced to leave Bucharest. They had had no news from her parents. They could not get in touch with them. They had only heard rumors that all the Jews in Czernowitz had been locked in a crowded ghetto and were going to be either deported beyond the Dniester or shot.

Just about this time, Joel learned about a ship preparing to sail to Palestine. It was advertised as a "luxury steamer" with double-occupancy state-rooms, two hot meals a day, and modern sanitary and medical facilities.

Ads started to appear in the newspapers. Tickets, which were expensive, were soon on sale at the ship's company office on Calea Victoriei, near the elegant Capşa restaurant. The ship, the Dorina, had been bought from a Greek shipowner, Nikos Papadoglu, by a Zionist organization for a great deal of money. Passengers would receive visas for landing in Palestine in Istanbul, where the ship had to dock before reaching her final destination.

Even though this made her an "illegal boat," Joel and many other Zionists were enthusiastic and full of hope. It was the only opportunity to get away. Furthermore, as members of a Zionist organization, he and Mathilda obtained tickets at a discount. He also was able to obtain a cheaper ticket for his mother, Josephine.

Joel was particularly proud that it was his Zionist organization, the Betar, that had bought the ship and was organizing the voyage. Since childhood he had always dreamt of going to Palestine. After the bloody Bucharest pogrom which had taken his father's life, he could barely wait to leave.

Joel was also pleased that, even though it was an illegal ship, the Romanian authorities had raised no objections. They had only stated that under no circumstances would they allow anybody who boarded the ship back into the country. Such individuals would be immediately punished and deported.

In contrast to Joel, Mathilda was much more troubled by their decision. Although she realized her situation was difficult and her life could be in danger, she worried about her parents and felt guilty for emigrating and leaving them behind.

She slept badly and had frightening dreams. One day she started to feel nauseous and faint. She had headaches. She started to crave foods which she had previously detested, like spicy sausages, doughnuts and bacon. Her period stopped and her breasts grew heavy and tight.

It was Stella who recognized her developing pregnancy. It changed everything in Mathilda's mind. Her doubts vanished. She knew now, for the sake of her child, she had to get on that boat.

This was not all. One night, as Mathilda finished washing the dishes and Joel was already in bed, the doorbell rang. Joel jumped out of bed and Mathilda came running to his room. They looked at each other anxiously. Who could it be so late at night? Had they come to take Mathilda away? There was a second ring. Only then did Joel go to open the door.

At first, he did not recognize the two old, thin and tired looking people standing in the doorway. Only as they stepped into the light did Joel and Mathilda see that they were facing Mathilda's parents.

They took off their coats, sat down and told their story. They said that almost miraculously they had been able to squeeze out of the ghetto. With the help of a policeman friend they had obtained new identity papers and traveled to Bucharest. They were so exhausted by the long trip they could barely finish their story.

Joel knew that the first thing he had to do for them was to get tickets on the boat using their new identity papers.

Many of Mathilda and Joel's friends became envious of them or wanted at least to change places with them when they learned about their decision to leave. One of them was Sorel, Stella's husband. He had survived the Iaşi pogrom and would have loved to join them. But Stella would never think of separating from her sister Nina and her friend, Doctor Georgescu. The voyage on the sea remained only a pipe dream for Sorel.

Even Adrian fantasized himself on the ship. It was not Switzerland or Lugano, still it represented a road to freedom. He knew that Nina would find it much too risky, particularly if Stella remained behind. Adrian admired Joel for his courage and determination and was slightly envious of him.

Of the whole family, it was only Joel and Mathilda with her parents and Joel's mother, Josephine, who would leave. The two Polish children, Boris and Rachel who were staying with Stella and Sorel were also going to accompany them as part of a children's transport.

The original date for the ship's departure had been set for September 30th, but it was later moved to October 8, and then to the end of October. The boat was in need of some minor repairs.

This allowed Joel to concentrate on selling and emptying both his own and his mother's apartments. They could bring only limited baggage on their trip.

Joel and Mathilda's apartment was not a problem, since it was not very large, nor was it too cluttered. Besides, they were lucky and found, with Doctor Georgescu's help, another young couple who wanted the apartment, were willing to wait for Joel and Mathilda's departure and could also use the furnishings of the home.

They had to work much harder emptying his mother's apartment, which was much larger, and filled with more furnishings and clothes. After his father's death in the pogrom, his mother had never touched any of his belongings. Getting rid of his father's clothes became Joel's responsibility.

When he opened the chest of drawers, the first thing he saw was a blue cashmere muffler, identical to the one his father had worn the day of the pogrom. (His father had been in the habit of buying duplicate pieces of clothing he liked.) When he saw the muffler and particularly when he touched the soft fabric, Joel felt transported to that grim day in January. He could suddenly hear and see all that had happened that morning in the slaughterhouse and in the forest. He covered his eyes and for a few minutes he had to sit down and catch his breath. Why did his father, a great patriot who had been decorated during the war and who was deeply loyal to his country of birth have to die such a cruel death?

For a while, he sat down lost in grief. It was only when his mother walked into the room that he remembered their plans to emigrate to sunnier shores.

It was now November 15th. The ship's departure had been postponed again, set back to the end of the month.

Joel had finished emptying his mother's apartment. She had moved in with him and Mathilda. At the same time, Mathilda's parents were also staying there so the space was very crowded. There was a bed or a couch in every room. Luckily, there were two bathrooms. Still, times for showers or baths had to be scheduled in advance. Cooking and eating was a different problem, since Mathilda's parents ate kosher food, while everyone else did not.

The parents never complained, but they never smiled. Every meal seemed a hardship for them. Every morning and every night, Mathilda's father wrapped himself in his tallit and prayed God to forgive him for his sins. Otherwise they stayed at home, hidden in the back room of the apartment with the curtains drawn. Although their forged ID papers looked quite legitimate, Joel didn't want his neighbors to become suspicious about the "new people" in the house. You never knew when a report from a nosy neighbor could lead to a police raid or an investigation, particularly now as rumors of deportations from Bucharest began to circulate.

A few days after November 15th, the date of the ship's departure was set for some time in December. All the tickets which had been sold were now cancelled. New tickets, much more expensive than the original ones, had to be purchased.

Joel was lucky. As a Zionist leader he still got tickets at a reduced price for himself, Mathilda and the two children. He had to stand in a long line at the company's ticket office near the Capşa restaurant for his mother and Mathilda's parents.

The news was bad. There were more and more deportations and massacres in the North-East of the country. The level of anxiety was high even in Bucharest.

The rush for tickets was so great people were camping in the courtyard of the travel society, hoping to be able to purchase new tickets. Even Joel almost missed the new sale.

In the end he managed to get three expensive tickets from the last available batch.

In this atmosphere of great tension, the family could barely wait for their departure. The organizers of the trip had issued an alluring prospectus, hoping to calm the anxiety of the passengers. The prospectus showed photos of staterooms with six beds and a powerful Diesel engine. Everybody was allowed to bring 20 kgs of luggage. A list of permitted items was published.

The prospectus also promised hot tea in the morning and warm meals for lunch and dinner. The authors added that the ship was provided with sufficient lifeboats, bathrooms, toilets and medical facilities, as well as possibilities for individual cooking arrangements.

Joel explained to his family that the Zionists, who had made this trip possible, were planning to divide the passengers into groups of twenty-five with a group leader to help organize food distribution, use of bathrooms, cultural activities, and division of responsibilities on board. "Actually," he told them in the end, "this is not exactly a luxury cruise. For a short period of time, we will have to live with 700 people in a limited space and without the comfort we have at home. But remember we'll be on our way to our own country—to a new life!" His eyes were shining. He smiled as he said these words.

Finally, on December 7, 1941—Joel, his family and the two Polish children—boarded the special train to

Constanța. When all the passengers were inside, the cars were sealed—all the windows and doors were locked and covered with metal bars just like the windows of a prison.

Everybody was surprised by these measures which they hadn't expected on this expensive voyage. When the train stopped in a small station before reaching Constanța, Mathilda and Joel saw a bunch of young men shoveling snow. Their clothes were torn and their hands were wrapped in rags. They had no gloves. When they saw the train, they stopped working and stared at the cars. Joel and Mathilda noticed the big yellow star each one wore and knew they were Jews, working in a forced labor camp. Joel realized with a start that, if he were not on this train, he too would end up working in a forced labor camp.

Early in the morning, after a long night's travel, the special train arrived in Constanța and stopped in the port near the Customs building. Nobody was allowed out of the sealed cars. They were locked in and guarded by soldiers armed with automatic rifles and guns. Joel's plan to visit the casino and then stop at the statue of Ovid, the great Roman poet who died in exile in the ancient harbor by the Black Sea, came to nought.

Locked in the train, he gazed out the window and saw nothing but an enormous refugee camp. Thousands of people of all ages and walks of life were milling around aimlessly, while others were crouching on the frozen ground or were huddled inside cardboard boxes or under makeshift tents.

Some looked foreign to him. They were blond and blue-eyed with fair skin. He remembered that German and Austrian Jews, even some Jews from Czechoslovakia had managed to sail down the Danube in hired German excursion boats in order to reach Constanţa and escape on the Black Sea.

It was very cold now. He remembered hearing that the Danube was frozen and some boats were stuck in the ice. For a minute he panicked when he imagined that their ship too might be stuck in ice—some place on the Danube, or might not even reach Constanţa and the Black Sea.

But these thoughts didn't last long. Suddenly the doors of the first car were opened, and twenty-five passengers were ordered out by armed soldiers for customs inspection.

The Customs room was an enormous hall in the basement of the Port Authority. It had many rows of large tables and a customs clerk was seated at each of them. Immediately after the passengers' tickets and ID cards were checked, they were told that the regulations had changed. They were allowed to take only 10 kg. of luggage with them and the rest had to be left behind. The decision as to what to take and what to abandon was made by the clerks, not by the travelers.

When Joel and Mathilda reached the table to which they were assigned, the agent told them to open their suitcases and take out their entire contents. He watched them closely as they were emptying their bags.

The customs clerk was a broad-shouldered stocky man with small, shrewd eyes behind thick eyeglasses. He was missing a front upper tooth, so that he made a whistling sound when he spoke. He wore a stained and frayed lab coat over his military uniform and a big fur hat on his head.

The clerk went slowly and methodically through the mound of things piled on his desk. He put to one side all the winter clothing, woolen sweaters, socks, hats, mittens, jackets and pants. He then took the china, cooking ware, new terrycloth towels, leather boots and heavy duty shoes; even the damask tablecloth which Joel and Mathilda had received as a wedding gift had to stay behind. When Joel tried to claim Leon's woolen muffler as a memento of his dead father, the officer refused, saying, "The muffler had now become 'national property' and could not be claimed by an alien."

The leather suitcases in which the luggage had been packed also had to stay behind. In the end, they gathered the remaining pieces of their belongings (weighing much less than 10 kgs.), wrapped them in a bed sheet, turning them into a bundle which they carried with them.

Before letting them go, the customs clerk had to check them for gold and diamonds. This was done by first patting them down thoroughly, then making them turn their pockets inside out. If nothing was found, the search continued. The clerk ripped open the hem and lining of their coats. Finally he cut off buttons to make sure that no gold coins or diamonds were hidden underneath.

When all this was finished, Joel and Mathilda were taken to the other end of the hall, where they met with the rest of their family.

Josephine, Joel's mother, was unhappy and tearful, since they had taken away her ivory hearing horn. Her customs inspector insisted that this was an old, precious, handcrafted art object, a "national treasure" which had to remain in the country. He could not be convinced that it was just a hearing aid, essential for the wellbeing of an old lady.

The inspector also took from her two big photo albums of family photos going back to her childhood. There were photos of her brother, Chief Rabbi Ariel Geller of London, as a five-year-old, photos of her and Leon's wedding and their honeymoon in Venice, and of Joel as a little boy on his hobby horse.

"These pictures can be used in espionage. They can be used to manufacture false passports and visas, so they cannot be taken on the ship," said the customs officer, as he also took away, without any explanation, her small china teapot with its cozy and her large soup terrine, which she had always used for family dinners on the holidays.

Mathilda's parents—who had come to Bucharest from the ghetto of Czernowitz—didn't have much luggage. Nevertheless the suspicious customs inspector, who didn't find any fault in their forged ID papers, took away her father's pocket watch and its gold chain and her mother's gold rimmed spectacles. The hem and the lining of their coats had been ripped open and their buttons were missing, having been cut off in the search for gold and diamonds.

Nevertheless, Mathilda's father didn't complain. He felt content that the customs clerk had not taken away his tallit, his prayer book and his phylacteries.

The only one not affected by the zeal of the customs officers was the Polish boy, Boris, whose small suitcase had remained untouched, and who was even permitted to take with him his mouth harmonica and his violin.

On December 12th, five days after they had left Bucharest in the special train, Joel, Mathilda and all the other travelers were led to the pier from which they would board the ship.

Nobody had seen the boat. What they discovered at the end of the quay was a small sailing vessel with two masts, but no sail. It looked like an old and frail boat, in serious disrepair and neglect, with a metal hull covered with rust.

"This boat will take us to our ship, right?" Joel asked a young soldier in charge of keeping order.

"What do you mean the boat which will take you to the ship? This is the ship! There is no other one!" the soldier said.

Joel couldn't believe him. It can't be! He thought, as he turned away and closed his eyes. The man is either making a bad joke, or he doesn't know what he is talking about.

But when Joel opened his eyes and looked again, he couldn't see any other ship.

As soon as he recognized the truth, he felt a nagging in his mind. How were the hundreds of people going to squeeze on this ship and live there for some time? And how was this old wreck going to be able to sail the rough seas as far as Palestine?

He felt a lump in his chest which made it hard to breathe. He almost choked. He couldn't speak. He could barely look at Mathilda. She said nothing. Her eyes were opened wide. She could only stare, without blinking, at the vessel in front of them.

In the next few minutes Joel realized that they were standing still. The whole column of travelers had stopped moving, as those at the head of the line refused to move forward and step on the gangplank.

Then there was a commotion: women started to scream and cry hysterically trying to break out of line and run back to the Customs building. Children joined them with their high-pitched voices. The whole procession would have ended in chaos, if the soldiers hadn't stopped them from breaking ranks. They forced them to climb the ramp.

It was late afternoon on December 12th, a very cold day, when Joel and his family boarded the ship. They were met by a second set of customs agents, who took additional items, such as bread, sugar, candy, biscuits, money, and whatever winter clothing they had left, from them.

On their way to the deck, Joel and Mathilda encountered the representative of the Zionist organization on board, who directed them to their family's sleeping quarters. He told Joel where to meet the other Zionist leaders—the "Ship's Committee"—on the boat.

It was not easy to reach their lodging quarters, since they were located three flights down, at the bottom of a steep and narrow staircase. There was no resemblance between the comfortable cabins shown in the prospectus and the narrow, wooden cages in which each family or group of single passengers were assigned to sleep.

These cages, which were only three-feet high, had to be used by five individuals. There were no beds. They had to sleep on the wooden floor. It turned out that some passengers had no place in the stalls. That is what happened to Boris, who had to sleep in the space outside the cages.

In addition, Joel soon discovered that sanitary conditions were also disappointing. There were only eight very primitive toilets—a simple hole in the floor—at the back and bottom of the ship. There were no medical facilities or first aid kits, only two small fresh water tanks, and only two lifeboats for 700 people.

It took a long time for everybody to settle in their bunks, since many people, such as Joel's mother and his in-laws—were so stunned by what they saw, they refused to descend the narrow staircase into the depths of the dark ship.

After his family was finally settled, Joel had a brief meeting with the other Zionist leaders, the Ship's Committee. The passengers were divided into groups of thirty individuals under the responsibility of one of the Zionist activists who would then work out a schedule for eating, washing, exercise, Hebrew studies and a precise time when each group could climb on deck, since the space there was so narrow it could accommodate only a limited number of people at one time without tipping the boat.

Later in the evening, after they had left their belongings in their sleeping quarters, Joel, Mathilda and the two Polish children climbed on deck to watch the ship raise anchor. As they saw the coastline vanish in the darkness, they joined the singing of Hatikvah, the anthem of the new land, which a group of youth had started to sing.

On the opposite side of the deck, by the railing, stood a solitary figure, wrapped in a tallit, dovening under the sky. At first, they wondered who it was. They walked toward him. As they came closer, they recognized Mathilda's father. He was saying the evening prayers and asking God's blessings for the tiny ship, the many passengers, and the long trip to Palestine.

Captain Garapnik and the first mate, Nissim, were sitting on the bridge, perched in the Captain's flimsy headquarters. They had supervised the raising of the anchor and the ship's sailing out of port, out of Constanţa, towed by a powerful tugboat.

It was cold and very windy. As they advanced into the open sea, the waves grew bigger and stronger, making the boat rock and roll in a dizzying way. Nevertheless, through the howling of the wind and the roaring of the sea, the two men on the bridge could hear the regular purr of the engine.

Captain Garapnik and the first mate shared a bottle of *mastika*. They didn't talk much. They emptied their glasses slowly and listened to the noise of the motor and to the roaring outside. Then the Captain decided to go to bed, leaving the first mate, Nissim, in charge of the boat.

A few hours passed. Even though he was sitting in a cramped, uncomfortable position, Nissim, had to fight his desire to drop off to sleep. He was shaken out of his drowsiness by something he heard or, more precisely, something he did not hear anymore—the purr of the engine. The motor had stopped working. He waited for a while, hoping that it was going to start again. But nothing happened. The engine remained silent. All he could hear was the wind and the sea.

He ran to the Captain and woke him up.

Half asleep and still drowsy from his drunken nap, Captain Garapnik put through an urgent call for help through the ship's weak and hesitant radio. He told Nissim to wake up the crew and ordered them to get rid of the water which had started to accumulate in the engine room. Without a working motor, the boat was drifting on the high sea, violently buffeted by the wind and the waves. Down below, in their bunker, Joel and his family were awakened by their neighbors' retching and vomiting. Mathilda's father got up, put on his tallit, opened his prayer book and started to doven.

For some time the Captain and crew were at a loss, wondering what to do next. They tried to send out another emergency message, but now the radio had stopped working, too. In the meantime they kept bailing water from the engine room.

Time went on. The ship kept drifting aimlessly in the sea. People became sicker and sicker; even the captain's spirits started to waver.

Suddenly, a light in the distance appeared. At first it was very faint, then it grew brighter and brighter.

To what did it belong? What could it be? As it came closer, they saw that it was a tugboat. They recognized the tugboat which had towed them out of Constanţa! It had now come to their rescue. The crew and captain of the tugboat had heard the earlier distress signal. When they reached the Dorina, the tugboat captain boarded the ship.

He had a short conference with Garapnik and Nissim and offered to have his mechanics fix the stricken engine for $7,500. This offer was passed onto the passengers via the Zionist team leaders. In a short time, a collection of wedding bands, bracelets, watches and lockets which belonged to the passengers but had escaped the zeal of the customs inspectors, was handed to Garapnik, who gave it to the tugboat captain. (Following so many inspections, nobody had any money left.)

Two mechanics from the rescue boat boarded the ship and started tinkering with the old, rusty engine. After strenuous efforts, they made it work.

With the engine now puffing and purring, the ship continued its route toward Turkey, out of the Black Sea. On Sunday, only two days later, near the entrance to the Bosporus, the motor fell silent again.

Left without power, the ship started drifting anew. There was danger ahead. Garapnik told Nissim that the water here had been seeded with German mines, aimed against Russian ships. He had heard that in order to protect their own fleet, the Turks had surrounded the mines with nets to which bells were attached.

As the Dorina approached the Bosporus, two crewmen perched on the masts heard the bells ringing and noticed nearby "nests" of mines. They immediately sent distress signals to a passing cargo ship.

But there was no response. The refugee ship drifted closer and closer to the mines. The Captain prepared to give the order to abandon ship. He told the crew that the danger from an exploding mine was greater than plunging into the freezing waters since they were not too far from the shore.

The crew was preparing to get the women and children into the rickety lifeboats, when salvation suddenly arrived. A Turkish tugboat under the banner of the crescent moon headed their way and towed them into Istanbul harbor. It was proof that the cargo ship had actually noticed them and alerted the seaport.

There was great excitement when they docked by the pier. Istanbul was lit like the World's Fair. Thousands of lights were reflected in the dark and calm water like in a mirror. It seemed to the passengers, who had lived for a year in total blackout, they had reached Paradise. Everybody, young and old, was now trying to get on deck. They felt happy and relieved of their worries. They were out of Romania. The engine was going to be fixed. Soon they would be heading toward Palestine.

Soon after they docked in Istanbul, the Captain communicated to the Port Authority that the ship's motor was not working and needed to be fixed or replaced. He wasn't allowed off the ship, nor was anybody else. A cordon of police boats surrounded and watched the Dorina, preventing her from having any contact with land.

Shortly after the Captain's message, two mechanics accompanied by several policemen climbed on board to inspect the engine. What they found convinced them that the Captain had told the truth. Their conclusion was that repairing the motor would cost about $5,000 and would take about one week. After that they could be off and on their way to Palestine.

A week passed and the boat remained anchored in the harbor. Most days Joel and Mathilda's family remained hunkered down in their stall. They were so hungry and cold, they stayed below deck in spite of the unbearable stench and lack of fresh air. Like everybody else on the ship, they could get only a meagre portion of biscuits each day. Even these provisions were getting smaller and smaller by the day.

Joel had taken part in a committee meeting with the Captain and the first mate to explore the situation, but no solution was found. As the ship was forced into complete isolation the specter of starvation haunted them.

But just as their plight seemed impossible to bear, there was sudden excitement on the bridge. Joel, the other team leaders and the entire crew were urgently ordered on deck by the Captain. As he stepped out in the open, Joel couldn't believe his eyes: a line of small fishing boats carrying sacks full of food had formed alongside the ship. Under the watchful eye of the police, the boatmen were hoisting their cargo to the men on deck.

When all the sacks of food were onboard, the Ship's Committee and the crew distributed them to the teams. It was hard work and took a long time, but for everybody on board it was like a miracle from heaven. The heavy sacks were filled with bread, sugar and cheese.

After that first morning, the mysterious deliveries continued every day or every other day. Sometimes, in addition to bread, sugar and cheese, the sacks also contained smoked fish or oranges.

But who was the unknown benefactor? It took almost two weeks until Zalman Bier, a short, middle-aged man with gray, wiry hair and very green eyes, was allowed to climb on board to meet the Captain and the Ship's Committee.

Zalman Bier was the head of the Jewish agency in Istanbul. The sacks of food delivered to the passengers of the Dorina were his brain child.

How did Zalman Bier connect with the ship? Everybody was wondering.

It was Nissim who told Joel how it happened. Late on the night of December 16, the police chief of the port of Istanbul, with whom he was friends, telephoned Bier to tell him that a new refugee ship from Constanța had docked in the harbor.

From that moment on, the new boat was all that mattered to Zalman. Due to his friendly relations with the harbor police and various food merchants, he was able to send the food packages to the ship.

But boarding a politically quarantined or illegal boat was a much more delicate problem. It could be solved only by slipping the necessary *baksheesh* in the appropriate hands at the right moment.

Zalman Bier was not merely the head of the Jewish agency in Istanbul, he was also a very wealthy and successful businessman who owned the largest chain of clothing and shoe stores in the land. He was born in Czernowitz when it still belonged to Romania. He came to Istanbul with his parents as a child. Because of his city of birth, he kept seeking out people from Czernowitz on every transport of refugees. He was delighted to meet Mathilda and her parents. He soon learned about Joel's mother missing her hearing aid and Mathilda's mother's lost eyeglasses. It didn't take him long to replace them. When he presented the old ladies with his gifts, they were so grateful and happy, they kept blessing him and calling him their "cherished son."

As there was no progress with the engine problems, life on board had to be organized for the long haul. In the committee meetings which took place on the ship, each team leader was given a chore, a special responsibility. As a pediatrician, married to a teacher, Joel and Mathilda were to take care of the children. Mathilda was to organize a school program in addition to teaching Hebrew, while Joel was to function both as a pediatrician and program director for "skits and entertainment." He often remembered the skits he organized with Silvia and her guitar for Nadia,

Corinna, Theo and their friends, back in Bucharest. As he thought of Silvia, he wondered what she was doing. What had happened to her?

It was now almost one year since the pogrom in Bucharest in which his father had lost his life and Silvia had aimed her pistol at him, trying to kill him. Thank goodness, when she recognized him, she became confused. She fell unconscious and had to be carried away.

What happened to her after that incident? Was she taken back to the mental hospital? Did she have shock treatment? Or did her Legionnaire boyfriend, Doctor Milo submit her to more hypnosis? Joel couldn't answer these questions. Instead he turned his attention to organizing a celebration for Hanukkah, which was right around the corner.

Despite all the hardships—the cold, the hunger, the filth, the pervasive stench, and lack of space—he put together a children's chorus and small orchestra formed by the children and adult musicians who had succeeded in bringing their instruments on board. He convinced Boris who had been able to keep his violin and two other children—one with a flute and one an accordion—to play as soloists. With the help of two crew members he built a small stage made of crates, on which Rachel, Boris' younger sister, could perform a spirited tap dance. The other children would then dance the hora.

Zalman Bier brought a large menorah with fake candles which was set up on deck and many dreidels for the children. The celebration was a big success and lifted everybody's spirits.

It was followed, a week later by Christmas dinner, and the sudden appearance of a small Christmas tree with red apples and golden nuts. It was brought on board by "Santa" Bier for the Captain and his crew. They had a big banquet with roast lamb and rice pilaf, olives, cabbage, wine and *cozonac*. Through the whole night, the crew sang Christmas carols in Romanian, Bulgarian and Greek.

Before the end of December, three weddings were celebrated on board by three different rabbis. They were all accompanied by the new orchestra and the children's chorus.

During all these festivities the policemen who were watching the ship brought their boats very close to Dorina so as to be able to listen and enjoy the lively concerts on board.

The last festivity, the New Year celebration, was sponsored and organized by the Captain. In the absence of colored lanterns, the whole ship was decorated with garlands of colored paper, provided by Zalman Bier.

In addition to their everyday menu, the Captain offered smoked fish, olives, oranges, figs and a few bottles of wine to his guests. The company invited to his table—which extended over most of the deck, included the entire crew, the Ship's Committee, the five rabbis on board, and the oldest passengers. Joel was included as a member of the Ship's Committee as was Mathilda, the teacher in charge. Boris and his little sister Rachel were invited since they had both performed as soloists. Josephine and Mathilda's parents were included as the oldest passengers on board, and Zalman Bier, of course, because he was Zalman Bier. The crew made the generators work that night so that the entire ship was flooded with light.

The festivity started on a serious note with the oldest rabbi speaking about the war and the destruction of the Jewish communities in many places in Europe. He then mentioned the massacres which were going on in their own land and prayed that the New Year would bring peace, ending the war and suffering. He finished his short talk by thanking the Captain for his courage and strength. Before sitting down, he prayed God for His protection and blessing.

Captain Garapnik was moved by the old rabbi's words. At midnight he got up and ordered that wine be poured in all glasses. Then, raising his own cup, he made a toast, thanking the crew and passengers for their discipline, hard work, and confidence in his leadership. With his right hand on his heart, he promised his guests that he was never going to abandon them and would not rest until the ship docked in Tel Aviv. After he ended his speech, he sang an old, sentimental Bulgarian ballad. He had a deep, melodious voice which came as a surprise to everyone and brought tears to their eyes.

When everybody went back to their sleeping quarters, Joel and Mathilda stayed on deck by themselves. In their crowded family bunker, they could never be alone. They looked at the festive harbor crowded with ships and yachts glittering with lights. The water too had turned into a sea of rainbows. Fireworks were bursting in the distance, and from the ships around them they could hear wine glasses clinking, champagne corks popping, dance music and laughter.

Joel held Mathilda very tight and rested his hand on her stomach. It was now bulging a little. Mathilda's waistline had thickened, in spite of the meagre diet. (Whenever he could, Zalman Bier sneaked a few sweets like baklava and *rahat lokum* to Joel for Mathilda, who then shared them secretly with the two Polish children.)

"How is he doing?" asked Joel.

"I think he is doing fine!" said Mathilda, smiling in the dark and covering Joel's hand with her own.

They didn't talk much, but they knew that they were thinking the same thoughts: how to name the child. Joel wanted to call him Leon, after his father, if he was a boy, and Leonie, if they had a girl.

Mathilda went along with him. But now, as she was leaning closely against him, her thoughts were flying ahead. She was imagining their life in a kibbutz, seeing herself picking oranges in an orange grove, while Joel was carrying the baby along in a small basket or strapped on his back . . .

They remained for a long time on the deserted deck watching the dazzling lights around them and a thin, silvery new moon rising on the horizon. Meanwhile their thoughts had wandered far away, lingering on the sun-drenched hills of Palestine.

A few days into January, as the distractions of the holidays were behind them, the mood on the ship changed. Some passengers started wondering when the engine would be repaired and how long would they remain at anchor in Istanbul.

The Captain, who had no answers, passed these questions on to the Port Authority. On January 10th, two mechanics supervised by an engineer came on board and inspected the engine anew. They returned after ten days and stated that the motor needed extensive repairs; important parts had to be replaced, while other parts needed to be ordered. The work would be ready by the end of the month, when the ship could leave and continue her voyage to Palestine.

But the mechanics didn't come back as promised, which made the Ship's Committee suspicious.

The Captain made a new complaint to the Port Authority. He was told that the new parts could not be found and the pieces which were available did not fit the ship's engine. They were either too small or too old. A new motor—they said—couldn't be used, since the engine space was too narrow.

The Captain wanted to speed up the departure. Backed by the Ship's committee and by Zalman Bier and his influential connections, he asked to be given another ship to sail to Palestine. This request too was turned down.

But the idea of getting on another ship had caught on. At the next Committee meeting, Joel and a few other young Zionists suggested that they set fire to their boat so as to force the authorities to transfer them to another ship. Joel and his friends had actually spoken with the captain of another ship anchored near them. The man had promised to take the passengers to Palestine if their ship was destroyed by the blaze. In the end, though, they all felt that setting fire to their boat was too dangerous, and the promise of a new ship too unreliable.

The committee then explored another way to get to Palestine, namely on land, traveling by train through Turkey and Syria. But this plan too was rejected by the authorities, since the passengers of the Dorina had no visas, and Turkey—which was under British pressure—refused transit through its land to anybody without a visa.

When he learned about this new refusal, Nissim, the first mate got very angry.

"Papadoglu, the original ship owner and broker, lied to us!" he told Joel. "He assured everybody that visas for Turkey and Palestine were waiting in Istanbul. As you see, it was a lie. He probably never tried to obtain the visas, since he knew the British wouldn't let us land in Palestine and the Turks would follow their orders. There is worse," he added. "A Bulgarian sailor who delivers food to our boat and knows Papadoglu well, told me the Dorina has never been a seaworthy vessel. In the past, she was nothing but a cattle barge with two masts, built at least one hundred years ago in the mid 1800's, to ferry live cattle along the Danube. Our famous so-called Diesel engine is not a Diesel engine at all, but a small, damaged contraption which belonged to a sunken boat. It was fished out of the Danube after resting on the bottom for nearly twenty years.

Papadoglu mounted the damaged motor on the cattle barge and refurbished the whole thing for a bargain price. When it was ready, he sold it to the Zionists for good money."

Nissim lit a cigarette, then spit on the floor and went on, "I, for one, have decided to get off this boat as soon as I can. She will never make it to Palestine."

Joel was deeply shocked by Nissim's words. But he couldn't believe him. Nobody could be so callous, so cruel, so money hungry! Even though the appearance of the ship and the severe engine problems confirmed Nissim's statements, Joel still had trouble believing him.

How about his fellow Zionists: where was their judgment? Didn't they check out the boat? Didn't they know what kind of person Papadoglu was? Didn't they know what they were getting into?

In the end, Joel had only one explanation: the Zionists probably weighed one danger against the other. They must have felt that getting on this rickety boat was less dangerous than staying in Romania.

Still, Joel had trouble with Nissim's story. Nissim was a sailor, and sailors were known for their fantastic tales. It was a byproduct of their profession. Joel remembered Ulysses' adventures in the Odyssey!

A few days later, he learned from Zalman Bier that the Captain had written a letter to the authorities asking to resign from the ship and to return to his country with his Bulgarian crew. He was afraid that, without a visa and as a citizen of an enemy country (Bulgaria had recently joined the Axis), if captured by the British, he and his crew would be detained as prisoners of war.

The Turkish authorities read Garapnik's letter and tried to find a substitute captain and crew. They were unsuccessful. Nobody wanted to sail to Palestine on a ship which had no landing permit from the British.

In addition, there were now other suspicions about the Captain. Some travelers feared that he was going to dock the ship on a Greek island, which was now occupied by the Nazis. As a Bulgarian, a citizen of a country allied with the Axis, this would be a good solution for him and his Bulgarian crew. It would mean sure death for the Jewish passengers.

In the first days of February, Mathilda started feeling unwell. She had severe fits of nausea, vomiting, and headaches which became progressively unbearable and painful cramping in her abdomen. She couldn't eat and she couldn't stand the stench of unwashed bodies, urine and feces which pervaded the boat. She was always running up on deck to catch some fresh air. Then, early one morning the cramps in her pelvis turned to sharp knives. The pain was accompanied by a thick, abundant hemorrhage. As she lost consciousness, Joel realized that she had suffered a sudden miscarriage.

He ran to Nissim and the Captain, who succeeded in having Mathilda placed on a police boat and taken to the Jewish hospital in Istanbul. Joel however was not allowed to accompany her. Nobody from the ship was permitted to set foot on land under any circumstance.

But it so happened that the doctor on call in the emergency room knew Zalman Bier and his involvement with the refugee ship. He put Mathilda through surgery immediately. As soon as she came out of anesthesia he called Zalman Bier who arrived quickly at the hospital, accompanied by his wife, Laura.

At first, in the recovery room, Mathilda was too weak to recognize Zalman Bier and speak to him. She was given a blood transfusion and intravenous fluids and allowed to sleep as long as she wanted.

From the first day, Zalman Bier and his wife Laura came to see her every day. As soon as she was able to eat, they brought her food prepared by Mrs. Bier and insisted that she not taste any of the hospital food. Zalman Bier was a very suspicious man: even though this was a Jewish hospital, it was not immune to "dirty play." The Turkish authorities—he said repeatedly—did not want any Jewish refugee from Romania in their land. And it would not be impossible to have Mathilda die suddenly in the hospital of what looked like a heart attack or an acute pulmonary embolism!

Due to the good medical treatment at the hospital and the food provided by the Biers, her health improved greatly within a week or two. In spite of this, Mathilda remained anxious and sad. She missed Joel and worried about her parents. She wanted to go back to the ship.

She felt guilty sleeping in a clean, comfortable bed, eating good food, and washing with soap and warm water when her loved ones were living in great misery and deprivation. She often cried, particularly when she was alone and sometimes even when the Biers visited.

Since the hospital was not far from the Topkapi Palace and the ship was anchored at the Sayaburnu dock, from her window she could see the two masts and a tiny portion of the bridge. Zalman Bier had brought her a pair of binoculars. She spent long hours pointing them in the direction of the pier. She watched the seagulls circling over the harbor and wished to turn into one of them.

Even though Mathilda begged him to let her return to the boat and the Turkish administration pressured the hospital to release her and send her back to the ship, Zalman could not accept this alternative. He had convinced the doctors in the hospital to diagnose her with various medical complications so that her continuous treatment and stay on the ward could be justified.

"I have a plan for you and for Joel," he told Mathilda. "I have assurances that it will be successful. But it demands that you stay here in Istanbul and not go back to the boat." He explained to her that he had started working on a plan to organize a children's transport from the ship, on land, by train, through Turkey and Syria.

"Somebody has to accompany the children's convoy. The best qualified would be Joel, as a pediatrician, and yourself, since you are already here, in Istanbul. We can add three more passports for your parents and Joel's mother, once we have permission for the sixty-five children on board," he said.

Zalman's plan was based on the fact that the British refused visas for Palestine to the Jews on the pretext that some of them may be German spies disguised as Jewish refugees. "With a transport of children younger than 18, this accusation cannot be sustained," he stated.

Quietly and without fanfare, the project of the children's convoy was submitted to the British and Turkish authorities. It was accepted on paper, but then unexpected complications appeared. Each administration in turn requested lists upon lists of specific and detailed information, claiming that it was indispensable for the release of passports and visas for each individual child.

Zalman Bier, who followed the procedures closely, learned that the lists had traveled from Istanbul to Ankara, from Ankara to London and from London back to Ankara or Istanbul. At this point nobody knew for sure where they were, as it was said that the lists had gotten lost in the shuffle. Then everything had to be started again from scratch.

At about the same time, Zalman Bier heard that there were new rumors circulating in the British Administration. Some officials were spreading news that the refugee ship, the Dorina, was the start of a giant wave of thousands and thousands of Jewish refugees headed toward Palestine.

According to the rumors, this dangerous wave of illegal ships had to be stopped immediately. In order to teach the refugees a lesson and to make an example, the ship now docked in Istanbul—the Dorina—had to be turned around and sent back to Constanța on the Black Sea, even if her passengers were going to be put to death by the Nazis.

Not everybody shared this point of view. Zalman Bier learned that there was some hesitation in both the Turkish and the British administrations. Some of the British and Turkish officials were less aggressive. They wanted to let the ship go on. They wanted at least to save the children. But all the news was confusing. It looked as if no final decision had been made. All the painstaking work had to be restarted from the beginning,

Meanwhile on board the ship—in the middle of February—as the Captain and the committee complained that nothing was being done with the engine, two new mechanics and an engineer arrived on the boat to test the motor. They tinkered around in the engine room. They lifted the motor out of its place and took it with them, saying that they were going to test it thoroughly, outside of the boat. When they brought it back, after several days, they told the Captain that everything was running smoothly.

But Garapnik was not convinced. He started the engine: it ran for ten minutes and stopped. For the next several days he kept calling the Port Authority for more repairs, but there was no response.

On February 23 toward noon, as Joel, Nissim and the Ship's Committee had joined the Captain for a short conference on the bridge, they saw a big, military tugboat approaching the Dorina. It was followed by many other, smaller police boats. Two uniformed men boarded the ship, pushing people out of their way. They were signaling the tugboat to throw them a rope.

Garapnik asked for an explanation but the men refused to talk to him or to explain what was going on. Some Zionist leaders became so angry they threw the policemen overboard.

This became the signal for the policemen in the small boats to climb on board and push everybody inside and down to the bottom of the boat. The men were armed with truncheons, pistols and guns. Whoever resisted was beaten and punched. Only the Captain with Nissim and Joel remained on the bridge, but they were guarded by two armed policemen and forbidden to move. They watched as the men on the tugboat threw a rope to the policemen on the ship.

The thick rope was then secured to the tugboat. Next, the policemen proceeded to cut the ship's anchor, letting the boat float freely on the water.

When this was done, the men climbed down to their boats. The large tugboat pulled the ship out of the harbor. It swung north, away from the Turkish coast, away from the Bosporus, into the Black Sea.

The military boat towed the ship for several hours, until they were far away from the Turkish coast and several miles out of Turkish waters. Then the policemen untied the rope and let the ship float without any direction. As predicted by the Captain, the engine did not work, nor did the radio or the generators.

Joel and the men on the bridge, as well as anyone who understood what was happening were seized with despair. Without an engine they were left to drift aimlessly. Without an anchor, they couldn't dock any place. Would a storm smash them against the rocks? Would they die of hunger and thirst on a calm sea? Joel kept asking himself these questions.

In a last effort, following the Captain's orders, he and the ship's leaders collected the passengers' bedsheets and painted on them the words: SOS, RESCUE US, JEWISH REFUGEES. They hung the sheets on the sides of the ship. Maybe they would be lucky, as they had been on their way to Istanbul, when they were rescued several times, Joel told himself.

But nothing happened. Boris, the young Polish boy, had come up on deck to help with hanging the sheets. The hours passed slowly, while the boat drifted along. Late in the evening, Joel fell asleep. Boris, who was sitting on deck next to him, fell asleep too.

The night was very quiet.

At dawn, when the explosion came, Joel was still asleep as was the Captain. According to Boris, they never woke up, but disappeared in the dark waters.

He himself, a strong, champion swimmer, was the only survivor of the wreck. He was lucky to find a piece of wood, to which he clung for many hours, until he was rescued by the fishermen of a small village on the coast.

He was lucky that he had the strength and endurance to keep swimming for a long time in the freezing waters, he later said.

After they found him and identified him, the Turkish authorities threw him in jail because he had no passport and no visa. For several months, the officials insisted on returning both him and Mathilda to Romania where, according to the Mareshal's warnings, they would be punished with death.

It was only due to Zalman Bier's tireless efforts and his friends in Washington that, after many months, they were allowed to travel to Palestine.

PURIM

ONE DAY AFTER THE SINKING of the Dorina, as the Rabbi prepared for the Purim ceremony at the Coral Temple in Bucharest, the telephone rang. (The Coral Temple was the only Jewish institution in the city to still have a telephone.) It was a long distance call, an international call from Istanbul.

"Hello, this is Zalman Bier in Istanbul. I am calling to tell you that yesterday the Dorina exploded and sank. There are no survivors."

Then the telephone went dead. The Rabbi shouted into the receiver, shook it forcefully, and dialed the operator. Nothing helped.

The telephone was dead. The Rabbi was in shock.

He was even more bewildered half an hour later, when a black car without license plates stopped in front of the temple. Four military men entered the synagogue, walked into the Rabbi's study and ordered him to follow them and climb into the car. They drove directly to the Presidential Palace; the commander of the group led the Rabbi to the office of the Mareshal.

As soon as the Rabbi stepped into the room, the Mareshal got up from his desk, greeted him with a nod and, without shaking hands, directed him to sit in one of the black leather armchairs.

The Mareshal was very agitated and kept pacing from one end of the room to the other. His freckled face was crimson; his red hair seemed ablaze.

Without any preliminary introduction, he told the Rabbi that he knew that the latter had received information about the sinking of the Dorina, since all the telephone conversations in the country were monitored.

"But even if you have this information, you are forbidden to mention it to anybody else. This is a military secret. If you don't respect this order, you and your wife will be shot as will the people with whom you have talked. This is the routine punishment for divulging military secrets in time of war."

The Mareshal had finally stopped his wandering through the room and had planted himself in front of the Rabbi. Standing very erect with his arms crossed over his chest, he added: "*And* we will know whether you have spoken to anybody or not. We will be watching you very closely. From now on, no more ships will be leaving for Palestine. As you can see, we made a big mistake by allowing the Dorina to sail."

The Mareshal stopped talking and seemed lost in thought, forgetting about the Rabbi. But after a short while he turned toward his guest and said, "This is all I have to tell you. You can go now, but remember: keep your lips sealed! Don't talk to anybody if you want to stay alive!"

The Rabbi was still in a state of shock when he arrived back at the temple. How was he going to celebrate the joyful feast of Purim after the terrible news about the wreckage? How could he lie to his congregation? For it seemed to him, by not telling them the truth and pretending nothing happened, he was betraying the faith they had in him. God had given him a heavy load to carry!

The Rabbi strongly felt that the martyrs on the ship should be mourned and that Kaddish should be said for them!

But he had no choice. God and fate were giving him a different message. Maybe the martyrs from the sunken ship should be celebrated on this holiday! After all, Purim was the day of Jewish victory over the cruel Haman. Maybe it was also a symbol of future victory over Hitler. It was not in vain that the *hamantaschen*, the Purim cookies made of nuts and honey, were now nicknamed "Hitlertaschen"!

These thoughts gave him courage. The Rabbi was always reading and studying the writings of the Jewish wise men, trying to understand God's puzzling and mysterious ways.

The next day, the Purim festivity was well attended by the large congregation. There was prayer and singing. The children performed a skit representing the story of Haman and Esther.

When the Rabbi saw Nadia, Corinna and Theo in their costumes of colored paper bedecked with shiny sequins, his thoughts went immediately to Joel. For it was Joel who had always organized the children's Purim skits.

The Rabbi had known Joel for many years. He had prepared him, as a boy, for his bar mitzvah. He still recalled his father, Leon's opposition to the ceremony. As a great

Romanian patriot, decorated in the war, he was opposed to any Jewish tradition. He believed that the Jewish problem could be solved only by total assimilation.

But Joel was different. He had attended services regularly for many years. Not too long ago he had married Mathilda in a ceremony conducted by the Rabbi himself.

On this Purim day, while watching Nadia play the role of Queen Esther, the Rabbi thought of the day, a few years ago, when she had been very sick and practically in a coma, he had performed a very ancient and controversial ritual, in which she was sold by her own parents to another couple who gave her a new name, so that she couldn't be recognized by the Angel of Death.

At that time, Adrian and Nina, Nadia's parents, had sold her to Leon and Josephine, Joel's parents. She had become their daughter and had another name. It was all done to deceive the Angel of Death.

But now, the Rabbi wondered, was the Prince of Darkness taking his revenge by first causing the death of his two sons and Leon, Joel's father, in last year's Bucharest pogrom? And now bringing about the death of Joel and his mother with the sinking of the Dorina?

We are all sinners, thought the Rabbi. When the mourner's Kaddish was said—it was now recited at all religious services for the many who had disappeared—the Rabbi prayed, in his heart, for the souls of all those who had perished with the ship. He asked God's forgiveness and blessing for himself.

Soon after Purim, rumors about the fate of the Dorina started to circulate. They had appeared earlier, but they were more numerous and more persistent now. Everybody had a story: people spoke about "sightings" of the Dorina travelers in Palestine, in Jerusalem, Haifa or Tel Aviv. Others had heard about sightings on the island of Cyprus or even Mauritius, where refugees from previous ships had been interned by the British. But nobody knew for sure where and how these rumors had originated. None of them was ever confirmed.

No direct news ever came from Mathilda, Boris or Zalman Bier, since no letter from abroad was permitted to reach anybody inside the country.

SPRING 1942

TIME PASSED. WHEN APRIL SHOWERS ended, spring arrived with an explosion of flowers and sunshine. The apricot, pear and cherry trees were wrapped in their delicate blossoms and the perfectly blue sky was the ideal backdrop for their beauty. In spite of air raids and bombardments, it was a radiant spring, and everybody agreed that they hadn't seen so many flowers in a very long time. On the terrace of the Stein family's attic, the geraniums, petunias and marigolds bloomed like never before.

Soon the ping-pong table was set up in its corner. As the school year was coming to a close and the long, empty summer loomed, Nadia became restless and bored. What was she going to do being cooped up in the small attic under the hot roof? Where could she go? Last year, at the beginning of the war, she couldn't go anywhere because of the daily air raids and bombardments. Suzy had taught her how to use a typewriter. They had hidden a secret machine from Adrian's office in the basement. The racial laws did not allow them to have a typewriter. Like Suzy's bicycle, this typewriter was so old it had never been registered.

Nadia had made great progress in typing. She was now almost as fast as Suzy, but she was not looking forward to perfecting her typing skills during the upcoming vacation. What else could she do?

Going to the local swimming pool was forbidden. Even the use of their own garden and pool was off limits since Doctor Ionescu and his family had taken over. It was all very gloomy.

In the middle of May there was a surprise. An announcement came from Professor Glassbein, the principal of the Jewish school, saying that the high school was allowed to send twenty students to a nearby village to collect linden flowers for the Army.

The village and surrounding forest of old linden trees were part of the Royal Estate. It had been the decision of the Queen to invite Jewish high school students to engage in this patriotic endeavor. It would allow them to get out of the suffocating city for three or four weeks of summer.

Nadia was thrilled. "We must go! We can't miss this opportunity!" she told her friend Dorothea.

"But your mother will never let you go! She would rather lock you up in the basement," said Dorothea.

"You're right. I forgot about my mother. Let me think. There must be a way to convince her or a way to get around this. There must be a way!" Nadia thought hard. She concentrated and frowned. After some time planning and scheming, she came up with a solution. Her face glowed when she turned toward Dorothea.

"I've got it. My mother always wants to know what other parents are doing. She watches them and then does what they do. So, if I tell my mother that your parents gave you permission to go, she'll let me go too! Besides, there is no telephone so they can't check with each other. They'll have to trust us."

Dorothea agreed and thought it was a brilliant idea. Both girls went home and presented their parents with their plan.

It turned out that Nadia had been right: even though both sets of parents were apprehensive, they allowed Nadia and Dorothea to take the trip to the country. They comforted themselves with the thought that, after all, the expedition was patronized by the Queen. The children were going to live on the Royal Estate and be supervised by the principal of the school. They would probably be in a safer place than in the city which was now attacked from the air twice a day, almost every day.

As the end of May came closer, Nadia and Dorothea became more and more excited. They had learned that boys from the Jewish high school on the next block were also joining them. They were very enthusiastic about this development.

On the morning of May 19th, the day of departure, they gathered at the main train station in front of the Gagel Bakery. Nadia came accompanied by Suzy, and Dorothea by her older sister, Dalia. Both girls felt relieved that they were chaperoned by their sisters and not by their parents: in this way their quiet manipulation remained a well hidden secret.

A noisy bunch of thirty adolescents, fifteen boys wearing short pants and sport shirts and fifteen girls in light cotton dresses, all carrying rucksacks and small valises, had gathered in front of the store. They were between 14 and

18 years old. Nadia and Dorothea were the youngest in the group.

Professor Glassbein, the principal of the girls' school who was also their math teacher, walked among the students and talked to all the girls. She was a woman in her fifties and had been famous for her beauty in her youth, but her face was now prematurely wrinkled. She was trying to remember their names and making sure they had brought enough clothing and essential toiletries for a month's duration.

Mr. Glassbein, her husband, a portly bald man who smoked a pipe and taught physics at the boys' school, was talking to them. He explained something about the basic organization and operation of the camp.

Then Nadia saw him—Mr. Gary Fisher. He was the tall, handsome supervisor of the boys and Mr. Glassbein's right hand assistant. Nadia couldn't believe her eyes. He was the exact image of Gary Cooper, a younger version of her movie idol. Tall, graceful, athletic, with the same harmonious and dreamy face, the same irresistible smile . . . and the same first name! Nadia was staring at him, spellbound, wondering whether she was dreaming.

She barely noticed when Sally Wolf, the dumpy young woman with freckles and red hair who was the girls' supervisor tried to say hello to her. She was so absorbed in the contemplation of her hero, she didn't pay attention when the group formed a long line and started advancing toward the waiting train. One more minute, she would have missed the departure.

At ten o'clock they all climbed into a car especially reserved for them. After a ride of about three hours, with frequent stops at small villages, they arrived at their destination.

The railway station at P consisted of a small red brick cottage next to an ancient fountain, flanked by tall linden trees and guarded by a fat pig and a flock of geese. The stationmaster, a short man who wore a wet handkerchief under his official red cap, kicked the pig out of the way. He signaled the conductor to make the train wait until everybody climbed down. He then led the visitors to a yellow bus waiting behind the station house. The bus was covered with dust and caked mud. The driver, who had the dark eyes and long black hair of a gypsy, was friendly and cheerful. He welcomed everybody to the village and whistled a lively folk tune throughout the short ride to the schoolhouse where they were going to stay.

The schoolhouse was a squat building, with whitewashed walls, arched windows and a red tile roof. The school principal, looking official in his dark suit, white shirt and red tie, and the janitor's wife, were waiting for them at the gate.

"Welcome to our place! Since you are the guests of the Queen, we will try to make you as comfortable as we can," said the principal. "Let me show you the premises before you unpack."

The high ceilinged classrooms had been turned into dormitories by pushing the children's desks against the wall, piling them high on top of each other, which left plenty of room for the straw mats for the new visitors. Naked light bulbs hung from the ceiling and heavy black curtains covered the windows at night because of the blackout. The walls were lined with wooden shelves with metal hooks where the newcomers could place their belongings. The boys were going to sleep in one classroom, the girls in another.

The only drawback was the absence of running water. Several very clean, white-washed wooden outhouses stood behind the building. The shower-and-bath installation consisted of a large watering can, a few buckets and a long green hose attached to the pump which stood in the front yard. The watering can and buckets were set up in the backyard behind a wall. The ground had been covered with cement in this space, but there was no roof.

They had lunch in the basement near the kitchen. They sat on wooden benches at a long table and ate an appetizer of fresh eggplant salad with tomatoes and onions, followed by large portions of steaming *mussaka*. The food was served in plates of heavy, white china. They could get seconds if they wanted. They had a dessert of strawberries and cream.

Nobody spoke during the meal: they hadn't eaten such tasty food in a long time and considered themselves privileged to be the guests of the Queen.

After lunch, Nadia joined a group of students led by Gary in a walk to the wood of linden trees. As she advanced under the old trees, she imagined that she had entered a holy shrine. The light was green and dim. The sky seemed far away, hidden by a moving ceiling of branches. Silence pervaded the hot afternoon, she could only hear the startled chirping of a bird from time to time. The perfume of the golden flowers clustered in the trees reminded her of incense burning in a church.

They followed the foot path until they came to the golden gates of the Queen's private garden. There were no guards so they sat down in the grass. They were so intimidated by the proximity of the Queen they spoke in whispers. In a short while they got up and walked back to the schoolhouse.

Early the next morning after a fine breakfast of fresh rolls with real butter, honey and large cups of strong coffee with warm milk, they went to work.

They had been arranged in pairs by their supervisors, a boy and a girl. The boy had to climb the tree and pick the linden flowers, while the girl collected the blooms, cleaned them of leaves and small twigs and placed them in a basket.

Nadia didn't like the boy with whom she had to work. George was a short, plump boy with glasses and a high-pitched voice. He liked to read comic books and had a passion for crossword puzzles. His backpack was filled with them. He always carried a few in his pockets. He was afraid of climbing trees and Nadia thought he was a wimp and shouldn't have come to camp at all.

By contrast, she admired Alex, the boy with whom Dorothea was working. He was tall and muscular and climbed trees like a cat. He could imitate the bird calls. He seemed to have lived all his life in a tree. He climbed all the way to the top and picked the best and biggest flowers. Dorothea's basket was quickly filled to the brim.

Not so Nadia's basket: the first two days George was able to climb to the lowest branches and pick the flowers within reach. On the third day this crop was exhausted. He had to use the ladder to climb higher. He tried, but as he hoisted himself up, he began to tremble and started to cry.

Nadia screamed at him, trying to make him climb higher. The angrier she got, the more he cried. She didn't know what to do. She told him she was going to ask for another companion.

When he heard this, he became very upset. "No, no!" he cried. "If you do that, they'll send me home, or they'll say something to my father and he'll beat me. My parents are great gymnasts and sports people. They get angry at me for being so clumsy and nearsighted. They sent me here after Professor Glassbein promised that he was going to make an athlete out of me."

Nadia looked at him with pity and disgust. What could she do? How to solve this problem?

"Well," she finally said, "we'll have to reverse our roles. I'll climb the tree and pick, you gather the flowers on the ground and put them in the basket. I don't mind doing this. As a matter of fact, I much prefer climbing than sitting on the ground with the basket. But the regulations are different: the boys must climb and the girls must sit. They make such a fuss about this!"

From that day on, every morning, George perched on a low branch making believe he was picking, while Nadia sat on the ground for a short time, until the inspection carried out by one of the supervisors was over. After that, they reversed roles: Nadia climbed high into the tree while

George sat on the ground and gathered the flowers she picked.

They carried their hampers home at noon and handed them to the two supervisors who took them to a special room where the flowers were spread on trays and left to dry. The perfume of the linden flowers was so strong in that room, that one couldn't stay there for more than a few minutes.

The janitor's wife told them that, a few years ago, a youth had lain down to rest in that room. But in a short time he fell into such a deep sleep that he was almost in a coma. Buckets of cold water didn't even wake him up. He had to be taken to the hospital to get his senses back.

The early afternoons were hard for Nadia. It was supposed to be "quiet time"—a few hours in which the students could rest, read or engage in quiet activity inside their rooms. There was a strict rule: Not to venture outside until about four-thirty when they could play volleyball in the schoolyard or go to the "beach"—a narrow strip of coarse sand and pebbles that bordered a rivulet nearby. But they were not allowed to go there alone. They were always to be accompanied by one of the supervisors.

After a week of boring afternoons during which everybody slept and snored on their straw mats, Nadia decided to sneak out to the beach. She would take her chances. She even told Dorothea about her plan and tried to convince her to come with her, but she refused, saying it was too risky.

Nadia followed her plan for a few days and was quite successful. She slipped on her bathing suit under her dress. She would then sneak out of the sleeping camp site and reached the little stream in no time at all. She took a dip in the shallow water, lay down on the sand to dry and watched the swallows and sandpipers circle overhead. In time she would get up and march back to the school building before anybody woke up and saw her.

But a few times, before going back, she took a long look at the small lake which lay further away. It was surrounded by tall reeds and weeping willows. The lake was part of the Queen's private property. It could be visited only under the supervision of one of the adults.

Nadia could barely wait for this opportunity. When nothing happened during her afternoon trips to the beach, she decided to explore the lake on her own. One sunny afternoon, after her stop at the brook, instead of getting dressed and going back to the school, she walked to the lake.

It wasn't far from the brook. She followed a narrow footpath which ran along the stream, crossed the remains of a wooden bridge and stopped at the edge of the lake. There was a narrow stretch of sand, bordered by patches of daffodils, forget-me-nots, and small, wild orchids. When she dove into the lake, the water felt smooth and cool. It was not clear and transparent like the sea, but dark green and opaque. She could not open her eyes: it felt painful and itchy.

Under her feet, the bottom was soft and slippery. It felt treacherous, making her afraid of sinking into the mud or being pulled into a whirlpool. Mysterious air bubbles came to the surface, like bubbles escaping from a boiling cauldron. She could hear the buzzing of insects and frogs croaking all around her.

But swimming made her feel light as a feather, happy to stretch her arms and legs and float in the water. She was renewed and refreshed when she stepped back on shore.

She sat on the sand to dry and watched the sandpipers chasing each other. When she got up ready to put on her clothes, she felt a strange heaviness on her back. When she tried to touch it with her hand, she encountered the slimy softness of a pack of leeches. She pulled one off and became aware of blood running down her side. Worse, there were leeches bunched and hanging in the middle of her back, where she couldn't reach.

What now?

She could not return to the school with her back covered with leeches, nor could she put on her clothes with the blood still running down. What could she do?

She needed help, but how to get it? Particularly since nobody should know where she had gone and what she had done.

She sat down on a rock and, absentmindedly traced figures in the sand with a stick, groping for a solution.

Nothing came. She was wondering whether, since she couldn't reach the leeches on her back, she should wait until they had their fill of blood and fell off on their own? This could take two or three hours or more!

As she sat there, helpless and worried, she heard somebody whistling in the distance. It was a familiar tune, a tune from the Merry Widow. The whistling came closer and she got up quickly, trying to hide behind a bush. It was too late: Gary, the handsome supervisor, had already seen her and hurried over.

"Why are you here? What are you doing here?" he asked, with a frown. "Don't you know you're not allowed to come here alone?"

He didn't wait for Nadia's answer: he saw the leeches on her back and blood trickling down her side.

"Don't move! Stay quiet!" he ordered. He picked a few large leaves from a bush and, with a firm grip, he removed the leeches one by one, making sure that no part of their body or mouthpiece was left in her skin. He covered the wound with the brown leaves, pressing hard on them to stop the bleeding.

Nadia felt a shiver of excitement when Gary's hand touched her back. It was so strong, it was almost painful. She closed her eyes and wished that he would keep his hand on her back forever.

"OK," he said. "You're fine now. Get dressed and go home. I won't say anything to anybody if you go home right away."

Nadia turned around to go back but, as she was leaving the lake behind, she saw two of the older students, Bernard and Sandu walking in the same direction Gary had gone. They were followed by another student, Zitta, and then by two others. They were all part of the oldest group of students. They were walking quickly and cautiously, looking around, as if afraid of being discovered by someone.

Where were they going? What were they up to?

Nadia became so intrigued by the mystery, instead of going home, she decided to follow them. Her desire to be close to Gary added to her decision.

It was easy to follow without being seen. She could hide behind the tall bushes which surrounded the lake.

She walked for some time on the narrow path, until she arrived near a round pavilion which was open on all sides and had a sloping roof.

Nadia stopped at some distance, crouching behind a bush. From here she could watch Gary who stood in the middle of the pavilion while the youngsters were seated on a long bench, which ran around the pavilion. She could observe them from here, without being noticed. Gary was speaking

He said, "Today I have a message for you from the world's children and from the International Students' Organization for Peace. They are condemning this war with our neighbor. They call it a criminal massacre. It kills and destroys thousands of people, including mothers and children! It destroys the treasures of culture and civilization and only brings evil and cruelty into the world. People of many nations can and should make friends with each other. We should all live forever in peace and harmony.

"This criminal war must come to an end! The country we are battling is NOT OUR ENEMY! It has NOT started the war. WE ARE THE ATTACKERS! WE have started this war! If WE had not attacked them, they would be friendly to us.

"We should spread this message as widely as we can, so that other people, all citizens and eventually the army will join us to stop the war."

The students made silent clapping gestures.

Then Gary went on, "In two days, when we meet again, I will tell you more about what we can do toward stopping this war. In the meantime, nobody should find out about our meetings. Be careful about your comings and goings!"

After that day, Nadia became completely obsessed with Gary. She could think only of him and tried to see him as much as she could. A few years ago she had felt this way about Skender, the tartar fisher boy from Eforie. Now, her feelings for Gary were much stronger. He was her hero—young, handsome, courageous. He followed her in her dreams, where he was her knight in shining armor.

She made sure that she attended all the secret meetings in the pavilion. She spied on Gary and the other students with much skill and succeeded in watching two other meetings without being discovered.

On the third gathering, she sneaked into her usual place without any difficulty and listened. Suddenly, just as Gary was explaining something important, Nadia heard a noise in the bushes near her. A big shepherd dog appeared and started growling, barking, and bearing its teeth.

Nadia got so frightened she lost her head. She jumped up and ran toward the pavilion, followed by the barking dog.

When they saw him, the students too got excited. Some climbed on the bench; others ran out of the pavilion. There was chaos. Only Gary remained calm and got the dog under control.

He then turned to Nadia and shook his finger at her. "All right, if you want to, you can be part of our group. You must make sure that nobody finds out about us and our meetings."

Some students were not happy with Gary's decision to accept Nadia. They said she was too young and immature. It was too risky to have her take part in their activity. Gary explained that, since she had discovered their secret, it was safer to make her a participant than to reject her.

Soon the end of their "vacation" was at hand. They met for the last time in the pavilion. Before leaving, Gary handed each of them a sealed envelope, ordering them to keep it hidden at all times. "There is dangerous material inside," he said. "You can pay with your life if you're not careful," he added, half joking, half serious. "I will get in touch with you after we arrive in Bucharest to tell you what to do with the envelopes. Again, do not mention a word to anybody about our meetings here and the envelopes I gave you."

Three weeks had passed since they had arrived in P. Nadia was sad to be going back home. She had found life in the camp very exciting, what with climbing trees in the morning and swimming in the lake in the afternoon in spite of the leeches. But best of all had been seeing Gary. Every day she looked forward to meeting him and she couldn't imagine life without him.

Besides, they had all thought that they were going to be here for another week. But the frequent air raids and bombings of nearby train stations and railway tracks made it necessary to leave without delay.

With much sadness, Nadia packed her small valise and rucksack, making sure that Gary's envelope was hidden at the bottom, under panties, socks and dirty underwear.

She had been happy here in this quiet village in the shade of this big forest of ancient trees. But her thoughts were always turning to Gary. When and how was she going to see him again? She would have to wait for him to get in touch with her, since she didn't have his address. While he could find her from the school records, she had no way of reaching him.

On Wednesday morning, after a last hearty breakfast of hot coffee with milk and fresh croissants with plenty of butter, honey and jam, they all rode to the railway stop where the stationmaster with his red cap made the train wait until they all got on board.

It was a quick ride. Back in the city, Nadia, Dorothea and Gary took the same tram. Gary was the first to get off at University Plaza. "I'll call you soon!" he whispered to

Nadia in a low voice so that Dorothea couldn't hear him. Nadia smiled and felt very happy with this promise.

Dorothea got off at Trajan Station and the next stop was Nadia's.

The day was hot. Even though she had had a good breakfast, Nadia felt hungry and thirsty by now. She couldn't wait to get home, get rid of her luggage and dirty clothes, drink a glass of cold water, and jump into the shower.

She walked slowly in the midday heat, dragging her feet and squinting to protect her eyes from the sun. When she turned the corner and got close to the house, she had a shock. There was her furniture, the furnishings from her own room, piled on top of an old, battered cart, pulled by a starving mule. There was her bed, bookcase, small desk, and two chairs. They were stacked high one on top of the other.

Why were they there? Where were they being taken? What did it all mean? She looked around, trying to find somebody she could talk to, but nobody was there. It was the middle of the day. The street was as deserted as if it were midnight.

Nadia took her valise and rucksack and climbed the stairs to the attic. The space was empty, abandoned. The furniture, lamps, carpets, paintings, pots and pans in the kitchen were all gone. Everything had vanished. And still—nobody! Not a soul.

Where was everybody?

Nadia could only think of the obvious: they had been deported. They must be far away, riding a crowded cattle train, or maybe they were locked up in a basement, awaiting deportation.

What was happening to them? And how about herself: what was going to happen to her? Were "they" going to come after her and take her away? Was she ever going to see her parents and Suzy again?

She drank some water and washed her face. Then she decided to go to Uncle Sorel and Aunt Stella. They must know where her parents were, what had happened to them.

She picked up her valise and rucksack and walked to the door. She slowly descended the stairs. It was very quiet. But when she reached the second floor, there was some noise. Somebody was speaking—a vaguely familiar voice. At first, she thought she was imagining it. Was it her father's voice? She must be dreaming! she thought.

At the bottom of the stairs, there he was, speaking to the peasant with the cart. Before she knew it, Nadia ran to her father, sobbing for joy. He held her tight and kissed her, and then talked to her, gently. "We have to go now. Your mother is waiting for us. Doctor Ionescu has taken the attic space for his family. We are moving to another apartment. Most of the furniture is already there."

Nadia was not happy with her new home. It was at the outskirts of the city, far away from everything and everybody. It was a small, cold-water flat, with an old fashioned terracotta stove in every room. To take a shower or bath, one had to light the fire under a tall metal boiler which looked to her like a vertical locomotive without wheels.

From her room, which she shared with Suzy and also served as the family dining room, all she could see was a gray wall and a roof covered with dark tiles. In the attic apartment there had been tall windows and a large terrace. Now she could see no trees and no sky from this place.

The worst was that she could not get in touch with Gary: since she had moved, he could not find her. With the school still closed for vacation, there was nobody around to tell her Gary's whereabouts.

A week later, when she visited Dorothea, she found out that Mr. and Mrs. Glassbein, the two professors who had been in charge of their trip, had been arrested. Nobody knew where they were.

"Yes," said Dorothea with an excited voice. "And so were Gary and a few older students who were in the camp with us. The police found Communist pamphlets and books in their apartments, money—bills of 5 and 10 lei—inscribed with antiwar and antigovernment slogans. I heard that they even found guns and explosives in Gary's basement!"

Nadia was so stunned she couldn't say anything. Dorothea went on, telling her that all the arrests had started after Bernard, the oldest student in the camp had handed a greengrocer a 10 lei bill, inscribed with the words: "STOP THIS WAR! DEATH TO THE MARESHAL!"

"Bernard had left the store. Afterwards when the greengrocer read the message on the bill, he ran into the street, caught up with Bernard, and hailed a policeman.

They took Bernard away for interrogation which, I heard," said Dorothea, "consisted of beatings and scalding with hot water. After that, Bernard gave them all the names he knew."

"What . . . what will happen next?" Nadia asked without looking at Dorothea. She felt faint, as if all her blood had drained out of her brain.

Dorothea shrugged. "I don't know. Nobody knows. But they say . . . 'nothing good!'" Then Dorothea stopped and looked at Nadia. "What is the matter with you? Are you sick? You look awfully pale!"

"Nothing is the matter. I just didn't have breakfast. I better go home and get some lunch."

As soon as she got home, Nadia locked herself in the bathroom with Gary's envelope. She opened it, and found a 10 lei bill, inscribed with the words: "DEATH TO FASCISM! STOP THIS CRIMINAL WAR!"

When she saw this, Nadia got so scared, that she immediately slipped the money back into the envelope, which she then hid at the bottom of a large drawer, under a pile of thick notebooks.

What should she do with this paper? Of course, the safest thing to do would be to destroy it, to rip it to pieces and flush them down the toilet. Make believe they never existed.

But she couldn't do that. She felt that, by doing so, she would betray Gary and all he stood for. At the same time, she became very afraid for herself: Bernard knew her. He was part of Gary's group at the camp. What if, under beatings and torture. he mentioned her name as one of the accomplices? Would they come after her, arrest her, and take her to prison? What then? But wait . . . She now remembered that, since she and her family had just moved, nobody knew their new address. She was safe—at least for now.

Still, Nadia kept obsessing over Gary's fate. She and Dorothea were following his trial. It was not going well: he and a few others were accused of having masterminded a "Judeo-Communist conspiracy." On this basis the prosecutors who represented the government asked for the death penalty for Gary, Bernard and Eliezer. The newspapers were making a big fuss of the trial, writing about it on the front page.

Lawyers for the defendants attempted to save them by showing that they were not Communists, but Zionists who were trying to protect the Jewish population. As the trial dragged on, there was some hope of success.

Meanwhile, bad news came from the front: the Romanian army was losing battles near the river Don. It had suffered many casualties. This made the Mareshal so furious that, without waiting for the end of the trial, he ordered the immediate execution of the three most important defendants, Gary, Bernard and Eliezer.

The Rabbi was urgently summoned to the prison to pray for the youngsters before their execution.

A few days later, the Rabbi visited Adrian and Nina and told them what had happened. Nadia tiptoed to the closed door and overheard the whole conversation.

"Early on Tuesday morning the soldiers escorted the three youths to the garden at the back of the prison, the so-called Grove of the Peach Trees," said the Rabbi. "The three walked erect and refused to be blindfolded.

"I said a blessing and prayed in silence for their innocent souls. When I finished, the captain gave the order to shoot. I heard the bullets whiz through the air and saw the young men fall. One soldier refused the order to shoot. He stood there, holding his gun, knowing quite well that he would be court martialed for this.

"There is still a trace of humanity in the world," the Rabbi said with a sigh.

The news of Gary's execution was devastating to Nadia. She became obsessed with his death. She kept seeing him lying in the grass in a puddle of blood. This vision was particularly troubling at night, when she went to bed. She had terrifying nightmares and screamed in her sleep.

She lost her appetite and started losing weight. She didn't laugh or sing anymore. Even Nina noticed that she had become more withdrawn and absent-minded. But when she asked her whether something was wrong, Nadia shook her head and said, "No, everything was fine." Then she would go to her room and make believe that she was reading a book. She couldn't tell anybody what was tormenting her. She would have liked to talk to the Rabbi, but she didn't trust him. She was afraid he was going to betray her to her parents.

Like many people in mourning, she wanted to go to the cemetery and lay a flower on Gary's grave. His place of burial was a secret: political criminals executed by the government were always buried in secret places, so that their graves could not become shrines of pilgrimage for their followers.

Sometimes Nadia pulled out Gary's envelope from the bottom of the drawer. She must do something with it, she told herself. He had given it to her for a purpose. However, she couldn't guess his instructions. She also couldn't make up her mind whether to do something or not.

A few days later she heard a rumor that the homes of all those who had been in the camp at P were going to be raided and searched. She knew now that she couldn't wait any longer; she had to make a decision. In her mind, she heard Gary's voice telling her that she had to go and spread the message. She pulled out the envelope, took the ten lei bill with the inscription, slipped it inside a thick book of poetry, and put the book inside a paper bag.

It was late afternoon when she left the house with the paper bag under her arm. She rode a bus and a tram to a park at the opposite end of the city. Even though Jews were not allowed to enter that park, she sat on a bench, near the children's sandboxes.

It was evening, the playground was empty and the birds were in their nests. In the distance, Nadia saw a policeman on horseback, and she wondered whether he would turn in her direction. But she didn't wait to find out. She placed the bag with the book on the bench, stood up, and marched out of the park. She looked back only once, to make sure that nobody was following her.

It was late when she walked into the dining room and supper was finished. Her mother and Suzy were washing the dishes, which was a complicated operation since only cold water was available. To soak the greasy plates, a pot of water had to be heated on the stove.

Nina was angry at Nadia's lateness and ordered her to wipe the dishes and place them in the cupboard. "You won't get any dinner tonight. Maybe it will teach you to come home on time," she scolded.

Nadia didn't say anything. She did what her mother told her. She didn't care about dinner. It was all a dream now.

In her mind, she heard Gary's voice, telling her that she had done the right thing. This was what she had to do, he was saying. She felt relieved, like a stone had rolled off her chest.

ZÜRICH, 1942

Doctor Georgescu sat down at his table to review his notes. He had taken a room with a balcony at the elegant hotel Baur au Lac in Zürich, where the International Conference of Psychiatry was going to take place.

The meeting was scheduled to open the next morning in the ballroom of the hotel. Victor was programmed to speak on the first day about his research with "Salep" and the good results he had obtained with this treatment. He had used Salep on men suffering from depression and sexual impotence.

He had started this research a long time ago during World War I when, as an army doctor, he noticed how many young men showed symptoms of depression and impotence. To his surprise, many were helped by the concentrated extract from the tubers of wild orchids! This essence was a condensed form of the familiar drink called Salep, very popular in the countries around the Black Sea.

Victor had continued this work after the war. He had refined and perfected the process of extraction. Sometimes, he had combined the treatment with hypnosis. (After all he remained a true disciple of his great mentor, Charcot.) He published his results in a few professional journals, but this was the first time he had been invited to present his work at an international conference.

Until recently he had labored alone in this area. He had been a solitary pioneer in a line of research for which nobody had any interest. Most psychiatrists devoted their attention to the fields of psychoanalysis, classic hypnosis, shock treatment, or, the latest "fad," Carl Jung's explorations of the collective unconscious. But now—since the beginning of the war—there seemed to be a general change in direction, which may have contributed to Victor's invitation to the conference.

This night he had eaten dinner downstairs in the terrace restaurant, which was located in the large park of the hotel, not too far from the lake. He enjoyed an unusual supper in eerie blue candlelight and admired the graceful movements of the waiters who served their guests with great elegance in almost total darkness. The whole terrace restaurant was lit only by small blue lanterns because of the blackout. Thank God for the full moon. It threw a pale silver glow on the tables, the walkways of the park and waters of the lake.

When he finished his dinner capped by café filtre and a glass of Remy Martin, he went back to his room. He sat down at the mahogany desk, lit his pipe and opened the folder with his notes. The first thing he saw was a sheet of paper with notes scribbled by Stella and a business card with the name, address and telephone number of Charles Kass from Baden, near Zürich. He had a similar business card in his pocket. As a matter of fact, he had already called Kass and had arranged a meeting with him for tomorrow early afternoon.

This meeting with Charles Kass was the other important reason for his trip to Switzerland. He had known Kass as Adrian's old friend and business associate from Brown Boveri in Switzerland. He had met him five years ago, when Charles Kass came hunting with the King in the Carpathian Mountains. Kass then stopped in Bucharest to see Adrian and later joined all of them at Sorel's birthday party.

While reading Stella's notes, Victor remembered his friends' urgings to find Kass and speak to him. "He was active in the International Red Cross during the Great War. Maybe he is still enrolled in the Red Cross organization. Maybe he can help!" they kept saying.

Victor thought about what Sorel had told him regarding the dying children at the Clinic and in the Jewish hospital. They came to the clinic undernourished and starving, at death's doorstep. They improved, with food, in the hospital. Then they went home, only to come back and die on the ward in a hospital bed. Their mothers had nothing to give them. Their fathers were in forced labor camps or deported far away in Transnistria.

For many years there had been a soup kitchen at the Moriah School, which functioned under Stella's supervision. But it was closed when the Wehrmacht occupied the building and turned it into a military hospital. A few soup kitchens remained open near some synagogues, but they were too small and too poor to be of real help.

Victor had assisted Stella and Sorel by renting, in his name, a building in the Jewish section of the city. A new soup kitchen, under Stella's direction, was installed there.

Next to it a Jewish walk-in-clinic was opened where Sorel could give immediate care to ailing children.

The funds for this operation came, at first, from donations made by the Jewish Community in Bucharest. When these funds were exhausted, the money came from the blue boxes of the Keren Kayemet Foundation. Victor knew that these savings were destined to buy land in Palestine. But this project could wait. It could be postponed. The new soup kitchen was a life and death emergency.

Nevertheless, as wonderful as it sounded, this project had limitations. Sometime soon, the Keren Kayemet money was also going to dry up and the starving people could no longer be helped.

"If nothing is done, we will all die of hunger, starting with the children!" Stella had declared in a moment of despair.

It was at this point that they decided to contact Charles Kass in Switzerland. Was he still active in the International Red Cross? They wondered if he could or would he be of help.

Stella, Sorel, and Adrian believed that it was a good decision. They had no other options. They hoped for positive results.

"I'll do it. I'll meet with Charles Kass!" Victor promised. But, skeptical by nature, he was reserved about the outcome of the meeting.

After he finished with Stella's notes, Victor reviewed his professional paper. He read for a while and decided to stop just as the clock at St. Peter's bell tower tolled midnight. He was tired and wanted to go to sleep. He switched off the light. Before going to bed he opened the door and stepped onto the balcony.

The full moon and the blackout of the city made the Zürichsee look more magical and mysterious than ever. A lonely sailboat was floating on the water. Snowcapped mountains shimmered in the distance.

As he stood on the balcony, Victor thought of Stella He wished that she could be here with him. They had always dreamt of taking a trip together to Switzerland, to Venice or to the Riviera. It had never happened.

He remembered how, five years ago, they had watched a golden sunset over the Black Sea at Eforie. Just like now, a lonely sailboat had been floating on the quiet sea. Soft music had reached them from the garden. They had danced, closely enlaced to the rhythm of an Argentinian tango.

The mechanical drone of an airplane, high up in the sky put an end to Victor's musings. He went to bed and slept deeply for the rest of the night.

Next morning, he had a light breakfast on his balcony, overlooking the lake. When he finished his croissant and café au lait, he went down to the conference hall. The president of the meeting, Professor Doctor Schultz greeted him and shook his hand. "I'm glad to see you! It's been a very long time!" he said. His bushy handlebar moustache trembled as he spoke.

Victor had a friendly chat with Doctors Bailey, Rieux and Johnson from London, Paris and Washington, whom he had met at other conferences. He was familiar with their work and publications. He enjoyed talking to them.

His presentation was received with much interest. Doctors in the audience asked many questions and wanted to know more details regarding the preparation and extraction of the substance, as well as more specifics regarding the dosage he used and the effectiveness of the treatment.

When the discussion was finished, Victor was stopped on the way out by a young man with very blue eyes and matching blue shirt.

"I am the representative of Geigy Pharmaceuticals. My name is Rolf Miess and I must talk to you about your work. Can we go to the bar and talk for a few minutes?"

Victor checked his watch and saw that he still had an hour until his meeting with Kass. He nodded and said, "Yes."

They went downstairs to the bar and chose a table in a quiet corner of the room. Victor ordered a cognac and a glass of cold water, and the young man ordered a halbe of Lowenbrau beer.

"As I mentioned before, I am the representative of Geigy Pharmaceuticals. My name is Rolf Miess," he said again, speaking French with a heavy German accent. "I have traveled all the way from Basel to be able to listen to your presentation and particularly to speak with you. The people at my company are impressed with your work and would like you to continue your research with us. We have followed your publications for several years and have found them both original and practical. We would like you to continue both the research and the production of this substance with us! Your Salep has certainly great commercial value, which can benefit both you and us.

"I must add, this is the right moment for it. Since the beginning of the war, the search for chemical substances which can act on the brain has greatly increased.

"As your work lies in this direction, you will enjoy many benefits—scientific, professional, financial and even personal—if you join us. You will have a department of your own with qualified and trained staff, an excellent salary as well as royalties from the sales of your products. We will provide good housing for you and your family, a car and driver if necessary, and so on and so forth."

He stopped talking for a minute, took two swallows of beer, and went on, "Here is my card, dear Professor. Please let me know if you have any questions. I hope that you will accept our invitation and join our company."

Victor felt his cheeks burning while listening to the young man's proposal. He was excited by this unexpected turn of events. He didn't know what to say so he took a long sip of cognac and then some cold water.

"Yes," he finally said. "I'll call you if I have any questions. Many thanks for your invitation. I must think it over before making a decision. I see your address and telephone number on the card."

"As a matter of fact, I will be here for the whole conference. You will certainly see me tonight at the banquet," said the young man as he stood up and said goodbye to Dr. Georgescu.

Victor sat down, lit his pipe and finished his cognac. He was smiling and his face was still flushed. He couldn't deny it: it felt good to be appreciated and wooed by a big company like Geigy Pharmaceuticals.

His thoughts were racing. The agent's promises kept spinning in his mind. He was particularly excited by the prospect of a well-staffed and well-equipped department in which he could initiate and conduct many new experiments.

He had not yet completely recovered from the news, when Charles Kass walked into the room. It was Charles who spotted Victor first. He waved to Victor and greeted him with a friendly *"Grüssgott!"*

In the five years since Victor had last seen him, he had not changed at all. On the contrary, he looked younger and more vigorous than ever. Tall and walking very erect, he wore a navy blue blazer with a hunting horn embroidered on his breast pocket, similar to the one he had worn when they had last met. As soon as he saw Victor, he smiled broadly. His white teeth lit up his face.

Victor remembered very clearly that, as an electrical engineer, Charles Kass had worked with Adrian at Brown Boveri in Switzerland. He remembered Charles' visit to Bucharest five years ago at Sorel's birthday party. He also remembered that Charles had many connections in Switzerland. He had been active in the International Red Cross during The Great War.

"I am glad to see you and to talk to you," said Charles as he sat down at the table. "How are Adrian and the family? We have very scarce news from the East. Only rumors we hear from refugees!"

Victor ordered another cognac and water for himself and a Lowenbrau beer for his guest. In a few words he told Charles everything that had happened to his friends in the past two years. He told him about the Legionnaire pogrom in Bucharest in the winter of 1941 and about the death of Leon, Joel Gold's father, in the massacre. He told him about the death trains and the pogrom in Iaşi which killed 12,000 people in the summer of 1941 and about Sorel's miraculous survival of that ordeal. He told him about the mysterious disappearance of the steamer Dorina and the questionable survival of any of its passengers, including Joel and his family. He also told him about Adrian losing his office, his car, his home and his right to earn a living.

Charles listened in silence. He didn't notice when his pipe went cold. He shook his head and sighed when Victor stopped talking.

"Life must be terrible for our Jewish friends! How do people survive without money and without food?"

"That is precisely why Adrian, Stella and Sorel wanted me to talk to you. We need your help." He went on telling Charles the grim stories of the starving children in Sorel's care. "Every day the clinic is more crowded with hungry and dying people. I have helped Stella and Sorel organize a central soup kitchen and a walk-in clinic. The local community has contributed as much money as they could to keep the center open. But they are running out of funds.

And if there is no help from outside, a catastrophe will surely happen!"

Victor stopped talking for a moment and stared at Charles. He then asked, "Weren't you once connected with the International Red Cross? I remember a story you told us, at Sorel's birthday party five years ago, about being stationed in the Carpathian Mountains as a medic for the International Red Cross during The Great War. You told us that it was then, you learned to love our mountains, our forests, and our wildlife. How about now: are you still in touch with the International Red Cross or anybody in that organization?"

Charles raised his eyebrows and put down his pipe. "How did you guess? I have just reactivated my membership in the IRC. Two days ago. Even though we, the Swiss, are not taking part in this war, some of us, like me, thought that it was time to get active again. I must tell you though— officially, the IRC refuses to deal with Jewish problems. They only deal with the problems of other refugees.

"However, I will introduce you to a good friend of mine, Serge Miller, who is the head of the Jewish Community of Switzerland. He knows much more about these problems than I do. I will take you to him as soon as I can."

"I am looking forward!" said Victor.

They finished their drinks and shook hands. Victor walked Charles to the door. They agreed to meet the next day.

At the evening banquet in the great ballroom, Victor received much attention. During cocktails, a number of doctors approached him and asked questions about Salep and the combined treatment of Salep and hypnosis. He received particular attention from a Mr. Fleischer, the representative of Hoffman La Roche pharmaceutical company. He was a middle-aged man with a bald head, gold-rimmed glasses, very sharp eyes, and a protruding stomach. From the cocktails to the end of the evening he clung to Victor like a shadow. He couldn't stop telling Victor how interested the doctors at his company were in his research and how much they wanted Victor to join them.

"I know that Geigy, our competitor, has made you a similar offer this morning. But if I were you," he said over a plate of steak au poivre, "I would pay no attention to them. They are a young company with no style and no history. They are newcomers on the market and nobody knows where they'll be next year, whether they'll be here or whether they'll go belly up. But I can promise you this. If you join us, you'll never be sorry. We will give you the best labs with the best equipment and the best people to work with. And, of course, you'll receive a great salary as well as royalties from the sales of our products. You'll have a good car, a beautiful home, and your family will live a carefree life. What else can you ask for?"

Mr. Fleischer stared at him with his sharp eyes. "What do you say? I bet you'll join our company! How could you turn down such an offer? But I understand that you need to think it over during the night. It's a big decision to make, even though I for one would know what to do!"

Victor listened and nodded from time to time. He didn't say yes but he didn't say no. He got tired of the man and felt relieved when the secretary of the conference came over to discuss some details regarding the publication of his paper.

Back in his room, Victor stepped out onto his balcony and looked at the lake in the moonlight. It was perfectly still. No sailboat was troubling the water. Only the mountains were standing guard in the distance. It all seemed unreal to him. He was living in a fairy tale.

So much enthusiasm and attention to his work was more than he had ever dreamt of! To have the offers of two leading drug companies in the world, it was hard to resist such temptation! As a matter of fact, he could see himself as the head of a busy research department. He had plans for other projects since there were many other plants whose fruits, roots and berries might produce healing juices when they were submitted to proper modern extraction methods. In combination with hypnosis, some of these substances could be of great medical value and heal other illnesses.

There was much to be done, if he had the appropriate facilities! He dreamt about this all his life, and now suddenly it was within reach.

But then his excitement went cold. His racing thoughts stopped spinning. What about Stella? He would have to leave her behind. Yes, he would have the greatest professional victory of his life, a stimulating career and all the riches he could imagine, but nobody to share them with!

He felt, without her, his life and his work would have no meaning. They had been together now for fifteen years. Victor had shared every thought, every project with Stella! He knew, beyond doubt, his life would be empty without her.

He remembered how they had first met at the military hospital in Bucharest. It happened many years ago, in 1916, during The Great War. He was the Chief of Surgery at the hospital, while she was volunteering as a nurse's aide. She was very pretty and so young. He thought she was someone's daughter. At that time he was married to Marguerite, a beautiful woman from the Romanian nobility.

After the war, Stella married Sorel Frühling, a young pediatrician. Soon afterwards, the two doctors, Victor and Sorel, started working together during a polio epidemic and became close friends. Two years later, Victor's wife died in a car accident.

Still, nothing would have happened between Stella and him, if they hadn't met, unexpectedly, one stormy night at a mountain refuge. Stella had hiked alone without Sorel from the little resort in the valley. Her husband was still busy with his practice in Bucharest.

Victor was at the refuge by himself. This accidental meeting was the beginning of a special romance between them.

At times, as the years passed, Stella felt guilty about their relationship and stopped seeing him. But during those episodes they both felt so miserable, they hurried back into each other's arms.

No, Victor concluded after these thoughts, still watching the lake from his balcony. He could not move to Switzerland and leave Stella behind.

The next afternoon at three o'clock, Victor joined Charles Kass in his open Rolls Royce in front of the hotel. They drove only a few blocks along the Limat River. Charles parked the car in a small plaza in the shade of an old chestnut tree. "We have to walk from here. It isn't far. The streets of this old section of town are too small for my car."

They turned left on a street with narrow houses which seemed to lean against each other. The tiles of their slanted roofs were covered with gray moss. The houses too had turned gray, like the moss, but they had flower boxes with colorful petunias and geraniums in their windows. Children were playing in the middle of the street since no cars were coming this way. Old trees were growing in small courtyards behind the houses. It seemed to Victor that here time had stopped or had even rolled back.

On the next block they saw a narrow store, filled with old books in many languages and different scripts. Next to it was a small music shop with old fashioned victrolas and ancient musical instruments.

The synagogue was two houses away. Serge Miller's home stood right behind it.

Charles rang the doorbell and a small woman with a pale face and a silk scarf tied over her hair opened the door.

She greeted them with a shy smile. Then she covered her mouth with her hand. She led them into a long room with small windows and heavy furniture. The room was dark. Everything inside was also dark: the leather-covered couch and armchairs, the mahogany desk, the floor to ceiling bookcases which lined the walls. A bronze menorah stood on the highest shelf of the bookcase.

A large portrait of Theodor Herzl, the founder of Zionism, hung near the window. The air was stale and there was a smell of moth balls.

The woman stepped out of the room. After a moment, Serge Miller, their host, walked in and greeted them. He was a slight man between 35 and 40, with delicate features, a sad, mournful look in his eyes, and deep lines on his forehead.

He was accompanied by a handsome young man with curly blond hair and dimples in his cheeks. He had a friendly smile and seemed to enjoy meeting the visitors.

"I am Serge Miller. I am the representative of the American Joint Distribution Committee, the 'Joint' or the 'JDC' in Europe," said the host shaking hands with his visitors.

He turned to Victor and said, "Your friend Charles, who is also an old friend of mine, has told me about the hardships of the Jewish community in Romania! Very little information about what is going on in Romania is reaching us here. I am grateful that people like you, like Charles and my friend Hans Waldo," he said pointing to the young man with blond curls, "people such as yourselves, who are not even Jewish, are making serious efforts to help us!

"Now, speaking about the heart of the matter, I mean obtaining the funds you need is not easy. The American Treasury Department refuses to send money to countries which are under Nazi occupation, or, worse, allied with the Nazis, like Romania.

"I hope to find a way around this obstacle: I will ask for more money for Switzerland, maybe even double the amount I was asking before. Then I will be able to send to Romania the amount you need.

"What I plan to do now is give Doctor Georgescu a letter for Adrian Stein, informing him of our participation in this project. The funds will be brought to your country by my friend Hans Waldo." He stopped and put his hand on the young man's shoulder. "He is a reporter and journalist by profession, who now doubles as a courier for the Swiss Embassy in Bucharest. He is a man I can totally trust. I have no secrets with him. Besides, he is a poet, a lyrical poet who has published two volumes of his own poetry and has another volume of translations of old Indian and Persian love poems. Here is his last volume of poetry and his translations of Eastern love poems—both inscribed with dedications, one for you," he told Victor, "and one for Adrian Stein in Bucharest."

While the man was talking, his wife brought a silver platter filled with slices of honey *leckeh* which she placed into artfully cut crystal dishes. She served each person three slices of honey cake. Then she went to the samovar which stood on the breakfront and poured tea for everyone in tall, delicate glasses.

"My wife Irina comes from Kiev in the Ukraine," said Serge. "Even though she is here in Switzerland for many years, she cannot conceive of a snack without a glass of tea. For her, life would be meaningless without a glass of Russian tea from the samovar."

He helped himself to a plate of honey cake and some tea. When he finished, he said he'd composed a letter for Victor to take to Adrian and Sorel in Bucharest and would read it out loud.

In a clear voice, he read a rather short message which detailed, in coded language, how the money transactions were going to be conducted and how communication between Adrian and Sorel in Bucharest and Serge Miller in Zürich was going to be assured. The intermediary for any communication and delivery of funds was going to be Hans Waldo, Serge Miller's old friend, who now served as courier for the Swiss Embassy.

After he finished reading, everybody seemed satisfied. Victor took the letter, checked it briefly and put it in his briefcase. When he turned around, he saw that a young boy, about eight years old, had walked into the room. He had deep set, slanted eyes like those of an oriental child, coarse, yellowish skin, and a very narrow forehead.

Down Syndrome! a mongoloid child! thought Victor.

The boy looked scared and confused for a moment. But Serge called him and he walked toward him.

"This is my son Dennis," he said, as he put his arm around the boy's shoulder. "He is now nine years old. I must tell you after he was born and I saw that he was not like other children, I thought it was a sign from God. I closed my lace factory although it was very successful because I felt I had to do something else. I didn't know what. Something more meaningful, I thought. So, when I received an invitation to the Annual Meeting of the Jewish World Congress in Geneva, I attended the session. It was there that I met the delegate of the Jewish Distribution Committee who was looking for a representative in Europe. He asked me to be their agent in this area. I accepted immediately.

"To this day, I still think that this was a sign from above. God wanted me to do this work! But," he added after he had a few sips of tea, "he doesn't always make it easy: not now and not in the past. Swiss laws are very conservative, both strict and punitive. They set up all kinds of obstacles, not unlike the laws of your Treasury Department which I mentioned earlier. And for Jews, things have never been easy here.

"The Swiss like our money, but they don't like us. If you come to the window, you can see the stone well in the courtyard next door. In the past, in 1550 or 1600 there was a rumor that the Jews had poisoned the well in order to murder the people in town. The news caused panic and turmoil in the city. Many Jews were hanged on this occasion and many others were driven out of the country. After some years they were needed again and called back. Thank God things have changed since then. Now we have almost the same rights as everybody else."

They went on talking about the Jews, the war and world politics. An hour later, Victor and Charles got up to leave, thanking Serge and his wife for their hospitality.

They walked a few blocks in silence. When they reached the car and got in, Charles turned toward Victor and said: "I try to understand you but I don't succeed. Why are you doing this? I mean, returning to Bucharest and trying to save these unfortunate people? I'm afraid you're making the same mistake Adrian made in 1936. He had a wonderful offer at Brown Boveri, but he turned it down. He couldn't convince his wife Nina to leave the rest of the family and come with him to Switzerland. Now, as you know, they are all in a terrible mess."

As he was listening to Charles, Victor thought, in reality, the indirect cause of their missed emigration was he, Victor. Nina wouldn't leave without her sister Stella and Stella wouldn't leave without him. By the time they all made up their minds to emigrate, it was too late. The Swiss border was closed to the Jews. But he couldn't tell this to his companion.

Meanwhile, Charles kept talking. "I know that in the last two days you have received two wonderful offers in Switzerland: one from Geigy and one from Hoffman La Roche. Rolf Miess, the young representative from Geigy, is my wife's cousin. He told us about the offers. Don't be a fool! Such opportunities only come once in a lifetime.

"I know from Adrian about your devotion to Stella, but they have two children and you must think of your future! What if you ignore these offers, you return to Romania, and one day Stella and Sorel leave for Palestine with their children? After all, Stella is married to Sorel. You are not part of the family. What then? Where does this leave you? There is only one solution to your problem, and you know what I mean!"

Victor turned around and looked Charles in the eyes.

"Yes, I know what you mean. I'm not a child. I know what I'm doing. Your scenario is not news to me. I've thought of everything. I have made my decision, and there is no need to talk about it anymore."

They continued their short trip in silence. When they stopped in front of the hotel, Charles stretched out his hand. "I wish you good luck," he said. "I am sure I will see you again."

OTHER PLACES

Soon after Victor Georgescu's return to Bucharest, the funds they had asked for started arriving. They were brought by Hans Waldo, who now visited Adrian at Stella and Sorel's apartment where Adrian had his office.

Everybody was happy to see Waldo. They always greeted him like a hero. Particularly happy to see him was Suzy, Adrian's oldest daughter, who helped her father with typing, correspondence, and other office jobs. She was smitten with the handsome young Waldo, as soon as she saw him. She was even more impressed when she learned he was a poet.

He too liked the tall, graceful girl with dreamy eyes. They soon started meeting not only in Adrian's office, but also on the wild bank of the lake which bordered the city.

As Suzy was a great lover of poetry, Waldo often read her his new poems, some of which he dedicated to her. He even gave her copies of his two published books, each of them inscribed with a loving dedication.

As time went by, the two young people grew closer and closer. Wado's visits to Bucharest lasted longer and became more frequent.

Meanwhile, Adrian, Sorel and Stella were busy organizing and expanding the soup kitchen and walk-in-clinic. The money they had received was barely sufficient to keep the operation going. But they hoped that more funds would follow.

However, an unexpected event took place that summer. Suddenly, the Mareshal ordered the Jews to make an immediate payment of 4 billion lei! His order stated that this was necessary to outfit the Romanian soldiers with new winter uniforms, warm boots, and modern weapons.

As the unofficial leader of the Jewish community, it was Adrian's responsibility to collect and provide the money. The magnitude of the order so infuriated him, he wrote an angry letter to the Mareshal and took it to the post office the same day.

"This is more than an insult to our community," he wrote. "Requesting this huge amount of money from our impoverished members under the threat of arrests and deportation is a sure sign of planned destruction. In no way can we be expected to obey this order."

The Mareshal's answer was quick. "You will pay for your words!" he wrote in a note that arrived a few days later. Indeed, in less than a week, four militiamen came to pick up Adrian in their van.

"You are under arrest. You will be deported to Transnistria. Order of the Mareshal!" said the officer in charge of the operation.

Nina was in a state of shock. Adrian hadn't told her a word about his correspondence with the Mareshal. In spite of her horror and consternation, she convinced the officer to come back a few hours later, so that they would have time to pack. She gave Adrian most of the food and all the money they had in the house. She put a few changes of good clothes and a spare pair of shoes in his valise and rucksack. Then she helped him tape to his body a hidden pouch in which she placed gold coins, two gold watches, gold cufflinks and precious earrings. When she was not in the room, Adrian slipped in two vials of cyanide Sorel had given him a few weeks earlier.

A few hours later, the officer and the policeman were back at the door. Adrian got in the car. After a short ride they stopped in front of Nadia's old Jewish school building. They had arrived. Adrian remembered the building had first been occupied by the Wehrmacht and later had been passed on to the Romanian authorities. Now he was led into a crowded classroom, filled with Jewish men, women and children.

The tall windows covered with paint for the blackout were closed. A weak light bulb hanging from the ceiling shed a dim light in the room. The noise was deafening, the air hot and suffocating.

People were sitting on the floor or on their luggage. They looked very tired. Their faces had taken a ghostly pallor. Adrian heard that some families had been sitting here for more than three days.

After he got used to the racket in the room, Adrian learned why the people sitting close to him were being deported to Transnistria. To his right, a young man called Martin Horowitz had been absent from forced labor— building a road on the outskirts of the city. He had been too sick to get out of bed. He was now being deported with his wife Roza, his mother, Sally, and his two daughters, Doris and Liliana.

The very thin woman at Adrian's left, Rebecca Saltzman, had been caught by a policeman trying to bribe the manager of a store to give her more sugar than was the official ration. Next to her, an old woman, Anna Kandell and her blind husband, Willy, had forgotten to pull the black curtains over their windows at night. They were accused of sabotage, espionage, and sending signals to the enemy. The punishment: deportation to Transnistria.

In front of Adrian were two teenagers, Nelly and Tony Katz who had been found on the street after curfew. They were now being deported together with their parents, Harry and Vera Katz.

Next to them sat Edy Gross, Nelly's boyfriend, who had been caught on the street with the girls during curfew. He and Nelly were very much in love. They held hands and kept gazing into each other's eyes.

Behind Edy was a large family of a still young, bearded man, Daniel Rispler wearing a yarmulka and black caftan. He was reading out of a red prayer book. His wife Marga, a fat young woman wearing a kerchief on her head, was caring for three small children and Daniel's father, Laurian. They were all being deported because they had no Bucharest ID papers. They were residents of another town.

To Adrian's left, was a distinguished old man, Max Wiener, and a little girl, Myriam. Adrian recognized the famous historian, who had written many books on various historical subjects. He was now being deported together with his son, Maurice, and daughter-in-law, Sonia, because books by Karl Marx and Lenin had been found in his library.

After speaking to his neighbors, Adrian sat quietly on his valise. He wondered how long were they going to stay in this hot, suffocating room. Where were they going to be sent? What part of Transnistria? How was he going to get in touch with Nina? He was obsessed by many questions with no answers.

Time passed very slowly. After about four hours, they were ordered to get up and were loaded into army trucks. They were driven to the city's freight railway station and pushed into the cattle cars of a waiting train.

There was chaos in the station. People were afraid to climb into the cars. They were afraid of being separated from each other, of losing their luggage, of being crushed to death by the crowd. They were screaming and wailing, while the soldiers were swearing and hitting them with the butts of their rifles.

Adrian found himself standing near a very sick man who had been brought from the hospital on a stretcher. His eyes were closed; he was barely breathing. His young daughter was crying and kept pleading with an officer to let her father die in the station. But it was in vain: the officer ordered two soldiers to throw the sick man into the cattle car, where he died even before the train was in motion.

Adrian was pushed into the same car with most of the families who had been sitting next to him in the classroom. They were crowded here, barely having enough space to sit on the floor. Once the door was bolted, it became pitch black and suffocating. The stench was unbearable. Children were crying, angry people were cursing and shouting. Next to him, Daniel Rispler, the young man with the yarmulka and the red prayer book kept saying, "Shemah Israel" in a loud voice, again and again, like a broken record.

In contrast, Max Wiener, the distinguished scholar prayed in a whisper. From time to time a deep sigh came from his lips.

After approximately two days of travel, the train stopped and the doors opened. They were in the middle of a cornfield. Adrian and the others were allowed to get off and relieve themselves among the cornstalks. They were content to breathe fresh air and didn't care about privacy. Before the doors were closed and the engine started again, people emptied the pots and buckets filled with human waste. Meanwhile the soldiers threw out the bodies of those who had died during the trip.

After six days of travel, they arrived in a small village with a bombed out station house. It no longer had a roof and all the windows were broken.

The travelers were exhausted, hungry and dirty. Adrian and the others were ordered to form a long column and march toward the village. But as it so happened, as they climbed off the cars, some families were separated and some parents, spouses or children, were forced onto another train. This was the fate of the children of the Horowitz family, Doris and Liliana, and the young Wiener couple, the son of the historian Max Wiener, parents of little Myriam.

When they couldn't find their loved ones, the deportees ran out of the column, shouting and crying, cursing and tearing their clothes. But the soldiers pushed them back, hitting them with their rifles and whips. When this didn't help, they started shooting into the crowd. Several people were instantly killed by the bullets.

As they marched into the village, Adrian noticed that he was surrounded by the same families he had met in Bucharest and with whom he had traveled on the train. When he looked around, he saw that the village had been completely destroyed: the small houses had no more windows or doors. Fences and roofs had disappeared. Even more stunning was the fact that the village was completely deserted. Not one human being was still living there. All he could see were packs of errant dogs and a river of rats scurrying in the ditches and on the road.

The weather had changed. Here it was cold and rainy. As the day progressed, Adrian and his companions from the train—about thirty people—took shelter for the night in one of the few houses which still had a remnant of a roof. The floor was very dirty and a dreadful stench filled the air.

The walls were splattered with blood. In between the bloodstains he found an inscription which said: "You who come here, say a kadish for Isac Goldenberg." Another inscription read: "We died for Kidush Hashem." A third one had written: "Here was murdered Arnold Davidsohn with his entire family."

It was then that he discovered the corpses. Indeed, there were many dead bodies in the rooms, the cellar, and the courtyard behind the house. It explained the unbearable stench. Adrian shuddered at the thought of the massacre which had taken place here. Was it going to happen again? Should he stay awake and keep watch? He was frightened of death. It was very near, surrounding him on all sides. He was so exhausted he collapsed and fell asleep on the miserable floor.

Early the next morning they were awakened by loudspeakers ordering them to assemble in the main square of the village. Here they were surrounded by armed soldiers on horseback. They had to form a long column and march toward the river Dniester.

In the crowd, Adrian recognized the faces of his old companions: Martin Horowitz, his mother and wife Sarah who were a few rows ahead of him. Next to them were the Katz family and Edy Gross, Nelly's boyfriend. The Risplers and others were further behind him.

They walked for many hours. When they came to a halt, Adrian heard people scream. He saw Martin Horowitz's wife and mother, as well as Rebecca Saltzman and many others run out of the column, turn back and refuse to keep walking. Nevertheless, the soldiers forced them to go on by pushing and hitting them. Soon Adrian understood why they had stopped. The marchers had reached an open grave, filled with hundreds of naked bodies. The stench was insufferable; the air heavy with death.

"These are the Jews who lived in the village of M, before we arrived," said Daniel Rispler, the young man with the red prayer book. "An officer told me that they were shot by his men a few days ago. Their clothes were taken by the peasants. Their houses were ransacked and burned. That's why the village is so deserted and ruined."

It was cold and rainy the whole day but they kept marching. In the evening, they stopped near a forest. The soldiers pushed them inside the woods. Some people were afraid and resisted, since they had heard rumors about murders of Jews in the forests.

Not far from Adrian, young Martin Horowitz and his wife Roza, who was still worrying about the fate of their daughters, started an argument with a soldier. They were afraid to advance into the wood. The noise of the discussion attracted the captain. He aimed his pistol at the young couple and fired. Both Martin and Roza fell to the ground dead.

Adrian lay down on his coat and covered himself with a woolen shawl Nina had packed for him, but the rain seeped through the fabric. He shivered the whole night. He woke up after a few hours and munched a piece of bread he had bought from a peasant during the march. It had not been cheap: he obtained the bread and some water in exchange for a gold tie clip.

He was still hungry and cold. He was so exhausted he went back to sleep. He dreamt about war, battles and shooting sprees. In the morning, he learned that a few of the old people, among them Daniel Rispler's old father, Laurian, had been dragged deep into the forest and had never come out again.

They continued their march toward the Dniester in the rain. Adrian could recognize the presence of the river by a thin line of fog in the distance.

Crossing the Dniester was frightening to all of them. There was a checkpoint staffed by officers and soldiers. Here the marchers had to empty their pockets and show all their personal documents and ID cards. Often these papers were taken away from them. They also had to drop their money, jewelry and watches into a bucket. They were often brutally searched, with beatings and blows. Adrian watched as Rebecca Saltzman, the very thin woman, failed to drop her left earring fast enough into the bucket. The soldier who was checking her lost patience and pulled so hard at her earring that the earlobe was torn. The woman shrieked in pain, but the soldier pushed her and forced her to keep walking.

Standing in line at the checkpoint, Adrian prepared himself for the search. When his turn came, he acted quickly. He slipped a gold coin between the pages of his ID booklet. The officer frowned, took the gold coin and dropped it into his pocket. Then he returned the booklet to Adrian and waved him through.

Other travelers were not so lucky. Not only were they robbed of their money and ID papers, many lost their luggage and other personal valuables. Max Wiener, the distinguished professor, was forced to throw his gold rimmed spectacles into the bucket.

When the ordeal of the checkpoint was over, they proceeded to cross the river. Adrian and most of the others were made to walk over a long and narrow bridge, a march which lasted many hours.

The remaining people were placed on barges. Two of these reached the opposite bank without trouble. But the last barge was very crowded. Too many people had been forced onto it.

The river was choppy, the boat was shaky, swaying dangerously from side to side. The people on board panicked and broke into a frenzy. They screamed and pushed and shoved each other so wildly the boat capsized and many fell overboard.

Adrian saw them float in the water. He recognized the blind man, Willy Kandell among them. Then he heard the shots. All around the wreckage, the river turned red with blood.

On the opposite bank of the Dniester, they continued their march in the cold rain. The soldiers on horseback pushed them to walk faster and faster. But the old people and the sick could not keep up. Adrian tried to help Sally Horowitz, Martin's mother, and Anna Kandell. But they couldn't walk and lagged behind. Threatened by the soldiers, Adrian had to abandon them on the side of the road.

When the distance between them and the column of marchers was big enough, volleys of shots were heard.

Adrian and the others held their breath: they knew what was happening and covered their ears.

They kept marching for days on end, having to walk between twenty and thirty kilometers every day. They were tired and starved, since they had almost nothing to eat or drink.

At night in his sleep, Adrian dreamt only about food—rich banquets with tables loaded with mountains of succulent roasts, vegetable soufflés, scrumptious desserts, free flowing champagne. Even in the daytime his mind was obsessed with the flavor of the finest delicacies he'd ever tasted. His mouth watered at these recollections.

Adrian knew that these were the first signs of starvation, which could progress into hallucinations and delirium. Losing his mind would be the end of everything. Was this going to happen to him?

He remembered the cyanide vials he was carrying with him. He took them out of his pouch and held them between his fingers. It would be so easy to break them and swallow their content! A few drops were sufficient. A number of people in their convoy—doctors, dentists and pharmacists—had already done it.

He couldn't make up his mind. Yes, he thought: it may be the right step to take. Things could only get worse. But something inside him held him back. He stopped himself from breaking the vials. He put them back in their wrappings and slipped them into the pouch.

The next day he met a peasant on the road who sold him a piece of bread and some water.

After several more days of marching in the rain, they arrived at a clearing in the woods. Here everything was wet: the trees, bushes, grass and tall reeds which covered the meadow. Under their feet, the soil felt slippery and soft. A soldier told the captain to stop the marchers and have them turn back since they had reached a treacherous marsh.

The captain didn't move. He told the soldiers to point their rifles at the first rows of the column and force the marchers to keep walking. "Dirty Kikes! You're here to die, not to live!" he shouted.

Adrian watched as two rows of people, among them Tony Katz, the youngest of the family, advanced into the clearing and slowly sank into the mud. At first they sank up to their knees, then to their hips, unable to raise themselves and reach solid ground.

The captain waited and watched. After a while, he ordered the marchers to turn around and take a different road. There was no help for those trapped in the mud. Later Adrian learned that twenty-eight people had drowned in the swamp.

The march continued for many more days. Adrian couldn't keep track any longer. One night, as they stopped not too far from the outskirts of a village, he was resting near the young couple, Nelly Katz and her boyfriend. Adrian was very fond of them. He particularly liked Nelly, who was a talented artist. She was always making sketches of her companions, even of the soldiers and drawing miniature landscapes. She was using any bit of paper she could find.

On this moonless night, the marchers stopped in an open field. As the night was chilly, they covered themselves with blankets and coats. It was very quiet and soon everybody went to sleep.

Suddenly, a loud commotion woke them up. Soldiers were stomping and running through the camp, screaming to wake them up. They were looking for young women to take to the officers' house in the village.

They tore the covers off the sleepers and pulled the women to their feet. The frightened people were screaming, fighting, and trying to run away.

Two soldiers stopped at the young couple near Adrian. They grabbed Nelly and dragged her along. Edy, her fiancé, clung to her, pulling her back and not letting go. The soldiers beat him with their rifle butts, until his head and his hands were covered with blood. He fell down. They took Nelly with them.

After they left, he crawled back to his place. Adrian could hear him sobbing and weeping for the rest of the night.

Late after midnight Nelly and the other women came back, stumbling in the darkness and crying, while the soldiers laughed at them.

In the morning, when everybody had to get up, the two young people did not move. Adrian called them, but there was no response. A soldier came and kicked them with his boot. They didn't move. He lifted the blanket and took a step back. He was in shock. The two people were lying in a puddle of blood. They had slit their wrists and escaped into death.

Adrian was saddened by the loss of his friends. As they kept marching without food, he suffered from severe hunger pangs. The thought of his vials of poison stirred again in his head. He was more afraid than ever of losing his mind. He had seen people becoming insane. One man, a lawyer, developed dementia because of the hunger. He ran into the village singing and dancing and was stoned to death by the peasants.

Where were they going? What was their destination? Or was there a destination at all? They kept asking themselves. Nobody knew. It had been kept a secret.

"We have to get to Moghilev, the capital city of Transnistria, if we want to stay alive!" said old Max Wiener. But it seemed to Adrian that they were far away from Moghilev and headed in the opposite direction. Besides, there were different opinions regarding the end point of their journey. Some people, among them Daniel Rispler, the religious man with the red prayer book, said they were headed toward the river Bug where they were going to be delivered to the SS. "Here, all of us will be shot. No one will escape." His wife thought that they were going to be abandoned in one of the deserted villages.

Max Wiener feared that they were going to be herded inside an old barn that would be set on fire. "We have to get to Moghilev if we want to stay alive!" he repeated.

They were all very weak and discouraged. In the last several days they had very little to eat. They had met few peasants and the price of a piece of bread and a sip of water was staggering. Many times the peasants didn't want money or jewelry. They asked for warm clothing or shoes, which the marchers had already given away earlier on their trip.

Now they were not only hungry and weak, but their shoes were torn, their clothes had turned to rags and they were infected with lice. But they had to keep marching another twenty or thirty kilometers each day.

With passing time, the rumors about being taken to the river Bug and delivered to the SS grew stronger. Everything they heard was terrifying and blood curdling.

They knew that the camps by the river Bug were run by the SS and the organization Todt. They had heard that no prisoner had ever come back alive from there.

"Jewish deportees are brought there to build bridges and pave roads," said Daniel Rispler. "I have heard when they finish their work or if they are too weak or sick to work, they are all shot by the SS. First they have to dig their own graves, then they are buried by the next group of arrivals, who will be shot and buried in turn, and so on."

"I also heard even though the SS expect them to work, the people don't get any food," said Max Wiener. "In one camp they ended up eating grass and the bark of trees. Then the commander fed them raw maize flour and raw potatoes. Their bellies puffed up from the indigestible meal. They died in terrible pain."

"This is not all," said Harry Katz who had joined the conversation. "I heard that in the camp of S the sick and the exhausted workers were all locked up in the synagogue. The building was doused with gasoline and then set on fire."

"But doesn't anybody try to escape, to run away?" asked Adrian.

Daniel Rispler smirked when he heard this question. "Yes, of course they try to run away. But the SS are very efficient. In most cases they catch up with the runaways. A punishment operation is then organized to teach everybody a lesson. The culprits are brought to the assembly place of the camp and hung with much fanfare or burned alive in front of all the deportees."

Silence followed this discussion. They couldn't speak any longer.

The marches went on without interruption. When they came near another deserted village, Adrian suggested to some of his companions they should ask the captain to let them stay in the village rather than take them to the Bug. He and Daniel Rispler collected gold coins, watches and jewelry from everyone and presented them as a gift to the captain. To their relief, the captain was pleased with the offer and accepted the deal.

The village of B was as ruined and deserted as other small villages they had passed: bombed and burnt houses without doors, windows and roofs. Even the walls were crumbling and ready to collapse.

There were no people in the village. It had been turned into a ghetto, and then the residents had been taken to the SS at the river Bug.

Adrian and the others were led to a separate section of the deserted village. They were crowded into whatever empty structures there were—pigsties, stables, barns and horse stalls. They were so tightly packed together, they barely had room to lie down. The camp was surrounded by barbed wire and patrolled by armed soldiers and police.

They couldn't drink water and couldn't wash. The nearest fountain was far beyond the barbed wire fence which they were forbidden to cross.

Some days, a few peasants came to a spot by the wire, under the chestnut tree, and traded water and bread for gold jewelry, watches and woolen clothes. The slices of bread grew smaller and smaller, but the price climbed higher and higher.

After a few weeks, the captain received new orders and he was moved to the front. His replacement was a cruel disciplinarian who always carried a long leather whip in his hand.

"This is your cemetery!" he told the prisoners as soon as he arrived. "We brought you here to die, not to live." He immediately ordered the soldiers to stop the peasants from coming to the fence.

After that, more people died every day.

It was unbearably hot now. Adrian was aware that the heat, the lack of food and water and the lice made everybody weaker and sicker. At first they lacked the energy to stand up or walk. They would sit in a corner, motionless, and stare into space. Then they would collapse and lie down with eyes closed. Often they would slip into a coma. It was hard to tell whether they were dead or alive. The first to succumb were the very young and the very old.

To Adrian's distress, among the sick was Max Wiener, the old professor from Bucharest. Until now, he and his five-year-old granddaughter, Myriam, had survived the long march and had made it to B. But here the old man was outdone. His strength abandoned him. He was no longer able to drag himself to the wire fence to buy bread from the peasants. Even though Adrian took care of him, he became weaker and sicker every day.

One morning, with his last trace of energy, he gave Adrian his battered valise. Then, from a hidden pocket in his underpants, he brought out a pouch filled with gold coins and diamonds. "Take these," he said as he gave them to Adrian "and promise me that you will take care of Myriam like your own child. You cannot abandon her!

I have sworn to her mother that I would rather die than abandon her! But God's will is stronger than our plans."

Adrian took his hand and assured him that he was going to take care of Myriam.

"Go to Moghilev! You must take Myriam with you to Moghilev!" the old man added in a whisper.

Then he closed his eyes. He seemed to rest peacefully. His hat had slipped to one side, revealing a gray layer of lice covering his hairline.

Half an hour later he was dead. His body remained in the same place, since the prisoners were not allowed to carry the corpses beyond the enclosure and the soldiers didn't care about the dead.

Adrian said Kadish for his friend, while Myriam sat on the ground, covering her face and crying into her hands. "Where did you go, Opa? Why did you leave me?" she kept repeating.

With the old man's money in his pocket and the responsibility of the little girl on his shoulders, it became clear to Adrian that he had to get out of here as soon as he could. Staying in this hell hole was sure death. Half the people with whom he had traveled were already dead. The other half were progressively slipping into a coma. Adrian himself felt quite weak, since he hadn't eaten anything in the last two days.

He had to get out of here, quickly; there was no question. But how?

Getting to Moghilev was dangerous. It was very far. Nevertheless, Adrian decided to go.

On a very dark night, he stuffed all his belongings in his large backpack and made sure that the bag with the diamonds was in a safe place. He then bent over Myriam and told her that she had to come with him. She couldn't stay here alone. At first she didn't want to go and pushed him away. She told him, "I'm staying here with Opa, he will open his eyes and will talk to me!" But when he scooped her up in his arms, she didn't resist. She was so small and so light that he had no trouble putting her on his back and slipping into the courtyard.

Sometime earlier, he had noticed a hole under the barbed wire fence, through which hungry dogs crawled into the camp and feasted on the corpses. The hole was quite deep and so well hidden by shrubbery, the guards hadn't seen it.

Adrian pushed Myriam through the opening. He then slid the backpack to the other side, bent down and crawled under the fence. The next minute they were outside the camp.

Adrian knew there was a curfew and nobody was allowed to be on the road after dark. He knew, if apprehended, both he and the child would be shot immediately.

Nevertheless, he started walking away from the camp. He stepped in the ditch which bordered the road, hiding under the tall bushes of wild blackberries. The night was pitch dark and very quiet. They could hear crickets singing in the grass.

They followed the road straight ahead. Adrian knew that there were houses, a small village further on, even though there were no lights because of the blackout. He wanted to get there before daybreak. It was too dangerous to be on the road in broad daylight.

But the trouble they now had was the dogs: they gathered in big, vicious packs and threatened to attack them. Their loud barking was also dangerous since it could attract attention to their presence. Adrian armed himself with rocks which he threw at the dogs.

After several hours of walking they reached the first house: it was a small hut with a thatched roof surrounded by a narrow courtyard. As they passed the house, the dogs in the courtyard started barking. The door opened and a man with a rifle appeared on the porch. "Go away or I shoot!" he screamed into the night.

Adrian had taken Myriam in his arms and they slipped carefully away into the ditch. After some time the dogs stopped barking and the night was quiet again.

They walked by a few more sleeping houses. Time was passing. Soon Adrian saw a narrow yellow band marking the horizon. With the approach of dawn, he decided that they must find a hiding place. They could not continue walking. Besides, he was so exhausted he could barely catch his breath.

Among the next buildings, he spotted a large mansion with a big courtyard behind the house. There was a narrow path between this house and the next, which led to the backyard. They followed the path, walking on tiptoe so as to make no noise.

They entered the courtyard and hid in the barn after first drinking water from a rain barrel which stood near the door. They climbed into the hayloft and fell into a very deep sleep.

Adrian was awakened by shouting and noise around him. When he opened his eyes he saw the ugly face of an angry man hovering over him. The man was screaming and ready to poke him with a pitchfork. "Get out of here, you dirty kike, or I'm going to kill you! You bloody bastard, get out or I'm calling the soldiers on you. They'll do to you what you deserve!"

Two other farmhands had appeared and they joined him in screaming and shoving their pitchforks at Adrian and Myriam. The little girl was crying hysterically.

Then, one of the men picked up an axe and walked toward Adrian, swinging it over his head. "Let's have fun with him and make the kike dance!" he shouted. "He should learn what it means to ignore regulations. I was a soldier once. I know what the soldiers would do if they found him. Come on, let's start! Don't be shy!"

He advanced toward Adrian, holding the axe ready for the blow, while the two others joined him with their pitchforks. They were very close, when a strong voice shouted, "Stop that at once! Where do you think you are? Put down those tools. Get out of here!" It was a loud, commanding voice. To Adrian's surprise, it was the voice of a woman.

A tall, lean woman had walked into the barn. Her gray hair was pulled back in a bun and her clear, transparent eyes were almost hard. She never blinked. When she spoke, she barely moved her lips. She wore riding pants and riding boots and held a pistol in one hand and a whip in the other. The men obeyed her at once. They dropped the axes and pitchforks and disappeared.

Once alone with the strangers, the woman told them to pick up their bundles and come into the house. She ordered the maid to run a warm bath for Adrian and then one for Myriam. She helped the maid prepare a hearty soup and hot sausages. She also packed bread and sausages for their voyage.

She then went to the closet, picked out a military uniform and gave it to Adrian. "This belonged to my husband. He was shot and killed in the first days of the war. The Mareshal made him a hero and gave him a big decoration," she said. "My husband didn't like this war. He was a civil engineer, but the Mareshal ordered him to build a strategic bridge over the Dniester. He didn't want to go to war, but he had no choice!"

Adrian thanked the woman for the food, the uniform and her hospitality, and wanted to give her some gold coins or jewelry, but she refused.

"I know who you are and I know that you're in danger. Also, you bring danger to those who try to help you. But—what can we do? It is important to save the life of our fellow humans. We cannot allow ourselves to turn into wild animals. It would be the end of the human race!"

She stopped talking and walked to the door.

"You must leave now, before the neighbors find out about you. My coachman will drive you and the girl to Moghilev. Of course, you will pay him for the ride.

"When you arrive in that city, you must find Sigmund Dorfman. He is the president of the Jewish community there. He was a friend of my husband's. Don't forget to mention our name. Goodbye now and good luck!" said the woman as she accompanied them to the carriage house.

The coachman, a tall man with a long beard, helped them into the carriage. "It's a long way to Moghilev!" he said when they were on the road. "We will have to ride slowly to protect the horses. If they get overheated or too exhausted, we'll be stuck on the highway in a hopeless situation."

They rode in silence. Not too far down the road they heard an explosion followed by gunshots and screams. When he turned to look, Adrian saw a big fire raging behind them. He asked the coachman whether it was the house of the woman they had just left.

"Yes," said the coachman. "The farmhands set fire to the mansion and probably killed her too. They believed that you and your daughter were still there and wanted to kill you. But Madam Stănescu had it coming to her. Today's attack had been a long time in coming. A few of the men who were working for her had been in the Iron Guard. They hated her because she helped Jewish fugitives. There was even a rumor that she had had a Jewish grandmother and had Jewish blood."

"But if you knew of this plan," said Adrian, "why didn't you warn her or help her flee?"

"You don't understand," said the coachman after a short pause. "I was never a Legionnaire myself and I don't approve of them. But I must watch my skin. I have a wife and three children to feed. If I had warned her and helped her flee, they would have known that it was me who betrayed them. They would have killed me too.

"It is bad enough," he added," that I am now left without a job. You see, I don't care about you Jews. I don't want to kill any of you. I'm a man with the fear of God and all I want is to make a living. My father was a priest and taught me the Ten Commandments. I venerate his memory and respect the Ten Commandments," he said

In the silence which followed, Adrian felt heartbroken for having caused the death of the woman who had rescued them. He looked at Myriam asleep in his arms and thought of Nadia, Suzy and Nina. He missed them so much! There was a great heaviness in his heart. Were they safe? What was happening to them? What was going on in Bucharest? He hadn't had any news since the day he had left. But maybe he'd learn more in a few days when he reached the city.

The journey to Moghilev took several days. After Adrian and Myriam finished the new provisions, Adrian gave money to the coachman. He bought fresh food for the three of them. Finally, on the fourth day they reached the outskirts of the city.

"We'll have to stop soon," said the driver. "I cannot bring the wagon into the city because they'll take it away, as well as the horses. The police have orders to requisition all horses and carriages for the army. But I'll drive you to the safest checkpoint where nobody will ask for your papers."

For some time they rode around the borders of the town. Then they stopped not far from a narrow street which was blocked by a barbed wire fence and a wooden kiosk occupied by an officer and a soldier.

"We have to wait here for an hour or two every day. At around three in the afternoon, the officer goes to the taverna around the corner to have his shot of țuică. He stays there for at least an hour and a half and returns to his post about two hours later.

"During this time, the checkpoint is manned by a soldier who cannot read or write so he never asks for identification papers. Besides, he wouldn't do this to you, since you look like a superior officer. He is a common soldier."

While they were waiting for the time to pass, the coachman went to the taverna to have a drink. When he came back, he brought with him a piece of paper with Sigmund Dorfman's office address and handed it to Adrian. In recognition, Adrian gave him one of the last gold coins he had in his pocket.

The city of Moghilev looked almost as ruined and devastated as the villages Adrian had seen on his journey. The only difference was the large crowd of people milling about in the streets. Every inch of space was crowded with people. Most of them were dishevelled and dressed in rags. Many looked famished and were begging for a piece of bread. Adrian couldn't have recognized anybody among these ghostly figures.

Many Romanian policemen, soldiers and a few German SS were also crowding the streets.

Dragging Myriam behind him and sometimes carrying her on his back, Adrian marched toward Dorfman's office building: he had to get there before the end of the day.

Sigmund Dorfman's office was located in a building just outside the ghetto. Two blocks away stood the ruins of the old synagogue, which had been burned and partly demolished. But Dorfman's office was in one of the few buildings in the city which was still standing intact—with a roof, chimneys, and all its windows undamaged. It looked like an old, solid mansion, a two-story building with a shingle roof.

There was a long line of people—most of them in rags—waiting in front of the entrance. Policemen and soldiers on horseback were keeping order, shouting at the crowd and hitting them with their whips.

Dressed in his military uniform, Adrian stepped to the front of the line. He was quickly ushered into the waiting room. Even though he was very tired, he made a great effort and pulled himself together for this meeting.

He didn't have to wait long: a few minutes later Sigmund Dorfman invited him into the main office. He was a tall man with a completely shaven head, dressed in a paramilitary uniform. He was wearing riding boots. His eyes were warm and lively, giving him a friendly appearance. There was an air of confidence about him, which made even the yellow star on his chest look like a military decoration. He looked with great interest at his visitor and the little girl.

"I am Adrian Stein from Bucharest. This is Myriam, Max Wiener's granddaughter, with whom I was in the camp of B. Her grandfather didn't survive, so I had to take her with me."

"Adrian Stein from Bucharest! I have heard so much about you!" cried Sigmund Dorfman. "Goodness gracious! We were looking for you for some time, and here you are! We knew that you had been deported, but we couldn't trace your whereabouts. There were so many bad rumors about you. Some people said you had drowned in the Dniester, others that you were shot dead on the way to the camp, and others that you had been taken to the Bug and delivered to the SS!

"Some people swore they saw your body floating in the Dniester and others that they were present and witnessed your execution. I didn't know what to believe, so I didn't believe anything. I am glad that none of these rumors is true, and that you are here with us in Moghilev.

"I think that you and the little girl should stay with us—with me and my family until you can go home to Bucharest."

Adrian barely had the strength to thank him before they walked across the street to Dorfman's private residence.

The next morning, the first thing Sigmund Dorfman did was to obtain permits of residence in Moghilev for the newcomers. These documents were expensive and hard to secure. But they were absolutely necessary, since those who didn't have them, could immediately be deported to the river Bug and delivered to the SS. But as he had been a high ranking officer in the Austrian army, Dorfman knew how to handle the military authorities. He was also helped by his friend, Captain Tudoran, a cousin of the governor of the Moghilev district. So it took only a very short time for Adrian and Myriam to get their permits of residence.

Soon after he moved into his new home, Adrian became very ill. He was exhausted and starved. During his stay in B, he had been infected with lice. Typhus developed without delay. He was now seriously ill. He ran a very high fever with unbearable headaches accompanied by convulsions. Sometimes he became extremely restless and tried to jump out of bed. They had no choice but to strap him to the railing. Other times he was very sluggish, didn't speak, refused to eat or drink anything and didn't recognize the people around him.

On some days his mind wandered. He called for Nina, Suzy and Nadia. He spoke to Fritz, the chauffeur, ordering him to prepare the car for a trip to the office or he thought that he was at the villa in Lugano, Switzerland, taking a boat ride on the lake.

He grew weaker and weaker every day. The doctors who came to see him said that he must be taken to the hospital and given intravenous injections to survive. It was the law. Patients suffering from typhus had to be taken to the hospital under threat of punishment or deportation. But

Captain Tudoran warned the family that the Mareshal had given a secret order never to let Adrian come home alive.

"If you put him in the hospital, he won't make it!" said the Captain.

"But if we keep him here without proper treatment he won't survive either!" said Sigmund Dorfman. It was a difficult decision to make. He consulted his wife, Yolanda, but she didn't know what to say. In the end, Captain Tudoran prevailed and Adrian remained home.

For many days he hovered between life and death. It took a long time for the Dorfmans to know whether they had made the right decision or not.

Meanwhile in Bucharest, immediately after Adrian's arrest, Nina, Stella, Sorel and Doctor Georgescu had informed Hans Waldo of Adrian's deportation. He lost no time and passed the news to Serge Miller and Charles Kass in Switzerland. This made the two men determined to organize a Red Cross visit to Transnistria with the ultimate goal of bringing Adrian back to Bucharest. They saw this expedition as both a fact finding and an aid bringing mission funded by the International Red Cross.

Since they knew that time was precious, Kass and Miller tried to rush the operation. But the formalities and preparations for the expedition turned out to be much lengthier and more complicated than they had anticipated.

Serge Miller struggled with the American Joint Distribution Committee which claimed to be out of funds. At the same time, the Swiss authorities had become suspicious of him and tried to put his entire program on hold.

Charles Kass too had to fight for the collaboration of the Red Cross that refused to give any aid to Jewish victims. Even though Charles Kass was a religious man with the fear of God, in this case he swore falsely pretending that the aid was intended for non-Jews. He knew that the life of so many people depended on this relief.

Finally, a few months after Adrian's arrest and deportation, Kass and Miller arrived in Bucharest bringing funds and large quantities of food and medicines. At this point, nobody knew anything about Adrian's fate or his whereabouts.

The two men's first visit was to Sorel and Stella's, where they were also met by Nina, Doctor Georgescu and Hans Waldo. Everybody was worried about Adrian. Nina couldn't stop crying. "I should have gone with him. I shouldn't have let him go alone," she kept repeating.

"You couldn't protect him and you couldn't help him," Stella and Sorel told her. But they couldn't stop her tears.

On this first meeting, they discussed a plan by which the two Swiss envoys would obtain permission from the Mareshal to travel to Transnistria. Victor Georgescu suggested that he himself—as the private physician of the Queen—and Professor Ursu, the Dean of the Medical School and an old high school friend of both Adrian and the Mareshal, visit the Mareshal and convince him to accept an urgent meeting with the Swiss delegates.

Everybody agreed to this plan.

On a warm September morning, Victor Georgescu picked up Professor Ursu and drove to the Presidential Palace. The Mareshal received them immediately. He was in a good mood. His visitors were impressed with his appearance. He was wearing a white, gala uniform with rich gold trimmings and a row of shiny military decorations. A blue silk sash spanned his chest. He was holding a gold and ruby inlaid ceremonial sword in his hand.

The Mareshal's appearance reminded Victor Georgescu of Napoleon's Imperial Coronation portrait. All that was missing was the mantle of white ermine and the Imperial crown.

"You didn't have to dress so formally for our visit!" said Professor Ursu. "We admire you for who you are, not for your regal uniform!"

The Mareshal was pleased with this compliment and explained that he was having his official portrait painted by the most famous artist in the country.

He took them to another room and showed them two easels with two different canvases. When he lifted the sheets which covered them, they saw a full length portrait of the Mareshal wearing the white gala uniform with the ceremonial sword attached to his belt. The second painting was a head and shoulder portrait of the Mareshal and Hitler together.

"The full length picture is going to be my new, official portrait," said the Mareshal. "The second one will be my Christmas gift for the Führer. I am convinced he will like it.

The artist is very gifted and Hitler surely knows something about painting!" he added with a wink. Doctor Georgescu and Professor Ursu agreed and complimented him on the portraits.

When they returned to the main office, the Mareshal took a bottle of Grand Marnier and three glasses from a shelf inside his desk.

"This is the best of France!" he said, as he clinked with his guests. "I stopped in Paris on my way back from Berlin," he added. "Still as beautiful as ever, even if La Ville Lumière is wrapped in the darkness of the blackout. But maybe one day . . ."

"That day is very far away," said Professor Ursu. "Right now we still have to face many months of war and darkness. A cold Russian winter awaits our troops," he added.

"I'm sorry to mention this, but warm uniforms, new equipment and weapons will be needed by our soldiers as well as blankets and medicines for our wounded men. There is an opportunity to get all this and extra funds right now," he said. He went on to tell the Mareshal about the visit of the Red Cross delegates. "They want to talk to you personally and make the offer directly to you. They could provide even more funds and goods in the future. All they want in exchange is to visit the camps in Transnistria and to bring Adrian Stein back to Bucharest."

The Mareshal didn't say anything. The professor wasn't sure if the Mareshal was listening but he went on in spite of the silence.

"As a matter of fact, in the case of Adrian Stein, why would you still keep him away rather than bring him home? If he is still alive, he is more of a liability in Transnistria, while he could be an asset here in Bucharest. Maybe we should remember that the war is far from ended and the United States is still very powerful!"

The Mareshal didn't answer. He poured more cognac in their glasses and went on praising the charm and beauty of Paris.

"Nothing beats a stroll on the grand boulevards, a promenade in the Jardin des Tuileries or an evening at Maxim's or the Folies Bergères!" He was so carried away with Paris that he got up and played the last hits of Maurice Chevalier and Edith Piaf on his victrola.

Victor Georgescu watched him in silence. It was all in vain! He told himself. Poor Adrian! Will we ever see him again? All the efforts of Charles Kass and Serge Miller were for naught.

There was a knock at the door. A young officer came in saying that the painter was waiting.

The Mareshal got up and saw his visitors to the door. He stopped in front of the mirror and arranged the decorations on his chest, while humming Maurice Chevalier's famous *"Tout va très bien Madame la Marquise."*

"Au revoir," he said, shaking the hands of his visitors while they thanked him for his hospitality.

They had almost reached the end of the corridor when he called them back. They stopped and turned around.

"Tell the Red Cross envoys to be at the presidential office tomorrow at 12 noon. I'll be waiting for them."

Charles Kass, Hans Waldo and two other members of the Red Cross mission arrived in Moghilev a few days later. They had traveled by military train and had been given a sleeping compartment for officers.

In addition to the funds they were bringing, they were also carrying cases of food, clothing, blankets and medicines for the people in the camps. Two cars of the train were filled with these supplies. The delegates were met at the train station by Sigmund Dorfman and Captain Tudoran.

As soon as the official formalities were over and the visitors were installed in the only standing hotel in the city, Charles Kass accompanied Dorfman to his home. When he walked in, he couldn't believe his eyes: Adrian was standing before him.

Kass was deeply moved by this unexpected encounter, since nobody had told him that Adrian was alive and staying here.

He had a shock when he first saw him. He almost didn't recognize him. Adrian looked frail and aged after his illness. He was very thin, his hair had turned gray, and his clothes were hanging on him. He looked like a shadow of himself. His face was white and small and his eyes seemed unusually large. But they were filled with the same sparkle as ever.

In spite of this shock, Charles Kass was happy to see him. "What a surprise to find you here! It feels like a miracle!" he said. "We didn't know where you were. As a matter of fact, we didn't know whether you were dead or alive. There were so many rumors!"

"I didn't know either whether I was dead or alive!" said Adrian, trying to make a joke. "But I must say it is a miracle to see you here in Moghilev, rather than in Zürich! And now I hope to go home without delay," he added.

But this was not yet possible. Adrian was still too weak to travel. In addition, little Myriam had disappeared and couldn't be found. Adrian wouldn't hear of returning to Bucharest without her.

Mrs. Dorfman was in tears, crying bitterly day and night, praying heaven for her return. "Oh! Mighty God, punish me for my sins, but let the little girl come back to our house."

Where could she be? How had she gotten lost? They kept asking themselves. The Dorfmans last remembered seeing her a few weeks before when Adrian was very ill and they had to decide whether to keep him at home or take him to the hospital. There had been a lot of confusion at that time. Strangers had come to the house and Myriam may have gotten scared and run away.

In the following days, Sigmund Dorfman, Charles Kass and Adrian, searched for her. Their first stop was the children's section of the Moghilev hospital.

As they walked into what looked like a bombed out building, all they saw were row upon row of dirty mattresses on the floor, or nothing but torn sheets and no mattresses. It was very quiet. Countless skeletal bodies were lying here, barely breathing or sunk in a coma. The three men looked at the children as closely as they could. Myriam was not among them.

From here they went to the orphanage.

This was a small partly ruined building, with no doors or windows. The many children between one year and eleven were sleeping on a raised platform. They were so crowded, they had no space to stretch out. They had no pillows, no blankets and no sheets. They were not wearing pajamas or nightgowns; they were covered in torn and dirty rags.

"They have no shoes either," said the young director of the orphanage, a skeletal-looking woman, dressed in a torn uniform, who coughed incessantly. "We have almost no food to give the children. Many of them wander out in the street and beg for food. Since they have no shoes and it is freezing outside in the winter as well as here in the building, they end up with frozen feet and cannot walk any longer. In addition, we are also invaded with big rats that attack the small children in their sleep."

Adrian and Dorfman walked slowly between the rows of famished children. At the end of the room, by the wall, they found Myriam. She was lying motionless, her eyes closed. She looked much smaller and younger than when Adrian last saw her.

He called her name, but she didn't answer. When he called her a second time, she opened her eyes and stared at him without recognition.

But Adrian didn't wait: "Come, come with me!" he said, as he bent down, scooped her in his arms and carried her home.

It took more than a week to nurse her back to health. During this time, whenever she heard the doorbell ring, she would run and hide under the bed. She was afraid that strangers would come and take her back to the orphanage.

Later, when she was less frightened, she told Adrian that one night she had dreamt that her grandfather, Max, was not dead, but had come to Moghilev and was waiting for her outside in the street. She sneaked out of the house to meet him. But she got scared by two big dogs that attacked her. She ran away from them and got lost. As she was wandering the streets, crying, a man and a woman asked her where she lived and where her parents were? She couldn't answer these questions and kept crying so they had taken her to the orphanage.

While Myriam and Adrian recovered, Dorfman and Captain Tudoran took the Swiss delegates on a tour of the camps near Moghilev. The food, the medicines and the clothing they brought were distributed and gone in no time at all.

Charles Kass looked at the empty containers and saw it as the beginning of a new adventure.

ISTANBUL

O N THAT SUMMER AFTERNOON, SUZY was looking forward to meeting Hans Waldo. At the end of the previous week, he had promised to come this Thursday.

Because he spent much time in Bucharest now, the Embassy had put a small Fiat at his disposal. He and Suzy had planned to drive out to the lake and have a picnic.

Waldo was going to bring the food—Swiss cheese, fresh rolls, ham, leberwurst and a few bottles of beer, for dessert, apples and milk chocolate. All these wonderful treats he could get through the Embassy, but they were not accessible on the market. In the past he had brought gourmet delicacies to the whole family.

It was a beautiful day and Suzy put on a light red summer dress with white polka dots and red stylish shoes with a pointed toe.

As she didn't want her parents to know that she was meeting Waldo, she told Nina that she was going to do some filing at the office and then to visit her friend Marcella.

Nina said, "OK" and then added, "Just watch the curfew and make sure that you're home before dark."

It was Nadia who commented on seeing her sister all dressed up. "You never wear this good dress and fine shoes when you go to visit Marcella!" she blurted out. "I bet you're meeting a beau . . . maybe Hans Waldo! He seems to be smitten with you!"

"Shut your big mouth!" Suzy retorted, putting her hand over her sister's mouth. Then she hurried downstairs and walked to the corner where Hans was going to meet her.

She didn't have to wait: as soon as she reached the corner, the blue Fiat stopped at the curb. It had been freshly washed and polished. It sparkled in the sunshine like a precious jewel.

Waldo stepped out of the car to greet her. He wore a white polo shirt with an open collar and light, shantung pants to match. He was tanned from playing tennis. His blond hair looked even more golden next to his bronzed face.

He smiled happily when he saw her and helped her climb into the car, next to the driver's seat. He quickly joined her. After locking the door, he took her hands in his own, raised them to his lips, and planted a kiss on every finger.

"*Grüssgott mein Liebchen!*" he said when he finished, while still holding her hands. He was smiling. She saw a dimple appear on his cheek. It made him look very charming.

He looks like a God or a movie star! He should be making movies, not wasting his time as a courier, Suzy told herself. She blushed at the thought that she was sitting next to a future movie star.

They didn't speak much while driving through the sun-drenched, dusty streets. Ever so often, when they stopped at a red light, he raised her hands to his lips and kissed her fingers. When they had to wait for the passage of a caravan of German tanks to clear the way, he pulled her close and kissed her on the neck.

After a while, they arrived at the lake which bordered the north end of the city. Waldo parked the car as close to the water as he could. Suzy got out, stretched her arms and her back, and took a deep breath. She closed her eyes and smelled with delight the perfume of the thousand roses that bloomed beyond the willow trees.

"Can you help me with the basket? Even better, take the blanket!" said Waldo as he lifted the lunch basket and a plaid blanket out of the car.

They walked to the small marina nearby and rented a white rowboat with two oars. Waldo rowed them to a deserted green island across the lake. Suzy leaned back on one of the benches and stared at the water and into the sky. "Just like the lakes in Switzerland! Oh! I wish we were in Lugano!" she whispered.

"Yes," nodded Waldo. "Just like Lugano! Only the mountains are missing."

They docked at the island and were greeted by a chorus of frogs and cicadas. Together they stretched the blanket on the grass and arranged sandwiches and apples on top. Waldo opened a bottle of beer and poured its content into the beakers.

"*Prosit*!" He cried. "Next picnic in Lugano!"

"Yes!" Suzy answered. "Next picnic in Lugano! You know," she added, "I've never been there, but it is the land of my dreams. My father bought an old, beautiful villa there and has promised to take us all there after the war! Or, even better, you and I should go and live there, after the war! I've brought some photos to show you. I'm sure you will like it," she said, as she took a handful of pictures out of her bag and gave them to Waldo.

"I actually know Lugano very well, since I was born and raised in Ticino. Living down there is really paradise! And this villa is magnificent. After the war, we should get married, move to Lugano and live in your villa!" Waldo said.

Then he drew Suzy close to him and kissed her.

"Are you serious? Do you mean that?" Suzy asked, as she scrambled out of his embrace.

"Yes, of course, I am very serious." He said. "And to convince you, here is the silver locket my mother gave me before she died." He handed her a tiny round box which contained a delicately crafted locket with the picture of a blond boy with curly hair.

"Take this as a token for *our* future."

Suzy was speechless. It must be a dream, she thought. Then Waldo took her in his arms and kissed her eyes, her lips and her ears. "After the war . . . we'll get married . . . we'll move to Lugano . . . we'll live in your villa . . . after the war . . ." He whispered between kisses. Suzy closed her eyes. It's a wonderful dream! She kept thinking as she surrendered to his embrace.

A few days later, Suzy was filing papers in the office. She kept thinking of Waldo and waiting for him. Only a few days had passed since their picnic on the lake and Suzy kept dreaming of it. She was wearing the new locket hidden under her blouse, stroking it from time to time. She didn't want Nina to see it and ask questions. But she could hear Waldo whispering into her ear. She could hear him clearly saying "after the war . . . we'll go to Lugano . . . we will live in your villa . . ." *After the war* were words people often used now when they spoke about the future!

Suzy slipped a thick file of papers into the drawer. They were copies of letters and memos her father, Adrian, had sent to the Mareshal, and the replies he had received.

There was another file with memos of various transactions. Waldo had asked her to show him these folders, since he needed them for his work. She had let him choose the papers he thought were important.

As she closed the drawer of the filing cabinet, she heard the doorbell. It must be Waldo, she thought, even though it was too early for him. She opened the door and took a step back. A tall, important looking, gray haired officer in full military uniform was facing her.

He gave her a military salute. "I am Captain Tudoran from Moghilev and I must speak urgently with Mr. Stein," he said. "Is Mr. Stein here? Can you tell him that I must see him immediately? He knows who I am."

"He is not here now, but he will be back soon. You can wait for him here!" Suzy said, leading him into the waiting room. She recognized his name: her father had mentioned him several times since his return from Transnistria. It was always mentioned with respect. She brought him a glass of cold water, which she placed in front of him.

He didn't have to wait long: Adrian, Sorel, Stella and Victor Georgescu arrived within a half hour. Hans Waldo appeared twenty minutes later. They always met here in the afternoon to keep in touch and discuss the events of the day.

Adrian was glad to see the Captain, but was also worried about possible bad news.

When they were all ready to listen, Captain Tudoran told them that he had been sent by his friend, Siegmund Dorfman, to inform them about the serious situation of the orphans in Moghilev and other camps. "It is a real catastrophe, I must tell you. Soon after the Moghilev orphanage was repaired and enlarged with the new funds, it was taken over by the Wehrmacht. Our staff was dismissed and the children scattered on the streets. Now they have no place to go and nothing to eat. They're dying by the hundreds on the streets and in backyards.

"My friend Dorfman has been fired from his position as president of the Jewish community, and nobody has replaced him.

"The children are sick, starving, and dying by the thousands. The Germans threaten to ship all the orphans to the river Bug. And we all know what that means. As a matter of fact, just before I left, I heard that the SS not only kill the children, but also bury the babies and toddlers alive! We must do something immediately. There is no time to sit back and wait!"

Adrian was horrified by this news as was everybody else. The Captain went on: "You must find a way to send these orphans to Palestine. There are thousands of them. I don't see how they can survive otherwise!"

"Palestine! Impossible!" Adrian and Sorel cried at the same time.

Adrian was dumbfounded. How were they going to send thousands of orphans to Palestine? It had been less than a year since the mysterious disappearance of the Dorina, the last boat bound for Palestine. Still, he remembered Myriam and the promise he had made to Max Wiener, her grandfather, on his deathbed in B. Adrian had heard a rumor that she had an aunt in Palestine, in Tel Aviv or Haifa. Being reunited with the aunt would certainly be best for Myriam!

"Palestine!" he said again, staring at the Captain. "It certainly is a great idea, but how the hell are we going to do that?"

"I don't know! I don't have the answer!" said the Captain.

"The Mareshal will never let the children leave. The British and Turks will never give them visas!" said Adrian. He stared at the Captain fixedly, as if trying to hypnotize him.

The officer stared back. "You must find a way to get the orphans to Palestine! Otherwise they will all die. This burden will be on your conscience for the rest of your life. You don't have much time: you must act now!"

A deep silence followed these words. Nobody moved and nobody spoke. Then Doctor Georgescu coughed and cleared his throat. "The Captain is right! We must do it and we have almost no time. We will start by writing a memo to the Mareshal. Without his permission, nothing can be done."

"We will need the approval of the Germans. Otherwise, they can stop the whole operation!" said Hans Waldo. "And we will need money too!" he added.

"And ships to get the kids at least to Istanbul," said Sorel. "We need to get in touch with Papadoglu again, as much as we hate the old crook. We can't do it without him."

"How about passage through Turkey to Palestine?" asked Stella. "Somebody will have to travel to Istanbul to talk to the Turks and the British and to alert the Jewish agency of our plan."

At the end of the evening, they were all excited and hopeful. Maybe they could still do something and save the orphans.

"You should stay out of this!" Nina told Adrian in the evening, when he explained the plan to help the orphans to her. "Don't you remember what happened to you last time when you wrote a memo to the Mareshal? I bet this time it will be worse. You just might not make it. Let the others do the risky work. Stay out of it!" she begged him.

"I can't," said Adrian. "This is my responsibility and I must see it through, no matter the risk." He reminded Nina of the promise he had made to old Max on his deathbed in the camp of B and his responsibility for Myriam. "You see, I cannot abandon Myriam and I cannot betray Max!" he said as he climbed into bed and switched off the light.

But Nina was not convinced. She spent a sleepless night, tossing and turning, without having the courage to start the discussion again. Adrian could not find any peace either. The image of the starving and dying children he had seen in the Moghilev hospital haunted him. It kept him from falling asleep.

The letter he wrote to the Mareshal the next morning was simple and direct. It described in detail the sufferings of the deported children, their lack of food, clothing and shelter, their illnesses and the sure death which awaited them if nothing was done very soon. "Thousands of orphans are dying already in the streets and backyards," he quoted Captain Tudoran. He added the killing of children by the SS on the banks of the river Bug. The only solution: emigration to Palestine. As in previous dealings with Romanian authorities, he also mentioned that financial and important material benefits would be provided to the Army and to the wounded soldiers if the emigration project was approved!

He sent the letter to the President early the next morning, Then the waiting began. He didn't know what to think or what to hope for.

To his relief and great joy, the emigration project was approved for 5,000 orphans of both parents under the age of 18 on the condition that the German Ambassador, Baron von L would give his approval.

When the project was submitted to the Ambassador (with the same promises of financial rewards), permission was granted. This time on the condition that the Chancellery of the Reich in Berlin would be in accord with the project.

"This is a simple formality. Nothing to worry about," Baron von L assured Victor Georgescu and Hans Waldo, who represented the Underground Jewish Council in these transactions.

The preparations for the emigration of 5,000 orphans started immediately. Lists of children in the numerous camps in Transnistria had to be made by the local Jewish communities. Ways of transporting them to Constanța or another point of departure had to be found. An adequate number of ships for 5,000 children had to be secured.

The issue of the port of departure required hard work and complex interventions, since the Mareshal was opposed to the use of any Romanian port of departure to Palestine. He ordered the organizers to use only Bulgarian ports for embarkation. Eventually this problem was solved. Constanța was named the main port of departure.

The question of the ships also had to be addressed. Most members of the Underground Jewish Council did not want to deal with Papadoglu again. His reputation had become that of a dangerous crook since there were rumors that the Dorina had been equipped with a nonfunctioning engine. The members of the Council tried to find another shipping magnate. But they were not successful. The German Army had requisitioned all seafaring ships. Only six small boats owned by Papadoglu were available to the Jews.

They would not trust Papadoglu's promise to obtain Turkish and British visas for the children. Rumors had reached them that the Dorina passengers had been held captive on the ship in Istanbul because they had no valid visas. Since the new plan was to get the orphans from Constanța to Istanbul by boat, and then through Turkey and Syria to Palestine by train, Turkish and British visas for every child were indispensable.

How to obtain these certificates? The only solution was for somebody to travel to Istanbul and engage in direct negotiations with the Turkish and British authorities. It was a clever idea; but who could they send? The Jews were not permitted to travel—not even from one city to the next. So who could be their delegate?

They searched for some time until Stella remembered Victor Georgescu's cousin, Paul Radin, a retired international lawyer and diplomat who held positions in several embassies during his career and had lived in Istanbul and England for many years. In addition, Paul Radin was a famous bridge champion, well known for his participation in international bridge tournaments.

He was tall and distinguished-looking, with wavy silver hair, always stylish, wearing a white handkerchief in his jacket pocket or a red carnation in his lapel. He gave off a pleasant scent of fresh aftershave from the house of Guerlain, embodying the quintessence of the successful Western diplomat.

He had been in Istanbul many times, knew Turkish ministers by their first names, and often dined at the club of the British consulate in Istanbul. He spoke perfect English and French and had studied at Cambridge while his father was the Romanian ambassador to Britain.

Victor Georgescu and Stella invited him to the next meeting of the Underground Jewish Council where he was briefed on the situation of the orphans and the plan to rescue them. Then Adrian handed him a list with the names of 5,000 children and a short list with the names of the six boats which were going to take them to Istanbul.

"From there," said Adrian "the children will travel by train through Turkey to Palestine. Once you arrive in Istanbul, you must contact the representative of the Jewish agency from Palestine, who will be in charge of the financial arrangements for the land transports. The best way to find this person is by getting in touch with the president of the Jewish community in Istanbul. I am sure that you will find him. In the meantime, we are all very grateful to you for undertaking this mission."

After these words, the group broke into applause. Paul Radin blushed and felt moved by their enthusiasm and by the faith they had in him.

The first thing he did after he had checked into the Park Hotel in Istanbul was to contact Zalman Bier, the president of the Jewish community of the city.

Paul Radin was pleased to see that the town had changed very little, almost not at all, since he was there eight years ago. It had the same noisy, chaotic, colorful and crowded streets, with oxen and donkey carts, overloaded buses and trams, maimed and blind beggars at every corner, street vendors offering *rahat locum* and sunflower seeds at the top of their voices. Mountains of rotting garbage and green melon rinds swarming with flies were piled high in the middle of fashionable boulevards

In contrast, his room at the Park Hotel was quiet and cool. There were thick rugs on the floor, a large brass bed with soft pillows, walls covered with red velvet, a large mahogany armoire with a venetian mirror, and red, brocade drapes covering the windows. The French doors opened onto a small balcony overgrown with geraniums in bloom. From here he could see the Sea of Marmara which was as blue as the sky and dotted with toy-like white boats.

Nothing has changed, he thought, with the exception of a large flag with a black swastika hanging from the building next door. It was the German Embassy, the bellboy had told him. He added that Von Pappen, the German Ambassador to Turkey, and his entourage always took their meals at the hotel restaurant.

In his conversation with Zalman Bier, the president of the Jewish community invited him to his house for dinner. He sent his shiny black Rolls Royce with his uniformed driver to pick him up from the hotel.

Bier's villa was located on top of a hill in Karakoy, the affluent residential quarter of the city. It was surrounded by a large park filled with exotic flowers. There was a small waterfall at the foot of a row of tall cypress trees. The straits of Bosporus were gleaming beyond the trees.

The door to the villa was opened by an aging valet with a monocle in his left eye. He greeted Paul Radin with a bow and led him to a low, overstuffed armchair. A few minutes later, his host, Zalman Bier burst into the room. He grabbed Radin's hand and shook it, asking him a hundred questions at once. It took Radin a few moments to adjust to Bier's boundless energy.

After Paul Radin explained the purpose of his visit, Bier told him that Chaim Labras, the president of the Jewish agency in Palestine would be joining them for dinner.

"He is a compassionate man who holds no grudges against the British for what happened with the Dorina. I, however, cannot forget nor forgive their crime. More than seven hundred innocent deaths were caused by their cruelty!"

With an angry voice he told Paul Radin the sad tale of the Dorina, from the arrival of the severely overcrowded and damaged ship, to its more than two-month detention in the port without permission of debarkation, to the fatal towing away of the paralyzed boat, ending with its mysterious explosion only a few miles from shore.

"It was the British who didn't allow the passengers to enter Palestine and who had ordered the Turkish authorities to detain the ship in the port. No," he added, shaking his head vigorously. "I will never forgive them and I have trouble dealing with them. Thank God, Chaim Labras is a different sort of man."

It was at this point of the conversation that Chaim Labras himself rang the doorbell and entered the room. He was a middle-aged man, completely bald, with a carefully trimmed goatee, wearing a bow tie, a suit and a vest in spite of the heat. The gold chain of his pocket watch hung over his prominent belly. He was born in Vienna and spoke French with a thick German accent.

"Glad to meet you and I wish I can be of help!" he said, shaking hands with the other two men.

They wasted no time with small talk and polite introductions. Over a dinner of cold *mezes* followed by kebabs on skewers washed down with Turkish *raki*, Paul Radin explained the grave situation of the orphans in Transnistria and the need to get them to Palestine as soon as possible.

"We need funds and we need Turkish and British visas for the voyage by train," said Paul Radin.

"Of course we will help you!" Bier and Labras assured him. "Zalman is friends with some powerful Turkish officials. I know the British Consul in residence. We will get you an official appointment with them in no time at all!" said Chaim Labras.

There was a moment of silence, as everybody concentrated on their spicy kebabs and tumblers of *raki*.

"We cannot have a repeat of the Dorina!" said Bier, after he swallowed the last mouthful of lamb. "The great irony and tragedy is that sixty-eight visa certificates for all the children on board had been approved, but were lost in the shuffle due to the negligence or the ill-will of the authorities. The children should have traveled to Palestine instead of ending up at the bottom of the Black Sea."

"We have sworn not to let this happen again," said Chaim Labras. "As a matter of fact there have been violent demonstrations against the British in Palestine because of the sinking of the Dorina. There have been assassination attempts against Sir M, the British governor of Palestine. He had to be moved out of the country because of these attacks! I have heard that even inside the British government there have been strong protests and much criticism for the mishandling of the Dorina. I hope that the official mood and attitude has changed drastically since the last year!" Zalman Bier and Paul Radin nodded in agreement with his words.

"Yes, and I almost forgot," Chaim Labras went on. "People from Haifa or Tel Aviv who have families in Romania came to see me and asked if I have any news. They have heard about the deportations and don't know if their loved ones are still alive. I have a neighbor, Mrs. Wiener who told me she has had no news from her family in Bucharest in a long time. She heard that many people had been deported and died in Transnistria. She has a young niece named Myriam. She and her husband would love to have Myriam come to Tel Aviv and stay with them. Many people in Europe have tried to send their children to Palestine, and I would love to be able to do something for these people!" said Labras.

"A strange coincidence," said Paul Radin. "There is a little girl, Myriam. I think her last name is Wiener. Adrian rescued her in Transnistria. She lost her entire family in the camps. Adrian was planning to send her to Palestine with the children's transport. It would be wonderful if her relatives in Haifa or Tel Aviv could be found! Maybe your neighbors are Myriam's uncle and aunt!"

They finished the dinner with baklava and bubbly champagne, followed by small cups of strong Turkish coffee.

Before the end of the evening, Zalman Bier suggested a game of bridge in the living room. They were joined by his wife Laura, a tall, statuesque woman with short, curly hair and many silver rings on her long fingers.

When the card game finished late in the evening, Paul Radin had won twice and he had let Laura Bier and Chaim Labras win one game each. He showed them some interesting bridge problems which he had solved and which had helped him win an international championship.

It was dark when they left. A half moon hung over the garden. The perfume of the exotic flowers filled the air and slow Turkish music could be heard from the street. Mysterious, illuminated ships appeared and disappeared on the water beyond the cypress trees.

When they got up to leave, Zalman Bier told Radin that his driver would take him home.

"But you know," he said, "you should not stay at the Park Hotel! Too close to the German headquarters! Besides, the entire Old City is unsafe. It is too dangerous and very difficult to patrol. It is full of agents and spies. There are daily reports of suspicious murders and dead bodies found in back alleys, in the rubble of the city walls, or in the backyards of hidden brothels. We don't know who may be watching you or following you and why. I understand that the Old City is much more appealing and picturesque and you may have good memories from other times. But it would be much safer to move to the modern quarters and stay in Karakoy. I have a safe house nearby where you can stay. I can provide you with a car and driver who can double as an armed bodyguard."

Paul Radin didn't like the idea of moving. The old city with its noise, its stench, its narrow alleys and small cafes where Turkish men played backgammon, drank black tea and smoked their *narghilea* was much dearer to him. He loved hearing the shrill call to prayer of muezzins from the minarets that pierced the cacophony of the city. But he felt that he had no choice but to follow Bier's recommendations.

Two days later there was another meeting this time at the clubhouse of the British consulate in Istanbul. This was an old, elegant mansion on the banks of the Bosporus. It had large, sunny terraces and a private beach decked out with chaise lounges shaded by red parasols.

In contrast to the façade, the interior of the mansion was a traditional British clubhouse, with large wood-paneled rooms, soft carpets, comfortable armchairs, leather couches, large chandeliers and green-shaded reading lamps.

They gathered in the conference room around a heavy mahogany table. A pot of Earl Grey tea and delicate china cups and saucers had been placed in the middle, surrounded by trays filled with finger sandwiches of cucumber and watercress.

Their host at the club was Sir Gregory Taylor, a young, athletic man known for his policy of trying to keep peace in the Middle East. He had been opposed to the Governor of Palestine's (Sir M) harsh measures against the passengers of the Dorina. But at that time he had no power against his opponents.

The fifth participant in the meeting was Ahmed Baiazid, a true descendant of the fabulous sultan. Like his famous ancestor, he had a long beard, an impressive black moustache, bushy eyebrows and bedroom eyes. Paul Radin could imagine him wearing a fez or turban. With the new regime of Kemal Ataturk, such attire was forbidden by law.

During the meeting it soon turned out that three out of the five men, Paul Radin, Sir Gregory Taylor and Ahmed Baiazid, had studied at Cambridge. Memories of punting on the Cam soon were the main subject of discussion and the three men felt that they belonged to the same close brotherhood. They shared old stories and had a good laugh.

Then as they sipped hot tea and munched cucumber sandwiches, Ahmed Baiazid approved the visas for 5,000 orphans, while the British diplomat, Sir Gregory Taylor, officially guaranteed their entry into Palestine.

"I don't want to be hunted down and assassinated by your angry warriors!" he told Zalman Bier and Chaim Labras at the end of the meeting. "Nor do I believe that Nazi spies are hiding among these children, as my predecessors did."

Paul Radin came home like a victorious general with the 5,000 approved certificates, train tickets and visas. He was celebrated by all his friends. He himself felt proud of his accomplishment.

Adrian, Stella, Sorel, Doctor Georgescu and the entire Underground Jewish Council were in a festive mood. They wasted no time when they got the good news and started working feverishly to get the children out of the camps and onto the ships. They called Hans Waldo and asked him to inform his friends in Zürich that new funds were urgently needed.

At the same time Adrian told Nina that he was particularly happy that a good solution had been found for Myriam. He thought it soon would be time to prepare her for the trip and reunification with her aunt in Tel Aviv.

A week after Paul Radin's return from Istanbul, Adrian received an official telegram from the Mareshal. He informed Adrian and the Underground Jewish Council that the Chancellery in Berlin had forbidden the orphans' emigration to Palestine. As a consequence, wrote the Mareshal, his government was also prohibiting any further plans for emigration.

Adrian was stunned and defeated. After a while he regained his fighting spirit. At the next meeting of the Underground Jewish Council which had been urgently called, he showed them the letter from the Mareshal. Then he read them the memo he had written, which went like this:

"Your Honor,

I was deeply saddened by your order to stop the preparations for the orphans' transport to Palestine. I want to remind you that the children we want to save are Romanian citizens, not Germans, so they should be entitled to benefit from Romanian laws and not have to abide by the laws of a foreign country. As a humble citizen, I beg you to reconsider your decision and allow these unfortunate children to travel to Palestine, rather than be murdered in the camps.

Signed: ADRIAN STEIN,
President of the Jewish Council."

Everybody approved of Adrian's letter, and he sent it to the Presidium the next morning. After that, all the Council members became hopeful again and resumed their work for the emigration of the children.

A black van with the small swastika flag on the engine stopped in front of Adrian's apartment Friday, near midnight. Four uniformed men, three SS and one Romanian officer entered the building and escorted Adrian to the van. It was still summer so he didn't take any warm clothing with him. He found Sorel and a few other members of the Underground Jewish Council sitting in the van, but they were not allowed to talk to each other. The windows of the van were blackened with paint so he didn't know where they were going. It was pitch dark inside the car, giving this mysterious abduction a feeling of doom.

The van made a few stops and more members of the Underground Jewish Council were brought inside. They were not allowed to talk to each other.

After some time, the car made two sharp turns and stopped. Adrian heard a heavy metal gate with squeaky hinges being opened. The car started again slowly and finally came to a halt.

When he climbed out, Adrian found himself in a large courtyard, surrounded by tall buildings on all sides. The courtyard and the buildings looked like an old armory and he recognized the military prison of Malmezon. He was led into one of the buildings and marched through a long corridor, until he reached a small room which was poorly lit where he had to surrender his wallet, jacket, belt, tie, socks and shoelaces. From here, he was led to another room, where a young soldier made him sit on a barber chair and shaved his head, leaving him completely bald. There was a large mirror on the wall in front of his chair, but it was covered with a sheet so he couldn't see his reflection.

When the shaving operation was finished, the barber and a guard attached a heavy chain to his ankles which restricted his movements. He was led by another guard through many long corridors and down several staircases.

He walked through a complicated underground labyrinth to the end of the world. The heavy chains hurt his ankles. Where was he going?

Was he going to be locked up forever in this deep, bottomless cellar? Was he heading to the bank of the Styx? He wondered.

Eventually, as he was getting exhausted and ready to collapse, they stopped in front of a metal door at the end of a dark corridor. The guard unlocked the door and they entered a tiny cell with a low ceiling, barely lit by a small bulb. A thin straw mattress lay on the floor and an ill smelling tin bucket stood in a corner. The air was heavy with the stench of human waste. A small window, installed near the ceiling, was covered with boards.

After the guard locked the door behind him, Adrian lay down on the mattress and tried to sleep. But the light of the bulb shone in his eyes and the heavy chains pulled at his feet, so he couldn't rest. Since his watch had been taken away from him, he lost all sense of time.

The next morning he received a small portion of cold *mămăligă* (corn mush) and a tinful of lukewarm water with some peas and pebbles inside. The food was handed to him through a slit in the door, which could be opened only from the outside.

After he finished eating, Adrian was taken by his guard for a long march, through different corridors and staircases than the night before. The chains at his ankles dragged him down and hurt his feet. "Where are we going?" He asked the guard. The man touched his lips with his index finger and didn't answer, indicating that Adrian should stop asking questions.

They walked through endless dark corridors and climbed many stairs. Then they crossed another deserted courtyard and entered a second building.

The guard opened a heavy door and Adrian found himself in a big, well lit room, with men standing or moving between tables and desks. Two soldiers in military uniform— one a German SS officer and the other a Romanian captain—stood with their backs toward him, talking to each other. Then the German officer turned around. To Adrian's great shock, he recognized Hans Waldo.

What was this: a dreadful, frightening nightmare or real life? Adrian wondered. But he wasn't left guessing for long. He was ordered to sit on a bench close to the desk of the two officers.

"Well," said the Romanian captain. "I am glad that we finally have the opportunity to discuss face to face the obnoxious crimes you and your accomplices have committed against our country. Thanks to the effort of Officer Hans Waldo, we have complete and concrete proof of your criminal activity."

He picked up a thick folder from his desk, pulled out a few sheets of paper, and gave them to Adrian who was horrified. He recognized duplicates of transcripts of discussions, transactions and letters of the Underground Jewish Council in which Waldo had participated. There were even copies of transactions in which he had not been involved. A Gestapo seal appeared in the lower left corner of every sheet, verifying that the entire folder had been read by the Gestapo.

Waldo was sitting in front of him at the desk with a smirk on his face. He was staring at Adrian but gave no sign of recognition.

"Adrian Stein," said the captain. "You must give us the names of all those who participated in your conspiracy! In addition, we want a list of those who are hiding weapons and where they are hiding them!"

"There is no conspiracy," said Adrian "We have no weapons."

"Did you hear what I said? The names of your co-conspirators and information about the weapons or your head will roll!" repeated the man. "You have the night to think it over," he added, before dismissing him.

Back in his cell, Adrian couldn't sleep. The burning light bulb kept him awake. His ankles were swollen and hurting from the heavy chains. But worse was the fear that some member of the Underground Jewish Council was going to crumble under pressure and make false statements, involving innocent family members in this nightmare.

The next day he was called again in front of the investigator and questioned. The same questions were repeated again and again for more than four hours. He was made to stand up straight the whole time. After four hours he was ordered to climb to the top of a steep ladder that nearly reached the ceiling and forced to concentrate on the same questions from this dangerous and unstable position, with the heavy chains still on his feet. He felt unsteady and lightheaded. He was convinced that he was going to fall and break his neck.

Back in his cell, the bad nights continued. If and when he fell asleep, he dreamt that Nina and his two daughters were brought to the prison and tortured. He dreamt that, without his knowledge, they had been deported to an unknown camp in Transnistria.

The investigation went on for many days without interruption. Sometimes he was awakened in the middle of the night, and, half asleep, dragged up to the torture chamber where he was asked the same questions. Often he was made to stand for many hours with the chains on his feet. Several times he collapsed under the strain. Then a bucket of cold water was poured over his face to revive him.

Other times he was whipped on the soles of his feet until the skin was lacerated, then ordered to run countless times around the room.

The questions were always the same: who else had participated in the conspiracy? where were the weapons? Sometimes he was told that the others had confessed and that it made no sense to resist the investigation.

Hans Waldo often sat at the desk and watched the proceedings with the same smirk. Sometimes he conferred in a low voice with his Romanian colleague. But he never said a word to the prisoner.

As time went by, Adrian felt weaker and weaker. His wounded feet were swollen and bleeding. He started thinking that this living hell was going to last forever. He began to wish for the vials of cyanide he had taken with him to Transnistria.

Then one day he was told that the investigation was finished and he was going to be taken to trial. The guard marched him to the barber shop where he received a shave and a shower. The chains were taken off his feet and his jacket, belt, tie, shoelaces and wallet were returned to him. He then walked the narrow corridor and up a steep staircase, until he reached the big door to the main courtyard.

Here the other members of the Underground Jewish Council who had come with him in the van were waiting. He barely recognized them: they looked like pale shadows of themselves. Sorel's face was white and he was leaning on crutches; his left leg had been amputated below the knee.

They didn't have to wait long. Several cars drove into the courtyard and stopped by the gate. Adrian looked, but couldn't believe his eyes: the first car was driven by Victor Georgescu, the second by Paul Radin and the other two by friends of Radin and Victor Georgescu.

What was this? Adrian wondered. Was it another part of the conspiracy in which trusted friends proved to be dangerous enemies? Were Paul Radin and Victor Georgescu connected with Hans Waldo? There was no time to answer these questions. The prisoners were told to climb into the cars and were driven away.

Adrian was dumbfounded. "What's going on? What is the meaning of this? Did they give us a temporary pass before taking us to trial? Or will we be deported instead of going to court?" he asked Victor Georgescu when they got home. "Neither," said Victor. "You have been released with no strings attached."

"How come?" asked Adrian, full of mistrust.

"Luck, I suppose," said Victor, with a mysterious grin. "Maybe you have a lucky star!"

"Seriously, what are you hiding from me?"

"All right, I will tell you, even though I promised to keep it a secret," said Victor Georgescu in a low voice. "Remember the Baroness von L, wife of the German ambassador? She got very sick with a toxic form of diphtheria and needed urgently a special type of serum which only I have in my lab. I keep it in case of an emergency for the King or the Queen. This time, a panicked Baron von L went to the Queen and asked for help. She called and asked me to give him some of the serum. I told the Queen I would release a dose of serum on condition that the members of the Underground Jewish Council held in the penitentiary would be freed immediately and sent home to their families with no strings attached!" Dr. Georgescu stopped talking and lit his pipe.

"Well, is it luck? Do you have a lucky star?" he asked after a pause.

"I don't know" said Adrian thoughtfully. "I don't know whether I have a lucky star, but I am lucky to have you!" He added as he took Victor's hand.

It was very early in the morning, the sun had not yet risen when Nadia got up to go to the bathroom. As usual, she didn't turn on the light. She knew her way with closed eyes.

But she stumbled on something which lay on the floor and rolled under her foot, making her trip and almost fall. She regained her balance and switched on the light. There was an empty flask of aspirins on the floor and an old flask of Nina's sleeping pills on Suzy's bedside table.

It seemed strange to Nadia. She called Suzy's name, but there was no response. She called again, but there was silence. She bent over her sister and shook her, but she didn't move. Then she noticed that Suzy's breathing was irregular and noisy like somebody who was drowning.

Nadia screamed and ran into her parents' bedroom. Adrian jumped out of bed, ran to Suzy and was quick to make a decision: they had no time to waste! Every second was precious! They had to get Suzy to the Jewish Hospital to have her stomach pumped. But they had no telephone to call an ambulance or to alert a doctor and there was a strict curfew for Jews. They were not allowed on the street before 7.30 AM.

Adrian didn't think of that. He rang the bell of his downstairs neighbor who was a Romanian teacher and asked for permission to use the telephone for this emergency. The man called the ambulance himself and they responded quickly to the Romanian caller. After a hefty *baksheesh* from Adrian, the driver agreed to take them to the Jewish hospital.

Meanwhile at home, Nina found an open letter written by Suzy lying on the table. The writing was clear, but here and there the paper was stained and the letters blurred. She must have cried while she was writing it, thought Nina.

As she was trying to read the letter, tears were gathering in her own eyes and blurred her vision. They ran down her cheeks and wet the paper.

> "My dearest parents,
> My heart breaks for inflicting so much pain on you. But the occurrence of the recent calamity—and only God knows what is in store for the future—is entirely my fault. It

was I who, in moments of weakness, trusted Hans Waldo, and believed him when he told me that he needed to read the files. Not only did I let him snoop around, but I trusted him and gave him important papers when he told me that they were needed for the success of the operations we were pursuing! I know now that, had I not been so thoughtless and had I talked to any of you, Waldo could not have gotten hold of the files and have tata arrested and tortured. It is entirely my fault that all your friends were arrested and tortured, and Uncle Sorel has lost his leg. God only knows what future dangers you will be exposed to because of me!

I feel so guilty for what I have done, I cannot live with myself anymore and I have no right to your love. Goodbye. It will be much better if I disappear!

Suzy."

Nina was paralyzed with pain. She couldn't move. All she could do was read the letter again and again. Tears ran down her cheeks, drenching the paper. She remembered when she had tried to kill herself by slashing her throat with a kitchen knife at the time of her mother's death. Luckily her father and brother, both doctors, had been able to rescue her.

She asked herself now whether Suzy had inherited a special inclination for suicide. Nina had heard that sometimes suicides occurred more frequently in certain families, and she was afraid of this. Even though she did not believe in God or religion, she found herself praying for a miracle.

At the hospital Suzy was immediately wheeled into the emergency room and her stomach was energetically pumped. Nevertheless, she remained unconscious for several hours, her breathing slow and shallow. It was obvious that the medicines had penetrated her brain, slowing down her breathing center.

Adrian sat by her bed, holding her hand which was cold and dry. He was frightened and felt very guilty. He shouldn't have used her as his assistant or he should have been more careful, giving her more guidance and supervision. She was still very young. He shouldn't have let her work so closely with Waldo.

Hans Waldo! blood rushed to his head and he clenched his fists. A wave of anger took hold of him. He knew that, if he met Waldo now, he would smash his face, crack his skull, and beat him to a pulp. He had no compassion for this man.

He got up and walked restlessly around the room. When he came back to the bed, he saw that Suzy had lifted her head and was watching him with open eyes.

THE ORPHANS AND THE TRAINS

THE CATTLE TRAINS CROWDED WITH orphans from Transnistria started rolling into the Bucharest freight station. They brought about two hundred children of various ages and in various conditions of health every day.

Stella, who was in charge of the young people's welfare, had her hands full. The orphans had to be lodged, fed, dressed, and those who were sick had to be treated. Stella proved to be an exceptionally competent organizer. She had mobilized an army of helpers and had prepared lodging, beds, clothing and food for the children even before their arrival.

Many of the women who assisted her in this operation were the wives, daughters or sisters of the members of the Underground Jewish Council. One young person who was particularly important to Stella and on whom she relied heavily was Suzy.

Stella went to see her immediately after her release from the hospital and, as soon as Suzy gained some strength, Stella had a long talk with her. "I understand very well what you went through," she said, "and I don't judge you or blame you in the least, nor does Sorel. What happened to him and to the others has nothing to do with you. It is Waldo alone,

Waldo himself who is the cruel villain! He fooled you and betrayed all of us, not only you! We have to forgive ourselves for this terrible misadventure! And you too have to learn to forgive yourself! We are fighting a war, and even though we are fighting to win the war, sometimes there are mistakes and heavy losses. We have to learn to deal with them, not let them pull us down. You can be an important soldier in our army, now!"

Suzy listened to Stella without saying a word. Her eyes filled with tears and she burst into sobs.

Stella sat next to her and took her hand in her own. Suzy cried for a while. When she calmed down, Stella explained to her that she needed Suzy to supervise and coordinate the complex work they had to do.

"I need you to be my right hand. I assure you, in the days to come, you won't have much time to think about Waldo!"

As she got up to leave, she embraced Suzy who was still wiping her tears.

Meanwhile, Adrian was following Suzy's recovery and was happy to see her working with Stella. He was still worried about Nina, who was very shaken by the recent events. His own arrest and imprisonment followed by Suzy's attempted suicide had taken their toll on Nina, leaving her frightened and often depressed. She ate very little, slept badly, and had migraine attacks.

After a few weeks, these daily concerns were suddenly pushed aside by an unexpected event. One morning, an electrical engineer who was working in a railroad station visited Adrian and told him that special trains were being prepared for the deportation of all the Jews of Romania to the extermination camp of Belzec in Poland. The engineer showed Adrian an article published in the German newspaper *Bukarester Tageblatt* with the title: *"Rumänien wird Judenfrei"* (Romania will be cleansed of Jews). He also told him that two similar articles with the same subject and similar titles had appeared in two other German newspapers, *Die Donauzeitung* published in Belgrade and *Der Völkisher Beobachter*, the organ of the German Nazi Party. The articles highlighted the fact that this action would make Romania the first country in Southeast Europe totally cleansed of Jews.

The deportation plan was to round up the Jews in a designated location, from where trains of fifty cars each would carry two thousand Jews every second day to the Belzec extermination camp. The Jews themselves would have to pay for their voyage.

The trains were ready to leave any day now and were only waiting for a sign from the Mareshal.

There was no time to waste. Adrian immediately spoke to Stella and Doctor Georgescu, who met with Doctor Stan, the Mareshal's personal physician on the same day. Doctor Stan was the director of the Home for Disabled Veterans, an institution which had recently received a substantial donation from the Jewish community.

He agreed to speak to the Mareshal about cancelling the deportations, but his intervention had no results.

Since time was short and danger was imminent, Adrian and the members of the Underground Jewish Council were forced to explore other alternatives. Doctor Georgescu spoke to his special patient, the Queen. She immediately alerted the King, Professor Ursu, the Dean of the Medical School, a few old school politicians and even the Head of the Church of Transylvania, Father Drăgan who had close ties to the Mareshal. It was well known that this cleric had unfriendly feelings toward the Jews.

The Queen's guests gathered at a festive luncheon at the Royal Palace given in honor of the head of the Church. After supper, the Holy Father agreed to meet with the Chief Rabbi of the country.

It was a long and dramatic meeting during which the rabbi made an emotional plea. He reminded the priest of the spiritual meaning of Christianity which was based on the love and respect for one's fellow man. He also told the pastor that, once in the Afterworld, he might be asked by the Almighty what he had done on this earth to save the lives of so many innocents.

"With a few simple words you could protect the life of hundreds of thousands of people!" the Rabbi said.

The Minister listened to the Rabbi in silence. Then he made up his mind to drive to the Mareshal's palace.

The Rabbi was left waiting for a miracle. Late in the evening, Father Drăgan finally let him know that the Mareshal had revoked the deportations.

By now the rumors of the projected transports had leaked into the Jewish community, and everybody was overjoyed with the cancellations. But the joy and relief were of short duration. By late September, early October, Adrian and the members of the Underground Jewish Council learned that the specter of the deportations had been revived. The Germans put heavy pressure on the Romanians.

Eichmann himself traveled to Bucharest to arrange with the Mareshal the last details of the transports.

As president of the Underground Jewish Council, Adrian was invited to meet with the German envoy responsible for Jewish affairs in order to facilitate the deportations. But he did not want to be involved in this matter and refused the visit with the Nazi official.

Shortly afterwards, in the middle of October, the order of deportation became very urgent. The minister of police told a friend who was a member of the Underground Jewish Council that the trains were ready. The transports were going to start within two days, early in the morning. The minister's friend, Doctor B, tried to convince the official to call the Mareshal and cancel the order. But the minister refused, saying it was too late. The Mareshal would not listen to him.

The friend kept insisting. After a long plea, late in the evening, he convinced the minister of police to invite Adrian to take part in the discussion.

When Adrian arrived, the minister greeted him with the words, "I don't know why you made the effort to come since nothing can be done at this hour. It is much too late. Nothing can be changed! There is no choice at this time!" he added.

"Yes, there is a choice! We always have choices," said Adrian, looking straight into the minister's eyes. "You know the old saying, 'When there is a will, there is a way.'" With these words, Adrian opened his briefcase and took out a brown velvet pouch. He handed it to the official, who opened it and found inside a heavy bronze key and a few sheets of paper.

"This is the key to my Villa in Lugano, Switzerland and the documents of ownership," said Adrian. "I give them to you. You can sell the villa or use it as you see fit. In addition, through our contacts abroad, we will provide the funds which are necessary to stop the deportations."

The minister took the key, examined it, frowned and didn't say anything. He got up and walked back and forth in silence.

He stopped by his chair, hesitated, and started pacing again. Finally he called one of his assistants and ordered him to write a letter to the Mareshal urging him to postpone the deportations because of "stormy weather."

When the memo was ready, the minister personally took it to the Mareshal. He instructed Adrian and the other visitor to wait there for his return.

The two men spent a sleepless, agonizing night. Finally, the next evening the Minister returned and told them that the deportations had been postponed.

Nina was waiting for Adrian when he came home late in the evening. She looked at him anxiously when he entered the room.

"We have lost our villa in Lugano, but we have gained a new lease on life!" he said as he took off his jacket and tie.

"I was worried to death about your whereabouts!" Nina said, with a trembling voice . . . "So many bad things have happened to you, not too long ago! They could have arrested you or deported you again!"

"No, no! I am here to stay!" cried Adrian as he took her in his arms and kissed her. Together, they stood by the window and stared into the dark night. Then they tiptoed into the other room to make sure that the girls were asleep.

"I am here to stay! Go to sleep and stop worrying!" Adrian whispered as they went to bed and turned off the light.

And indeed, he was right: in spite of German pressure and threats, after the minister of police and the authorities took possession of the Villa in Lugano and collected the Jewish funds from Switzerland, there were no more discussions or plans for deportation to Belzec or other camps.

EPILOGUE

W HEN THE IMMEDIATE DANGER SUBSIDED, Adrian and the Underground Jewish Council renewed their battle for the emigration of the orphans. It was an uphill struggle since Eichmann and the Germans were continuously delaying the operation.

Myriam Wiener finally sailed to Istanbul in the beginning of February 1944 on the first ship of Jewish orphans out of Constanța.

Earlier, the fierce battle for Stalingrad raged in the East. After the big city fell, many Romanian patriots started doubting their faith in the war. The Red Army progressed relentlessly toward the borders of the country. Bucharest and the oil fields of Ploești were under savage bombardments by British and Americans forces.

At the beginning of 1944, the Mareshal called the leaders of the Underground Jewish Council and asked them to write letters to the Allies in an attempt to settle a lenient peace.

But it was too late. On August 23, 1944, after the Russian troops had marched into the country, the King arrested the Mareshal, ordered the troops to turn against the Germans and signed an armistice with the Soviets and the Allies.

The German troops stationed in Bucharest fought with the Romanian army. After their military leader jumped out of his hotel window, the dejected German soldiers surrendered to the Romanian troops.

The months which followed the armistice were a time of hope and rejoicing. In spite of the heavy losses and countless destruction, everybody relished and celebrated the end of the war.

Foreign embassies which had been closed, now reopened and the black market bloomed. It was flooded with American cigarettes, whiskey, gin, silk stockings, coffee, chocolate and chewing gum. Nightclubs and bars were open until late in the night. Live jazz bands filled the air with the beat of their drums and the primal call of the saxophones.

Soon after the truce, Adrian hired a lawyer, and, after eight months of negotiations, regained possession of his house and his garden. However, he was never able to redeem his office, his car, and, of course, Nadia's bicycle.

Doctor Ionescu, the neighbor from across the street who had taken his house, was now reduced to living in Adrian's cold water flat. (He never recovered his own, original home.)

As far as others who had been close to Adrian and his family, Hans Waldo had been arrested and was going to be tried as a war criminal.

In contrast, Doctor Georgescu had a time of great success and satisfaction. His work was in great demand: the two Swiss companies which had been interested in him, contacted him again and made tempting proposals.

It was a difficult decision, as Victor Georgescu did not want to separate from Stella. As for Sorel, he was dead set on emigrating to Palestine. After the amputation of his right leg in the prison of Malmezon, he did not want to remain in the country. But Stella could not cut herself off from Doctor Georgescu and her sister Nina.

For many months they kept meeting and trying to find a solution, without success. The situation was more complicated now, since their old friend from Switzerland, Charles Kass, who in the past had promised to help, had fallen ill and was out of reach.

Time went on and the trial of the Mareshal approached. It was set for the middle of May 1946. A few months before that date, the defense lawyers contacted Adrian and asked him to testify in the case.

All those close to him—Nina, Stella, Sorel, Victor Georgescu and even Professor Ursu—strongly advised him not to take part in the trial.

"It is too dangerous to get mixed up in this!" they kept saying. "And besides, you won't be able to save the Mareshal from the wrath of the Russians and the vindictiveness of the Communists!"

But they couldn't convince Adrian.

"The Mareshal stopped the deportations to Belzec. By doing so, he saved the lives of 300,000 Jews!" Adrian said.

"He never really stopped the deportations, he only postponed them!" Sorel replied.

"Never mind!" said Adrian. "Because of him, many people are still alive. He allowed the orphans to sail to Palestine," he added.

"Yes, after raising many obstacles and dragging his feet, which caused the death of thousands of children!" said Doctor Georgescu and Professor Ursu.

"He allowed us, the Jews of Bucharest to live without the Yellow Star. Ultimately he took the implementation of the Final Solution in his own hands rather than let the SS do their dirty work which *killed all the Jews* in other countries," said Adrian.

"But it was he who ordered the pogrom in Iași, the deportations to Transnistria including your own deportation and arrest, not to mention the massacre of tens of thousands of Jews in Odessa. He is a war criminal!" cried Stella.

"Yes, you are right," said Adrian. "But humanity must prevail even in the trial of a war criminal."

Nina and the others were angry at him and tried to stop him from testifying. Only the Rabbi understood and gave him support. Adrian presented testimony in the trial on May 19, 1946. As predicted, his deposition had no effect.

The Mareshal was executed by a firing squad on June 1, 1946, on the grounds of the Jilava prison.

Slowly, almost imperceptibly, as the months went by, Soviet influence became stronger and stronger in the country. It culminated in a Communist coup at the end of 1947, which forced the King to abdicate and flee to Switzerland.

Suddenly, Adrian found himself once again in danger: massive arrests followed the coup. Adrian was blacklisted because of his testimony at the trial of the Mareshal.

Together with Nina and Nadia, each of them carrying a small valise, they left in a hurry for Paris. Nina was heartbroken. Suzy had refused to join them, since she was engaged to a young, radical physicist, who dreamt of a bright, Communist future in Romania.

Once in Paris, Adrian set up an electrical engineering firm. But soon after his arrival, he contacted the World Jewish Congress. After two years he became one of the leaders of the organization.

Nina, however, spent many unhappy years, since she could not resign herself to her separation from Suzy and her sister Stella.

Meanwhile, back in Romania, Sorel and Stella were in great trouble. Known as Zionists, they were accused by the Communists of "betraying the country" and of being "spies and evil agents working for an enemy power."

They were arrested and sentenced to thirty years of solitary confinement. Now, in spite of the Communist regime, the prosecutors at their trial were the same individuals who had interrogated Sorel and Adrian at the prison of Malmezon under the orders of the Gestapo.

For five years, nobody knew where Stella and Sorel were and whether they were dead or alive. There were rumors that Sorel had died following an infection which had spread from the site of his amputation. Other rumors claimed that Stella had gone blind, after a severe blow to her head. But these rumors were never confirmed.

Three years after Stalin's death, they were released and expelled to Israel within twenty-four hours. Their children, Corinna and Theo, were not allowed to travel with them. They were permitted to emigrate only many years later.

At about the same time, Doctor Georgescu also joined them in Tel Aviv. He had been replaced as director of the mental hospital and professor of psychiatry by his young assistant, Doctor Eugen Milo, soon after the Communist coup of 1947. The authorities viewed Doctor Georgescu with suspicion because of his long association with the Queen and his friendship with known Zionists.

In contrast, Doctor Eugen Milo and Silvia, his fiancée, had become such fervent and devoted Communists, their Legionnaire past had been completely forgotten.

After his arrival in Israel, Stella and Sorel helped Doctor Georgescu set up a private practice. Sometime later, he became professor of psychiatry at Hadassah University. However, his dream of perfecting and manufacturing Salep as a pharmaceutical product never became a reality.

Stella and Sorel's presence in Israel was a blessing not only for Victor Georgescu, but also for Nina in Paris. She could now visit with her sister at least twice a year and stay as long as she wanted. (It was some consolation for her when her daughter Nadia decided to settle in the United States.) In time, even Suzy, who was one of the last six thousand Jews still living in Romania, was able to come to see her parents and relatives for several short visits.

Finally, about forty years after Adrian's death, a sum of money equivalent to the value of the Lugano Villa was restored to Nadia, Suzy and their children by the Holocaust Claims Tribunal. This reminded Nadia of those years of turmoil. It made her think, with longing, about her wonderful bicycle, the winged Pegasus.

THE END